The Years of the City . . .

". . . is a tightly-focused drama . . . infinitely moving . . . rendered with intensity of feeling. . . . *The Years of the City* has a generosity of spirit which may be unfamiliar to readers of Frederik Pohl's more cynical works. . . . The result so clearly and consistently conveys Pohl's humanism that one must conclude that structure and style have been consciously bent toward this end, with remarkable success. *The Years of the City* is superior Pohl, which is to say that it is writing of the highest order."

—*Locus*

The Years of the City . . .

". . . is about Pohl's inventive, utopian visions of the city, and he has written it in a clear, clever, rapidly paced and economical style. . . . [C]onsistently interesting, rich in imagery and very smoothly, professionally done."

—*Publishers Weekly*

"In the hands of a master such as Frederik Pohl, sci-fi isn't just kid stuff about pointy-headed creatures from extraterrestrial space dropping in for a beer, or about intergalactic warfare between the black hats and the white hats, planetary division. Instead, the reader's imagination is encouraged to take wing about the shortfall of intelligence on our mundane earth."

—*The New York Times Book Review*

FREDERIK POHL

THE YEARS OF THE CITY

PUBLISHED BY POCKET BOOKS NEW YORK

FOR BETTY ANNE HULL
WITH SEVEN YEARS OF LOVE

 POCKET BOOKS, a division of Simon & Schuster, Inc.
1230 Avenue of the Americas, New York, N.Y. 10020

Copyright © 1984 by Frederik Pohl
Cover artwork copyright © 1985 Paul Lehr

Library of Congress Catalog Card Number: 84-128

ISBN: 0-671-46047-1

First Pocket Books mass-market printing August, 1985

10 9 8 7 6 5 4 3 2 1

POCKET and colophon are registered trademarks of Simon & Schuster, Inc.

Printed in the U.S.A.

contents

introduction

ALTHOUGH I'VE lived half my life in semi-rural suburbs, and even a few stretches in places as notably unurban as Harlem, Pennsylvania, and Canadian, Texas, I think of myself as a city boy. Actually, I'm even rather proud of it. I like cities. I respect them, and I think they contribute massively to the art, culture, learning and invention of the human race. As things now stand, the world's cities are obviously having a hard time. I worry that they might become an endangered species, for if the cities are allowed to decline I think it will cost us all dearly.

Herein these worries—and these hopes, and even prayers—have become a science-fiction novel.

Since I earn my living by writing science fiction, I've done a lot of thinking about the future of cities (and of everything else). In this particular case, however, I can trace the long chain of free association that led to this book to one particular incident after a cocktail party in early 1973. Among the guests was the then Mayor of New York City, John V. Lindsay. As it happened, we left the party at the same time, heading in the same direction, and His Honor courteously offered my wife and me a lift in the official limousine. Science-fiction writers are not bashful. I took the occasion to tell him some of my thoughts about the governance of the city. Somewhere along the line I expressed to him my opinion that he had the hardest job in the world, because New York City seemed to me simply too sprawly and too diverse to be governed by one central authority.

Nonsense! said Lindsay. New York City's only problem was its unfairly puny tax base. If the city could only manage to keep its fair proportion of the tax revenues it *generates—much of which are bled off by the State of New York to other counties in the state and by the feds to other states of the U.S.A.—the future would be fascinating, exemplary and golden. And he went on to tell me some of his hopes and dreams for the city (none of which appear in this book).*

He just about convinced me. But a few days later the headlines announced that, contrary to expectations, he had decided not to run for another term. So maybe I convinced him a little bit, too.

—Frederik Pohl

I AM WHAT YOU MIGHT CALL YOUR AVERAGE New Yorker. I move fast, I talk tough, I breathe soot and carbon monoxide. I live in a place where the garbage trucks and police cars keep me awake all night and it's worth your life to cross a street, and I pay through the nose to do it—monstrous taxes and preposterous rents are my way of life. I wouldn't change. This is where the action is. Even if the action turns out to be a good chance of being mugged and a near certainty that my apartment will be robbed every two or three years, I'm part of the action. There's only one thing that scares me. I've seen, every month, some new crime or strike or catastrophe, and what I fear is that some day they'll all happen together . . . and that will be the day

when new york hit the fan

Shire Brandon, thirty-four, was very young to be a widower, but that was what he was. He was a good man, the kind of good man who lets himself be stuck for jury duty when he really could get out of it if he wanted to, and that, too, was what he was doing, though his job needed him. He had a daughter who was thinking a lot about suicide and he lived in a city that seemed to be heading the same way, though not necessarily on purpose. In fact, that was its biggest problem. It seemed to have no collective plan at all, though Brandon thought he knew how to help it design one. Brandon loved them both, inexpertly. With both there was a difficulty in communicating that love. For his daughter, he could not find the words, while the city simply did not listen.

1

Perhaps the city was too huge to hear any single voice. New York is big. There's a square mile of it for every day in the year, almost exactly—there being three hundred sixty-five and change of each. There are five boroughs of the city, each one of which is also a county of the State of New York. There are twenty islands big enough to build on—it's almost all islands, you see. For this reason years ago, when Boston put up its Pru, it advertised the skyscraper as the tallest building on the continent of North America. So it was, Manhattan being no part of the main. The Bronx is firmly attached to the continent, but who builds in the Bronx?

New York is an old city, at least for its hemisphere. It was first visited (first by a European, that is, because dark skins don't count) by Giovanni Verrazano in 1524 (but he didn't get to name any of its parts—that was reserved for Henry Hudson eighty years later, because Italians didn't count either)—unless it was by some stubborn Viking in an oared longboat or some lost Irishman in a wicker curragh. It has been visited many, many times since. By almost everybody. In Washington's day it was a tiny town and not much worth visiting. He disliked it—would have burned it if the Congress had let him (but he didn't have to, because rioting New Yorkers did it as soon as he left). Before that, only Indians. And not many of them. Before that—well, it wasn't any town at all some umpty million years earlier, not only because there weren't any people to inhabit it but because it lay under some of the biggest damned mountains the planet Earth has ever spawned. They didn't last. Nothing lasts. The mountains crumbled (they say even Gibraltar may tumble) and the trickle of the rain and the flow of the rivers planed those mountains flat. Twice. More than twice. This planet squeezes mountains out of its crust like a young man pinching a blackhead, and the waters wash them away, everywhere, endlessly. At least, endlessly until the planet cools. And meanwhile, in this "now,"

2

the city's here, and widely hated, and widely envied, for it is the Big Apple. You listen to the lullaby of (or give your regards to) Broadway's rhythm, where everybody dances, but sometimes on air on the shores of Collect Pond.

Because the island of Manhattan is so beautifully surrounded by water, deep and flowing, the original planners saw no need to leave room for parks. Later generations disagreed, so they're there, lots of them, big ones and beautiful to walk in—if you dare. "Smoke? Hey, *smoke?*" cry the pushers, scaring the kids off the swings and the seniors away from the cement checker tables. Before Central Park was a park it was a shantytown for the city's despairing poor. Before Washington Square was a park it was a potter's field where the anonymous and friendless dead were pushed into the ground out of sight—not very far out of sight, because when the earthmovers came in to beautify it they broke right through the crust and crunched the pauper bones. The White Way is Gayer than ever, with its parade of militants in lavender shirts. There are more rats than people on Manhattan island, and the city trembles ever precariously between bankruptcy and boom. More than one kind of "boom," to be sure, because when someone has a bomb to plant it is in New York City that they like best to plant it—why would anybody bother to bomb Los Angeles? The city has seen, heard and smelled everything: draft riots and glaciers, garbage strikes and the worse stink of burning slaves, tickertape parades and stock-market crashes. New York is where the money is. To the extent that money is power (a very considerable extent) it is the brass-knuckled fist of might. The United Nations building stands on what was once the city's biggest slaughterhouse. A car with a DPL plate is parked by every fire hydrant, and the city's poor are—well, not really *poor,* if measured against Calcutta or the Latin-American barrios, but certainly impoverished in hope and purpose. Of course there's crime. There always has been.

A Dutchman was scalped on lower Broadway in 1643 by the Indians. The Dutch retaliated, making the score for that particular engagement Indians 1, Dutch 200. If New York is no longer the murder capital of the nation, having lost the crown to places in Florida, Arizona and Texas, it is also not a place where you stroll in the park to view a lunar eclipse, because what gets eclipsed may well be you. New York City is despised. It is feared. It is even often loved, but mostly it is there, a fact too large to be erased. Both "city" and "civilization" come from the same Latin root, *civitas,* and you can't have one without the other.

So here is the city, in this large "now," and here are some of the people in it, a North Carolina teen-ager getting off at the Port Authority Bus Terminal, a real-estate developer who thinks of himself as a futurologically sound conserver of urban values, a think-tank employee who believes he knows how to solve all the city's problems, a terrorist, a child contemplating suicide, a woman with a mission and a really mean tongue, a million, several million others. Sticks and stones don't make the city. People do. Each one pulls his own way for his own reasons, noble or mean or most often just irrelevant, but there is a vector result that makes it move. It never stops.

So here are four of those people, three visible and one standing at the window of a hallway across the street to watch what goes on. The one we are looking at most closely now is the one who thinks he knows how to solve all the city's problems—by means of social inventions—inventions which permit people to get their hands on the levers of government, in particular. That is what he does with his working time, but just now he isn't working at it because he has been interrupted by the requirements of an earlier social invention. He is on jury duty. He isn't getting along with that very fast, either, because of another social invention of considerable antiquity. The person across the street has put a bomb in the building. The thinker's name is Shire

4

Brandon. He has all the foregoing on his mind, plus the fact that his daughter, Jo-Anne, is upset because her mother has disappeared. And, oh, yes, there's also a garbage strike.

The trial was a kind of low-key oratorio, indignant yelping from the defendant's attorney cross-examining, hostile response in a mumbled contralto from the plaintiff on the stand, antiphonal interjections by her lawyer—hardly enough to keep a jury awake, or even the judge, when to the auditory portion of the program was added a divertissement in mime. A policeman came sidling into the courtroom. He moved with that special calm that said that he had a lot to be calm about, and he whispered inaudibly to the bailiff, who muttered to the clerk, who jumped up to tell the judge something the judge was shocked to hear. That was no longer a whisper, though Brandon couldn't make out the words from the jury box. All the calm had been used up with the patrolman, too. Everybody in the courtroom froze where he was. The judge banged his gavel. "There's been a phone call," he said loudly. "We've been warned there is a bomb on the premises. Follow the officer out of the building in an orderly way and—and—and wait for further instructions." Everybody unfroze at once. Choking gasp from the fat woman next to Brandon, scared giggle from the plaintiff's attorney, and from the black man in the silk suit a loud "Shee-*it*." "Move it, God damn it," bawled the cop, mime no more, and somehow, not with panic but with a lot of confusion, all of them were out the door and down the wide, shallow marble steps and out into the steamy, late-summer New York air.

No one dawdled. No one protested being herded across the street into the park, although the place stank terribly—most of the grass was covered with ten-foot-high stacks of black plastic garbage bags. The rats had been at them, and maybe the bag ladies and the derelicts from along the Bowery, too, because at least half of them were spilling their contents. Partly in self-defense against the stench, mostly out of pent-up nicotine hunger, Brandon was pulling out his cigarettes as he moved. So were half the others spilling out of the Municipal Building, and as he patted his pockets for a match somebody put a slim Dunhill under his nose. It was the black man in the silk suit. And here, at last, our three New Yorkers are together—or almost together, because Brandon hadn't seen the third person yet, being busy with introductions to the second one—

"I'm Dan de Harcourt."

"Hello, Mr. Harcourt, I'm—"

"No, no, not Harcourt, *dee* Harcourt."

—whom he recognized, or almost recognized. Somewhere? Where? Oh, sure. Dan de Harcourt was the one who was always on the telephone in the jury room, while they were all waiting to be called, and Brandon was one of the three, five, sometimes ten people in line waiting for him to get off. What de Harcourt was *doing* on the phone so long (when Brandon was anxious to call his office, or even more anxious to call his child) was not clear, although in one of the arguments about that at the head of the line Brandon had heard the word "investments." You didn't actually think of a twenty-two-year-old black man as an investor, Brandon thought, but this one looked like money—the silk suit, the Guccis, the whiff of Aramis as he lit Brandon's cigarette.

It wasn't a place for conversation. They were jostled and moved along; the crowd was moving of its own volition, too, as individual members tried to get away from the stink of refuse from the sea-food restaurant, only to find themselves moving toward the garbage of the pizza parlor down the block. On the steps of the Municipal Building uniformed cops and some men in plain clothes—FBI?—were leading leashed dogs inside —explosives sniffers?

It was a major annoyance for everyone concerned,

but it was also exciting. If it hadn't been for the stink of the garbage, it might almost have been fun. There was a Channel 2 van already in position at the edge of the square, with a cherry-picker camera panning the crowd —there was a very good chance, thought everyone there, that he might turn up on the six o'clock news. Channel 7 had a hand-held camera and somebody familiar—Tom Snyder?—talking to a policeman with a gold shield on the steps of the building, and WPIX's truck was just edging in. These people wouldn't be wasting their time on a false alarm—thought everyone in the crowd—and so to the excitement there was added the smallest hint of danger; and everyone put on his best face in case the cameras were turned his way, so that he might join the host of heroes—Julius and Ethel Rosenberg, the Reverend Sun Myung Moon, senators, bankers, bank robbers—who had gone before them to appear on TV cameras in this place.

Brandon edged his way toward them, like everyone else, though (he told himself) his motives were different, and almost stumbled over a slight elderly man in glasses like the bottoms of pop bottles. "Mr. Feigerman," he cried, pleased. "I didn't expect to find you here!"

Since de Rintelen Feigerman's relationship to Shire Brandon was a very small part of his life, not to mention that Feigerman was all but blind, it took him a moment to respond. At the Jefferson Commonwealth Institute for Governmental Studies de Rintelen Feigerman was a member of the Board, on premises only at the bi-monthly meetings, an occasional conference and the Christmas party; in those surroundings he recognized the Goals and Strategies Committee chair, but not in the hot miasma of Foley Square during a bomb threat. Still, he managed to place the dim face. "Ah, yes, the Universal Town Meeting man," he said, offering his hand. "How's the project coming along?"

Now, a proper answer to that would have required

7

Brandon to report on at least a dozen aspects and ramifications of the matter. The Universal Town Meeting itself was complicated enough, and Brandon wasn't at all sure that Feigerman knew what it was about, other than that it involved using the electronic media to get all the people of New York City talking together. The preliminary discussions with the radio and TV stations were another—actually, were twenty-two other —areas, for each station proposed its own ground rules. But, beyond that, it would be necessary to explain that none of it was coming along, just now, because of the fact that Brandon was stuck on a lengthy divorce trial, and that his private life was in a shambles. It was a tribute to Brandon's organized mind that he managed to compress quite a lot of that into three or four sentences, with the help of a gesture toward the TV crews (exemplifying the way the electronic media could keep a community in touch with its million parts) and to the piles of garbage, as examples of the sort of problems UTM would be able to solve.

It was a tribute to old man Feigerman's powers of comprehension that he grasped at least enough of what Brandon was saying to ask the most pertinent question —although, as he had learned from long experience in having knotty problems brought to him, the most pertinent question didn't necessarily require having heard any of the explanations. It was only:

"What do you need to have happen to get the thing going again?"

"Help from City Hall," Brandon said promptly, and searched Feigerman's face for a reaction. But you could never get one through those thick, distorting lenses. He went on, "The stations are only stalling—nobody wants to be the first to give away a whole night's time. But they all know the FCC will give them brownie points for it. So if the Mayor would put in a word it might get them off the dime."

And then he realized that at least part of the reason

he wasn't getting a reaction was that the old man was in distress. The heat, the stench, the crowds—Mr. Feigerman was looking very pale.

Mean-hearted, hostile New York—all the same, as soon as the nearest cop saw what was happening he went racing off for an ambulance man with oxygen, and the eight people squeezed onto a six-seat bench all got up so Mr. Feigerman could stretch out, and even backed away to give him room; and the black man with the Dunhill lighter took off his silk jacket to fan Mr. Feigerman with it . . . and by the time the policeman got back with the oxygen Mr. Feigerman was sitting up and his color was back, and a captain of police with a bullhorn was announcing from the steps that the bomb call had been a hoax.

So everyone trooped back to what they had been doing. Mr. Feigerman got a second-reading approval of his environmental impact statement for the new apartments on the Queens side of the East River, Mrs. Madeleine Finster got her freedom from Mr. Finster, along with custody of their son and their house, and at least two of the city's problems had been solved that day. To be sure, there were others. The garbage still mounted, the police were threatening blue flu if their new contract didn't give them more money than the firemen and an uptown IRT express, stopped for a malfunctioning red light at 23rd Street, was struck from behind by another train egged on by a malfunctioning green—eight dead, more than two hundred injured, and traffic so badly tied up that Shire Brandon had no hope of getting to the office even after his case was completed downtown.

And then, when Brandon got home, his daughter Jo-Anne was crying desolately in the middle of the living room.

Crying wasn't a surprise. She had cried on and off for weeks, ever since the early-morning private garbage collector found her mother on the sidewalk. The two plainclothes cops who were with Brandon's daughter, they were a surprise. Having accepted that they were there, and having observed that every book that had once been in the wall shelves was now tumbled on the floor, it was no surprise at all for Brandon to learn that while Jo-Anne was in school and he was performing his civic duty in the Municipal Building, their apartment had been burglarized.

> My name is Gwenna Anderson, but they call me Vanilla Fudge because I'm the only one of Dandy's whores that's white. When Dandy came up to me in the Port Authority Bus Terminal and said he'd give me a lift to wherever I was going, I knew where I was going. I was ready. I was fifteen years old, but that doesn't mean I didn't know what a pimp was. There weren't any pimps in the diner in North Carolina. Just the counterman. And the busboy and the short-order cooks and a couple of customers at night when business was slow, and if I'm still earning my living on my back at least it's on a bed, not on those greasy duckboards in the kitchen. And my feet don't hurt.

The burglars hadn't taken the beds at least, though they'd unmade them and ripped open two pillows to look for hidden money, so when Brandon woke up the bed at least was unchanged. Jo-Anne was standing in his doorway, holding his discharge certificate from the United States Army. "I was putting things away," she said, "and I found this. I don't know where it goes."

In order to remember that the apartment had been robbed, Brandon had to reason backward from what Jo-Anne had said. "Anywhere, honey," he said, looking around. Yes, it wasn't a dream; the stuff that had been pulled out of bureau drawers and thrown on the floor was all back—in one drawer or another—but his bedside TV was gone, and the empty box that had once held his cufflinks and wedding ring was standing on his night table. There wasn't any *Today Show* to watch while they ate their breakfast, either, because that TV was gone, too, and so was his roll of postage stamps and Jo-Anne's eighteen silver quarters hoarded since the currency change and her portable typewriter and even her china pig—contents, she thought, maybe as much as fifty dollars, because she'd been saving for skis. The super, Mr. Rozak, came in while they were eating to see how they were bearing up, and behind him one of the neighbors, that Mr. Becquerel from the fourth floor. Both seemed to think it was the Pins from across the street. The police didn't seem to have any theory at all, or much hope of ever seeing any of the stolen property back. When Brandon finished shaving and came out of his room Jo-Anne was standing by the window, watching what the Pins were doing that day. "Don't be late for school," he said automatically, but as he came up beside her he saw that the morning's performance was interesting. Their across-the-street neighbors were what was termed "Persons in Need of Supervision"—Pins, for short—which meant that they were graduates of a reformatory, a jail or an asylum. They were all young, all male, all black. It had been Brandon's opinion that they weren't really bad neighbors, not counting an unpredictable amount of noise at odd times, but they did do strange things. This morning's noise was a yo-heave-ho sort of grunting and yelling as three or four of them were rocking somebody's parked Chrysler Imperial back and forth. Whoever parked it had not bothered with the hand brake—or with the sign that said *No Parking, Social Services Vehicles Only*.

"Honey," he said, "I'd like to leave a little early this morning, because I want to pick up some stuff on 42d Street—"

"I'm ready, Daddy," she said. She punched the elevator button while he double-locked the door—the second lock had been installed at ten o'clock the night

11

before, and he had explained to his daughter what "locking the barn door after the horse is stolen" meant.

"Give you a lift to school," he said, as he said every morning, and,

"Thanks, Daddy," she said, as she said every morning, as though the issue had never been in doubt. When they got out to the sidewalk the Pins had got their prey out into the middle of the street. Unfortunately, the steering geometry had caused the car's wheels to track themselves straight. Since no one could get in to turn the steering wheel, it could not be moved in any direction now except straight forward and straight back, and so the block was clogged with cars, most of them blowing their horns, and they had to walk to the corner to find a cab.

Coming into the garment center the taxi inched along. Then, for three changes of the traffic light, it didn't move at all, because a tractor-trailer trying to make a turn had blocked the intersection. "I'll walk from here," Brandon said through the wire mesh that was supposed to keep cabbies from being mugged and, who knew, perhaps sometimes did. He tipped the man a dollar. It was not enough to forestall the muttering of a hack driver abandoned by his passenger in a gridlock.

Brandon was not actually in any hurry. The situation report he was going to pick up at the old McGraw-Hill Building on West 42d Street was going to fill up his morning, but before Brandon was willing to get to thinking about that there were a whole congeries of other things he had to think about.

The problem with problems was in deciding which of them to tackle first. That was conventional wisdom, exemplified for Shire Brandon by Dr. Jessica Grai, the Director of Life Style Analysis, and his opposite number at the foundation. Given any request at all, Dr. Grai's response was, "I have only one stack of priorities and there's only one top to it—where does this go?" But in Brandon's experience problems didn't come in stacks. They came in concentric shells, like black holes in the universe. You not only couldn't deal with the core problems, you couldn't even see them after a while through the layers of others that had enveloped them, though they were still there and hurting. So, strolling up Eighth Avenue from the old green Art Deco building on West 42d Street, Brandon's attention was used up in trying to remember what the core problems were. Outside of them all was the problem of getting ready for the afternoon Plans Committee. Just under that the burglary. Somewhere close to the outer layers the resolve to finish some of the interrupted conversations he had had with Jo-Anne: whether she should go to the pajama party at her friends'; why the Pins were the way they were; why, even when it was in the high eighties, it was right to refrain from air-conditioning, even though the noise of the air-conditioners was what made all the rest of the tenants in their building more tolerant of the Pins' noise than they might have been; the gnawing worry that he might be impotent, because even the hot-pants hookers didn't strike him as attractive . . . it was all jumbled together, roiling around inside the surface worries. But the core was not in doubt. It was the fact that Jo-Anne was upset, and the core of *that* was a quasar bright enough to shine through all the layers outside. It was tough times for a man when his wife went six stories airborne. It was even tougher for a ten-year-old girl, particularly when it was the ten-year-old who had been wakened first by the sirens and found that all that remained of Mommy was a note that said:

I love you both, but all the lies are making me crazy.
I have to get out of this situation.

Love, Maude

And, of course, when Brandon woke up to find his wife a suicide, the hardest thing to deal with was not the child's hysteria but the undodgeable, but also unanswerable, question: "What 'lies' was she talking about, Daddy?"

He had to answer her sometime—but not, please God, for a few more years.

The Jefferson Commonwealth Building was a plagiarism from that pleasantest of office structures, the Rockefeller on East 42d Street. It was thirty stories tall, and the portion of it nearest the street was a garden. The street wall was three hundred vertical feet of glass. Behind the glass was a bower. There was a gently flowing stream, with pink-and-white and golden carp moving restlessly through it. There were ti-flowers from Hawaii, and a banyan; there was a grove of half a dozen banana and orange trees, and almost every week there were half a dozen tree-ripened oranges or a hand or two of firm green bananas for the secretaries to take home. Winter or summer, the little tropic paradise on Eighth Avenue stayed at seventy-eight degrees, and passersby, sweltering or frozen or drenched, would gaze enviously in at heaven. Only gaze. If you had no business with the Institute, you couldn't pass the guard at the door.

What Brandon wanted to do at that moment was get a cheese Danish from the coffee wagon and sit under the banyan tree, watching the carp chase his crumbs. He resisted the temptation. When you worked for a think-tank, you tried harder than in any Fortune 500 corporation to look like an alert, efficient executive. So he sent his secretary, Kim Hwa, for the coffee and Danish, and his research associate, Al Plugmann, off to Xerox the situation report, and received them both on his little lanai on the eighteenth floor.

If Brandon could pull together a coherent list of recommendations for the Plans meeting, their report would be laid before the Advisory Commission—which in turn would bring it up at the Mayor's Study Group, which might actually pass it on to the Mayor—the half-dozen electoral reform schemes that had formed Brandon's doctoral dissertation, become a well reviewed (though infrequently read) university press book and thus been directly responsible for his appointment as Goals and Strategies Director for the Jefferson. They included:

The Universal Town Meeting, which, through the use of electronic media and random-access interviewing of ordinary citizens, might achieve a decision-making assembly comparable to the New England town meetings or the old Greek agora—on a scale of tens of millions of people.

The Five Per Cent Solution, by means of which individual citizens willing to pay a five per cent surcharge on their income taxes could direct that the whole of their taxes be directed to whichever function of government they thought most important.

The Citizens' Grand Jury, with the same statutory authority as those used in preparing criminal indictments, but with the authority to subpoena and question all the departments of government and quasi-governmental agencies, and to prepare recommendations for the Universal Town Meeting.

The Cafeteria Municipal Budget, in which each citizen was given a stipulated amount of services free— and if he chose to take them in the form of parks and swimming pools rather than schools for his children or open-air concerts, could indicate his choices by having a "credit card" punched each time he used a service.

There were others. Brandon had spent three years dreaming them up, while Maude and his veterans' benefits supported them and Jo-Anne was learning to walk and talk and get along without diapers, and in some ways it had been the happiest time of his life. But only seven inventions had survived his dissertation advisor, and only four of those had got past the Advisory Commission of the Jefferson.

All these social inventions—these crackbrained schemes, the first people he had applied to for a job had called them—had been fun to create, and they had achieved every goal he had hoped for them, as a starving, overage graduate student, except for one. No one in any kind of civil authority had ever shown any interest at all in putting any one of them into practice.

But the Advisory Commission might start things going at last, if only he could put together a proper report. So Brandon made the effort, reading, making notes, dictating sections into Kim's Stenorette. It wasn't easy, for his mind did not want to think about public policy, only about private calamity. He found himself daydreaming, looking across the angle of the building to the other lanais, where people were working on a hundred jobs—many of them female people— quite a few of them dressed for the outdoors summer and the indoors tropics, in short skirts or even shorts; he marked where smooth thigh, pale or cocoa or coffee cream, disappeared under a typing table, and wished that he felt more interest in any of them. . . .

And was caught staring up the dress of a woman on the floor above by Simon Moberly, the ancient and honorable Director of the Institute. "What are you doing *here?*" the Director demanded, staring around the lanai in horror.

"Why, it's just more convenient. There are fewer interruptions—"

"I don't mean out here, I mean why are you here instead of down at City Hall? Didn't you get my message? Saul Wassermann's expecting you."

"Why— Why— Nobody told me," said Brandon.

"It was Mr. Feigerman who arranged it—said he'd spoken to you about it yesterday. Very intelligent of you to bring it up that way, though of course generally speaking communications with members of the Advisory Commission ought to be confined to proper channels —no," cried the Director, recollecting himself, "there's

16

no time to talk about that. You're due down there in forty minutes, Shire! And you certainly don't want to keep Saul *Wassermann* waiting!"

Certainly no one wanted to keep Saul *Wassermann* waiting. He was one of those through whom power flowed. It was Saul who programmed the Mayor, Saul who was the knob of the Mayor's door and the hearing-aid in the Mayor's ear, Saul who carried in his head the map of the maze you must solve to make the vast city political machine turn over. Touch base with the union heads. Get a money promise from the bankers. Placate the power brokers from the boroughs and the neighbor-hoods, especially the ones that were not sharing in this particular milking of the public cow. Find a city coun-cilman to introduce the ordinance, explain it to the clerks and the legislative assistants, clear it with Albany if the state was involved, fill in the city's congressmen so that Washington would throw up no roadblocks, persuade the civic associations and the taxpayers' groups to endorse if possible, or at least to look the other way as this one went by—recruit; neutralize; horse-trade; coax . . . and then, if you were lucky, the gears would engage and the machine would turn, and out would come your new subway line, or park, or auditorium, or agency. Perhaps the machinery of gov-ernment could function without people like Saul Was-sermann. No one knew. The experiment had never been tried. In cities or nations, under dictators or mayors or kings, there was always the technician who knew where to find the levers of power. Sometimes he was camouflaged and mild, a Colonel House or a Harry Hopkins. Sometimes flamboyant: Haldeman, Raspu-tin, Talleyrand. Or Saul Wassermann.

Saul Wassermann was out of the Talleyrand-Rasputin taxon. He wore conspicuously the trappings of power. His office was as large as the Mayor's, and when the two met it was Saul who set the time.

He set the time for Shire Brandon, too, by keeping Brandon waiting for an hour and twenty minutes in a room without a window or a decent chair.

When Brandon at last got into the room the waiting wasn't over, because Wassermann was talking on the telephone, turned around in his chair, looking out across City Hall Park at the hot afternoon city. Even inside the building you could smell the garbage strike, because City Hall Park had its ten feet of stacked garbage. There was no chair near the desk. Having no choice, Brandon simply stood uncomfortably until Wassermann turned, slammed the phone into its cradle and looked at him. "Thanks for coming, Brandon," he said agreeably. "What have you got for me?"

It was the moment. Brandon had rehearsed his speech, and he began it well. "This is the basic prospectus," he said, dropping two hundred odd Xeroxed pages on Wassermann's desk. "I don't expect you to read it all—we academics get wordy. It makes several main points. First, it is people's perception of facts, more than the facts themselves, that govern their behavior. Second, behind most of the strikes and unrest in the city, in fact in the world, lies a perception of unfairness and helplessness—people believe that they are not getting a fair share of the world's goods, and at the same time that they have no good way to change that. Third, there is a reality behind most of the perceptions. The good things are not distributed evenly, and most people do not have any good way of affecting events. All this is prefatory, and it's all covered in the first five pages—but you probably are aware of all this already."

Wassermann nodded: *get along with it.* "So what we propose," Brandon lectured, a little faster, "is to cure this helplessness—this *anomie,* as it is called—by giving the average man some opportunity to exercise real control over the world he lives in. In a community as large as this no individual's share of control can be large. But each one can be made to feel, because he can be allowed to have, *some* actual authority. This is accomplished by giving him an opportunity to determine to some extent how his own tax payments are spent—this is called 'The Five Per Cent Solution'—and to select which government functions other than the absolute essentials he wishes to make use of—the 'Cafeteria Budget'—and to take part in large decision making through the Universal Town Meeting."

He was saying it all quite well, Brandon told himself, but at the same time he could not help observing that Wassermann was not growing in enthusiasm. The charm level was dropping inch by inch; the impatience index rising, bit by bit. "There are," Brandon went on, summarizing now, "a number of other proposals. The Selective Service Legislature. The Citizens' Grand Jury. The——"

"Excuse me," said Wassermann, and although he was still polite Brandon recognized he had lost him. "Let me see if I've got this right. All these things you're recommending, they're about different ways of running the government?"

"Basically, yes," Brandon admitted.

"Uh-huh," said Wassermann. He pawed through papers on his desk for a moment until he found what he wanted. He thought for a second, then lifted his eyes to Brandon. "The reason I agreed to see you was I got a call from Feigerman & Tisdale. They're pretty important in this city. Their construction projects are all over the place, and they're well built and well run. They've got some pretty far-reaching ideas for projects the city should get into, so when Mr. Feigerman's people said I should talk to you I jumped at the chance."

"And I appreciate it," said Brandon.

"But this isn't what I expected," Wassermann said kindly. "What I was hoping for from you was tangible things. We average losing thirteen thousand jobs in manufacturing a year. Give me something that makes jobs. We've priced apartments out of all reason and we still can't house all the people that want to live here.

Give me some housing plans. Political theories don't give me. I can't collect taxes on political theories." He pulled open a drawer and lifted out a thick red folder. "Here's something Mr. Feigerman had drawn up for us a few months ago. Why don't you take it back to the Foundation? Let your people look it over. See if there are ways to make any of it happen. Then come back and see me again," he said, rising to shake Brandon's hand, "if there's any point to it."

The Director was not angry, because the Director never allowed himself to get angry. He was just very, very disappointed. "I had hoped," he said faintly, "that this would be a breakthrough for us. What were these proposals that Mr. Feigerman's office gave the Mayor?"

"Hardware," said Brandon bitterly, "hardware and construction." He stirred the folder, in its handsome plastic cover held on with a silken cord, with the embossed words *Feigerman & Tisdale, Engineering*.

"Like Mr. Feigerman's East River project?" the Director inquired. "Because I'm bound to say that the idea of putting a whole apartment city on the Queens bank strikes me as maximum use of amenities for everyone."

"Everything!" said Brandon, and it pretty nearly was. Half of them were things you were accustomed to see only on the cover of *Popular Mechanics*. A project for rebuilding the subways as maglevs. A project for constructing new prisons in depressed areas of the cities—new industry for the unemployed, good use of worthless land, easy access for the families of the prisoners (who very likely, though the proposal did not explicitly point it out, were already living in those same depressed areas—and a supplementary notion of putting them underground for the multiple purposes of saving energy, reducing the chances of escape and sparing the law-abiding neighbors, if any, the necessity of looking at them). There were proposals for building

a dome over the island of Manhattan, harnessing the
tides of the Lower Bay for electrical energy, damming
Long Island Sound to turn it into a freshwater lake,
cooling the city's buildings in summer heat by pumping
deep-aquifer cold water through its air-conditioners
and double-decking the city's main avenues with pedestrian malls. Every one of them was far out. But every
one was buttressed with pages of feasibility studies and
cost-benefit accounting.

"I'm bound to say," said the Director, "that some of
these are quite ingenious." He was looking at a page on
the Princeton Ice Pond, suggesting the use of snow-
blowers in winter to create and store ice for summer
cooling.

"The one I like," Brandon said gloomily, "is the
car-use meter. Every car has one, and it's radio-
controlled by zone—the closer you are to the center of
town, the more it costs you to have your car there. It's
an English idea."

The Director nodded sagely. "But they need it as
much in London as we do here, and if they're not using
it there must be terrible bugs in it. I imagine we'd find
that true of most of these studies, eh, Shire? Impractical dreams, filled with conceptual faults?"

Brandon shook his head. "I'm afraid it's a work of
genius," he declared.

And so it was, if not so much for what it proposed,
then for what it left unsuggested. There was not a word
in it about any of the sort of social inventions that
Brandon had included. There was no suggestion of
political change at all. As far as F & T's recommendations were concerned, the City of New York would for
its entire future life go on having a Mayor, a City
Council, five Borough Presidents and a political club on
every block. The pressure-cooker of special-interest
lobbying and political muscle would steam right on
forever. So most of the decision making would be in the
hands of professionals . . . and the true genius of writing the report as F & T had done, Brandon perceived,

was that the Saul Wassermanns were an integral part of the F & T future, while in the sort of world he strove to create they would have no place. "You know what we did?" Brandon asked. "We offered Saul Wassermann a plan for his own elimination. No wonder he didn't like it!"

I'm Maude Brandon, and I know it was damn foolishness for me to get myself pregnant while my husband was still in Vietnam. But I thought he was dead. He was good about it, when he came back. He said if it hadn't been for the war we'd be having a child about now, so this would be the child. He said if we moved to another city there wouldn't be any friends or neighbors to start adding up dates, and with his veterans' benefits he could go back to graduate school and we'd start a new life and no one would ever know the difference. But it turned out there was one person who could know the difference, by adding up dates, as soon as she was old enough.

And the city went on doing its thing. The subways were slow, because the repercussions of the accident had not yet been cleared away, and the garbage continued to mount and stink. In a loft on Worth Street a raddled junkie (she had been Class of '79 at Barnard) stuffed firecracker powder into a Band-Aid box and dreamed of plutonium. A pimp with a gravel voice looked incredulously at the diamond ring his girl had brought him as a peace offering, and knocked her down. It was his way of telling her to take it back and bring money instead. Fifteen Italian boys in Brooklyn surrounded a black mailman, sliding their heavy belts out of the loops. He was allowed to deliver mail in the white neighborhood, but he had made the mistake of drinking a Coke in their favorite candy store, and that was not allowed. And at the same time on East 58th Street a writer was tapping the last lines of his finest novel into a word processor, a delegate to the United Nations was about to propose a viable nuclear arms control and, in dirty, rickety old Bellevue Hospital, a surgeon with eight hundred thousand dollars' worth of lasers and instrumentation and a ten-person team of highly skilled colleagues, was removing a tumor from the spinal cord of a Bowery derelict. For nothing.

So it was in New York. So it was in all cities everywhere, but New York was the *schwerpunkt*. It is not only etymology that makes "city" = "civilization." A village can support a store, a policeman and a post office. A town, more stores, a fire department and perhaps a movie theater. But these are only the beach froth of the great wave of civilization. To support specialized hospitals and specialized schools, an opera company or two, a symphony orchestra, night clubs, museums, great libraries, a choice of churches, sports teams, convention centers, an infinitely varied labor force, an access to instant capital, quick public transportation, shops that hold anything you might want, shops that offer what you need at any hour of any day, hookers, heroes, homosexuals, psychoanalysts, circuses, forensic pathologists and foreign diplomats—to support all these things and people, to provide a means and an outlet for all the manifold "civilized" activities of human beings what is necessary is critical mass. When enough of all these things come together we have civilization, and the place where we find it is called a "city."

The cost is steep, in every coin, but the city is an indispensable expense.

To the task of solving Brandon's burglary the city applied its forces. They were impressive, even if inadequate.

The first suspects, of course, were the Pins. It was Brandon's first guess, and his daughter's, and the building superintendent's, and that of the police. You could not say the police weren't painstaking. They

23

dusted every flat surface for prints. They knocked on every door to see if neighbors in the building had seen or heard anything. They made Brandon search out sales receipts and warranties, and copied down the numbers of every appliance they could.

You could not say, either, that they were encouraging. When the burglary detective came back to report that he had no report he volunteered that not one stolen article in a hundred was ever recovered. "Most of the ones we do get when we bust a burglar never get back to their rightful owners anyway," he added. "Can't identify them. So they get auctioned off by the Police Property Custodian."

They were standing by the window where the main television set had once been. Across the street the Pins were engaging in their usual pursuits of an August afternoon. Two of them were squared off, a good ten feet apart. One was in a John L. Sullivan boxing pose, the other with his feet spread and pointed outward, like an Oriental frieze of a temple dancer. No blood seemed likely to be spilled. The detective looked at them with the technical appraisal of a tank officer observing a hill which, at that moment, he does not have to take. "If they're the ones that took our things," said Jo-Anne thoughtfully, "can't you just go over there and look for them?"

"Not without a warrant, honey, and we don't have probable cause. Anyway, they've probably moved it all out by now." But he didn't want to discuss the Pins, except in generalities. They were Persons in Need of Supervision, all right, but he wouldn't commit himself on what they needed to be supervised for. Yes, they had been institutionalized. A proper concern for the Pins' civil rights didn't allow him to say for what—but just what the hell, Mr. Brandon, do you think young black kids get institutionalized for? Mugging? Rape? Drugs? Yes. All of the above. Most of the Pins had begun accumulating a green sheet before they were twelve. The fact that they were now in a halfway house didn't mean that they had reformed. It only meant at most that somebody, somewhere, thought there was some hope they would.

But as the detective left it was clear that he was not that person.

If you added up the replacement value of everything that was taken it came to nearly two thousand dollars. But that was an insurance-type figure, not a real one. The living-room TV set had been expensive when Brandon bought it for the tenth wedding anniversary, but its picture tube was about to go and the tuning strips had worn so that you could hardly get some channels at all. Jo-Anne's pink clock-radio with the Donald Duck stencils had been with her since she was five, and frequently dropped. The most serious damage was internal. Particularly to Jo-Anne. Children grow up by meeting challenges, but if the challenges are too severe they can't be met. She no longer asked difficult questions about her mother. She had given up writing those long, chatty letters that there was no way to mail. She spent more and more time in her room with the door closed and when Brandon, worried, coaxed her out to talk out her feelings she simply stared him down. I'm all *right*, Daddy, for the heaven's sake! But she wasn't.

So what was Brandon to do? It was not through his own decision that he was a single parent, without ever having learned how to be one. He humbled himself to ask Jessie Grai for advice—after all, she had a doctorate in psychology—but the Director of Life Style Analysis had never had a family. Brandon got better advice out of Ann Landers, whom he read religiously. The best advice he got was all to the same effect: Spend time with the child. Encourage her to talk. Try to be cheerful around her, but don't give her special consideration—make her do her chores and study her homework. And, again and above all, spend time with her. But the obstacle to that was Jo-Anne herself. For the heaven's sake, Daddy, *no,* I don't want you to take your vacation now so that we can go to Disney World! Thank you, Daddy, but I've been to all the museums on class trips. No, thank you, Daddy, there isn't any movie I want to see right now. On the last hot, muggy Saturday before school started he persuaded her at least to take a walk by the river with him, and unprotestingly she made tuna-fish salad sandwiches and filled a thermos with orange juice. Down at the far end of the block two of the Pins were having one of their long-range arguments, one on one curb, the other one across the street. What the argument was about was impossible to tell. Even in the echoing canyon of the block's high-rise concrete walls you could not quite make out the words, or at least never more than one of them, so what Brandon heard was only, "Mumble FUCKIN mumble mumble FUCKIN mumble FUCK mumble mumble FUCK." Jo-Anne gave no sign of hearing. She took her father's hand when they crossed the avenue and politely refused to let him carry her shoulder-bag with their lunch, and when they were seated on a fairly clean concrete block at the edge of a more or less abandoned pier she listened attentively as he pointed out the seaplane coming in for a landing, the pleasure boats, the Circle Line excursion vessel, the tugs prodding along their strings of barges, the bridges north and south across the river.

The advantage of a meal, when you are with a ten-year-old daughter who doesn't want to talk about the things that are bothering her, is that it gives you something to do for many minutes. The disadvantage is that when it is over you are out of programming. "The last time we were here," Brandon offered as they were finishing the sandwiches, "remember, Mommy wanted to go up in a seaplane."

"I remember," said Jo-Anne in a neutral voice, and then, brightly, "Look, Daddy, it's beginning to rain."

26

Brandon was equal to the occasion. They retreated under the shelter of the East River Drive, where more of the great square concrete blocks had been left to keep cars from driving into the parking spaces without paying for them. The blocks were dusty here. They didn't get the usual blessing of being rinsed off in rains, so all the airborne solid matter that settled on everything in the city not only settled there, it stayed. Brandon wiped off a block as best he could with their paper napkins. Even so, Jo-Anne's shorts would have to go in the wash.

It wasn't quite as nice as by the water in the sunshine. The smell of tar and wetness was diluted by smells of gas and burned-off tires and old, undisturbed dirt; weeks before the space had been one of the city's best hidey-holes for uncollected garbage, and there were still traces of that in the air. But Jo-Anne was as happy as she ever was, these days. Being out in a thunderstorm was an adventure. Across the East River they could see, through sheets of rain, a newspaper printing plant, the tower of a radio transmitter, the blot that had once been the Navy Yard—and even a stretch of green, somehow overlooked in the industrial building of the past centuries. If de Rintelen Feigerman's plans went through, all that would be wiped out by the pastel towers of East River East. Eighteen hundred apartments to a unit. Twelve units projected. Allowing for the standard two point two persons per unit, nearly fifty thousand people would be living there in the next five years, swimming in their five great pools, playing on their racket-ball courts, shopping in their self-contained supermarkets and drugstores and boutiques, skimming (if the money held out) by hovercraft across the East River to Wall Street or 42d Street to their jobs, and providing an interesting spectator sport for the welfare families in the Jacob Riis houses on the Manhattan side of the river. It was possible, Brandon acknowledged to himself, that Feigerman and Tisdale and Saul Wassermann had the right of it. There would be a lot of jobs in East River East. Given the choice between fifteen hundred well paying jobs and some airy-fairy fantasy about making civic decisions justly and with the participation of all, which would strike him as most valuable —assuming he were Feigerman, Tisdale or Wassermann, with the responsibilities they bore for making money either by building the city or providing funds to run it?

"It's raining pretty hard now, Daddy," said Jo-Anne. It occurred to Brandon that, considering his purpose in being with the child was to encourage her to talk out her feelings, he had been letting the conversation slide pretty badly. It hadn't seemed to trouble the child. She was entertaining herself by looking around the unfamiliar surroundings. As the rain grew stronger it leaked through the seams in the roadway overhead, and water came down in sheets where the seams had worn thin. There were drainspouts, but mostly they were bone dry—plugged up since God knew when, with God knew what. The whole city was well overdue for repair and reconstruction, Brandon realized. You couldn't blame Wassermann for wondering where the money was going to come from. . . .

He was doing it again. "What do you say, sweet?" he asked. "Want to try walking home in the rain?"

"Oh, wow!" she cried, adventure on top of adventure. She immediately discovered reasons why it was not only a good idea but indispensable—the rain was too warm to do them any physical harm, everything they had on, both of them, could pop right in the washing machine, and most of all she had to get ready for the birthday party that Brandon had completely forgotten about that afternoon. They weren't the only ones in the rain. There were joggers, ignoring anything that came between them and their therapy, splashing at every step. There were Hispanic kids on bicycles, doing figure-eights and curlicues on the nearly traffic-free street. One of them slid in the water, and fell, leaping up immediately with a grin as though he had planned that trick all along, and Jo-Anne grinned happily back.

But the rain was really intense. It filled Brandon's eyes. Across the river he could no longer see the radio transmitter towers, and the boats slinking in to the landing at 23d Street, sails furled, caught in the storm, were only gray shadows. He wondered where the seaplanes went when the weather got bad—none were in sight. It was the sort of thing he would have liked to talk over with Jo-Anne, but what stopped him was that it wasn't what he thought he *ought* to talk to her about. And yet, the real stuff—it was too hard! Ever since the suicide he had tried to be sensitive to every one of Jo-Anne's moods, looking for the right one to spark the talk that would heal all wounds, expose all sores, make the child informed and happy—as if it were possible to be both at once! But the right mood never came. When Jo-Anne was happy, it was a shame to spoil her mood. When she was not, he was reluctant to make her feel worse.

They paused at the corner of the avenue, smiling at each other through the downpour, as an extended family in front of them organized their forces to cross the street. There were four or five kids, including babies in strollers, and several grown-up women. Even the kids in the strollers had little umbrellas over their heads.

Why, thought Brandon, affectionately regarding his daughter, she doesn't seem upset at all, does she? Maybe the best thing to do is to butt out. Maybe she'll come to ask questions in her own time, and maybe what I should do is leave her to do it. So maybe I shouldn't press for a heavy daddy-kid talk that neither of us is really going to enjoy. . . .

Perhaps it was not good advice that Brandon gave himself, but it had one great advantage besides being easy to carry out. It did not add to his pain—at a time when pain had been pushed below the surface of his mind, most of the time, but was always known to be there and ready to boil out again at any moment.

I wasn't exactly the last man out of Ton Son Nhut airport, but I only missed it by about seventy-two hours. They kept me for a while in Waikiki, along with a couple thousand other late departures from the Nam, and it was like a honeymoon time. No bride, of course. Maude was still in San Francisco. She sounded funny when I phoned her from Honolulu, but I didn't think much of it—after all, we hadn't seen each other for a year and a half—until I got to Oakland. She was five months pregnant. It wasn't easy to handle. I made a decision—I don't know if it was the right one. I said we would move to New York and I would bring up the child as my own, and I did. I can't say it didn't bother me. What I didn't realize was that, for ten years, it bothered Maude even more.

Six times a day the mail boys made their rounds of the building. What they bore was not usually mail. It was interoffice memos, Xerox copies of policy statements, flagged issues of the three hundred periodicals the Institute subscribed to, each with a rubber-stamped distribution list so that, easily by the first of April, everybody would have had a chance to see the January issues. When Brandon heard his outer door open he called from the balcony, "Bring it out here, please." And the bearer did, but it wasn't the mail boy. It was the Director himself, smiling through his meringue of white beard.

"I thought I'd better bring this in person," he said, handing over the eighth or tenth Xeroxed revision of the afternoon's Commission meeting agenda. That was all he said. He stood beaming, and from the tilt of his eyebrows and the lilt of his voice Brandon knew that there was some kind of good news on the agenda. It took him only a moment to find it:

Item III-a. Dr. Brandon. Presentation of Universal Town Meeting Concept.

"Why," said Brandon, as much astonished as pleased, "that's great! I thought the whole project was down the tube."

"Inelegant," tittered the Director, "but not inexact. However, you've got a reprieve, Shire. Mr. Feigerman himself phoned and asked that we make time for it."

It was good news . . . but it caught Brandon unaware. "I haven't prepared anything," he said. The Director shrugged winsomely. "I mean, I don't know what angle to take."

"Be brilliant," the Director advised. "Think about the city as organism. Consider all its life processes. Survival, ingestion, elimination, reproduction—but listen to me," he said, laughing at himself, "trying to tell you what to say! I'm sure you'll be fine." On that note he left. It was one of the Director's least endearing traits that he allowed himself to speak only in allegory and innuendo, but expected from his subordinates blueprints.

So Brandon spent the next ninety minutes on his lanai, working notes into shape for a presentation. He was keenly conscious of the clock. Even so, it was not until he became conscious of a disturbance far below that he realized he had actually finished the job. It wasn't complete. It didn't give all the details. But it was all he would be allowed to say under Item III-a anyway. He stood up and stretched. Down below, among the banana trees and the purling waters, the security guard was repelling an invasion of the caterer's men, attempting an illicit shortcut with the food for the luncheon meeting, instead of going around the block to the service entrance. "Here goes," said Brandon—to himself, or to the banana trees—and headed for the washroom to comb his hair for the show.

When I die they won't have to put up a tombstone, because my tombstones are all over the city. Office buildings, hotels, condos, trade centers; I don't design them, but I build them. I don't mean just that I hire the workers and buy the steel. You don't build a skyscraper on the land you've acquired, you build it in the courtrooms and the city agencies, getting federal grants and municipal waivers, suing to reverse some Landmark Commission ruling, trading airspace for amenities—I'm good at that. I usually win, because I know what's good for the city and besides I have a right. They owe me. They owe me because I paid my dues when my B-24 crashed and burned and my eyes have never been right since; they owe me because I never would have had the chance if I hadn't married Paul Tisdale's widowed daughter to start the firm. They owe me because I grew up in the slums with the good old Dutch name of de Rintelen Feigerman. So I had to learn to fight when I was five, and I haven't stopped.

"Hello, Mr. Feigerman," said Brandon, coming into the dining hall.

The old man looked up at him. "Yes?" He didn't offer his hand and, considering the dim way he peered around the room, Brandon was far from sure he was recognized. He introduced himself, and got another, "Yes?"

The old man wasn't really that old, no more than middle sixties, but his thick glasses and slow, squinting stare made him look worse than he was. Brandon made conversation—that was what you were supposed to do before the Advisory Commission luncheons, that was why they were luncheons, with drinks on the sideboard, instead of simple meetings. Feigerman's responses were not hostile. They simply did not go beyond yes or no, and it made little difference what Brandon ventured. To the question whether Feigerman was fully recovered from his upset the day of the fake bomb, a declarative yes. To Brandon's random observation that he had been looking across the East River at the place where Feigerman proposed to build East River East, an interrogative one. Only when Brandon asked if he could get Feigerman a drink did he get a shake of the head and then a whole sentence: "My wife's the one you ought to be talking to."

But just then everyone was being seated, and the chance didn't come. There were extra chairs around the table, and Brandon was far down from where the Feigermans sat, next to a young woman who at once wanted to know how the Cafeteria budget would affect the bargaining power of municipal employees.

There were eleven members of the Advisory Commission, and for a wonder they were all present—more than all, because de Rintelen Feigerman had brought his wife; they were twenty-one at table. The woman on his right, Brandon discovered, was named Maggie Moscowitz, there as a stand-in for the Commission's spokesman for organized labor, the President of the Transit Workers Union. "Contract bargaining," she pointed out, "isn't a privilege; it's guaranteed by law. What happens if, say, a lot of people decide they don't want to ride the subway and the revenues fall off? Is the city going to make up the difference? And out of what?"

"That doesn't change," Brandon protested, pointing out that there was already a deficit on the transit system that had to be made up by tax money. "Anyway, the subway's probably the last thing that would be hurt—it's the libraries and museums that are going to need special protection." She allowed him to tell her what the special protection provisions were, but all she said was, occasionally, to pass the salt.

When she switched to Dr. Grai, on her other side, Brandon kept his eye on the Feigermans. Jocelyn

Feigerman was, if anything, older than her husband, he decided. She was not a pretty woman, but she was a striking one—tall, ash-blonde, looking as self-assured and poised in person as she did on the posters of her with a child or a happy unwed mother that advertised her mission against abortion. She didn't speak much, but when she did it was in a lecture-platform voice that carried easily down to the foot of the table. Brandon listened shamelessly, but none of it seemed to have to do with him. He applied himself to his meal.

The lunch was far more elaborate than usual, chilled white wine and napkin-wrapped red added to the usual Cokes and coffee urn. The Director was going out of his way to make a good impression on the Commission. It would have helped to have a larger room. This one was definitely overcrowded, especially as Maynard Mecke-ridge, the banker, would not refrain from smoking his cigar and Jocelyn Feigerman had not only invited herself along with her husband, but had brought a dark, agile young man as a sort of secretary. Mrs. Feigerman kept her goff busy. It was "Hersch, more wine, please," and, "Hersch, phone the airline and confirm my flight this afternoon," and when poor Hersch was not running errands he was kept busy fanning Meckeridge's cigar smoke away from his boss.

The makeup of the Commission included someone in social services—Msgr. Bredy, doubling as the authority on religion—an international commodities broker, the representative of Halbfleisch Frères. Taxation and law was an attorney named Milt White; politics and entertainment subsumed in the single person of ex-Senator Sandstrom, who backed shows. No Embassy hostess ever sorted her place cards more carefully than the Institute had chosen its Commission. Besides the outside commissioners there were the three in-house resident geniuses, Brandon, Jessie Grai and the Director himself. Of course, the Commission was not the Institute's only activity. At any given moment the Institute fielded at least a score of committees, commissions, task forces and study teams. They varied drastically in size, scope and function, but they all had one element in common. The Director was on all of them.

"III-a" had seemed like a nice remote agenda item when Brandon glanced at it, but he had not fully realized that Item I was only Msgr. Bredy's benediction and Item II took no more time than to propose a motion to dispense with the reading of the minutes, and so, while the drafted waitresses from the typing pool were still clearing away dishes, he was standing at the head of the table.

Since it was de Rintelen Feigerman who had been responsible for putting the presentation on the agenda, Brandon spoke to Feigerman. It wasn't satisfactory. Behind Feigerman's thick, tinted glasses there were no eyes to be seen. "The Universal Town Meeting," said Brandon, wondering whether Feigerman was looking at him—or even awake, "is a synthesis of sociology, communications theory and computer studies. What it promises to do is to make it possible for a city the size of New York, seven or eight million people, to participate in an interactive, two-way discussion of problem-solving in the same way that the New England town meetings did in the past. The UTM makes use of the redundant communications facilities available in the city: seven VHF and a large number of UHF television channels, approximately one hundred AM and FM radio stations—I beg your pardon?"

Feigerman's own interest, if any, was still not visible, but his wife had raised her hand. "I wondered, had you considered cable?" she asked.

"As a matter of fact, yes, but it could have only a limited usefulness—as you will see," said Brandon, intending a small but hopefully inoffensive reproof. "Let me sketch a scenario that might actually be employed right now. As you know, the city has been having a series of confrontations with its unions, particularly in the uniformed services. There is a logical impossibility in agreeing to terms, in that the police want their pay scale to reflect the fact that they have the highest risk and occupational hazard of any service, and that the firemen want pay parity with the police; you can't agree to both. Now, how do we solve this? We invite the entire city to take part. A major television channel provides a studio where, let us say, the City Council is gathered. Everyone can watch. At the same time, AM radio stations are assigned to provide simultaneous translation in Spanish, Japanese, Yiddish, Chinese, Italian and whatever other languages have a large enough constituency in the city to justify their use. Did you have another question, Mrs. Feigerman?"

"Yes. How about a referendum on moral issues?"

Brandon looked to the Director for help, but got only a resigned twinkle. "I'm not sure I understand, Mrs. Feigerman."

"In that case I'll explain. As you know, I am active in the right-to-life movement. We feel there should be a constitutional amendment banning abortion, and we are quite sure that if the issue were properly presented a large majority of voters would agree with us. My question—in fact, the reason why I asked to be here today—is whether your procedure can help us."

The table had become very quiet. Even the banker had stopped puffing on his cigar, and the conscripted waitresses were standing by the door, waiting to see how Dr. Brandon would get himself out of this. Dr. Brandon was curious about that, too. Dr. Brandon had fairly hard-held political opinions, and they did not include sympathy with the anti-abortion forces; in Dr. Brandon's view, they were made up of elderly troglodytes who didn't want other people to have any fun. He said, "I actually haven't considered it in that way, Mrs. Feigerman. It is a tool for mediation, not for persuasion."

"Exactly," she said, nodding. "Mediation is what I'm talking about. Not brain-washing, if that's what you're thinking. A simple public airing of the pros and cons. If it will make you feel better, don't think of it simply as a right-to-life proposition. There are many other moral issues that need a full and frank public discussion. Drugs. Street crime. The rights of victims. The concept of capital punishment, not to mention—"

Whatever else Mrs. Feigerman was going to mention she didn't mention, because there was one other major issue that she had left out, but would not stay left out. It mentioned itself.

The mention was a sudden sharp crack and grumbling roar, and then a crashing of fragile falling things amid a chorus of screams. Brandon, reprieved while leaning toward Mrs. Feigerman, turned just in time to see the great glass outside wall of the Institute Building separate itself into jigsaw shards and slip down out of sight. A pressure wave hit them, even inside the board room, making papers on the great pale conference table flutter and slide.

Brandon was the first to the railing, staring down into the great atrium. The tropical plants that had never felt outside air were crushed under the fallen wall, and the carp pool was turning pink with someone's blood. There was a crushed-icicle heap of shattered glass on the benches, and under it were human beings. Four of them that Brandon's shocked eyes could see, and one of them still horribly, miraculously alive.

Terrorists, of course. Some terrorists. Any terrorists; and the bomb they had used this time was no fake and no toy.

The bomb had been more than a block away, planted under the hood of a parked car in one of the theater blocks leading to Times Square. The driver and a passenger had been killed instantly, of course—had been much more than merely "killed," because there were body bags with some of their parts all around the smoking scrapheap that had been a 1982 Volvo. It could not have been intended just for them. The overkill was immense. Forty or fifty people were taken away to hospitals, mostly cut by flying glass and debris. At least fifteen were known to be dead, five of them inside the Institute.

If the uniformed services of the city were meditating strike, they didn't show it. The first emergency vehicle screamed in, tires crunching on the broken glass, in less than a minute. Minutes later the street was pyrotechnic with the flashing red, white and blue lights of fire trucks, police cars and ambulances. There was not room on the block for all of them; traffic was blocked on four side streets, and on Eighth Avenue from 42d Street north.

The damage was enormous. Theater marquees were sagging or down. Burglar alarms were ringing all up and down the street from locked doors nudged open or sometimes shattered by the blast. A post office truck with its side crunched in had rammed a cruising taxi and had come to rest nose-deep in a parked sports car. A huge, gray limousine had been half a block away, but part of the engine block from the bomb car had been hurled through its windshield; the chauffeur was dead, his passenger already in some hospital's emergency-care unit. Hub caps, broken glass and unidentifiable rubble mingled with the dirt in the street, and much of the sludge was red with blood. There was steam and smoke from burning vehicles, and fire hoses snaking in every direction across the street. A sleazy hotel at the corner had lost its awning to the overpressure from the bomb, and a woman on a stretcher, extracted from the splintered glass of the hotel's street-front window, was being transported to an ambulance. All that showed of her was her calm, perplexed face, eyes wide open and dismayed, as an ambulance attendant walked beside her with a bottle of plasma held high and the tube vanishing under the blanket. A youth with his head bandaged like The Invisible Man was being led to a police emergency van.

No one was being allowed to leave the Institute. The balconies were full. The staff and visitors hung fascinated over the rails, shivering in the damp winds that came in through the naked space where the plate glass had been, watching the disaster teams at work. No one talked about the bombing itself. It was a phenomenon too huge to articulate in sentences. What they talked about was whose protest it was—the Puerto Rican Nationalists? some Black Power revolutionaries? the Palestinians, the Irish, the Croats? It could have been almost anyone, for there did not seem to be a cause so quixotic or a hope so forlorn that some band of assassins was not prepared to set off a bomb for it. They had to wait half an hour before the emergency crews had everything in hand—well, not in hand, really, but as near as you could hope for in a city block where some of the rubble was still being picked apart, like deadly-sharp jackstraws, to look for more victims underneath. Then at last the Institute's people were allowed out, the stronger and haler first, the secretaries and the frailer among the visitors held back. When Brandon got past the still functioning door, averting his eyes from the pink glass where the doorkeeper had been unfortunate enough to stand, he discovered it was raining. He stood for a moment, waiting to be told when it was safe to cross the street, and Jocelyn Tisdale Feigerman picked her way toward him, her face creased with fury. "Now you see what animals they are!" she cried. "They should be treated like the vermin they are! Looking at this, how can anyone deny that we need the death penalty back?" She wrinkled her nose at the stench of a smoldering seat cushion, thrown from perhaps the original bomb car itself, swerved to avoid a chained bicycle bent by a car that had gone up on the sidewalk. "When I see the Mayor," she continued, as much to Brandon as to anyone—actually, to an invisible audience at some not-yet-convened women's-club meeting—"I'm going to tell him once and for all that we need more police and a lot tougher laws for terrorists!"

Brandon moved way, but departing the sound of Jocelyn Feigerman's voice brought him into the range of a black man who was bemoaning the gash the chained bicycle had left on the side of his chalk-white Mercedes. "Would you *look* at it?" he appealed, as much to Brandon as to anyone. "How'm I going to get that fucker out? And I can't even open my damn *door.*" It was a day for addressing unseen audiences. The man looked vaguely familiar to Brandon, but no more than vaguely familiar, for both of them had long since forgotten the previous bomb scare that had brought them together. Brandon moved a step farther along the sidewalk. There was a tour bus at the corner, undamaged but trapped in the traffic, with Japanese tourists standing engrossed at its door, snapping pictures of the carnage and the bank on the corner with its windows blown out and workmen already beginning to fit sheets of plywood into the vacant spaces. No doubt they kept the plywood on hand all the time, Brandon mused—

And heard a crash and screams from behind him, and turned. A remaining chunk of glass from the great glass wall of the Institute had swung itself loose from the upper stories and crashed to the ground, tearing with it a strip of metal framing. The glass had miraculously missed all the people there. The metal framing did not. It struck down an elderly man just coming out of the door.

It was Jocelyn Feigerman who was screaming the loudest, and her husband who had been smitten by the falling metal. "Oh, God!" she cried, "get a doctor!"

And suddenly the scene was no longer a spectacle to Brandon but something much closer to his own fragile self. The victims were not impersonal objects, after all. One was old Sullivan, the doorguard at the Institute, another de Rintelen Feigerman. It was people he knew who were among the dead, the shattered, the very nearly dying. . . .

It could even have been himself.

And across the street the owner of the gashed Mercedes was jumping over bits of rubble as he raged toward a young woman who was staring fascinated at the scene. She wore a fake-fur coat over hot pants; her name was Gwenna, but everyone in her area of employment called her Vanilla Fudge. Her employment consisted of patrolling that block of Eighth Avenue until some cruising john rented her for a quick trick, and her area was not at the moment productive because of the bombing. "Now, Nillie," cried the black man as he reached her, "why the fuck you just standin there? How the fuck you gonna make a dollar that way?" His voice sounded like crushed rock; it wasn't so much his temperament as the fact that a competitor had once cut into his larynx with a switchblade knife. But it was also partly his temperament, and Vanilla Fudge replied only cautiously.

"But, Dandy, honey, there isn't anybody looking for a date right now."

"Aw, shee-*it*," he groaned. "Don't you understand *nothin?* What you do now, you get you ass over to Lexington Avenue, hear? I come after you in one hour, and you better have some good news!"

"Sure, Dandy," the girl said obediently, but hesitated. "Dandy? Is it all right if I go over to the hospital to see how Lucy Box is? She got really cut up in the hotel. . . ."

"If you want to see really cut up," snarled Dan de Harcourt, "you just stand there one more *minute.*" And scowled after Vanilla Fudge as she click-clacked away in her high heels. He shook his head. A big scratch on the Mercedes, one of his best bitches in the hospital, the other three gaping at the sideshow instead of turning tricks—what a shit of a day it was!

And not only for Dan de Harcourt. The shockwave of the explosion sent ripples all over the city. Those who had theater tickets for that block had to make other plans for the evening. Three young girls from Milwaukee, on the way to the ice show at the Radio City Music Hall, found themselves in hospital beds instead. A playwright coming out of a bar had just had the epiphany of a perfect comedy scene for his second act when the bomb went off; he was wholly unharmed by the explosion, but he never could remember those comic lines again. Appointments were missed, relatives jumped on planes or buses or into cars to attend victims in the hospital or the morgue—for the ripples did not stop at the city; one of the dead was a city councilman from Chicago, and his absence precipitated a terrible fight for leadership of his ward; some of the Japanese tourists sent postcards home that caused fifty other prospective Japanese tourists to head for Australia instead of the U.S.A.

But by and by the ripples faded away. The shows reopened, the debris was cleared away, the widows remarried. Over the next few weeks the great glass window of the Institute was slowly replaced. De Rintelen Feigerman was slowly patched together again and released from the hospital, though that took longer and the repair was less complete. New shocks dulled the memory of the old. There were other bombs—not as big, but much more recent, so the perspective of time enlarged them. There were other wild-card catastrophes and crises. The Friday Firebug appeared in Brooklyn, setting blazes in apartment buildings in Bensonhurst and Brownsville and East New York while the occupants were davening at Friday evening services in their temples. A nut murderer took prostitutes to the best hotels in the city and left their dismembered bodies for the maid to find—terrifying Vanilla Fudge, causing Dan de Harcourt to fulminate against the quality of police protection; a nut rapist chose only female police officers for his victims; a nut basketball fan waited patiently outside Madison Square Garden for weeks for the opportunity to shoot a visiting team's star center, and only managed at the last to wing another fan before being arrested. The garbagemen hadn't really ended their strike, only recessed it for ninety days, and as the deadline got closer and the negotiators got entrenched in positions far apart, the city began to smell again as collections slowed. The transit workers wanted hazard pay, as the old system began to develop more and more faults; but the city couldn't settle with the transit workers because every other group of city employees was waiting to see what came of their effort. If one group of city workers got one more dollar in their paychecks, everybody else on the city payroll took that dollar as guaranteed and was willing to strike to collect it, and the city was running low on dollars. A water main burst, and for three weeks a hundred and fifty thousand people were boiling rusty sludge to get something to drink until it was fixed; the police began to suffer from blue flu as the firemen seemed to be getting close to attaining pay parity; a whale washed up on Brighton Beach and its decay smote ten thousand nearby apartment dwellers for two weeks, while the sanitmen and the Coast Guard argued over who was to take it away; a hotel fire killed three, Legionnaire's disease struck a dozen in a Capuchin monastery in Queens; a Cuban refugee set himself on fire in front of the UN; two rival tongs settling drug territories decimated a dim sum joint in Chinatown, Terrorist Hijacks LaGuardia Shuttle, Mystery Sniper Shocks Midtown, Gay Love Nest Murderer Confesses, Ex-Hubby Slays Three, Power Brownout Probable, Welfare Funds Run Out, Schools Close as Arsonist Strikes. You don't really need a bomb to destroy a city. You only need to take your hands off the controls for a minute, and the city will destroy itself.

As the weather got colder the Pins retreated inside their house. The handball court down the block didn't get used very often. Now and then, on a Sunday, a big bus with a *Charter* sign over its windshield would come and take them away for a while. Otherwise they seemed to stay in their rooms. At least during the summer, with their music boxes playing and their constant sparring and yelling on the stoop, they had seemed high-spirited. As the weather cooled, so did their spirits. So did Brandon's. So, for reasons she did not seem to want to discuss, did his daughter's; for that matter, so did the city's. Righteous indignation ebbed into sullen rage.

It was the despondency of the city that Brandon was paid to study, but it was his daughter's that disturbed him most. She served his breakfast every morning. She took her turn with him in cooking the evening meal and doing the dishes. She kept her room cleaner than she ever had, and on Saturday mornings he often woke to hear the buzz of the vacuum cleaner as she did the living room. But she wouldn't talk. There had been twenty-four hours of sobbing and fright when she realized how close her father had been to the bombing, and then she closed up again. Brandon worried. The people he worked with noticed it, and on their regular Thursday morning, eating brioche and drinking coffee on his lanai, the Director said so directly—as directly as the Director ever said anything. "You look," he said, staring dreamily out at the new glass window, "as though you're not getting enough sleep, Shire. Really you should be quite encouraged."

Brandon searched his memory to find what it was he should be encouraged about without success. "Mrs. Feigerman," beamed the Director. "She's very interested in the UTM."

Brandon paused with the coffee cup halfway to the saucer. "But she misunderstands completely!" he protested. "The Universal Town Meeting is a forum for bargaining and horse-trading! It would be ideal for the present situation in New York, so that all the parties at interest could talk out their differences and work out areas of agreement—but she thinks of it as a publicity device." The Director shrugged, nodded, raised an eyebrow humorously and buttered a roll, all at the same time; he did not, however, put his thoughts into words. "I mean," Brandon went on, trying again to fill the gaps that the Director left in any conversation, "it's the wrong tool for the job—even assuming that job should be done. And I should tell you, Director, that I am not in sympathy with the anti-abortion movement. I realize that she has very good connections in City Hall, and that her sponsorship would be very helpful—" The Director nodded enthusiastically, approving the fact that Brandon had taken his meaning at last. "But I would hate to see UTM employed for a purpose it wasn't meant for, and probably would fail at."

He stopped there, because the Director had put down his roll and was gazing dreamily out over the gardens at the traffic outside. It seemed he was about to speak.

And so he was. "Do you see," he meditated, "how the streets of the city resemble the circulatory system of an animal?" He waited for an answer.

"I suppose they do," Brandon acknowledged.

"It's such a help," the Director sighed, "to think of it that way, don't you think? Not a few million individuals organized into pressure groups, but an organism. Well," he beamed, rising, "I'm glad we've had this chance to clarify our positions, Shire. Wasn't that Jessie Grai coming in down there a minute ago? What a wonderful person she is, my boy, and so helpful in dealing with the problems of young people." And, with a pat and a smile, he was gone.

Up to a point, Brandon had acquired the skill of deciphering the Director's ellipses. The one about Jessie Grai was easy enough to figure out; it was only the way the Director said it that made it a little tricky. So Brandon sought her out. "You're a psychologist,

Jessie," he said, "and I've got a little psychological problem with my daughter."

She heard him out patiently, then nodded. "You have to distinguish between healthy reactions and bad ones, Shire. Jo-Anne has had a couple of pretty bad traumas—the bombing here, the burglary of your apartment, above all her mother's death. Of course she's reacting. That doesn't make her sick. She'd be sick if she didn't."

"So I should—"

"Go on being her father," Grai nodded. "Love her, and let her know that you do, and when she wants to talk let her. Of course, you could get professional help if you wanted to. It's easier for a child to talk to a professional stranger than to a parent, at least when the parent is part of the problem—I don't mean you are doing anything wrong, Shire, only that to Jo-Anne her parents are not so much individuals as part of a package deal. It's hard for her to separate her feelings about you from her feelings about her mother. But that's up to you."

Brandon thanked her gloomily—of course it was up to him, that was the problem; it was up to him, and he didn't know what to do. Still . . . to go on being her father, to love her and let her know that he loved her, those weren't too hard to do, even if unoriginal. It did not occur to Brandon that Grai's advice might have been quite different if he had given her a little more information.

The other part of the Director's fuzzy directive was harder. Think of the city as an organism?

Well, sure. Cities metabolized, like organisms. They breathe, they eat, they sweat, they excrete. Given a chance, they grow and, if somehow they are prevented from doing any of these vital things, they are very likely to die.

It was not an original thought. It was certainly not a new one. City planners—and the common run of human beings, for that matter—had thought of cities in that way for years. They hadn't always realized the implications of that thought, of course; that was why so many cityscapes from about 1920 showed tall, skinny skyscrapers dominating the scene—that was so everyone could have an outside window, or something like it, and so the city could breathe. But that was before air-conditioning. That was before Buckminster Fuller, reasoning from energy considerations, declared the skyscraper a disaster. If you wanted, said Fuller, to design a nearly perfect radiator—which was to say, a system that would waste as much energy as it possibly could—you would come up with something very like the skyline of almost any city in the world. Especially New York, for it had started the fashion; but everywhere else, too, as rapidly as the others could catch up. With a maximum of surface area to a minimum of contained volume, so that heat soaked in as fast as possible in summer and fled with chilling speed in winter, the skyscraper was the embodiment of ultimate energy waste.

So—think of city as organism, Brandon instructed himself. Think of it as a living creature, say a bear. What does a bear do to keep from being frozen or boiled?

The bear has two strategies. Clothe itself in fur; dig into a cave in winter.

The same strategies were open to City-Bear, and Brandon knew where to find out about them. He pulled out the Feigerman & Tisdale report and studied it. Yes. His memory had been correct; the strategies were there. City-Bear could enclose itself, like the fur of an animal, in a thermally opaque coat—as Buckminster Fuller proposed, a great dome over the city. Or City-Bear could bury itself in a deep cave, where the worst winter winds could not follow. Below the ground the temperature is steady and bearable all year round—thus the art of "terratecture," to take advantage of this free gift.

Not entirely free, Brandon discovered. Cities do not

need only to be protected from outside heat. They generate heat of their own—from industry, from home heating, from their vehicles—and that was why New York City was generally a degree or two warmer than its neighbors in winter, and why landlocked interior cities like Saint Louis left the "footprint" of that extra warmth in altered precipitation patterns that could be measured for many miles downwind. Not all the city heat was from industry or space heating. Quite a lot, Brandon was astonished to learn, was from its human inhabitants. Each human being generates about thirty watts of heat energy, day in and day out; for a city of six million that is nearly two hundred thermal gigawatts, about like half a million electric space-heaters going all the time. All animals did that. That was one of the reasons animals got no bigger than they were. The blue whale was the largest animal who ever lived, but he lived in a sea of coolant fluid. Big land animals, with only air to carry away the heat they stoked inside themselves, had to develop radiators—fins, wings, the spikes of stegosaurus, the lolling tongue of a panting dog—to keep them alive, and even so no land mammal could match the size of those who lived in the sea. Bear the size of the blue whale would die of heat stroke, even at the North Pole. . . .

Brandon realized his attention was wandering. This was not what the Director had meant him to do . . . probably wasn't . . . well, you seldom could tell exactly what the Director meant you to do.

City as organism?

Why, yes. There was another sense. When an organism is in health its parts share the work of keeping it alive—so do a city's; when an organism's parts begin one by one to fail, it becomes ill—so does a city. But when the parts of the creature begin to fight against each other it does not matter which of them wins. Before long they all die. The name of the condition is cancer; and, in that sense, the Director's insight was sound. There was a malignancy in the city, and if it could not be controlled or cured the life of the city was at an end.

Because my name is Millicent they called me "the Red Mill." Not a put-down. Nobody did that to me twice, anyway. My parents came from Arizona and my grandparents were cowboys, and we know how to protect ourselves. It's not just ourselves, it's the poor, the oppressed, the downtrodden that need protecting, and that's what I'm good at. The Times Square bomb was mine. The locker bombs are mine. The letter bombs are mine. When my great-grandfather fought the railroads, he did it with a Colt .45 Peacemaker. They called it "the equalizer" because, although my grandfather was a little bit of a man, with one of those strapped to his belt he could stand up against the meanest, toughest yard bull the railroads could hire. Well, now we have a different kind of equalizer—plastic explosive and the Molotov cocktail—and I'm the one who makes them!

On the first of December the sanitmen began an East Side-West Side slowdown. Mondays, Tuesdays and Wednesdays they picked up the garbage east of Fifth Avenue, the other days of the week west; if the city didn't get down to serious bargaining, they threatened, the East Side–West Side would soon be all around the town. The subway men called off a go-slow of their own, but not much was gained for the city's woes because the bus drivers started a work to rule. This meant that no bus left the garages if its windshield wipers weren't working and its lights were not all operational—whether it was ever used or not. It also meant that no bus driver allowed a passenger on or off unless he could get his bus in within the legally required eighteen inches of the curb, which on some runs meant never. The city expanded its vocabulary of diagnostic terms:

Blue flu. Police calling in sick because they didn't—yet—want to go on strike.

Work to rule. Enforcement of every rule on the books, regardless of how impractical.

Gridlock. An insoluble traffic jam caused by vehicles getting stuck in intersections so that no movement in any direction is possible.

Deadlock. The situation produced when one set of non-negotiable demands conflicts with another, so that no resolution can be reached.

And the newest coinage of all:

Medlock. Spelled like "meddle," pronounced like "needle," it was the word for what happened when all the city unions went to arbitration and the mediators themselves struck to protest the work load.

Shire Brandon hadn't gone to church since he was fourteen. When asked, he called himself a "secular humanist"—meaning that he believed in morality and a benign approach to his fellow humans, but rejected the notion of a supernatural God—but, considering the city's problems, he could have wished for one. At the Institute's Friday-evening depressurizing session, when everyone broke off work early and the top staffers joined the Director for a drink, he said as much. The Director beamed mistily. "I am reminded," he said, peering over the top of his fluted glass of *fino,* "of a joke that went around during the Second World War. It had to do with the Allies invading Europe, but I think it could be adapted . . . yes. Here is the joke:

"There are two ways the city can solve its problems, a miraculous and supernatural way, and one that is relatively more probable. One way is that the Lord God shall appear over Herald Square and shower down loaves, fishes and manna in such quantities that everybody can pick up enough to sell to Philadelphia and get rich; that's the probable way. The other way is the fantastically supernatural way, requiring a miracle to get it to happen, and that is that the city shall sit down and reach agreements within itself."

Brandon usually laughed at the Director's jokes, even when they were wooly-headed; but not at that one.

I was Hermann Gebtsen's son Erich, a carpenter by trade. For twenty-six years I was working hard in America and earning a good wage, even in the War when it was not good to be a German. In 1929 there was a Crash. I was not harmed, for every week I put money in the bank. In 1931 the bank closed. I could not pay my rent, so the landlord locked my room and kept my tools. I could not look for work then. I found food the grocers had thrown out. To sleep I had made a room with cardboard boxes on the fire escape of a movie house. No one bothered me, for the movie house was out of business, too.

"Put your coat on, honey," Brandon called to his daughter. "I'll be ready in a minute." And then to the telephone: "Well, certainly, Simon, I'll be there for the meeting with Mr. Feigerman. Yes, I know the snow's getting bad, but—What?" Jo-Anne, who already had her coat on, waited patiently for her father to finish. She knew it was the Director; her father was never so patient with any other caller, just as he was about to leave in the morning. Jo-Anne had met the Director twice, once at the previous year's staff Christmas party, once at the summer picnic in Central Park. She had formed an image of him that was partly Wizard of Oz and partly Santa Claus; he was the one who gave out the mesh stockings of sticky hard candy and fragile, inappropriate toys; but he was also the one who caused her father to scowl and grimace at the telephone with the effort of keeping his voice calm and reasonable.

The phone had caught him just as he was about to leave. He was standing by the bookcase in his boots and fur-collared coat and Cossack hat; he didn't seem to mind that he was sweating in the steam-heated apartment, but Jo-Anne was less comfortable than he.

Boots, leggings, down zipper-jacket, lined hood—she was dressed for the Arctic, and nothing she had been able to say had convinced her father that if her mother had been there she would have had to wear less. She pulled the door to and fro; the squeak attracted her father's attention and he nodded permission for her to go on ahead of him.

Even the vestibule was too warm for the bundled-up child. She pushed her way out onto the sidewalk, wondering why Mr. Rozak the super wasn't standing inside to polish the doorknobs and remind the tenants that Christmas was coming.

Then she stopped and stood very still, because she saw why not. Mr. Rozak was standing at the edge of the sidewalk in his down vest, bare arms exposed, hatless; he must have been cold, but he wasn't paying attention to that. His attention was concentrated across the street.

It was the Pins again, of course. It was the particular Pin Jo-Anne called the Smasher, because he liked to pick bottles out of the trash awaiting collection and toss them high into the air to crash into the middle of the street. He wasn't crashing bottles this morning. It looked as though he were getting set to crash himself. He was sitting on a window ledge on the top story, swinging his legs and staring at the slow, fine snow as it came down. The air was cold and damp and the boy was wearing only cutoffs and a tee-shirt. He didn't seem to notice.

The superintendent discovered Jo-Anne beside him and looked down, grinning. "What do you think of that guy, honey? The little ba——the guy," he corrected himself, "wants to jump. Go ahead, I say! What a jerk!" The Pin had shifted his gaze and, noticing them, waved dreamily. He wore nothing on his feet. His bare toes flexed as though he were testing pool water before jumping in. And he was collecting an audience. A taxi-driver had stopped to look up, and behind him cars were beginning to collect; a couple of early morning dog-walkers were staring, and some schoolgirls on their way to the parochial school were calling to him. "Go on," bawled Mr. Rozak, grinning. "Jump, why don't you?" He wasn't the only one egging the boy on. From another window of the Pin house, a floor down and two rooms away, one of the other inmates had stuck his head out to peer up. It was a violent verbal burst, but as usual Jo-Anne could make out only a couple of words: "Mumble FUCKIN mumble mumble FUCKIN JUMP!"

But then the Pin-pusher came unhurriedly out of the house. He was a man about forty. There was easily two hundred and forty pounds of him, though he wasn't very tall. In the moments when the Pins seemed about to come unstuck—roughly once a week—it was the Pin-pusher who kept the worst explosions from happening. He did now. "You, Malcolm!" he called clearly. "You get you ass inside *now.*"

And that was all there was to it, except that when Mr. Rozak turned, grinning, to Jo-Anne to complain that the show was over his face suddenly froze. "Oh, *shit,*" he groaned. "You're the Brandon kid, aren't you?"

When Brandon came out a minute later the Pins were back in their house, the dog-walkers had walked on, Rozak the super was busily shoveling snow in the alleyway and Jo-Anne stood silently waiting for him. He noticed that her expression was stiff and strained, but she did not seem to want to tell him why. "I've got to get a move on, honey, so—" He paused, mouth open, gazing reproachfully at the sky. "Good God, it's really snowing!"

When my mother air-mailed herself out the window she was all sprawled out on the sidewalk and they did just like in the movies. They drew an outline all around her body before they let the ambulance take her away. I always thought they did that with chalk, but they used some kind of grease pencil and, even though Mr. Ruzik washed it away, I could still see it there for weeks. I tried to tell Daddy about it, but he didn't want to hear. I wish he would talk to me more, because I know something's wrong. My friend thinks I might be adopted, but I don't think so. I think it might be even something worse.

Snowing it really was. The streets were slippery. Not very slippery yet, but then they didn't have to be very anything to make the traffic tangles even worse ensnarled. As soon as Brandon got his daughter to her school he paid off the taxi and headed for the subway to save time.

It didn't save time. The motorman hit a red signal just outside the 34th Street station. As the rule books ordered, he came to a full stop—and then, as the rule books also ordered (but no one in his right mind had ever bothered to comply), he proceeded to climb down from his cab and make a complete circuit of the train, all ten cars, resetting the brakes on every wheel by hand before starting up again; thus "work to rule" spelled out. Brandon arrived at the Institute to find the Director sitting pale and reproachful by his desk. He bent his head in the general direction of Brandon's apologies, but it was like a Rodin marble doing it—the attitude was one of attention, but if there were thoughts going on in that stony brain they did not concern reasons for tardiness. "I had hoped," said the Director to the air over the garden, "that you would be here in time to discuss funding with Mr. Feigerman. It did not go well, Shire. Mr. Feigerman feels that your program conflicts with F & T's recommendations, as I told you on the phone. He was quite upset. Since he's not entirely recovered from that terrible bombing I couldn't ask him to wait." He sighed. "Perhaps you would have been able to present your case better than I. If you had been here."

"Director, the whole city's tied up this morning—"

The marble head inclined again. "No final decision has been reached, of course. But next month, at the Annual Meeting—" he spread his hands. "I don't think I'll join you for coffee this morning, Shire. So much to do."

So much to do for the Director, maybe, but what was there to do for Shire Brandon? Decoding the Director's comments as best he could, it sounded very much as though his job was in trouble. The word "funding" had appeared in what the Director said, and that was a word of great significance to an academic who did not have tenure and whose job was secure for him only as long as the job itself continued to exist. What a crying shame, thought Brandon, taking the large view; what a pity that just now, when the city was convulsing itself in a more than usually tetanic paroxysm, the programs that could cure it were about to be terminated! And indeed the city was in bad shape. His secretary's radio, going all day long, kept throwing up alarming items. Offices were closing early because of the storm. A storm warning had been changed by slow degrees to a blizzard alert, and something over ten inches was forecast for the next twenty-four hours. All the airports were still open, but there were thirty-minute delays at Kennedy and Newark, and an hour or more at LaGuardia. And if Washington and Wilmington were a guide to what New York had to expect as the center of the low plowed stubbornly up the Coast, it was going to be bad indeed—a tanker was in trouble off Hatteras, and at least five deaths had already been reported in Virginia and the Delmarva peninsula.

At four o'clock the word came through that the Director had ordered the office closed for the weekend and everyone was invited to get home before the worst of the storm hit. Brandon had no objection to complying. But as he was putting his desk in order the phone rang. "This is Jocelyn Feigerman," said the commanding voice in his ear. "I wonder if you can come by to see me this afternoon. You sure it won't take you out of your way? Good. In twenty minutes, then."

It was only half a dozen blocks from the Institute to the old green steel and glass skyscraper that housed Feigerman & Tisdale in three large floors, but it took more than twenty minutes. At that, walking was faster than driving; there were long lines of cars inching along Eighth Avenue, trying to get into the Lincoln Tunnel, which for some reason was having unusual troubles. By the time Brandon got out of the elevator his shoe-tops had scooped up snow and slush from the streets and the muscles around his eyes were sore from squinting against the driving flakes. Jocelyn Feigerman offered him tea against the cold, and then was direct. "My husband," she said, "tells me you were not able to meet him this morning."

No obvious response occurred to Brandon except to say that he was sorry for being late—but the snow picky-ticking against the window explained that. He didn't need to make a response, as it turned out. "I thought," said Mrs. Feigerman, "that you would have had the sense to come and see me after our last meeting. You know that I'm interested in your project."

The untenured academic pricked up his ears. The idealist compressed his jaw. Warring impulses inside Shire Brandon battled briefly, and then he shook his head. "Mrs. Feigerman," he said, "the Universal Town Meeting is designed for exactly what we see going on in New York City right now—and in every other city in the world, and in most non-urban places, too. It is a way of getting the whole population of the area to consider its problems and to make whatever compromises and adjustments are necessary. That's all it is."

Jocelyn Feigerman frowned. "I don't think you explained it very clearly," she said. "I understood it to be a sort of referendum."

He said patiently, "A referendum, Mrs. Feigerman, is a lot like a presidential election. By the time the question gets on the ballot it has been formalized and complicated, and half the voters don't know what it's about and most of the other half agree with part of it and disagree with another part and could go either way. There's no chance to bargain in a referendum, Mrs. Feigerman, and that's what UTM is all about. Bargaining."

"You said it was a way of getting significant reforms accomplished, Mr. Brandon."

"Yes! Right! In the manner of a New England town meeting, with tradeoffs of penalties and benefits. For worthwhile reforms."

Mrs. Feigerman pursed her lips. "Would you look at that picture, Mr. Brandon?" she said, indicating a poster on the wall. It was two persons, Mrs. Feigerman herself and an angelic-faced little girl. Brandon had long since noticed its presence without looking at it very carefully; now he saw, with shock, that the little girl had no arms. "Her life, Mr. Brandon, is a worthwhile reform! And if your Universal Town Meeting can help save children like her from being murdered in the womb, then I want it done."

The granite face thawed. "Now, Mr. Brandon," she said, "tell me how we are going to go about getting your scheme adopted for the benefit of mine."

The subway got him as far as 23d Street, but the buses were hopeless and there was, of course, no such thing as a visible taxi. So Brandon slogged through the deepening snow all the way across town, wondering how he had got himself into promising to work out Jocelyn Feigerman's UTM.

There wasn't really a question. He had got himself into it in the same way that Albert Einstein had found himself urging the construction of an atomic bomb, that Werner Von Braun's aim at the stars had missed and hit London, that scientists all over the world found themselves going along with causes not their own. When you have invented something truly remarkable, you want to see if it will work.

The conversation could easily have gone a different way, Brandon told himself. He could have temporized, stalled, got out with his research program intact but no specific commitment to help the right-to-lifers . . . if he had been deft enough. He could have honeyed the old girl along. She was the real muscle behind F & T now, with her husband still recuperating from the severe damage of the bomb blast.

But he hadn't.

The going was really bad now. With the sanitmen's strike he had not expected to see any snowplows—and indeed there were almost none; but somebody had made at least a pass or two on the main north-south avenues. Not enough to make travel easy for the cars, which were just inching along when they moved at all. Enough to throw up drifts along the curbs, entombing parked cars and making pedestrians like Brandon into alpinists. He was glad enough to turn into his own block.

It was full dark, and the streetlights had a bluish aura—the snow, Brandon thought, without quite being able to figure out cause and effect. Certainly the snow was intensifying every hour. There were no pedestrians in sight, and on this quiet side street no cars moving either. The house of the Pins was mostly dark—as it always was; what they did with themselves in there Brandon could not guess. His own building was brighter, though there was no one in the lobby.

There was no one in his apartment, either. Jo-Anne was not at home.

That was impossible! Jo-Anne was *always* at home when he got back from the office! She would stay at school for her after-hours classes, the piano, the ballet, the swimming club; there was one every day, and every one of them had the kindness to end at five, just in time for Jo-Anne to get her regular lift back to the apartment and be there when Brandon came in the door. She never failed. It was impossible that she should not be there!

But it was true.

> Name is Malcolm White. They bust me twice for possession and the third time for selling, so the damn judge says he tired of seeing my face in his courtroom and he puts me away. Wasn't bad. Came out, and they stick me in this turkey house way damn downtown, don't know a soul, got nothing to do, I'd rather be back at the place. They're going to learn me some skills and get me a slave. They say. Don't do it, though. They don't ever do what they say they're going to do, except bust my ass. They do that fine.

Jo-Anne wasn't in the apartment, and Brandon was becoming very nearly frantic. She hadn't left any note, but there was a message. It was spread on his bed. After the apartment was robbed and Brandon's locked file was broken open, he had replaced it with a new strongbox. The new strongbox came equipped with two keys. Jo-Anne had found one of them where he had hidden it, Scotch-taped to the bottom of his desk drawer. It was not the copy of *Penthouse* that interested her, nor his financial records, nor the handful of stock and savings certificates. There were two things that had taken her attention, and she had left them on his bed. One was her birth certificate. The other was Brandon's Army discharge, with his service record.

Jo-Anne had paid close attention in her Sex Education classes. She knew that the gestation period for human babies was nine months. She knew what that implied.

So Brandon sat in the apartment, with all the lights on, still wearing his coat, with the slush melting down into his socks, cradling the telephone and listening to the endless ringing of the 911 emergency number. It was a good day for emergencies in New York City. He counted more than forty rings, and still no human voice answering, while his eyes were fixed firmly on the doorknob in the hope that he could will it to turn, and his mind was rebelliously refusing his orders to be calm. In the other room the radio he had automatically turned on was furnishing not music but bulletins of disaster: A tractor-trailer had jackknifed on the Jersey exit ramp of the Lincoln Tunnel, and all lanes were blocked. The LIRR had annulled half its trains, and the remaining ones were subject to two-hour delays. All the airports were closed. No cars were allowed on the George Washington, Tappan Zee or Verrazano bridges, and the East River bridges were just crawling. As was the slow ring of the 911 phone; and Brandon couldn't stand waiting any longer. He couldn't stand waiting for the elevator, either, and took the fire stairs two at a time down to the superintendent's apartment.

The super had his TV going instead of a radio, but the words were not any more pleasing. Not just the weather. A bomb had been reported in Grand Central, with twenty thousand stuck commuters evacuated into the snow; a fire on the West Side was burning out of control because the few working firemen couldn't get through the snow and abandoned cars to reach it. "Oh, sure, I saw Joie," said the super, but he didn't sound reassuring. "She was, uh, crying." He hesitated. "I think that black guy this morning got her kind of upset." Brandon listened as Rozak told him about the Pin in the window with his—threatened? pretended?—with his almost-jump, and cursed himself for not understanding, for not asking Jo-Anne what the matter was, for—for everything that had happened in the past year, a catalogue too long for him to rehearse. "Then when her school was closed—"

"What's that about her school?"

"They sent the kids right home, didn't you know? Because of the storm, I guess—anyway, she came back about nine-thirty, and then right after lunch I saw her go out. That's when she was crying, Mr. Brandon. Listen," he said helpfully, "it's probably nothing, but maybe you should call the cops."

"Call them! I tried the 911 number, they're always busy!"

"Don't fool with that 911, call the precinct. Use my phone. The number's on the wall right over it—there, go ahead."

Numbly, Brandon did as he was told. The wait for the local precinct was interminable too, but he hung on doggedly because he had no better idea, while the superintendent and his wife conversed in low tones, in whatever the language was that they had been born to.

He was absolutely certain that, in this day with the city destroying itself, the police would take very little interest in one more missing little girl. He was right. When at last he got the desk sergeant it was only the mention of Mr. Rozak's name that got him even the cursory attention of taking a description for the missing persons report. At least that was something! Something to laugh over when she came home, he thought, maybe even something to use to instruct her with, when she understood from that act how frightened he had been.

"Mr. Brandon?"

He realized he was still holding the phone, although the desk sergeant had long since rung off. "What?"

The superintendent was wearing a curious expression, halfway between a funeral mourner's and the intended reassurance of a visitor to a patient in intensive care. "My wife says one of the tenants told her something."

He seemed reluctant to get it out. "What?" barked Brandon.

"Well, maybe it's nothing, but—anyway, the woman in 2-H said she saw a girl in the Pins' house across the street." He hesitated. "It didn't look like there was anything wrong with her exactly," he added, "but she was a white girl, and it was kind of funny. The tenant said she sort of just lay in the open window for a while, and then this black guy grabbed her and pulled her in."

The fat old Pin-pusher listened for a moment, one foot blocking the door, then he opened it wide. "Your daughter ain't here, Mister," he said, "but you come on upstairs. Ask the boys if they seen anything. Then I'll show you something."

Brandon had often wondered what the inside of that bleak four-story building with the bare flagpole was like. It was spartan-neat. The halls were sterile white, linoleum tile on the floors, nothing on the walls but a lettered placard at each bedroom door—occupants' names and what looked like a duty roster—nothing in the way of furniture anywhere. At each door black faces peered out at Brandon and Mr. Rozak and the fat keeper. They weren't hostile, or even curious. They just looked. In the fourth-floor front the keeper led them into a room with three metal beds, a bureau, a couple of old chests of drawers, pictures of Mean Joe Green and Herschel Walker taped to the walls. The Pin-pusher nodded to the young men in the room and reached under the bed. What he pulled out was what looked at first like a crumpled Macy's Parade balloon, small size. It seemed to have yellow hair.

"This what the lady saw?" asked the pusher, shaking it out to show what it was. A rubber doll, life size. One of those sex things that you saw in the 42nd Street porn shops.

The Pins, at least, were enjoying themselves. When they saw the faces of Brandon and the super their laughter was considerable, and they relayed a blow-by-blow description of everything that was happening, at the top of their voices, to the other inhabitants of the Pins house. Brandon stood there listening; how terribly the tragedies of life turned into farce! One of the Pins had hidden the doll belonging to another; the robbed Pin had threatened to jump out the window until he got it back; then the robber had threatened to throw the doll out—it was all sordid and—and, yes, funny.

But the super stopped listening. He was standing by the window, gazing across the street into his own apartment building. He said, "For the love of God."

It took Brandon a moment to figure out which apartment Rozak was looking at but, after all, there wasn't much doubt. One was far brighter than any of the others. It seemed to have at least a dozen lights going in each room—desk lights, high-intensity tensors, floor lights in several different designs. It was the corner apartment on the fourth floor—the one belonging to Mr. Becquerel, Brandon realized, the nice man who worked at the United Nations or something—and it was radiant. From across the street Brandon could see into the living room, as far as the kitchenette and the hall foyer, into the bedroom with its unmade queen-sized bed and chests burdened with appliances.

In the middle of urgent woes, Brandon paused to look. It was almost prurience. There was a sly, sneaky pleasure in peering into the private life of a casual acquaintance. Mr. Becquerel had to be quite a television fan, for there were three sets in the living room alone, plus two whole tape video decks and a couple of cameras; you'd never have guessed that about Mr. Becquerel! But that evanescent thought was swallowed up in a swift realization. His own apartment was almost as open to inspection. The window drapes, that looked opaque from inside the room, were not much more than theatrical scrim when the light was inside. All those times he had thought himself alone and unobserved, doing private things and personal—for how many of those times had he amused an audience of Pins? The view into his own apartment was no more obscured than into Becquerel's, with its bright lights scattered all over, among the TV sets, and the stereos, and the word processors, and the Cuisinarts and the electric typewriters—

And suddenly Brandon realized that that bright pink

clock-radio had been his daughter's. It had not, after all, been the Pins who had burglarized his apartment.

Mr. Rozak was thrilled—almost thrilled enough to forget about Brandon's missing child—thrilled enough to insist on calling the information in to his friend on the precinct desk, and then to urge Brandon to have dinner with him and his family, to stop worrying, to take it easy because nine times out of ten missing kids just turned up all by themselves a couple of hours late, why, he remembered himself when he was a little kid just in America he took the wrong subway and found himself at Main Street, Flushing, without a dime in his pocket to get back on the subway or make a phone call . . . it was all well intentioned, and all wholly repugnant to Brandon. The last thing he wanted was to be looked at by people who didn't share his worry.

And there was always the chance that Jo-Anne indeed might call. Which presented him with a whole new set of problems. Inspiration: To call the parents of all of her classmates, one after another, on the chance that Jo-Anne had sheltered with one of them. Drawback: What if she tried to call him when the phone was busy? Would a ten-year-old have the tenacity to keep trying until she got an answer? Would she be in a position where that was possible? Brandon felt a sudden explosion of furious rage at Becquerel, who had stolen his telephone-answering machine; why, maybe Jo-Anne had tried to call a hundred times and not been able to leave a message!

He resisted the impulse to dash there and make Becquerel disgorge his loot—even with the added attraction of punching the man's face in.

By midnight he had gone as far with the list of possible refuges as he could—the last two parents he had called had been got out of bed to answer the phone and, while they were sympathetic, they were also annoyed. And no word. All night the radio by his bed and the TV in the living room had been broadcasting the tidings of disaster—a twenty-three-car pileup on the Long Island Expressway (but since no car could go more than ten miles an hour in the storm, no lives lost), subways still operating where they were underground but irregular or absent entirely where they were in the open, people stuck in railroad stations (trains annulled or indefinitely delayed), stuck in bus stations, stuck in airports, every hotel jammed and people stuck in lobbies . . . stuck. The whole city was stuck. Nothing moved. He was barely aware of the change when he heard a plow in his own block, but he was too sunk in despair to go to the window and look.

When the policeman knocked on the door he felt a surge of terror. "Is it—have you found my daughter?" he choked out.

The officer was wiping snow off his glasses, an elderly man with gold braid on his cap. He looked puzzled. "Are you Shire Brandon?" And at the nod, "I'm sorry, I don't know anything about your daughter. You're a hard man to reach, Mr. Brandon. We've been trying to call you all night."

"I see." Energy poured out of Brandon. He felt himself slump. "Well, if it's the burglary loot, it's in the apartment next door. I don't know if he's still at home, but—"

"Not burglary either, Mr. Brandon. It's the Mayor. He wants you downtown right away, and he sent me to get you."

Brandon hadn't ridden in a truck since the Nam and never in one that had a snowplow rigging—there was not much plowing of snow going on in Vietnam. There was not much going on this time, either. The truck's principal job was to get Brandon and the police captain down to City Hall. It only plowed where plowing might help it to make better time, usually because abandoned cars blocked the center of the avenues. Huddled in the noise, between the driver and the police captain, Brandon shouted into the captain's ear, sentence by sentence, his worries about his daughter. In exchange he got the same statistic his superintendent had offered him, finding it no more reassuring.

The space just in front of City Hall had been plowed, and two plows were still there, along with fifteen or twenty other vehicles, most of them with chauffeurs inside keeping the motors running and moving the limousines out of the way of the plows from time to time. The captain climbed down first and, as he held the door for Brandon, he said, "One thing I didn't understand. You said your daughter had some special reason to be upset—do you mind telling me what it was?"

Brandon stopped with the snow beating against his face. Did he mind? It was the statement that had never crossed his lips to anyone in this city—to anyone anywhere. But was there any reason to keep it secret now?

He licked snow from his mouth and said, "She's not my child. She found that out this morning."

"Um." The policeman nodded, his face showing that reservation of judgment which displays a judgment already made. People who kept secrets from their kids! "I wouldn't worry too much about that. Adopted children learn to deal with it—"

"She's not adopted. She . . ." He hesitated, then plunged into it. "My wife got pregnant when I was in Nam. Jo-Anne never knew. I didn't know what to tell her."

What the policeman said in return Brandon didn't know—something reassuring, maybe something sympathetic. Maybe he said nothing at all, not even goodby, because Brandon was hardly aware of what anyone said to him, or where he was. He was thinking not even of Jo-Anne, not even of his wife; he was remembering those hours in the waiting room of the hospital, trying to read *Time* while all the time he was wondering who the baby's father was . . . whether the baby would

resemble him . . . yes, more than anything else, what
color the baby would be. It wasn't race prejudice that
obsessed him with that question. It was the difficulty,
no, the impossibility, of pretending that the child was
his own if it were conspicuously of a different color—a
practical matter, not a question of bigotry.

He told himself that.

The Hall was busier this late night of a blizzard, when
all sensible people were in their homes, than usually of
a weekday afternoon. No one seemed to know exactly
why Shire Brandon was here. He was ushered to a seat
by a woman wearing a right-to-life button, given a cup
of instant coffee by a man from Gay Lib and a
newspaper to look at by a woman from the Haitian-
American Friendship Society. The big waiting room
was full of people, all of them talking to each other,
none of them known to Brandon. Brandon didn't want
to talk to any of them. The only person he wanted to
talk to was not here. He approached the woman who
had told him to wait, leaning across her desk to be
heard as he asked to use the telephone. You could
always tell when you were on the losing end. "I don't
know," she said, shaking her head. "It's taxpayers'
money that's involved and I'm responsible for it."

"I'll pay!"

"It's not that easy. I'll have to make out a
miscellaneous-funds-received slip and channel it
through Non-Tax Accounts and—" But ultimately he
was allowed to make his call. Of course, there was no
answer at his apartment; that had been too much to
hope for. When he was explaining to the super about
the note he would like Mr. Rozak to leave on his door
and how to reach him if he heard something, anything
at all, about Jo-Anne, somebody tapped him on his
shoulder.

He got off the phone and turned to see a young man
with a wispy beard and a sheepskin jacket over a wool
turtleneck; he must have been sweating in this over-

heated room. "Are you Shire Brandon? My name is John Harvey and I'm in charge of hooking up your broadcast."

"My *broadcast?*"

The young man nodded. "Come on down to the studio. See if you like the way I've got it fixed up."

He tugged Brandon out of the room, snapping a plastic ID badge on his coat. He kept on talking, but it was always over his shoulder and there was so much noise in City Hall that Brandon could catch only occasional words. John Harvey didn't wait for elevators. He led Brandon two steps at a time down the fire stairs, past police guards, through a passageway that smelled as bad as any other New York cellar these days, for City Hall's garbage wasn't picked up either.

The City Hall television studio was in what had once been the press room. It had none of the amenities of the big broadcasting networks. One corner was made into a sort of talk-show set, with a peeling mural of the New York City skyline on the wall and two chairs before the backdrop. Cameras and lights on teetery metal stands faced the chairs. "This is for the Mayor and his guest," Harvey announced. "We feed to the WNYC studio over in the Municipal Building, and from there the video goes to Two, Four, Five, Nine, Eleven and Thirteen, and the audio goes by telephone to the simultaneous translators—we've got eight of them, including Japanese, Chinese and Arabic. Air time is ten o'clock tomorrow morning for the Mayor, but we're going to have bulletins on all the stations, AM, FM, TV, the works, starting right now. How do you like it?"

"My God," said Shire Brandon.

How did he like it? It was not easy to say. How had he liked it when Blanche Ehler, wandering away with him from the high-school picnic, had let him know that it was all right if, for the first time in his life, he wanted to go all the way? Thrilled, scared—mostly unbelieving. Harvey didn't wait for an answer. He only grinned and led Brandon over to tap on a door. Was it really happening? Would the Universal Town Meeting really get its first full-scale trial—in circumstances like these, where the eyes of the world were on New York's agonies, and no one anywhere could fail to see it happening?

The door led to—surprisingly—what looked like an ordinary Holiday Inn hotel room. The only unusual things about it were the police lieutenant at the door, who nodded to Harvey and let him knock, and the fact that, once the door was open and Brandon could see inside, he observed there were no windows. There were four or five people inside. Brandon recognized the Mayor, Saul Wassermann and the lone woman, Jocelyn Feigerman . . . and at once his mood changed. Nervous expectancy disappeared. Thudding comprehension drove it away.

They didn't go in. The door closed and Harvey drew Brandon a few yards down the hall. "He'll be right with us," he promised. "Now. Do you have the picture? Did I tell you about the remotes? We'll have mobile-unit vans from the commercial stations at the TWU headquarters, and the hotels where the firemen and the police unions are meeting. We short-hop the signals by microwave to the collection point, then by wire to the studios. We're covering all the major municipal unions, and—what's the matter?"

"What does Jocelyn Feigerman have to do with this?" Brandon demanded.

John Harvey's face changed. The lips drew closed, the corners of the mouth drew down, the eyebrows lifted. "Oh, yeah," he said after a moment. "Saul said you might give us a hard time about that."

"I asked you a question!"

Harvey said patiently, "She's your rabbi, Brandon. Why do you think we're doing this? It goes by clout, and she's got it."

Brandon had time to get his thoughts together. He

nodded. "Right, I understand that, but *what* are we doing?"

"What? What's the matter, Brandon, don't you pay attention? It's this Universal Town Meeting thing—"

"But for what purpose? Are you figuring some public-relations thing like a telethon for outlawing abortion, or a real UTM? Why do you want remotes at the union headquarters?"

"Shit, man! They're the ones that speak for the municipal workers!"

"But the whole *point* is to let people speak for *themselves*. What about remotes from the citizens at large? What about—" He broke off as Saul Wassermann came out, talking over his shoulder, and looking like a man who had no time to waste. "I think you're doing it all wrong!" said Brandon, now to Wassermann. "You're missing the point of the whole thing!"

"Oh," groaned Wassermann, "*shit*. Harvey! Get this monkey out of here!"

But Brandon shook off the bearded man's hand. "You didn't listen!" he shouted. "The UTM isn't an exercise in brain-washing! It's a way to give the people real control over what's happening! Not a chance to hear more bullshit from the Mayor. Not a way for the special-interest people to divide up the public treasury. Free give and take, with every human being in the city getting an equal chance to say what he wants to say and vote on what he wants done . . . that's the Universal Town Meeting, and that's the only way it can make a difference!" He knew that he was shouting. He *enjoyed* shouting. He enjoyed the fact that heads were turning all up and down the hall, that the cameramen had popped out of the TV studio to listen and the police lieutenant, frowning, was coming a step or two closer. He did not know that the Mayor himself was among them until he turned and saw His Honor standing there.

You could not tell anything from the Mayor's expression. You couldn't tell much from his tone, either, because neither one varied much—the half-smile at the worst of times, the fumbly, school-teacherly inflections of the voice even at the best. He wasn't looking at Brandon. He was not looking at Saul Wassermann, either, although his words were addressed to him. "Tell me, Saul," he said to the air, "what did we get this man down here for?"

It was a rhetorical question, but of the special kind that required a rhetorical answer. Wassermann obliged. "Because Mrs. Feigerman suggested that he might be able to help us with this Universal Town Meeting. Because you said we couldn't be any worse off, and we might as well try anything. Because the Governor says the National Guard can't get into the city with the roads the way they are, and because you're running for re-election next year."

The Mayor nodded. "All of those things are still true, Saul," he observed. "If we try this thing out, we don't want somebody saying later that we didn't give it a fair chance."

"No," Wassermann agreed. He only glanced momentarily at Brandon, but Brandon's heart jumped. He knew, but could not believe, what was coming next. It came.

"So give the son of a bitch what he wants," said the Mayor.

I was John Barrett, ship's chandler, fearing God and loving the King. We sold stores from a shop in South Street, my nigger and me, and it was good business. Two cargoes in three for North America came to South Street. I treated him good, but he didn't appreciate it. He tried to run off. He left the stove unbanked. The chimney touched off the laths and the building burned to the ground. I was ruined, and the city worse than I for my nigger was not alone. Yet two weeks later they rounded up him and the other rebel slaves. That day I went up to Collect Pond to see, and they burned him, too.

It was true that the city had never been in worse shape. Nothing unprecedented had happened. There was not one of the things that had gone wrong that hadn't gone wrong before—even often before. But never before had it all hit the fan at once. Strikes and storm, bureaucratic muddling and individual citizens' stubborn resentments, terrorists and hoodlums had all combined to stretch the strength of the city as far as it could go. Farther. In places it had snapped. The fire in Hell's Kitchen, only blocks away from Times Square and Broadway, would have been a bad one at any time, but the few working firemen could not get their equipment past the clogged streets unplowed by the few working sanitmen, and the winds fanned it and the flames spread. And in Bedford-Stuyvesant eight kids ventured out of a housing development to crack the windows of a liquor store, and on Fifth Avenue a shivering Puerto Rican with fury in his heart tried to set off a package of dynamite in front of a bank but succeeded mainly in blowing himself away—almost completely; and in one of the city's most fashionable hotels a woman from West Palm Beach was raped, robbed of her jewels and murdered. Almost. Both tourist and terrorist actually retained a spark of life.

And so did the city. There was looting and robbery, oh, yes! But only small groups or individuals did it in scattered places. It was too cold for mobs to form. There were crimes committed and no police to stop them; but not too many victims ventured forth, and business was bad for the muggers and stickup men.

For hookers it was worse. Vanilla Fudge peered out of a coffee shop on Eighth Avenue and wished urgently that her pimp would show up. If he did there was the chance that he would bust her ass for hanging around the coffee shop when she ought to be out working. But there was also the chance that he would tell her to forget it, take the night off, go to a movie, maybe even stay home and watch television. Along with stage actors, teachers of college evening courses and maîtres d'hôtel, hookers were permanently deprived of prime-time TV. There were nights when Vanilla thought she would die for not knowing what was happening on *Dallas* and *Hill Street Blues*.

After she had made up her mind and was pulling one foot after another out of the snow she thought she had made it up the wrong way. There were no cruising cars with Jersey licenses on the avenue, and certainly no pedestrians looking for a date. She could hear sirens from the big fire off toward Tenth Avenue and see the glow in the snowy sky; apart from that the city seemed depopulated. Down to the south she could see flashing green-and-white lights—a stray snowplow trying to keep the intersection clear at 42nd Street, perhaps. A *screeeep* and whine from the next block showed where some trapped motorist was rocking his car on a slick—not successfully, it seemed.

"Yay. Nillie!"

Vanilla jumped and almost fell in the snow. "Gee, Dandy," she panted, twisting around to regain her balance. "You really scared me."

"You too scared to hustle, girl?" Dandy's voice was always growly; tonight it was so rasping she could hardly understand him.

She offered: "There's nobody around, hon, you can see that."

"What I see's a lazy whore. You check out those bars, hear?"

"Aw, Dandy, you know they'll just chase me out—"

"You going to worry about that? You worry about what I'll do!"

What Vanilla Fudge expected then was that he would hit her. So he did, but his hand was open, the blow landed on the small of her back; it was more of a playful spank than anything else. "You don't do any good in the bars, you go work the bus terminal," he ordered. "I be looking for you there." But he wasn't even looking at her.

She stared after him as, holding up the skirts of his

coat like a dowager, he waded through the drifts and turned the corner. Dandy's heart wasn't in his business tonight. That probably meant he had other business on his mind. Vanilla Fudge hoped it wasn't anything too stupid—or too dangerous.

Dandy wasn't strong enough or maybe brave enough to do any good in more violent kinds of crime; every time he tried it he got hurt. Pimping suited him just right. He wasn't really mean enough to be a great success as a pimp, either. He couldn't hold much of a stable—had lost all but two to harder competition as soon as business began to pick up after Thanksgiving, had got rid of the only other girl when she began mainlining. Dandy wouldn't put up with hard drugs; add him up altogether, and he was missing most of the skills his job usually entailed. But that was all right with Vanilla Fudge. Add her up altogether, and she was well enough content with her life—

Except when the weather was this bad.

The bars were crowded, but she wasn't welcome in any of them. Anyway, nobody wanted to go out in the snow to score. It was going to be just the same in the bus terminal, of course, but at least it was going to be warm in there. Nillie turned south, looking forward to maybe a cup of coffee and a chance to slip her wet boots off.

There were a couple of figures across the street.

She hesitated, then decided to walk by them—Dandy would be a lot gladder to see her if she could turn at least one trick. Through the snow she couldn't see anything much about them except that one was tall and one was short. As Nillie crossed the street with long, deep strides the tall one went inside the building, and left the shorter one standing there.

By now the water inside Nillie's boots felt like it was freezing. They were red leather, for looks, not for keeping cold and wet out, and the fake-fur jacket protected only the top part of her body. She slid and sloshed through the snow, wishing for jeans—even for red flannel underwear. God knew what Dandy would say if she turned up for work in that kind of clothes! Of course, it didn't matter tonight, because there wasn't going to be any call to get bare in a hurry—

The remaining figure on the sidewalk was just standing there, and it was a child. A little girl.

Nillie glanced at her enviously as she went by. Scarf, leggings, fat mittens—that was the way to dress tonight! "Hi, sweetie," she said, and walked on a few steps before looking back.

Vanilla Fudge wasn't in the habit of stopping her patrol for kids. If there was one thing that Dandy would think worse than wearing red flannels, it would be to be seen talking to a child. But who was there to see? So Nillie turned around in her own footprints and stepped back to the little girl.

"Hon, what are you doing out here this time of night?" she demanded.

And the child began to cry.

I'm Timothy Beyley, pumper-driver for McClanahan's fire brigade. It was the week before Christmas, 1835. It was bitter cold. The North River froze over, the wells froze, the hydrants froze, the cisterns froze. The only way we could get water was to drive out on the ice of the river and chop a hole. So the ten of us pumped into the box of Nix's pumper, and Nix pumped to Marion's, and so on all the way to the fire, up around John and Broadway. But it wasn't enough. We lost them all. Every house on Broadway burned, clear to the Battery.

Jo-Anne knew what a prostitute was, more or less. That is, she knew what they did, though she didn't really understand why anybody would pay them to do it. But Jo-Anne was a city kid, growing up with city smarts. However naive her father might think her, the jokes the older kids made about the women who hung around street corners on Lexington Avenue and down toward Cooper Square had stayed in her mind. She knew that this young woman in the stained red boots and short skirt was not a fashion model.

But what she saw when she looked at Vanilla Fudge was her mother. Her mother had done it, whatever "it" signified exactly, in probably just the same way this young woman did it. The jokes and Sex Ed classes had not left in Jo-Anne's mind any clear distinction between an unfaithful wife and a whore. This didn't dispose her against her mother, it made her willing to bury her head in the fake-fur jacket and cry. "Aw, honey," said Vanilla, patting her head through the knitted cap, and, "Come on, sweetie, tell me what's the matter."

And then, when the child began to tell her about the school letting out early because of the storm, and going back to her apartment and wanting to find out the truth about her mother—mostly about herself—Vanilla Fudge said, "Hey, is this going to be a *long* story? Because we might as well go down to the Port Authority and get warm, all right? Sure. Now you take my hand—no, wait a minute. You mind taking off one of those pretty little mittens, hon? 'Cause then, see, I'll put that one on here, and you keep the other one on there, and we'll put our hands in my pocket like this, the ones that are left over—"

"I'm a bastard," said Jo-Anne, and began to cry again.

So the bare hands had to come out of the pocket so that Vanilla could hug the little girl and let her cry a little while longer.

When they got started again Jo-Anne began to talk. She didn't stop. Scuffling and plowing through the snow, tripping over garbage-can lids and other bulky trash hidden in the drifts, she managed to get her story out a sentence at a time. And Nillie squeezed the hand in her pocket and nodded and listened. She could see the little girl doggedly searching till she found what she sought, but did not want to find. Bastard! Her daddy no daddy, and her mother filled with so much—hate? hate of the child who had wrecked her life?—of some passion, anyway, strong enough for her to kill herself to get away.

So then there was nothing for Jo-Anne to do but flee the house she had no real right to be in.

For hours she had wandered aimlessly through the suffering, storm-struck streets of midtown Manhattan. She didn't think out her problem. She held it away from her. She was warm enough, in her bundled-up snow-suit; she had money enough, from the store she had begun to accumulate in the new piggy bank, to feed herself when she got hungry. A Big Mac and fries here, a Coke and a hot dog there—the things that Mommy had rationed out sparingly all her life, but what right did Mommy have to dictate to her now? She even had money for a movie, and sat through two showings of a film in which cops and dope dealers pursued each other all over the city. It didn't matter that she saw it twice. Really, she hadn't seen it even once, because she spent much of the time crying.

When she came out, conscience and training took over from misery and she tried to call her father at home. The phone was busy. It kept on being busy, every ten or fifteen minutes as she wandered from booth to booth, and then it didn't answer at all. She knew it was getting late—could he have gone out somewhere at this hour? Did he somehow know it was she who was calling, and if so was he punishing her by refusing to answer? She was wise enough to know that the second possibility was too bizarre to be true—but so was the first!

Another movie? But the next theater she passed was closed by the storm, and anyway the money was getting low. There wasn't much traffic any more, she realized, and not even very many pedestrians, and it was very dark. She began to be scared.

In a city with numbered streets and avenues it was impossible for her to be lost, but when she found street signs not snowed illegible she realized she was a long way from familiar places. Home was out of the question for her now; she was too tired to undertake a walk of fifty or sixty blocks. But her father's office was nearer. Nearer but out of reach. When she finally floundered her way there the man at the door was not old Mr. Sullivan, whom she knew—and who, she remembered, was dead. It was a stranger. He seemed friendly enough but all he would give her was advice—"Go home, kid. I can't let you in, they'd fire me!" Certainly he would have changed his mind if she had begged, or even explained—but she didn't know that.

And then Nillie had come along.

Jo-Anne and Vanilla Fudge paused at the 42nd Street intersection while a snowplow roared and scraped in front of them. They watched it silently, waiting to cross. It wasn't trying to ease traffic flow—that was impossible. It was only trying to clear space so that the abandoned buses that had not been able to make the ramps of the Port Authority Bus Terminal would have a place to get out of the way. It wasn't succeeding; the job was impossible. City buses, long-distance Trailways and Greyhound monsters, trucks, taxis, passenger cars, police cars were all tangled together. The bus terminal had been the hub of one of the busiest traffic complexes in the world, and all the vehicles at last had surrendered to the storm. What it looked like more than anything else was the plastic snow under a two-year-old's Christmas tree. The presents had been opened. The toy vehicles were scattered heedlessly—and the person who put them there had been sent off to bed, abandoning them for Daddy and Mommy to pick up. But Daddy and Mommy were not equal to the task. "Honey," said Vanilla Fudge as they got ready to cross, "do you know what an abortion is?"

"Sure I do!"—indignantly.

"Then you ought to count your blessings, because suppose your mother had decided not to have you?"

Jo-Anne brought up sharp on the sidewalk, staring

up with her mouth hanging open. Nillie nodded. "Was your daddy mean to her?" Jo-Anne shook her head. "Or to you? No, I didn't think so. So she just screwed up her life some way. People do that, honey. I know you're hurting, but don't you think he's hurting too? Looks to me like the two of you need each other—now come on in here and let's get warmed up!"

The snow was coming down a little more slowly, the wind a hair less violent, but Jo-Anne was still frozen as they pushed at the revolving door. It didn't push easily. It would not turn until, grumbling, the family of Hispanics whose bus to Bayonne had never left inched out of the way. Once inside, it was hard to move.

There didn't seem to be room for two more in the terminal. Every wall had some body propped against it, trying to sleep. Every bench, countertop or stair had someone stretched out; so did most of the floor. All the escalators were stopped and filled with people except for two—once they had been stopped, too, but then the trapped crowd so clogged them that no one could get up or down; so the sleepers had been dislodged and the motors started again to keep them clear. "Gee," said Vanilla Fudge, wrinkling her nose, "you could catch something from the air here." She gazed around, frowning. It wasn't just the dense, smokey, sweaty air that was troubling her, but the little girl read her mind.

"I'll be all right here," she said. "Honest. I'll just keep calling home till my Daddy answers, then he'll tell me what to do."

"You sure?"

"Sure I'm sure."

"Well. . . ." But the child was safe enough here. "I could find a cop," Nillie offered. Jo-Anne shook her head wisely.

"They don't want to bother about me right now."

"Well, that's true enough." Nillie looked around and found a part of the floor less congested than most. It took a little squirming and shoving, but she made room for the little girl. When Jo-Anne was obediently seated, Nillie steadied herself with one hand on the girl's head and, one at a time, pulled the red boots off. "My feet are freezing," she complained, looking around. "Well. You stay right here, I mean as much as you can. You'll be all right here." Had she just said that? Seemed almost as though she had, but her mind was no longer on the little girl. It was Dandy she was thinking about now.

"You'll be fine," she said, and picked her barefoot way to the escalator.

Jo-Anne nodded after her. The nod didn't mean agreement. It only meant that she understood the woman didn't want to take any further responsibility for her. Should she go to sleep? But she wasn't really sleepy, for some reason. Her mother would have said overtired. Besides, it was noisy—people arguing, somebody snoring, over her head a TV monitor with a rock band blaring, though there was no picture, only the legend: *Stay tuned for special bulletin.* Jo-Anne watched Vanilla Fudge go. Then, getting up as quietly as she could so as not to wake the fat lady sleeping next to her, she followed, up the one moving escalator, tortuously through the crowd on the second level. Some of the stores were still open—a coffee shop, an ice-cream parlor, a bar—but apparently just to make room for the stranded. They seemed to have run out of anything to sell. Jo-Anne hesitated at the ladies' room. The line was forbidding. But the need was urgent.

By the time she emerged from the washroom Vanilla Fudge was of course long gone. Jo-Anne was beginning to tired, but there was a row of phone booths just across the way. That was another long line, but Jo-Anne's conscience was bothering her badly. It was almost a relief when there was no answer at her apartment.

She hunted for a better place to sit down, and found one neglected by most people because it wasn't very warm. It was one of the loading docks, only scantily protected from the outside air. Not a problem for a young girl in a snowsuit and two sweaters. She didn't much like the looks of her neighbors, who were passing a brown-paper bag around as though it were something to drink. But it wasn't as noisy here.

Sleep overcame her—until she woke up because somebody's hand was inside her snowsuit. It was a man, older than her father and far larger. He smelled bad, breath and body, and he had not shaved for a long time. And the others who had shared the place seemed to be asleep—no, seemed to be *pretending* to be asleep.

Jo-Anne screamed.

The man shifted position quickly, thrusting his face into her neck. His other hand was on her throat. "You shut up, sweetie, or I squeeze!" he rasped.

It wasn't a bluff. He not only was willing to do it, he was already doing it. That didn't stop Jo-Anne from trying to scream again; she was shocked and disoriented, and she would have screamed her head off if the pressure on her throat hadn't turned it into a harsh rattling bellow.

But someone evidently heard. The man, swearing, turned, hurling her into the door to the bus bay. When she got herself turned around enough to see, there was another man there, a tall, young, black man in a red beret. He had the would-be molester in a choke hold, and he was glaring down at her. Then the fury on his face tempered to recognition.

She knew him, too. It was the Smasher, the Pin from across the street.

At eleven A.M. Shire Brandon had passed the point of being sleepy. They had moved the center of operations from the City Hall to one of the big network studios in midtown.

It was really happening! Ever since two A.M. every radio and television station in the city had been running standby teasers, announcing that the Universal Town Meeting would begin at noon. Mobile camera crews were spotted around the city, ready to pick up remotes. It was no problem to get them there; they were the same crews who had been covering the storm, all night long and the day before; the overtime and double-penalty overtime bills were going to be fearsome, but the crews were all in position. The Mayor, just now being made up after four hours of sleep, had cut a tape to announce what was happening; the City Council had been somehow collected and brought together in City Hall; the bargaining teams for all the struck and go-slow unions had been assembled; translators were on hand in the assigned radio stations, drafted from the United Nations; even the Director had been bundled up out of his warm apartment on Central Park West and brought down to the studio, where he twittered and beamed and got in everybody's way. "Oh, Shire," he said ecstatically, "it's looking good, isn't it?"

Part of the reason the world was looking good—at least better—was that the snow had tapered off. A few of the north-south avenues in Manhattan were very nearly open again; progress had even been made on a few of the major cross streets, and the subways were running everywhere there were subways. It would be sometime before the Els and the tunnels and bridges were of any use to anyone, but at least there was movement again.

Brandon took his seat in the control room, nursing a cardboard carton of machine coffee. It was long since cold, and it hadn't been very good in the first place, but every time he remembered he had it he wet his lips with it. "All remotes on line," said the assistant director. "Tapes ready," said the technical director. "Stand by," said the director, nodding; and then, as the clock showed precisely ten seconds before the hour, he nodded. "Roll Eight," he said.

Brandon listened to the seconds countdown—nine, eight, seven—and then the director said, "Take Eight!"

From somewhere a picture emerged on the screen. It was the Mayor, repeating his tape. "Today," he said, "we are going to try to settle our differences, not sweep them under the rug. We are going to talk about the things that are crippling our city, and listen to all the proposals that are being made to settle them. Then you, the citizens, are going to help us decide. I say 'help' only because there is no provision in law for making this sort of community decision making binding, but I assure you that your voice will count. From time to time today there will be a vote. The way you vote is by calling a number on your telephone. Nobody will answer, but counters will register how many people call up on that number—one number for yes, one number for no. If there is a clear majority for either side we'll take that as the voice of the people and then the City Council, which is now sitting in session ready to act, will do what is necessary. They aren't *bound* to do what you say, but I assure you they will be listening intently. Those are the ground rules—"

Somebody was touching Brandon's shoulder. "Yes? What is it?"

A network security man was handing him a folded slip of paper. "Message for you, Mr. Brandon."

"Thank you." There had been dozens of messages; one more could wait. Brandon listened on:

"—the event there's no clear majority, then we go back to the bargaining committees or to individuals chosen at random among all you listeners and viewers. If you are selected to be on the air, you will have exactly thirty seconds to say what you want to say— speak in favor of one side or the other, make an alternative selection, suggest a modification—it's your time, you can use it any way you want to. But thirty seconds is all you've got—"

"They said it was important, Mr. Brandon." The security guard was still standing there.

"Oh, all right." But he took his time unfolding it, watching the Mayor explain how each new suggestion would be offered to the viewers at large for voting, and the ones that seemed to command a favorable vote would be embodied in the next major vote. "The first thing we have to deal with," the Mayor declared, "is the strike of our public servants. So first we will hear from the chief negotiator for the policemen—"

But then Brandon heard no more, because his eyes had fallen to the message form. It said:

> A man named Willbur Perkins, who says he is a neighbor of yours, says your daughter is in the Port Authority Bus Terminal, main waiting room, south terminal, ground level. He says she is well and unharmed, but very tired, and he will stay with her until you get there.

It is an exceptional parent who can be just to all his children equally. You try to give each one what he needs; that's basic minimum. You give each what he deserves—that's fair; and you give all what love directs —that's parenting. And when there's a conflict? When Bobby needs to be taken to his guitar lesson at the same time as Sue has to get to cheerleader practice? When there's enough money for Chet's teeth or Maisie's wedding, but not enough for both? What do you do then?

You do the best you can. And so Brandon divided himself between his two children the best way he could, though neither was a child of his flesh—the weary ten-year-old who needed comforting and caring and reassurance, and the child of his mind and heart that was even now naked to the inspection of ten million strangers. And they were inspecting it. They were *using* it! The way from the network to the bus terminal was a twenty-minute walk through crowded city streets— usually—but on this day it was nearly an hour, and detouring through as many office buildings and hotel lobbies as he could manage; faster than the choked streets, and warmer. And in every one, or every one that was open at all, someone had put up a television set and there were people gathered around. Listening.

Arguing. Proposing. And, now and then, agreeing. Voices caught his ear, fragments, some from the crowds, some from the TV monitors. A cop: "—get along without more money, but, Jesus, could you make the job a little *easier?* Get people not to *fight* us?" A Hispanic: "Is *wrong,* how they say you have to be so big to get to be a fireman—I swear, I can climb a ladder faster than those turkeys!" A union leader on the TV screen: "You want us to be *reasonable?* You tell the *members* to be reasonable! They don't want to hear reasons why they can't get, they just want to *have!*" And all the long way, trudging through snow, slipping on wet tile lobby floors, dodging through service entrances, wending his way around tow-trucks tugging at abandoned cars—all that way Brandon was filled with love and pride and worry, an undistributed welling of emotion that was linked with his daughter and with his project and left him wet-eyed when he reached Jo-Anne and caught her up in his arms. All he said was, "The subway's running again. Let's go home." And all she answered was, "All right, Daddy." And hand in hand they hurried through the crowds and out into the city that was digging itself, slowly digging but surely digging, digging itself out of the wrack of the storm.

YOU KNOW WHAT A "SLUMLORD" IS? IT'S ME. Me and people like me that saved our dough and looked for real estate to invest it in. Well, where can you find anything you can afford to buy? The slums, that's where. And then the tenants expect you to give them sauna baths and swimming pools and a new paint job every six months, and the city won't let you raise the rents, so what do you do? Sure, I've had a few violations. Maybe they don't get all the hot water they want and it's hard to get the exterminators in every time somebody sees a bug, but what do they expect? That's not the worse thing. The worst thing is when they have one of those Universal Town Meetings and decide to rebuild the whole neighborhood, and then what happens to your investment? They call it progress! But actually I'm the first casualty of

The Greening of Bed-stuy

I Marcus Garvey de Harcourt's last class of the day was H.E., meaning "Health Education," meaning climbing up ropes in the smelly, bare gymnasium of P.S. 388. It was a matter of honor with him to avoid that when he could. Today he could. He had a note from his father that would get him out of school, and besides it was a raid day. The police were in the school. It was a drug bust, or possibly a weapons search; or maybe some fragile old American History teacher had passed the terror point at the uproar in his class and called for help. Whatever. The police were in the school, and the door monitors were knotted at the stairwells, listening to the sounds of scuffling upstairs. It was a break he didn't really need, because at the best of times the door monitors at P.S. 388 were instructed not to try too hard to keep the students in—else they simply wouldn't show up at all.

Once across the street Marcus ducked behind the tall mound of garbage bags to see which of his schoolmates —or teachers!—would come out in handcuffs, but that was a disappointment because the cops came out alone. This time, at least, the cops had found nothing worth an arrest—meaning, no doubt, that the problem was over and the teacher involved wouldn't, or didn't dare to, identify the culprits.

One-forty, and his father had ordered him to be ready to leave for the prison by two o'clock. No problem. He threaded his way past the *Construction— All Traffic Detour* signs on Nostrand Avenue, climbed one of the great soil heaps, gazed longingly at the rows of earth-moving machines, silenced by some sort of work stoppage, and rummaged in the dirt for something to throw at them. There was plenty. There were pieces of bulldozed homes in that tip, Art Deco storefronts from the 1920s, bay-window frames from the 1900s, sweat-equity cinderblocks from the 1980s, all crushed together. Marcus found a china doorknob, just right. When it struck the nearest parked backhoe it splintered with a crash.

They said Bedford-Stuyvesant was a jungle, and maybe it was. It was the jungle that young Marcus de Harcourt had lived all his life in. He didn't fear it—was wary of parts of it, sure, but it was all familiar. And it was filled with interesting creatures, mostly known to Marcus, Marcus known to a few of them—like the young men in clerical collars outside the Franciscan mission. They waved to him from across the road. Bloody Bess at the corner didn't wave. As he passed her she was having a perfectly reasonable, if agitated, conversation: "She having an a*bort*ion. She having an in*flatable* abortion. He having intercourse with her ten *times*, so she having it." The only odd part was that she was talking to a fire hydrant. The bearded man in a doorway, head pillowed on a sack of garbage, didn't wave either, but that was because he was asleep. Marcus considered stealing his shoes and hiding them, but you never knew about these doorway dudes. Sometimes they were cops. Besides, when he looked closer at the shoes he didn't want to touch them.

One forty-five by the clock on the top of the Williamsburgh Bank Building, and time to move along. He trotted and swaggered along the open cut of the Long Island Rail Road yards. Down below were the concrete railguides with their silent, silver seams of metal. Marcus kicked hubcaps until he found a loose one. He pried it off, one eye open for cops, and then scaled it down onto the tracks. Its momentum carried it down to crash against the concrete guide strip, but the magnetic levitation had it already. It was beginning to move sidewise before it struck. It picked up speed, wobbling up and down in the field, showering sparks as it struck against the rail, until the maglev steadied it. It was out of sight into the Atlantic Avenue tunnel in a moment and Marcus, pleased, looked up again at the bank clock. One fifty-five; he was already late, but not late enough for a taste of the cat if he hurried. So he hurried.

Marcus Garvey de Harcourt's neighborhood did not look bleak to him. It looked like the place where he had always lived, although of course all the big construction machines were new. Marcus understood that the project was going to change the neighborhood drastically—they said for the better. He had seen the model of the way Bedford-Stuyvesant was going to look, had listened to politicians brag about it on television, had been told about it over and over in school. It would be really nice, he accepted, but it wasn't nice yet. Between the burned-out tenements and the vacant lots of the year before and the current bare excavations and half-finished structures there was not much to choose, except that now the rats had been disturbed in their dwellings and were more often seen creeping across the sidewalks and digging into the trash heaps. Marcus ran the last six blocks to his father's candy store, past the big breeder powerplant that fed a quarter of Brooklyn with electricity, cutting across the scarred open spaces, ducking through the barbed wire and trotting between the rows of tall towers that one day would be windmills. He paused at the corner to survey the situation. The big black car wasn't there, which was good. His mother wasn't waiting for him outside the store, either; but as he reached the door, panting a little harder than necessary to show how fast he'd been running, she opened it for him. His father was there, too, with his coat on already. He didn't speak, but looked up at the clock behind the soda fountain. "Damn, Marcus," his mother said crossly, "you know your daddy don't like to be kept waiting, what's the matter with you?"

"Wouldn't let me out no sooner, Nillic."

His father glanced at him, then at the storeroom door. Behind it, Marcus knew, the cat-o'-nine-tails was hanging. Marcus's mother said, "You want trouble, Marcus, you know damn well he's gone give it to you."

"No trouble, Nillie. Couldn't help it, could I?" There wasn't any sense in arguing the question, because the old man either would get the cat out or wouldn't. Most likely he wouldn't, because this thing at the prison was important to him and he wouldn't want to waste any more time, but either way it was out of Marcus's hands.

The old man jerked his head at Marcus and limped out of the store. He didn't speak. He never did talk much, because it hurt him to try. At the curb he lifted an imperious hand. A cruising gypsy cab pulled up, surprising Marcus. His father did not walk very well on the kneecaps that had once been methodically crushed, but the place they were going was only about a dozen blocks away. You had to sell a lot of Sunday newspapers to make the price of a cab fare. Marcus didn't comment. He spoke to his father almost as seldom as his father spoke to him. He hopped in, scrunched himself against the opposite side of the seat, and gazed out of the window as his father ordered, "Nathanael Greene Institute, fast."

Because the Nathanael Greene Institute for Men was built underground, the approach to it looked like the entrance to a park. Nathanael Greene wasn't a park. It had forty-eight hundred residents and a staff of fifty-three hundred to attend them. Each resident had a nearly private room with a television set, toilet facilities and air-conditioning, and its construction cost, more than eighty-five thousand dollars per room, slightly exceeded the cost of building a first-class hotel. Nathanael Greene was not a hotel, either, and most of its luxuries were also utilitarian: the air-conditioning ducts were partly so that tear gas or sternutants could be administered to any part of the structure; the limit of two persons per cell was to prevent rioting. Nathanael Greene was a place to work, with a production line of microelectronic components; a place to learn, with optional classes in everything from remedial English to table tennis; a place to improve oneself, with non-optional programs designed to correct even the most severe character flaws. Such as murder, robbery and rape. Nathanael Greene had very little turnover among its occupants. The average resident remained there eleven years, eight months and some days. If he left earlier, he usually found himself in a far less attractive place—an Alaskan stockade, for example, or a gas chamber. Nathanael Greene was not a place where just anyone could go. You had to earn it, with at least four felonies of average grade, or one or two really good ones, murder two and up. Major General Nathanael Greene of Potowomut, Rhode Island, the Quaker commander whose only experience of penology had been to preside over the court-martial of John André, might not have approved the use of his name for New York City's most maximal of maximum-security prisons. But as he had been dead for more than two centuries his opinion was not registered.

Of course there was a line of prison visitors, nearly a hundred people waiting to reach the kiosk that looked like a movie theater's box office. Most were poorly dressed, more than half black, all of them surly at being kept waiting. Marcus's father nudged him toward the big Bed-Stuy model as he limped to take his place in the queue. The boy did what was expected of him. He skipped over to study the model. It was a huger, more detailed copy of the one in the public library. Marcus tried to locate the place where his father's candy store was, but would not be any longer once the project was completed. He circled it carefully, according to orders, but when he had done that he had run out of orders and his father was still far down the waiting line.

Marcus took a chance and let himself drift along the graveled path, farther and farther away from the line of visitors. What the top of Nathanael Greene looked like was a rather eccentric farm; you had no feeling, strolling between the railings that fenced off soybeans on one side and tomato vines on the other, that you were walking over the heads of ten thousand convicts and guards. It looked as much like Marcus's concept of the South African plains as anything else, and he imagined himself a black warrior infiltrating from one of the black republics toward Cape Town—except that the concrete igloos really were machine-gun posts, not termite nests, and the guard who yelled at him to go back carried a real rifle. A group of convicts, he saw, was busy hand-setting pinetree seedlings into plowed rows. Christmas trees for sale in a year or two, probably. They would not be allowed to grow very tall, because nothing on this parklike roof of the prison was allowed to grow high enough to interfere with the guards' field of fire. A squint at the bank clock told him that if he didn't get inside the prison pretty soon he was going to be late for his after-hours job with old Mr.

Feigerman and his whee-clickety-beep machinery; a glance at his father told him it was time to hurry back into line.

But his father hadn't noticed. His father was staring straight ahead, and when they moved up a few steps his limp was very bad. Marcus felt a warning stab of worry, and turned just in time to see a long, black car disappearing around the corner and out of sight.

There were a lot of long, black cars in the world, but not very many that could make his father limp more painfully. For Marcus there was no doubt that the car was the one that the scar-faced man used, the one who came around to the candy store now and then to make sure the numbers and the handbook that kept them eating were being attended to; the one who always gave him candy, and always made his father's limp worse and his gravelly voice harder to understand; and it was not good news at all for Marcus to know that this man had interested himself in Marcus's visit to the prison.

When they got to the head of the line the woman gave them an argument. She wore old-fashioned tinted glasses, concealing her eyes. Her voice was shrill, and made worse by the speaker system that let them talk through the bulletproof glass. "You any relative of the inmate?" she demanded, the glasses disagreeably aimed toward Marcus's father.

"No, ma'am." The voice was hoarse and gravelly, but understandable—Nillie had told the boy that his father was lucky to be able to talk at all, after what they did to his throat. "Not *relative,* exactly. But kind of family," he explained, his expression apologetic, his tone deferential, "'cause little Marcus here's his kid, and my wife's sister's his mother. But no, ma'am, no *blood* relation."

"Then you can't see him," she said positively, glasses flashing. "The only visitors permitted are immediate family, no exceptions."

Marcus's father was very good at wheedling, and very good at knowing when other tactics were better. "See him?" he cried in his gravelly voice, expression outraged. "What would I want to see the son of a bitch for? Why, he ruined my wife's sister's life! But the man's got a right to see his own kid, don't he?"

The woman pursed her lips, and the glasses shone first on Marcus's father, then on the boy. "You'll have to get permission from the chief duty officer," she declared. "Window Eight."

The chief duty officer was young, black, bald and male, and he opened the door of his tiny cubicle and allowed them in, studying Marcus carefully. "Who is it you want to see here, Marc?"

"My father," the boy said promptly, according to script. "I ain't seen him since I was little. Name's Marcus, not Marc," he added.

"Marcus, then." The officer touched buttons on his console, and the file photograph of Inmate Booking Number 838-10647 sprang up. HARVEY John T., sentenced to three consecutive terms of twelve to twenty years each for murder one, all three homicides committed during the commission of a major felony— in this case, the robbery of a liquor store. There was not much resemblance between the inmate and the boy. The inmate was stout, middle-aged, bearded—and white. The boy was none of those things. Still, his skin color was light enough to permit one white parent. "This your daddy, Marcus?"

"Yes, sir, that's him," said Marcus, peering at the stranger on the screen.

"Do you know what he's here for?"

"Yes, sir. He here because he broke the law. But he still my daddy."

"That's right, Marcus," sighed the duty officer, and stamped the pass. He handed it to Marcus's father. "This is for the boy, not you. You can escort the boy as far as the visiting section, but you can't go in. You'll be able to see through the windows, though," he added, but did not add that so would everybody else, most especially the guards.

The pass let them into the elevator, and the elevator took them down and down, eight floors below the surface of the ground, with an obligatory stop at the fourth level while an armed guard checked the passes again. Nathanael Greene Institute did not call itself escape-proof, because there is no such thing; but it had designed in a great many safeguards to make escape unlikely. Every prisoner wore a magnetically coded ankle band, so his location was known to the central computers at every minute of the day; visitors like Marcus and his father were given, and obliged to wear, badges with a quite different magnetic imprint; the visiting area was nowhere near the doors to the outside world, and in fact even the elevators that served it were isolated from the main body of the prison. And as Marcus left his father in a sealed waiting room, two guards surrounded him and led him away to a private room. A rather friendly, but thorough, matron helped undress him and went through everything he possessed, looking for a message, an illicit gift, anything. Then he was conducted to the bare room with the wooden chairs and the steel screen dividing them.

Marcus had been well rehearsed in what to say and do, and he had no trouble picking out Inmate 838-10647 from his photograph. "Hello, da," he said, with just enough quaver in his voice to be plausible for the watching guards.

"Hello, Marcus," said his putative father, leaning toward the steel screen as a father might on seeing his long-lost son. The lines for the interview had also been well rehearsed, and Marcus was prepared to be asked how his mother was, how he was doing in school, whether he had a job to help his ma out. None of that was any trouble to respond to, and Marcus was able to study this heavy-set, stern-looking white man who was playing the part of his father as he told him about

Nillie's arthritis and her part-time job as companion to old Mr. Feigerman's dying wife; about how well he had done on the test on William Shakespeare's *Julius Caesar* and his B+ grade in history; about his own job that his ma had got him with Mr. Feigerman himself, the blind man with the funny machinery that let him see, sort of, and even work as a consulting engineer on the Bed-Stuy project . . . all the same he was glad when it was over, and he could get out of that place. Toward the end he got to thinking about the eighty feet of rock and steel and convicts and guards over his head, and it had seemed to be closing in on him. The guards at Nathanael Greene had an average of ten years on the job, and they had had experience before of kids running errands that adults could not do, so they searched him again on the way out. Marcus submitted peacefully. They didn't find anything, of course, because there hadn't been anything to find. On that visit.

II Marcus's after-school job was waiting impatiently for him. The name of the job was de Rintelen Feigerman, and he was a very old man as well as quite a strange-looking one. Mr. Feigerman was in a wheelchair. This was not so much because his legs were worn out—they were not, quite—as because of the amount of machinery he had to carry with him. He wore a spangled sweatband around his thin, long hair, supporting a lacy metallic structure. His eyes were closed. Closed permanently. There were no eyeballs in the sockets any more, just plastic marbles that kept them from looking sunken, and behind where the eyeballs had been there was a surgical wasteland where his entire visual system had been cut out and thrown away. The operation saved his life when it was done, but it removed Feigerman permanently from the class of people who could ever hope to see again. Transplants worked for some. The only transplant that could change things for Feigerman was a whole new head.

And yet, as Marcus came up the hill, the white old head turned toward him and Feigerman called him by name. "You're late, Marcus," he complained in his shrill old-man's voice.

"I'm sorry, Mr. Feigerman. They made me stay after school."

"Who's that 'they' you keep talking about, Marcus? Never mind. I was thinking of some falafel. What do you say to that?"

Actually Marcus had been thinking of a Big Mac for himself, but that would mean making two stops, in different directions. "Falafel sounds good enough to me, Mr. Feigerman," he said, and took the bills the old man expertly shuffled out of his wallet, the singles unfolded, the fives creased at one corner for identification, the tens at two. "I'll tell Julius I'm here," he promised, and started down the long hill toward the limousine that waited on Myrtle Avenue.

The old man touched the buttons that swung his chair around. He could not really see down the hill, toward where the project was being born. The machinery that replaced his eyes was not too bad at short range, but beyond the edge of the paved area atop Fort Greene Park it was of no use at all. But he didn't need eyes to know what was going on—to know that not much was. Half the project was silent. By turning up his hearing aid and switching to the parabolic microphone he could hear the distant scream of the turbines at the breeder reactor and the chomp and roar of the power shovels where excavation was still happening, underlain with the fainter sounds of intervening traffic. But the bulldozers weren't moving. Their crews were spending the week at home, waiting to be told when payroll money would be available again. Bad. Worse than it seemed, because if they didn't get the word soon the best of them would be drifting off to other jobs where the funds were already in the bank, not waiting for a bunch of politicians to get their shit together and pass the bill—if, indeed, the politicians were going to. That was the worst part of all; because Feigerman admitted to himself that that part was not sure at all. It was a nice, sunny day in Fort Greene Park, but there were too many worries in it for it to be enjoyed—including the one special troubling thing, in a quite different area, that Feigerman was trying not to think about.

While they ate their late lunch, or early dinner, or whatever the meal was that they had formed the habit of sharing after Marcus's school got out, the boy did his job. "They've got one wall of the pumphouse poured," he reported, squinting out over the distant, scarred landscape that had once been a normal, scarred Brooklyn neighborhood. Silently the old man handed him the field glasses and Marcus confirmed what he had said. "Yeah, the pumphouse is coming along, and—and— they're digging for the shit pit, all right. But no bulldozers. Just sitting there, Mr. Feigerman; I guess they didn't turn loose your money yet. I don't see why they want to do that, anyway."

"Do what?"

"Make another hill there. They got this one right here already."

"This one's the wrong shape," Feigerman said, not impatiently—he liked the boy, welcomed his questions, wished he had had a real son of his own sometimes— since the semi-real stepson he had had no detectable love for his adopted father. "Besides, this one is historic, so they don't want to build windmills on top of it. George Washington held the British off right here— read the inscription on the monument sometime." He licked some of the falafel juice off his lip and Marcus, unbidden, unfolded a paper napkin and dabbed the missed spatters off the old man's bristly chin. Feigerman clicked in his long-range optical scanners in place of the sonar and gazed out over the city, but of course he could see only vague shapes without detail. "It's a big thing," he said—as much to the unheeding city as to Marcus.

"I know it is, Mr. Feigerman. Gonna make things real nice for Bed-Stuy."

"I hope so." But it was more than a hope. In Feigerman's mind it was certain: the energy-sufficient, self-contained urban area that he had lobbied for for more than twenty years. It was wonderful that it was going in in Brooklyn, so close to his home. Of course, that was just luck—and a few influential friends. The project could have been built anywhere—which is to say, in any thoroughly blighted urban neighborhood, where landlords were walking away from their tenements. And those were the good landlords; the bad ones were torching their buildings for the insurance. South Bronx wanted it. So did three neighborhoods in Chicago, three in Detroit, almost all of Newark, half of Philadelphia—yes, it could have been almost anywhere. Brooklyn won the prize for two reasons. One was the clout of the influential political friends. The other was its soft alluvial soil. What Brooklyn was made of, basically, was the rubble the glaciers had pushed ahead of them in the last Ice Age, filled in with silt from the rivers. It cut like cheese.

When Bed-Stuy was done it would not have to import one kilowatt-hour of energy from anywhere else—not from Ontario Hydro, not from Appalachia, not from the chancy and riot-torn oil fields of the Arab states. Not from anywhere. Winter heating would come from the thermal aquifer storage, in the natural brine reservoirs under the city, nine hundred feet down. Summer cooling would help to warm the aquifers up again, topped off with extra chill from the ice-ponds. By using ice and water to store heat and cold the summer air-conditioning and winter heating peaks wouldn't happen, which meant that maximum capacity could be less. Low enough to be well within the design parameters of the windmills, the methane generators from the shit pit and all the other renewable-resource sources; and the ghetto would bloom. Bedford-Stuyvesant was a demonstration project. If it worked there would be more, all over the country, and Watts and Libertyville and the Ironbound and the Northside would get their chances—and it would work!

But it was not, of course, likely that de Rintelen Feigerman would be around to see those second-generation heavens.

Reminded of mortality, Feigerman raised his wrist to his ear and his watch beeped the time. "I have to get going now," he said. "My wife's going to die this evening."

"She made up her mind to do it, Mr. Feigerman?"

"It looks that way. I'm sorry about that; I guess your mother will be out of a job. Has she got any plans, outside of helping out in the store?"

"Friend of my daddy's, he says he can get her work as a bag lady."

Feigerman sighed; but it was not, after all, his problem. "Take us on down the hill, Marcus," he said. "The car ought to be back by now."

"All right, Mr. Feigerman." Marcus disengaged the electric motor and turned the wheelchair toward the steep path. "Seems funny, though."

"What seems funny, Marcus?"

"Picking the time you're going to die."

"I suppose it is," Feigerman said thoughtfully, listening to the chatter of teen-agers on a park bench and the distant grumble of traffic. Marcus was a careful wheelchair handler, but Feigerman kept his hand near the brake anyway. "The time to die," he said, "is the day when you've put off root-canal work as long as possible, and you're running out of clean clothes, and you're beginning to need a haircut." And he was getting close enough to that time, he thought, as he heard his driver, Julius, call a greeting.

There was a confusion at Mercy General Hospital, because they seemed to have misplaced his wife.

Feigerman waited in his wheelchair, watching the orderlies steer the gurneys from room to room, the nurses punching in data and queries to their monitors as they walked the halls, the paramedics making their rounds with pharmaceuticals and enema tubes, while Marcus raced off to find out what had happened. He came back, puffing. "They moved her," he reported. "Fifth floor. Room 583."

Jocelyn Feigerman had been taken out of the intensive-care section, because the care she needed now was too intensive for that. In fact, in any significant sense of the word, her body was dead. Her brainwaves were still just dandy. But of the body itself, with its myriad factories for processing materials and its machines for keeping itself going, there was left only a shell. External machines pumped her blood and filtered it, and moved what was left of her lungs. None of that was new, and not even particularly serious. Fatal, yes. Sooner or later the systems would fail. But that time could be put off for days, weeks, months—there were people in hospices all around the country who had been maintained for actual years—as long as the bills were paid—as long as they, or their relatives, did not call a halt. Jocelyn Feigerman's case was worse than theirs. It could be tolerated that she could never leave the bed, could remain awake only for an hour or so at a time, could eat only through IVs and could talk only through a machine; but when she could no longer *think* there was no more reason to live. And that time was approaching. The minute trace materials like acetylcholine and noradrenaline that governed the functioning of the brain cells themselves were dwindling within her, as tiny groups of cells in places buried deep in the brain, places with names like the locus coeruleus and the nucleus basalis of Meynert, began to die. Memory was weakening. Habits of thought and behavior were deserting her. The missing chemicals could be restored, for a time, from pharmaceuticals; but that postponement was sharply limited by side effects as bad as the disease.

It was time for her to die.

So the hospital had moved her to a sunny large room in a corner, gaily painted, filled with flowers, with chairs for visitors and three-D landscape photographs on the walls, all surrounding the engineering marvel that was the bed she lay in. The room was terribly expensive—an unimportant fact, because it was never occupied except by the most terminal of cases, and rarely for more than a few hours.

As Feigerman rolled in the room was filled with people—half a dozen of them, not counting Marcus or himself. Or the still figure on the bed, almost hidden in its life-support systems. There was his daughter-in-law Gloria, tiny and fast-talking, engaged in an argument with a solid, bearded dark-skinned man Feigerman recognized as the Borough President of Brooklyn. There was his stepson, now an elderly man, smoking a cigarette by the window and gazing contemplatively at the shrouded form of his mother. There was a doctor, stethoscope around his neck, tube looped through his lapel, all the emblems of his office visibly ready, though there was not in fact much for him to do but listen to the argument between Gloria and Borough President Haisal—a nurse—a notary public, with his computer terminal already out and ready on a desk by the wall. It was a noisy room. You could not hear the hiss of Jocelyn Feigerman's artificial lung or the purr of her dialysis machine under the conversation, and she was not speaking. Asleep, Feigerman thought—or hoped so. Everybody had to die, but to set one's own time for it seemed horribly coldblooded. . . . He raised his chin and addressed the room at large: "What are we waiting for?"

His stepson, David, stabbed his cigarette out in a fern pot and answered. "Mother wanted Nillie here for some reason."

"She's got a right," Gloria flashed, interrupted her argument with Haisal to start one with her husband. Haisal was of Arab stock, from the Palestinian neighborhoods along Atlantic Avenue; Gloria was Vietnamese, brought to the United States when she was a scared and sick three-year-old; it was queer to hear the New York–American voices come out of the exotic faces. "Father! Haisal says they're going to go to referendum."

Feigerman felt a sudden surge of anger. He wheeled his chair closer toward the arguing couple. "What the hell, Haisal? You've got the votes in Albany!"

"Now, Rinty," the Arab protested. "You know how these things work. There's a lot of pressure—"

"You've got plenty of pressure yourself!"

"Please, Rinty," he boomed. "You know what Bed-Stuy means to me, don't you think I'm doing everything I can?"

"I do not."

Haisal made a hissing sound of annoyance. "What is this, Rinty? Gloria asked me to come here because you need a magistrate for your wife's testamentation, not to fight about money for the project! This is a deathbed gathering. Where's your respect?"

"Where's your sense of honor?" Gloria demanded. "You promised, Haisal!"

"I do what I can," the Borough President growled. "It's going to have to go to referendum, and that's all there is to it—now let's get going on this goddamn testamentation, can we?"

"We have to wait for Vanilla de Harcourt," Feigerman snapped, "and anyway, Haisal—what is it?"

From the doorway, the nurse said, "She's here, Mr. Feigerman. Just came in."

"Then we go ahead," said Haisal irritably. "Quiet down, everybody. Sam, you ready to take all this down? Doctor, can you wake her up?"

The room became still as the notary public turned on

his monitor and the doctor and nurse gave Jocelyn Feigerman the gentle electric nudge that would rouse her. Then the Borough President spoke:

"Mrs. Feigerman, this is Agbal Haisal. Do you hear me?"

On the CRT over her bed there was a quick pulsing of alpha waves, and a tinny voice said, "Yes." It wasn't Jocelyn's voice, of course, since she had none. It was synthesized speech, generated electronically, controlled not by the nerves that led to the paralyzed vocal cords but by practiced manipulation of the brain's alpha rhythms, and its vocabulary was very small.

"I will ask the doctor to explain your medical situation to you, as we discussed," said Haisal formally, "and if you have any question simply say 'No.' Go ahead, doctor."

The young resident cleared his throat, frowning over his notes. He wanted to get this exactly right; it was his first case of this kind. "Mrs. Feigerman," he began, "in addition to the gross physical problems you are aware of, you have been diagnosed as being in the early stages of Alzheimer's syndrome, sometimes called senile dementia. The laboratory has demonstrated fibrous protein deposits in your brain, which are increasing in size and number. This condition is progressive and at present irreversible, and the prognosis is loss of memory, loss of control of behavior, psychotic episodes and death. I have discussed this with you earlier, and repeat it now so that you may answer this question. Do you understand your condition?"

Pause. Flicker of lines in the CRT. "Yes."

"Thank you, doctor," rumbled the Borough President. "In that case, Mrs. Feigerman—Joss—I have a series of questions to ask you, and they may sound repetitive but they're what the law says a magistrate has to ask. First, do you know why we are here?"

"Yes."

"Are you aware that you are suffering from physical

conditions which will bring about irreversible brain damage and death within an estimated time of less than thirty days?"

"Yes."

"Then, Mrs. Feigerman," he said solemnly, "your options are as follows. One. You may continue as you are, in which case you will continue on the life-support systems until brainscan and induction tests indicate you are brain-dead, with no further medical procedures available. Two. You may elect to terminate life-support systems at this time, or at any later time you choose, as a voluntary matter, without further medical procedures. Three. You may elect to terminate life-support and enter voluntary cryonic suspension. In this case you should be informed that the prognosis is uncertain but that the necessary financial and physical arrangements have been made for your storage and to attempt to cure and revive you when and if such procedures become available.

"I will now ask you if you accept one of these alternatives."

The pause was quite long this time, and Feigerman was suddenly aware that he was very tired. Perhaps it was more than fatigue; it might have been even bereavement, for although he had no desire to shriek or rend his clothes he felt the dismal certainty that a part of his life was being taken away from him. It had not always been a happy part. It was many years since it had been a sensually obsessive part . . . but it had been his. He tried to make out the vague images before him to see if his wife's eyes were open, at least, but the detail was very inadequate. . . . "Yes," said the tinny voice at last, without emotion, or emphasis. Or life. It was, almost literally, a voice from the grave; and it was hard to remember how very alive that wasted body had once been.

"In that case, Mrs. Feigerman, is it Alternative Number One, continuing as you are?"

"No."

"Is it Alternative Number Two, terminating life-support without further procedures?"

"No."

"Is it Alternative Number Three, terminating life-support and entering cryonic suspension?"

"Yes." A long sigh from everyone in the room; none of them could help himself.

The Borough President went on: "Thank you, Mrs. Feigerman. I must now ask you to make a choice. You may elect to enter neurocryonic suspension, which is to say the freezing of your head and brain only. Or you may elect whole-body suspension. Your doctor has explained to you that the damage suffered by your body has been so extensive that any revival and repair is quite unlikely in the next years or even decades. On the other hand, suspension of the head and brain only entails the necessity for providing an entire body for you at some future day, through cloning, through grafting of a whole new donor body to your head and brain or through some other procedure at present unknown. No such procedures exist at present. This decision is entirely yours to make, Mrs. Feigerman; your next of kin have been consulted and agree to implement whatever choice you make. Have you understood all this, Mrs. Feigerman?"

"Yes."

Haisal sighed heavily. "Very well, Joss, I will now ask you which alternative you prefer. Do you accept Alternative Number One, the cryonic suspension of head and brain only?"

"No."

"Do you accept whole-body suspension, then?"

"Yes."

"So be it," rumbled the Borough President heavily, and signed to the notary public. The man slipped the hard-copy transparency out of his monitor, pressed his thumb in one corner and passed it around to the witnesses to do the same. "Now," said the Borough President, "I think we'll leave the family to say their good-bys." He gathered up the notary, the nurse and Marcus's mother with his eyes; and to the doctor he signaled, his lips forming the words: *"Then pull the plug."*

III On the first morning of de Rintelen Feigerman's new life as a widower, he awoke with a shock, and then a terrible sense of loss. The loss was not the loss of his wife; even in his dreams he had accepted that Jocelyn was dead, or if not exactly dead certainly both legally and practically no longer alive in the sense that he was. The shock was that he had not dreamed that he was blind. In Rinty's dreams he could always see. That was a given: everyone could see. Human beings saw, just as they breathed and ate and shit. So in his dreams he experienced, without particularly remarking on it, the glowing red and green headlamps of an IRT subway train coming into the Clark Street station, and the silent fall of great white snowflakes over the East River, and the yellow heat of summer sun on a beach, and women's blue eyes, and stars, and clouds. It was only when he woke up that it was always darkness.

Rosalyn, his big old weimarian, growled softly from beside the bed as Feigerman sat up. There was no significance to the growl, except that it was her way of letting Feigerman know where she was. He reached down and touched her shaggy head, finding it just where it ought to be, right under his descending hand. He didn't really need the morning growl any more. He could pretty nearly locate her by the smell, because Rosalyn was becoming quite an old dog. "Lie," he said, and heard her whuffle obediently as she lay down again beside his bed. He was aware of a need to go to the bathroom, but there was a need before that. He picked up the handset from the bedside table, listened to the beeps that told him the time, pressed the code that connected him to his office. "Rinty here," he said. "Situation report, please."

"Good morning, Mr. Feigerman," said the night duty officer. He knew her voice, a pretty young woman, or one whose face felt smooth and regular under his fingers and whose hair was short and soft. Janice something. "Today's weather, no problems. Overnight maintenance on schedule; no major outages. Shift supervisors are reporting in now, and we anticipate full crews. We've been getting, though," she added, a note of concern creeping into her voice, "a lot of queries from the furloughed crews. They want to know when they're going to go back to work."

"I wish I could tell them, Janice. Talk to you later." He hung up, sighed and got ready for the memorized trip to the toilet, the shower, the coffee pot—he could already feel the heat from it as it automatically began to brew his first morning cup—and all the other blind man's chores. He had to face them every morning, and the most difficult was summoning up the resolution to get through one more day.

Rinty Feigerman had lived in this apartment for more than thirty years. As soon as Jocelyn's son, David, was out of the house they had bought this condo in Brooklyn Heights. It was big and luxurious, high up in what had once been a fashionable Brooklyn hotel, when Brooklyn had still considered itself remote enough from The City to want its own hotels. Fashionable people stopped staying there in the thirties and forties. In the fifties and sixties it had become a welfare hotel, where the city's poor huddled up in rooms that, every year, grew shabbier and smelled worse, as the big dining restaurant, the swimming pool, the health club, the saunas, the meeting rooms, the rooftop night club withered and died. Then a developer turned it into apartments. It was Rinty Feigerman who picked the place, studying the view and the builders' plans while he still had eyes that worked. But Jocelyn had furnished it. She had put in end tables and planters, thick rugs on slippery floors, a kitchen like a machine shop, with blenders and food processors and every automatic machine in the catalogue. When Feigerman lost his eyes, every one of those things became a boobytrap.

For the first couple of years Jocelyn grimly replaced candy dishes and lamps as they crashed. She had not quite accepted the fact that the problem was not going to get better. After the damage toll began to be substantial, the week a whole tray of porcelain figures smashed to the floor and a coffeemaker burned itself out until the electrical reek woke her up, Jocelyn, sullen but thorough, attacked the job of blindproofing their home. The living spaces she kept ornate. Rinty stayed out of them, except on the well established routes from door to door. They wound up with three separate establishments. One was for company. One was Jocelyn's own space, formerly dainty but in the last two years more like a hospital suite. And the rest was Feigerman's own: a bedroom, a bath, a guest room converted into a study, a guest bath rebuilt into a barebones kitchen, all crafted for someone who preferred using only his sense of touch. And the terrace.

For a blind man with a seeing-eye dog, that was maybe the best thing of all. It had started out flagstoned, with two tiny evergreens in wooden pots. Jocelyn's son had had a better idea, and so he filled it from wall to wall with twenty cubic yards of topsoil. It grew grass, though nothing much else, and so became a perfect dog's toilet. No one had to walk Rosalyn in the morning. Rinty opened the thermal French windows, Rosalyn paced gravely out; when she had done what she had to do she scratched to come back in, and then lay attentively near her master until he called her to put on her harness. Feigerman always accoutered Rosalyn before he did himself. He wondered if she disliked it as much as he did, but of course he had no way to know. Rosalyn never complained. Not even when he was so busy working that he forgot to feed her for hours past her time; she would take food from no one else, and he supposed that if he continued to forget she would simply starve. Not even now, when she was so slow and tired so quickly that he left her home on almost every day, except when guilt made him take her—and a human being like the boy Marcus, for insurance—for a walk in a park. He stood in the open doorway, letting the morning sun warm his face, trying to believe that he could see at least a reddening of the darkness under his eyelids, until Rosalyn came back and whined softly as she put her cold nose in his hand.

Someone was in the apartment. Feigerman hadn't put his hearing aid on because, as he told himself, he wasn't really *deaf*, just a little hard of hearing; but he had not heard the door. He opened the door to his own room and called, "Is that you, Gloria?"

"No, Mr. Feigerman, it's me. Nillie. Want me to fix you a cup of coffee?"

"I've got some in here. Wait a minute." He reached for the robe at the foot of his bed, slid into it, tied it over his skinny belly—how could he be so thin and yet so flabby?—and invited her in. When she had poured herself a cup out of his own supply and was sitting in the armchair by the terrace window he said, "I'll be sorry to be losing you, Nillie. Have you got something else lined up?"

"Yes I do, Mr. Feigerman. There's a job in the recycling plant, just the right hours, too, so don't worry about me."

"Of course I'd like Marcus to keep on guiding me, if that's all right."

"Surely, Mr. Feigerman." Pause. "I'm really sorry about Mrs. Feigerman."

"Yes." He had not really figured out how to approach that particular subject. If your wife was dead, that was one thing; if she was sick, but there was some hope of recovery, that was another. A wife now resting at a temperature about a dozen degrees above absolute zero was something else. Not to mention the five or six years as her aging body began to deteriorate—or the years before that when their aging marriage was doing the same. Jocelyn's life was political and dedicated. His was no less dedicated, but his social objectives were carried out in bricks, steel and mortar instead of laws. The two life styles did not match well—"I beg your pardon?"

"I said I'm going to clear my stuff out of Mrs. Feigerman's room now, Mr. Feigerman."

"Oh, sure. Go ahead, Nillie." He realized he had been sitting silent, his coffee cooling, while his mind circled around the difficulties and problems in his world. And he realized, too, if a bit tardily, that Vanilla Fudge de Harcourt's voice had sounded strained. Particularly when she mentioned her son. Small puzzle. Sighing, Feigerman fumbled his way to the sink, poured the cold coffee away and set himself to the job of dressing.

"Dressing," for Rinty Feigerman, was not just a matter of clothes. He also had to put on the artificial vision system, which he disliked, and postponed as long as he could every day. It wasn't any good for reading, little better for getting around his rooms. Information Feigerman took in through braille and through audio tapes, the voices of the readers electronically chopped to speed them up to triple speed, without raising the frequency to chipmunk chirps. Nearly everything he chose to do in his rooms he could do without the vision system. He could speak on the phone. He could listen to the radio. He could dictate, he could typewrite; he could even work his computer console, with its audio and tactile readouts, at least for word-processing and mathematics, though the graphics functions were of no use at all to him any more. Feigerman was never able to see the grand designs he helped to create, except in the form of models. There were plenty of those, made in the shops of the consultancy firm he owned with his stepson; but it was not the same as being able to look down on, say, the future Bed-Stuy in the God's-eye view of every sighted person. At the computer he was quite deft, as artificial speech synthesizers read him the numbers he punched into the keyboard and the results that flashed on the CRT, now usually turned off. Of course, he did not really need to see, or even to feel a model of, Bed-Stuy. The whole plan was stored in his mind. . . . He was stalling again, he realized.

No help for it. He patted Rosalyn and sat down on the foot of his bed, reaching out for the gear.

The first step was to strap the tickler to his chest. Between the nipples, in a rectangular field seven inches across and five deep, a stiff brush of electrical contacts touched his skin. Feigerman had never been a hairy man, but even so, once a week or so, he had to shave what few sparse hairs grew there to make sure the contacts worked. Then the shirt went on, and the pants, and the jacket with the heavy-duty pocket that held most of the electronics and the flat, dense battery. Then he would reach down under the bed to where he had left the battery itself recharging all night long, pull it gingerly from the charger, clip it to the gadget's leads and slip it into the pocket. Then came the crown. Feigerman had never seen the crown, but it felt like the sort of tiara dowagers used to wear to be presented to the Queen. It wasn't heavy. The straps that held it made it possible to wear it over a wool cap in winter, or attached to a simple yarmulke in warm weather. It beeped at a frequency most people couldn't hear, though young children's ears could sometimes pick it up—Marcus claimed to hear it, and there was no doubt that Rosalyn did. When he first got the improved model the dog whined all the time it was on—perhaps, Feigerman thought, because she knew it was taking her job away from her.

When he turned the unit on now, she didn't whine, but he could feel her move restlessly against his leg as he sat and let the impressions reach his brain. It had taken a lot of practice. The returning echo of the beeps was picked up, analyzed and converted into a mosaic that the ticklers drew across his chest with a pattern of tiny electric shocks. Even now it was not easy to read, and after a long day there was more pain than information in it; but it served. For a long time the patterns had meant nothing at all to Feigerman, except as a sort of demented practical joke someone was playing on him with tiny cattle-prods. But the teacher promised he would learn to read it in time. And he did. Distance and size were hard to estimate from the prickling little shocks until he came to realize that the sonar's image of a parked car covering a certain area of his chest had to represent a real vehicle ten feet away. When he became accustomed to the sonar he didn't really need Rosalyn very much, and she was already beginning to limp on long walks. But he kept her. He had grown to like the dog, and did not want to see her among the technologically unemployed. . . . Then the coat; then the shoes; then Feigerman was ready to summon his driver and be taken to the offices in the Williamsburgh Bank Building for one more day of dealing with the world.

It was ever so much better, Feigerman's teacher had said, than the way things were for the unsighted even a few years earlier. Better than being dead, anyway, in Feigerman's estimation. Marginally so.

By the time Feigerman was at his office in the Williamsburgh Bank Building he was almost cheerful, mostly because his driver was in a good mood. Julius was a suspended cop; he had been a moonlighting cop, working for Feigerman only in his off-duty hours, until his suspension. The suspension was because he had been caught in a surprise blood test with marginal levels of tetrahydrocannabinol breakdown products in his system. Julius claimed he was innocent. Feigerman thought it didn't matter, since everybody was doing it, cops and all; and what made Julius's mood high was that his rabbi had phoned to say the charges were going to be dropped. So he joked and laughed all the way to the office, and left Feigerman still smiling as he got out of the elevator and beeped his way to his desk, answering the good-mornings of the staff all the way.

The first thing to do was to get out of the heaviest part of the harness again, which he did with one hand while he was reaching for his stepson's intercom button with the other. "David?" he called, lifting off the headpiece. "I'm in and, listen, I'm going to need another driver next week. Julius is getting reinstated."

"That's good," said the voice of his stepson, although that voice hardly ever sounded as though it found anything good. "I need you for a conference in half an hour, Dad."

Dad. Feigerman paused in the act of rubbing the imprinted red lines on his forehead, scowling. "Dad" was something new for David. Was it because his mother's death had reminded him that they were a family? David didn't seem to show any other effect. If he had shed one tear it had not been in Feigerman's presence. That wasn't surprising, maybe, because David's mother had devoted far more of her attention to her political causes than to her son. Or her daughter-in-law. Or, for that matter, to her husband. . . . "What kind of conference?" Feigerman asked.

There was a definite note of strain in David's voice, part wheedling, part defiant. "It's a man from S. G. & H."

"And who are S. G. & H. when they're home?"

"They're investment bankers. They're also the people who own all the legislators from Buffalo to Rochester, and the ones who can get the Bed-Stuy money out of committee."

Feigerman leaned back, the scowl deepening. There was enough tension in David's voice to make him wish he could see David's face. But that was doubly impossible—"The man from S. G. & H. wouldn't be named Gambiage, would he?"

"That's the one."

"He's a goddamn gangster!"

"He's never been convicted but, yes, I would agree

with you, Dad." The truculence was suppressed, but the wheedling was almost naked now. "All you have to do is listen to him, you know. His people have been buying utility stock options, and naturally he has an interest in Bed-Stuy—"

"I know what that interest is! He wants to own it!"

"He wants a piece of it, probably. Dad? I know how you feel—but don't you want to get it built?"

Feigerman breathed out slowly. "I'll see him when he comes in," he said, and snapped the connection.

If he had only thirty minutes before a very unpleasant task, he needed to get ready for it. He reached to the gadget beside his chair and switched it on. It was his third set of eyes, the only ones that were any good at all over a distance exceeding a few yards. They had another advantage. Feigerman called them his daydreaming eyes, because they were the ones that allowed him to see what wasn't there—yet.

Feigerman had designed it himself, and the machine on and around his desk had cost more than three hundred thousand dollars—less than half recouped when he licensed it for manufacture. It was not a mass-market item. Even the production models cost more than a hundred thousand, and there were no models which were in any sense portable. The size constraints could not be removed by engineering brilliance; they were built in to the limitations of the human finger.

The heart of the device was a photon-multiplier video camera that captured whatever was before it, located the areas of contrast, expressed them digitally, canceled out features too small to be displayed within its limits of resolution; and did it all twice, electronically splitting the images to produce stereo. Then it drove a pinboard matrix of two hundred by two hundred elements, each one a rounded plastic cylinder thinner than a toothpick—forty thousand pixels all told, each one thrust out of the matrix board a distance ranging anywhere from not at all to just over a quarter of an inch.

What came out of it all was a bas-relief that Feigerman could run his fingers over, as he might gently touch the face of a friend.

Feigerman could, in fact, recognize faces from it, and so could nearly a hundred other blind people well connected enough to be given or rich enough to buy the device. He could even read expressions—sometimes. He could, even, take a "snapshot"—freeze the relief at any point, to study in motionless form as long as he liked. What was astonishing was that even sighted persons could recognize the faces, too; and it was not just faces. Feigerman had no use for paintings on the walls, but if he wanted to "behold" the Rocky Mountains or the surface of the Moon his device had their stereo-tactile images stored in digital form, and a simple command let him trace with his fingers the Donner Pass or walk along the slopes of Tycho.

What he chose to do this morning, waiting for the gangster to show up and ruin his day, maybe even ruin his project!, was to "look out the window."

For that the electronic camera mounted behind his chair was not good enough. The electronic "pupillary distance" was too small for a stereoscopic image. But he had mounted a pair of cameras high up on the wall of the observation deck of the building, and when he switched over to them all of Bedford-Stuyvesant rippled under his fingers.

What Feigerman felt with his fingers was not really much unlike the surface of the Moon. There were the craters of excavation, for the underground apartment dwellings that would house two hundred thousand human beings and for the garment workshops, the electronic assembly plants and all the other clean, undegrading industries that would give the two hundred thousand people work to do. There were the existing structures—the tenements not yet torn down, the guardhouses atop Nathanael Greene, the derelict factories, the containment shell over the breeder reactor, the Long Island Rail Road lines—a late shoppers' express came hissing in on its maglev suspension, and the ripple of its passage tickled his fingers. There were the projects begun and the projects now going up—he recognized the slow, steady turn of a crane as it hoisted preformed concrete slabs onto the thermal water basin.

And there were the silent rows of dumpsters and diggers, backhoes and augers, that were not moving at all because of the lack of funds.

De Rintelen Feigerman didn't count up his years anymore. Now that his wife was a rimey corpsicle somewhere under Inwood no one alive knew the total; but everyone knew that it was a lot of years. There could not be very many more. Feigerman was used to delays. You did not make a career of major construction in the most complicated city in the world without accepting long time overruns. But this one time in all his life he was not patient, for every minute wasted was a minute taken off what had to be a slender reserve.

And this was his masterpiece. East River East was just one more big damn housing development. The Inwood Freezer complex was only a cold-storage plant. Nathanael Greene was just another jail. But Bed-Stuy—

Bed-Stuy was the closest human beings could come to heaven on earth. The original idea wasn't his; he had ferreted it out from old publications and dusty data-chips; somebody named Charles Engelke had described a way of making a small suburban community self-sufficient for energy as far back as the 1970s—but who was interested in suburbs after that? Somebody else had pointed out that the blighted areas of American cities, the South Bronxes and the Detroits, could be rebuilt in new, human ways. But it was de Rintelen Feigerman who put it all together, and had the muscle, the *auteur* prestige, the political connections, the access to capital—had all the things that could make the dreams come true. Solar energy. Solar energy used in a thousand different ways: to heat water in the summer and pump it down into rechargeable lenses of fossil water far under the surface; the new hot water squeezes out the old cool, and the cool water that comes up drives summer air-conditioning. In winter the pumps go the other way, and the hot summer water warms the homes. Solar energy as photovoltaics, for driving electronic equipment. Solar energy as wind, also for generating electricity, more typically for pumping water in and out of the thermal aquifers. Solar energy, most of all, for the thing it was best equipped to do—domestic heating. Feigerman made an adjustment, and under his fingers the vista of Bed-Stuy grew from what it was to what it would be, as his datastore fed in the picture of the completed project.

Even forty thousand pixels could not give much detail in a plan that encompassed more than a square mile. Each element represented something about the size of a truck; a pedestrian, a fire hydrant, even a parked car was simply too tiny to be seen.

But what a glorious view! Feigerman's fingers rested lovingly on the huge, aerodynamically formed hill that would enclose the surface-level water store and support the wind engines that would do the pumping. The smaller dome for the ice pond, where freezing winter temperatures would provide low-temperature reserves for summer cooling, even for food-processing. The milder slope that hid the great methane digesters— perhaps he loved the methane digesters best of all, for what could be more elegant than to take the most obnoxious of human by-products—shit!—and turn it into the most valuable of human resources—fuel? All the sewage of the homes and offices and factories would come here, to join with the lesser, but considerable, wastes from the men's prison next to it. The shit would stew itself into sludge and methane; the heat of the process would kill off all the bacteria; the sludge would feed the farms, the methane would burn for process heat. Industries like glass-making, needing the precise heating that gas could produce better than anything else, would find cheap and reliable supplies—meaning jobs—meaning more self-sufficiency—meaning—

Feigerman sighed and brought himself back to reality. At command, the future Utopia melted away under his fingers and he was touching the pattern of Bed-Stuy as it was. The methane generator was still only an ugly hole in the ground next to the prison. The great wind hill was no more than a ragged Stonehenge circle of concrete, open at the top. The idle construction machinery was still ranked along a roadway—

"I didn't want to disturb you, so I just let myself in, okay?"

The blind man started, twisted in his chair, banged his head against the support for the camera behind him. He was trying to do two things at once, to reach for the sonar crown that would let him see this intruder, to switch the tactile matrix back to the inside cameras so that he could feel him. The man said gently, amusedly, "You don't need that gadget, Feigerman. It's me, Mr. Gambiage. We've got business to talk."

Feigerman abandoned the search for the coronet; the camera behind his head had caught the image of his visitor, and Feigerman could feel it under his fingers. "Sit down, Mr. Gambiage," he said—pointedly, because the man was already sitting down. He moved silently enough! "You're holding up my money," he said. "Is that what you want to talk about?"

The image rippled under his fingers as Gambiage made an impatient gesture. "We're not going to crap around," he informed Feigerman. "I can get your money loose from Albany, no problem, or I can hold it up forever, and that's no problem too. On the other hand, you could cost me a lot of money, so I'm offering you a deal."

Feigerman let him talk. The tactile impression of

Gambiage did not tell much about the man. Feigerman knew, because the news reports said so, that Gambiage was about fifty years old. He could feel that the man was short and heavy-set, but that his features were sharp and strong. Classic nose. Heavy brows. Stubborn broad chin. But were his eyes mean or warm? Was his expression smile or leer or grimace? Gambiage's voice was soft and, queerly, his accent was educated under the street-talk grammar. It could even be Ivy League—after all, there was nothing to say that the sons of the godfathers couldn't go to college. And Feigerman had to admit that the man smelled good, smelled of washed hair and expensive leather shoes and the best of after-shave lotion. He could hear the faint sound of movement as Gambiage made himself comfortable as he went on talking: could smell, could hear, could feel . . . could be frightened. For this man represented a kind of power that could not be ignored.

Feigerman had dealt with the mob before—you could not be involved in large construction in America without finding you had them for partners in a thousand ways. The unions; the suppliers; the politicians—the city planners, the building inspectors, the code writers —wherever a thousand-dollar bribe could get a million-dollar vote or approval or license, there the mob was. It did not always control. But it could not be set aside. The ways of dealing with the mob were only two, you went along or you fought. Feigerman had done both.

But this time he could do neither. He couldn't fight, because he didn't have time left in his life for a prolonged battle. And he couldn't go along with what came to nothing less than the perversion of the dream.

"It's the co-generation thing," Gambiage explained. "You make your own power, you cost the utilities a fortune. I've got stock options. They're not going to be worth shit if the price doesn't go up, and you're the one that's keeping the price from going up."

"Mr. Gambiage, the whole point of the Bed-Stuy project is to be self-sufficient in energy so that—"

"I said we're not going to crap around," Gambiage reminded him. "Now we're going to talk deal. You're going to change your recommendations. You'll agree to selling all the power-generating facilities to the utilities. Then I'll recommend to my friends in Albany that they release your funds, and everything goes smoothly from there on. And I'll make it more attractive to you. I'll sell you my stock options for fifty thousand shares for what I paid for them. Thirty cents a share, for purchase at ninety-one and a quarter."

Feigerman didn't respond at once. He turned to his data processor and punched out the commands for a stock quotation. As he held the little earpiece to his ear the sexless synthesized-speech voice said: "Consolidated Metropolitan Utilities current sale, eighty-five."

"Eighty-five!" Feigerman repeated.

"Right," said Gambiage, and his voice was smiling. "That's what you cost me so far, Feigerman. Now get a projection with us owning the co-generation facilities and see what you get. We make it a hundred and ten, anyway."

Feigerman didn't bother to check that; there would be no point in lying about it. He simply punched out a simple problem in arithmetic: $110 − (91.25 + .30)$—say 1% for brokers' fees, × 50,000. And the voice whispered, "Nine hundred thirteen thousand two hundred seventy-five dollars."

He was being offered a bribe of nearly a million dollars.

A million dollars. It had been a legacy of less than a tenth of that that had put him through school and given him the capital to start his career in the first place. It was a magic number. Never mind that his assets were already considerably more than that. Never mind that money was not of much use to a man who was already too old to spend what he had. A million dollars! And simply for making a decision that could be well argued as being the right thing to do in any case.

It was very easy to see how Mr. Gambiage exercised

his power. But out loud Feigerman said, his voice cracking, "How many shares have you got left? A million or two?"

"My associates and I have quite a few, yes."

"Do you know we could all go to jail for that?"

"Feigerman," said Gambiage wearily, "that's what you pay lawyers for. The whole transaction can be handled offshore anyway, in any name you like. No U.S. laws violated. Grand Cayman is where the options are registered right now."

"What happens if I say no?"

With his fingers on the bas-relief, Feigerman could feel the ripple of motion as Gambiage shrugged. "Then Albany doesn't release the funds, the project dies and the stock bounces back to where it belongs. Maybe a hundred."

"And the reason you come to me," Feigerman said, clarifying the point, "is that you think I come cheaper than a couple of dozen legislators."

"Somewhat cheaper, yes. But the bottom line comes out good for me and my associates anyway." The needles tickled Feigerman's palm as the man stood up; irritably Feigerman froze the image. "I'll be in touch," Gambiage promised, and left.

It would be, Feigerman calculated, not more than three minutes before his stepson would be on the intercom.

He wasn't ready for that. He slapped the privacy switch, cutting off calls, locking the door.

The important thing, now, was to decide what was the important thing forever. To get the project built? Or to get it built in a fashion in which he could take smug and virtuous personal pride?

Feigerman knew what he wanted—he wanted that sense of triumph and virtue that would carry him through that not-long-to-be-delayed deathbed scene, for which he found himself rehearsing almost every day. His task now was to reconcile himself to second best—or to find a way to achieve the best. He could fight, of course. The major battles had been long won. The general outlines of the project had been approved, the land acquired, the blueprints drawn, the construction begun. Whatever Gambiage might now deploy in the way of bribed legislators or court injunctions—or whatever other strategies he could command, of which there were thousands—in the long run the game would go to Feigerman—

Except that Feigerman might well not be alive to see his victory.

He sighed and released the hold button; and of course his stepson's voice sounded at once, angry: "Don't cut me off like that, Dad. Why did you cut me off? What did he say?"

"He wants to be our partner, David."

"Dad! Dad, he already *is* our partner. Are you going to change the recommendation?"

"What I'm going to do is think about it for a while." He paused, then added on impulse, "David? Have you been picking up any stock options lately?"

Silence for a moment. Then, "Your seeing-eye kid is here," said David, and hung up.

When Marc came in to help Mr. Feigerman get ready he was prepared for a bad time. The other guy, Mr. Tisdale, was all in a sweat and grumbling to himself about trouble; the trouble centered around old Feigerman, so maybe the day's walk was off, maybe he'd be in a bad mood—at his age, maybe he'd be having a stroke or something.

But actually he was none of those things. He was struggling to put his camera thing on his head by himself, but spoke quite cheerfully: "Hello, Marcus. You ready for a little walk?"

"Sure thing, Mr. Feigerman." Marc came around behind Feigerman to snap the straps for him, and his glance fell on that pinboard thing the old man used to see.

"What's the matter?" Feigerman said sharply.

"Aw, nothing," said Marc, but it was a lie. He had no trouble recognizing the face on the pinboard. It was not a face he would forget. He had seen it many times before, arriving at his father's candy store in the black limousine.

IV Inmate 838-10647 HARVEY John T. did not merely have one of the best jobs in Nathanael Greene Institute for Men, he had two of them. In the afternoons he had yard detail, up on the surface. That was partly because of his towering seniority in the prison, mostly because he had been able to produce medical records to show that he needed sunshine and open air every day. Inmate Harvey had no trouble producing just about any medical records he liked. In the mornings he worked in the library. That was partly seniority, too, but even more because of his special skills with data-processors. Inmate Harvey's library work generally involved fixing the data-retrieval system when it broke down, once in a while checking out books for other inmates. This morning he was busy at something else. It was like putting together a jigsaw puzzle. Under the eyes of two angry guards and the worried head librarian, Harvey was painfully assembling the shards of broken glass that had once been a ten-by-twenty-six-inch window in the locked bookshelves. When it was whole it had kept a shelf of "restricted" books safe—books that most of the inmates were not permitted to have because they were politically dangerous. Now that it was a clutter of razor-sharp fragments it was something that inmates were even less permitted to have, because they were dangerous, period. On the edge of Harvey's desk, watched by a third guard, sat the two other inmates whose scuffling had broken the glass. One had a bleeding nose. The other had a bleeding hand. Their names were Esposito and La Croy, and neither of them looked particularly worried—either by their injuries or by the forty-eight-hour loss of privileges that was the inevitable penalty for fighting.

Those were small prices to pay for the chance of escape.

Hardly anyone ever escaped from Nathanael Greene. Of course, a lot of inmates tried. Every inmate knew that there were exactly three ways to do it, and that two of them were obvious and the other one impossible.

The obvious ways, obviously, were the ways through which people normally exited the prison—the "visitors' gate," which was also where supplies came in and manufactured products and waste went out; and the high-security "prisoner-transfer gate." Trusties lucky enough to be working on the surface, farming or cutting grass, could pretty nearly walk right out of the visitors' gate. Sometimes they made the try; but electronic surveillance caught them every time. The prisoner-transfer facility had been a little easier—three times there had been a successful escape that way, usually with fake transfer orders. But after the third time the system was changed and that way looked to be closed permanently.

Scratch the two obvious ways. The only way left was the impossible one. To wit, leaving the prison through some other exit.

What made that impossible was that there wasn't any. Nathanael Greene was underground. You could try to dig a tunnel if you wanted to, but there wasn't anywhere to tunnel to nearer than a hundred yards—mostly straight up—and besides there were the geophones. The same echo-sounding devices that located oil domes and seismic faults could locate a tunnel—usually in the first three yards—assuming any prisoner could escape the twenty-four-hour electronic surveillance long enough to start digging in the first place.

That was why it was impossible, for almost everyone,

almost all the time. But inmates still hoped—as Esposito and La Croy hoped. And even took chances, as Eposito and La Croy were willing to do; because there never was a perfect system, and if there was anyone who could find a way through the safeguards of Nathanael Greene it was Inmate 838-10647 HARVEY John T.

He never did get the jigsaw put back together to suit the guards, but after two hours of trying, after he had crunched some of the pieces twice with his foot and it was obvious that no one was ever going to reconstruct the pane properly any more, the guards settled for picking up all the pieces they could find and marching Esposito and La Croy away. They had no reason to hassle Inmate Harvey. That didn't stop them from threatening, of course. But when the lunch-break signal sounded they let him go.

The trip from the library to his cell took three flights of stairs and six long corridors, and Harvey did it all on his own. So did every other prisoner, because no matter where they were or what they were doing the master locator file tagged them in and out every time they came to a checkpoint. You lifted your leg to present the ID on your ankle to the optical scanner. The scanner made sure you were you by voice prints or pattern recognition of face or form, sometimes even by smell. It queried the master file to find out if you were supposed to be going where you were going, and if all was in order you simply walked right through. The whole process took no longer than opening an ordinary door, and you didn't screw around if you could help it because, anyway, you were under continuous closed-circuit surveillance all the time. Inmate Harvey, carrying his book and his clean librarian's shirt, nodding to acquaintances hurrying along the same corridors and exchanging comments about the methane stink that was beginning to pervade the entire prison, reached his cell in less than five minutes.

His cellmate was a man named Angelo Muzzi, and he

was waiting for Harvey. "Gimme," said Moots, extending his hand for the copy of *God-Emperor of Dune*.

Harvey entered the cell warily—you watched yourself with Muzzi. "You're fuckin up the whole plan," he pointed out. "You don't need this." But he handed the volume over just the same, and watched Muzzi open it to the page where the shard of glass lay.

"It's too fuckin short, asshole," Muzzi growled. He wasn't particularly angry. He always talked that way. He ripped a couple of pages out of the book, folded them over and wrapped them around the thick end of the glass sliver. When he held it as though for stabbing, about three inches of razor-edged stiletto protruded from his fist—sharp, deadly and invisible to the prison's metal detectors. "Too fuckin short," he repeated fiercely, but his eyes were gleaming with what passed in Muzzi for pleasure.

"It's the best I could do." Harvey didn't bother to tell him how long he had sat with the fragments, pretending to try to reconstruct a complete pane; Muzzi wouldn't be interested. But he offered, "The screws were going to give me a twenty-four." Muzzi would be interested in that.

And he was. "Shithead! Did you fuck up your meet with the kid?" This time the voice was dangerous and Harvey was quick in defense.

"No, it's cool, Moots, that's not till Thursday. I was just telling you why that was the best I could do."

"You told me. Now shut up." Harvey didn't wait to see where Muzzi would conceal the weapon. He didn't want to know. Fortunately he and Muzzi didn't eat on the same shift, so Harvey left without looking back.

The thing was, Muzzi didn't need the shiv. It would be useless in the first stages. When it stopped being useless it would be unnecessary. But you didn't argue with Muzzi. Not when he told you to steal him a glass blade. Not when he added more people to the plan and made two of them break the glass to get it. Not ever. It wasn't just that Muzzi's connections made the whole project possible, it was the man himself. "Man" was the wrong word. Muzzi was a rabid animal.

Tuesday lunch was always the same: sloppy-joe sandwiches, salad from the surface farm or the hothouse, milk. What they called "milk," anyway; it had never seen a cow, being made of vegetable fats and whitener. What made it worse than usual was the methane stink from where the digging of the new sewer pits had seeped through the soil into the cellblocks themselves. Harvey didn't join in the catcalls or complaints, didn't let sticky soup from the sloppy-joes spill on the floor or accidentally drop a meatball into the Jell-o. He didn't do any of the things the other inmates did to indicate their displeasure, because the last thing Harvey wanted was to get even a slap-on-the-wrist twenty-four-hour loss of privileges just now. All the same, he suffered with every bite. Inmate Harvey was used to better things.

Inmate 838-10647 HARVEY John T. had a record that went back thirty years, to when he was a bright and skinny kid. He hadn't intended to get into violence. He started out as a Phone-Phreak, rival of the semi-legendary Captain Crunch. When Ma Bell got mad enough to put the Captain in jail, young Johnny Harvey got the message. Making free phone calls to the Pope on his blue box just wasn't worth it, so he looked for less painful ways to have fun. He found them in proprietary computer programs. Johnny Harvey could wreck anybody's security. No matter how many traps Apple built into its software, Johnny Harvey could bypass them in a week, and make copies and be passing them out, like popcorn, to all his friends before the company knew they'd been screwed. Apple even got desperate enough to offer him a job—don't crack our security programs, design them—but that got boring. So did program-swiping. For a while Harvey worked for the city, mostly on the programs for electronic voting and the Universal Town Meeting, but that was kind of boring, too, in the long run, and then somebody came along with more larceny in his heart than Harvey had ever owned, and saw what treasures the young man could unlock.

He unlocked six big ones. Two were major payoffs from insurance companies on life policies that had never existed, on assureds who had never been born. Three were sales of stock Harvey had never owned, except in the tampered datastore of a brokerage house's computers. One was a cash transfer from branch to branch of a bank that thought its codes could never be compromised.

When the bank found out how wrong it was, it set a trap. The next time Harvey tried to collect a quarter of a million dollars that didn't belong to him, the teller scratched her nose in just the right way and two plainclothes bank security officers took Johnny Harvey away.

Since it was a white-collar crime and nobody loves a bank anyway, the prosecutor didn't dare go for a jury trial. He let Harvey go for a plea-bargained reduced charge. No one was really mad. They just put him away for eighteen months. But they put him in Attica, world's finest finishing school for street crime and buggery. After that Harvey couldn't get a job, and the codes had got a lot tougher, and, by and large, the easiest way he could find to support the habit he had picked up in stir was with a gun.

And when that went wrong, and they put him away again, and he got out once more, the situation hadn't improved. He tried the same project. This time things went very wrong, and when he finished trying to shoot his way out of a stakeout there were three people dead. One of the victims was a cop. One was a pregnant shopper. The third was her three-year-old kid. Well, the forgiving State of New York could make a deal on a homicide or two, but this time they were calling him "Mad Dog" on the six o'clock news, and he was convicted in public opinion before the first juror was called. He was looking at three consecutive twenty-five-to-life sentences. If he was the most model of prisoners, he could hope to get out two months past his one hundred and ninth birthday.

That wasn't good enough.

So Johnny Harvey summoned up his resources. He still had his winning ways with a computer, and Nathanael Greene was a computer-controlled prison. The central file always knew where every inmate was and whether he had a right to be there, because at every door, every stair, every cell there was a checkpoint. Each inmate's anklet ID checked him in and out for all the hours of his sentence, everywhere.

That wasn't good enough, either, but then two more events filled out the pattern. The first was when his first cellmate, No Meat, stuck his hand in the microwave oven. It was Harvey's fault, in a way. He had told No Meat how to bypass the oven's safety interlocks. But he hadn't really thought No Meat would carry his protest against prison diet that far until he didn't show up at evening lockup, and the screw told him No Meat was now well on his way to a different kind of institution, and the next day Harvey got a new companion. His name was Muzzi, and he looked a lot like bad news. He was short and scowling. He came into the cell as though he were returning to a summer home and unsatisfied with the way the caretakers had kept it up, and Harvey was cast in the role of the caretaker. His first words to Harvey were: "You're too fucking old. I don't screw anybody over twenty-two." What struck Harvey most strongly, even more than the violence and the paranoid brutality in the man, was his smell: a sort of catbox rancor, overlaid with expensive men's cologne. What struck Harvey later on, when Muzzi finished explaining to him who he was and how Harvey was going to behave, was that here was a man who was well connected. Not just connected, but holding. Muzzi was serving his sentence without the clemency he could have had in a minute for a little testimony. Muzzi chose instead to serve his time. So he was owed; and by somebody big.

The other event was that excavation started, no more than ten yards from the retaining walls of the prison, for the Bed-Stuy methane generating pit.

On Thursday morning Inmate 838-10647 HARVEY John T. returned to his cell after breakfast, along with all the other inmates in his cellblock, for morning showdown. Bedding stripped. Mattress on the floor. Personal-effects locker open. Inmates standing by the door. As always, the guards strolled past in teams of three. Usually there was just a quick glance into each cell. Sometimes a random dash and a shakedown: body search, sometimes going over the mattress with hand-held metal detectors, sometimes even taking it away to the lab and replacing it with a new one, or rather an even older, worse-stained, fouler-smelling one off the pallet the trusty pulled behind them. Harvey and Muzzi stood impassively as they went by. This time the reviews didn't bother them; but from the end of the cellblock Harvey could hear cursing and whining. Somebody, possibly the black kid who had just come in, had been caught with contraband.

Then, for some minutes, nothing, until the speaker grilles rattled and said, "All inmates, proceed to your duty stations."

Muzzi's work in the bakery was one way, Harvey's library the other. They didn't say good-by to each other. They didn't speak at all.

Harvey was not surprised when, toward the end of his morning shift, the speaker in the library defied the *Quiet!* signs and blared, "Six Four Seven Harvey! Report to Visitors' Center!"

The well connected Muzzi had used his connections well. He had procured them a reception party to be waiting once they were outside the prison. He had procured a couple of assistants to manufacture the plastic explosive and help with the digging—and, of course, to get him his personal shiv as well. He had also procured for Harvey a "son" to serve as a courier, and not a bad son at that. The kid even reminded Harvey a little bit of himself at that age—not counting color, anyway. Not counting their family backgrounds, either, which were Short Hills versus Bed-Stuy, and certainly not counting parentage—in Harvey's case a pair of college teachers, in Marcus's a retired hooker and her pimp. It was hard to see any resemblance at all, to be truthful, except that the young Johnny Harvey and the young Marcus de Harcourt shared the lively, bursting curiosity about the world and everything that made it go. So when Marcus came in he was right in character to be bubbling, "I seen the model of Bed-Stuy, Dad! Boy! There's some neat stuff there—they got windmills that're gonna pump hot and cold water, they got a place to turn sewage into gas, they got solar panels and an ice pond—"

"Which did you like best?" Harvey asked, and promptly the answer came back:

"The windmills!"

And that was the heart of the visit, the rest was just window-dressing.

Because Harvey had an artist's urge for perfection he took pleasure in spinning out the talk to its full half hour. He asked Marcus all about his school, and about his Mom, and about his Cousin Will and his Aunt Flo and half a dozen other made-up relatives. The boy was quick at making up answers, because he too obviously enjoyed playing the game. When it was time to go Harvey reached around the desk and hugged him, and of course the guard reacted. "Oh, hell, Harvey," she sighed—not unpleasantly, because she didn't believe in shaming a man before his kid. "You know better than that. Now we got to frisk you both."

"That's all right," said Harvey generously. It was. He wasn't carrying anything that he wasn't supposed to, of course, and neither was the boy. Any more.

An excuse to clean up around the model on his afternoon shift, a pretext to return to the library after dinner—Harvey's glib tongue was good enough for both, though not without some sweat. He was carrying, now; if he had happened to hit a routine stop-and-search with the contraband in his possession . . . But he didn't. Before bedcheck that night Harvey's part was done. The chip was in place in the library computer.

The chip Marcus had smuggled in wasn't exactly a chip. It was a planar-doped barrier, a layer cake with gallium arsenide for the cake and fillings of silicon and beryllium. Once Harvey had retrieved it from the niche under the model windmills and slipped it into place in the library terminal, it took only a few simple commands—"Just checking," he grinned at the night duty officer in the library—and the chip had redefined for the master computer a whole series of its instructions.

So, back in his cell, Harvey stretched out and grinned happily at the ceiling. Even Muzzi was smiling, or as close to smiling as he ever got. They were ready. Esposito had already stolen the vaseline and the other chemicals to make plastic. La Croy had the hammers, the shovels and the spike to make a hole in the wall for the plastic charge.

And the chip was in place.

It functioned perfectly, as Harvey had designed it to do, which meant that at that moment it did nothing at all. As each inmate passed a checkpoint, his ankle ID registered his presence and was checked against the master file of what inmates were permitted to be in what locations at which times. In the seven and a half hours after Harvey did his job, about a dozen inmates came up wrong on the computer. Their sector doors locked hard until a human guard ambled by to check it out. Three of the inmates were stoned. One was simply an incorrigible trouble-maker who had no business being in a nice place like Nathanael Greene. The others all had good excuses. None of them was Inmate 838-10647 HARVEY John T. Neither he nor any of his three confederates had tripped any alert, and they never would again. The computer registered their various presences readily enough. When it consulted the file of any one of them it was redirected to a special instruction table which informed it that Inmates Harvey, Muzzi, Esposito and La Croy were permitted to be any place they chose to be at any time. When it sought any one of them in his cell and registered an absence, the same redirection told it that this particular indication of absence was to be treated as registering present. The computer did not question any of that. Neither did the guards. The function of the guards was not really to guard anything, only to enforce the commands of the computer—and now and then, to be sure, to see that none of the inmates dumbly or deliberately jammed the optical scanners by kicking their IDs in backward, thus locking everybody in everywhere. The guards didn't ask questions, since they were as sure as any bank or brokerage firm that the computer would not fail.

And were about to learn the same lesson from Johnny Harvey.

So at five o'clock the next morning all four of them had strolled to a cell in the east wing of Nathanael Greene, part of the block that had been evacuated while the outside digging for the Bed-Stuy shit pit was going on. "Do it, fuckheads," Muzzi ordered, licking his lips, as Esposito held the spike and La Croy got ready to strike the first blow. "I'll be back in ten minutes."

He was fondling the paper-wrapped shiv, and Harvey had a dismal feeling. "We all really ought to stay right here, Moots," he offered.

Muzzi said, without malice: "I got business with a guard." And he was gone.

"Oh, shit," sighed Harvey, and nodded to La Croy to swing the hammer.

Since no one else was in that wing, no one heard. Or no one but the geophone, which relayed the information to the central computer, where the same chip informed it that the digging noises were part of the excavation for the shit pit. The geophone heard the sound of the plastic going off in the drillhole five minutes later, too, and reported it, and got the same response; and they were through the wall. All that remained was furious digging for about a dozen yards. When they were well begun Muzzi came staggering back, holding his face, his jaw at an unusual angle. "Fuckin cockthucker thapped me," he groaned. "Get the fuckin hole dug!" And dig they did, frantic shoveling, now and then noisy and nervewracking sledge-hammering as they hit a rock, and all the time Muzzi ranting and complaining as he held his fractured jaw: the shiv had been too short, it had broken off, the fuckin guard fought back, Muzzi had had to strangle the fucker to teach him a fuckin lesson for giving him a fuckin hard time—Harvey began to panic; the grand plan was going all to pieces because this raving maniac was part of it—

And they made it through the dirt and broke out into open space, into the excavation. Out onto a narrow plank walk over four stories of open steelwork. To a ladder and up it, five stories up, all the way to the surface, seeing buildings, seeing city streets, seeing the lightening pre-dawn sky, and it was working, it was all working after all!

They even saw the black car that was waiting where it was supposed to wait, with its clothes and guns and money—

And then it all went wrong again—Jesus, Harvey moaned, how *terribly* wrong—as a construction-site security guard, who did not have a computer to tell him what to do, observed four men clambering out of the excavation, and tried to stop them.

It was too bad for him. But the shots gave the alarm, and the noise and the commotion were too much for the person in the black car, and it rolled away and around the corner and there they were, Esposito dead, Muzzi with a bullet in his ass, out of the prison, free—but also alone in a world that hated them.

V Marcus was early at Mr. Feigerman's office, not just early because the errand he had to run couldn't wait, but too early for Mr. Feigerman to stand for it. He couldn't help himself. All the way from the candy store his feet kept hurrying him, although his head told him to slow down. His feet knew what they were doing. They were scared.

So was the rest of Marcus Garvey de Harcourt. It was bad to be summoned out of school because his father had been hurt. It was worse that when he got to the candy store his father was in a stretcher, a paramedic hovering by, while two cops questioned him angrily and dangerously. The store had been robbed, Marcus gathered. The robbers were not just robbers, they were escaped prisoners from Nathanael Greene; and they had held up the store, beaten up his father, stolen all the money and ridden off in a commandeered panel truck with Jersey plates. None of that really scared Marcus. It was only the normal perils of the jungle, surprising only because his father was known to be under the protection of someone big. It did not occur to Marcus that the story was a whole, huge lie until his father waved the cops away so he could whisper to his son. What he whispered was, "Around the corner. Mr. Gambiage. Do what he say." It was serious—so serious that Dandy de Harcourt didn't bother to threaten

Marcus with the cat, because he knew the boy would understand that any punishment for failure would be a lot worse. That was when he began to be scared; and what finished the job was when Mr. Gambiage snatched him into the black car and told him what he had to do.

So he took the knapsack and the orders and went trotting off, and if the boy warrior did not wet his pants with fear it was only because he was too scared to pee. He had been told that a diversion had been organized. The diversion was beginning to take shape all around him, people in threes and fours hurrying toward the heart of the Bed-Stuy project, some carrying banners, some huddled on the sidewalk as they lettered new ones. It made slow going, but not slow enough; he got to the Williamsburgh Bank Building more than ninety minutes before he was expected, and that was too early. The best thing to do was to pee himself a break in the twenty-ninth floor men's room to collect his thoughts and calm himself down, but a security guard followed him in and stood behind him at the urinal. "What's in the backpack, kid?" the guard asked, not very aggressively.

Marcus took his time answering. It was a good thing he'd finally managed to get tall enough for the man-sized urinals, because there weren't any kid-sized ones here. He urinated at a comfortable pace, and when he was quite finished and his fly glitched shut he turned and said, "I'm Mr. de Rintelen Feigerman's personal assistant, and these are things for Mr. Feigerman." The guard was a small man. He was lighter skinned than Marcus, but for a minute there he looked a lot like Dandy getting ready to reach for the cat.

Then he relaxed and grinned. "Aw, hell, sure. Mr. Feigerman's seeing-eye kid, that right?" He didn't wait for an answer, but reached under his web belt and pulled out a pack of cigarettes. "If you see anybody coming in, kid, you give a real loud cough, you hear?" he ordered, just like Dandy, and disappeared into a stall. In a moment Marcus smelled weed. Cheap chickenshit, he said, but not out loud, because he knew there was no hope that a guard working for Mr. Feigerman would offer a hit to Feigerman's young protégé, no matter how much the protégé needed to steady his nerves.

In the waiting room of Feigerman & Tisdale Engineering Associates Marcus dusted off his best society manners before he approached the receptionist. It was, "Mr. Feigerman's expecting me, sir," and, "I know I'm too early, sir," and, "I'll just sit over here out of the way, so please don't disturb Mr. Feigerman, sir." So of course the receptionist relayed it all to Feigerman practically at once, and Marcus was ushered into the old man's presence nearly an hour before his time. But not into the big office with the useless huge windows. Feigerman was down where he liked to be, in his model room, and he turned toward the boy at once, his headset wheeling and clicking away. "I heard about your dad, Marcus," he said anxiously. "I hope he's all right."

"Just beaten up pretty bad, Mr. Feigerman. They're taking him to the hospital, but they say he'll be okay."

"Terrible, terrible. Those animals. I hope the police catch them."

"Yes, sir," said Marcus, not bothering to tell Mr. Feigerman that it was not likely to have been the escaped convicts that had done the beating as much as one of Mr. Gambiage's associates, just to make the story look good.

"Terrible," Feigerman repeated. "And there's some kind of demonstration going on against the Bed-Stuy project, did you see it? I swear, Marcus," he said, not waiting for an answer, "I don't know how Gambiage gets these people out! They must know what he is. And they have to know, too, that the project is for their own good, don't they?"

"Sure they do," said Marcus, again refraining from

the obvious: the project could do them good, but not nearly as much good, or bad, as Gambiage could do them. "We going to go take a look at it?"

"Oh, yes," said Feigerman, but not with enthusiasm; it was a bad day for the old man, Marcus could see, and if it hadn't been for the nagging terror in his own mind he would have felt sympathy. Feigerman reached out to fondle a sixteenth-scale model of one of the wind rotors and brightened. "You haven't been down here lately, Marcus. Would you like me to show you around?"

If Marcus had been able to afford the truth he would surely have said yes, because almost the best part of working for Mr. Feigerman was seeing the working models of the windmills, the thermal aquifer storage with oil substituting for the water, the really truly working photovoltaics that registered a current when you turned a light on them—all of them, actually. And there was something new, an Erector-set construction of glass tubing with something like Freon turning itself into vapor at the bottom and bubbling up through a column of water and pulling the water along, then the water passing through another tube and a turbine on the way down to generate more power.

Feigerman's sonar eyes could not tell him what someone was thinking, but he could see where Marcus was looking. "That's what we call the wopperator," he said proudly. "It can use warm underground water to circulate that fluid all winter long, boiling another fluid at the bottom and condensing it again at the top—what's the matter?" he added anxiously, seeing that Marcus was shaking his head.

"It's Dandy," Marcus explained. "Before they took him away he told me I had to deliver some cigarettes for him—they're good customers, over by the power plant—"

Feigerman was disappointed, then annoyed. "Oh, hell, boy, what are you telling me? Cigarettes don't come in tin cans."

Fuck the old bastard! Sometimes you forgot that he saw things in a different way, and that metal would give off a conspicuous echo even inside a canvas backpack. "Sure, Mr. Feigerman," Marcus improvised, "but there's two containers of coffee there, too. And Dandy said he'd get the cat out if it got there cold."

"Oh, hell." Since Feigerman wasn't much good at reading other people's expressions, perhaps in compensation his own face showed few. But it was clear this time that he was disappointed. He said in resignation, "I don't want to get you in trouble with your dad, Marcus, especially after those thugs beat him up. Sam!" he called to the modelmaker chief, standing silent across the room. "Call down for my car, will you?" But all the way down in the elevator he was silent and obviously depressed. No more than Marcus, who was not only depressed but scared; not only scared but despairing, because he was beginning to understand that sooner or later somebody was going to connect his visits to the prison with the fact that the escaped prisoners had just happened to stop at his father's candy store . . . and so, very likely, this was the last time he would spend with Mr. Feigerman.

Julius was waiting for them with the car, illegally parked right in front of the main entrance because it had begun to rain. Mr. Feigerman's machine was doing its whee-clickety-beep thing and he turned his head restlessly about, but the sonar did not work through the windows of the limousine. "There's a lot of people out there," said Marcus, trying to help without upsetting the old man.

"I can hear that, damn it! What are they doing?"

What they were doing was shouting and chanting, and there were a lot more of them than Marcus had expected. Old man Feigerman was not satisfied. Blind he might be, but his otoliths were in fine shape; he could feel the pattern of acceleration and deceleration, and knew that the driver, Julius, was having a hard time getting through crowds. "Is it that maniac Gambiage's demonstration?" he demanded.

Marcus said apologetically, "I guess that's it, Mr. Feigerman. There's a lot of them carrying signs."

"Read me the signs, damn it!"

Obediently Marcus rattled off the nearest few. There was a *Give Bed-Stuy Freedom of Choice!* and a *Salvemos nuestras casas!* and *Jobs, Not Theories!* and two or three that made specific reference to Mr. Feigerman himself, which Marcus did not read aloud. Or have to. As they inched along, block by block, the yelling got louder and more personal. "Listen, Feigerman," bawled one man, leaning over the hood of the car, "Bed-Stuy's our home—love it or leave it!" And old man Feigerman, looking even older than usual, sank back on the seat, gnawing his thumb.

The rain did not seem to slow anybody down—not anybody, of all the dozens of different kinds of anybodies thronging the streets. There were dozens, even hundreds, of the neighborhood characters—five or six tottering winos, fat old Bloody Bess the moocher, even two young brothers from the Franciscan rescue mission, swinging their rain-soaked signs and shouting— Marcus could make out neither the slogans nor the signs, because they seemed to be in Latin. There were solid clumps of blue-collars, some of them construction workers, some from the truckers and the airline drivers; there were people who looked like bank clerks and people who looked like store salespersons—put them all together and it was a tremendous testimonial to Mr. Gambiage's ability to whip up a spontaneous riot on a moment's notice. And they were not all pacific. Ahead there was a whine of sirens and a plop of tear-gas shells from where the construction equipment stood idle.

"They're getting rough," bawled Julius over his shoulder, and he looked worried. "Looks like they're smashing the backhoes!"

Mr. Feigerman nodded without answering, but his

140

face looked terribly drawn. Marcus, looking at him, began to worry that the old man was not up to this sort of ordeal—if, indeed, Marcus was himself. He craned his neck to peer at the clock on the Williamsburgh Bank Building and gritted his teeth. They were running very late, and it was not the kind of errand where an excuse would get you off. It didn't get faster. A block along a police trike whined up beside them, scattering a gaggle of high-school girls shouting, "Soak the rich, help the poor, make Bed-Stuy an open door!" The cop ran down his window and yelled across at Julius, then recognized him as a fellow policeman and peered into the back to see Mr. Feigerman.

"You sure you want to go in here?" he demanded. There was a tone of outrage in his voice—a beat cop who had spent the first hour of his shift expecting to find desperate escaped convicts, received the welcome word that they were probably across the Hudson River and then been confronted with a quick, dirty and huge burgeoning riot.

Julius referred the question to higher authority. "What do you say, Mr. Feigerman?" he called over his shoulder. "Any minute now some of these thugs are going to start thinking about turning cars over."

Feigerman shook his head. "I want to see what they're doing," he said, his voice shrill and unhappy. "But maybe not you, Marcus. Maybe you ought to get out and go back."

The boy stiffened. "Aw, no, please, Mr. Feigerman!" he begged. "I got to deliver this, uh, coffee—and anyway," he improvised, "I'd be scared to be alone in that bunch! I'm a lot better off with you and Julius!" It was a doubtful thesis at best, but the cop in the trike was too busy to argue and Mr. Feigerman too full of woe. Only Julius was shaking his head as he wormed the big car through the ever narrower spaces between the yelling, chanting groups. But as they crossed the Long Island Rail Road tracks the crowds thinned. "Down there," Marcus ordered, leaning forward.

"Over between the power plant and the shit pit, the stuff's for the guards at the excavation—"

Julius paused to crane his neck around and stare at Marcus, but when Feigerman didn't protest he obediently turned the car down a rutted, chewed-up street. Feigerman gasped, as the car jolted over potholes, "Damn that Gambiage! I thought he was still planning to buy me off—why does he do this now?"

Marcus did not answer, but he could have guessed that it had something to do with the stuff in his backpack. "Right by the guard shack," he directed, and Julius turned into an entrance with a wire-mesh gate. A man in uniform came strolling out. "Got the stuff for us, kid?" he asked, chewing on a straw, his hand resting on the butt of a gun.

"Yes, sir!" cried Marcus, shucking the pack and rolling down the window, delighted to get his errand run so peacefully.

But it didn't stay peaceful long. Julius was staring at the man in guard's uniform, and, with increasing concern, at the quiet excavation and the absence of anyone else. Before Marcus could get the pack off Julius shouted, "Son of a bitch, it's Jack La Croy—get down, Mr. Feigerman!" And he was reaching for his gun.

But not fast enough. La Croy had the guard's gun, and he had not taken his hand off it. The shot went into Julius's throat, right between the Adam's apple and the chin, and spatters of blood flew back to strike Marcus's face like hot little raindrops. Two other men boiled out of the guard shack, one limping and swearing, the other Marcus's pretend-father, his face scared and dangerous. As La Croy pushed Julius out of the way and shoved himself behind the wheel the other two jumped into the back of the car, fat, fearsome Muzzi reaching for the backpack of weapons and money with an expression of savage joy. . . .

And from behind them, a sudden roar of an engine and the quick zap of a siren.

Everybody was shouting at once. Marcus, crushed under the weight of the killer Muzzi, could not see what was happening, but he could feel the car surge forward, stop, spin and make a dash in another direction. There was a sudden lurch and crash as they broke through something, and then it stopped and the men were out of the car, firing at something behind them. Julius would never get back on the force, Marcus thought, struggling to wipe the blood off his face—and whether he himself would live through the next hour was at best an open question.

For Johnny Harvey everything had begun going terribly wrong even before they broke through the wall, and gone downhill ever since. It was just luck they'd been able to kill the security guard and get his gun, just luck that they'd been able to hide in a place where there was a telephone, long enough for Muzzi to make his phone call on the secret number and beg, or threaten, the big man to get them out. The arrangements were complicated—a delivery of guns and money, a faked holdup to send the cops in the wrong direction, a whomped-up riot to keep the cops busy —but they'd been working pretty well, and that was luck, too, lots of luck, more than they had a right to expect—

But the luck had run out.

When the boy came with the guns it was bad luck that the driver was an off-duty cop who recognized La Croy, worse luck still that there was a police car right behind them. La Croy did the only thing he could do. There was no way out of the street they were in except back past the cops, and that was impossible. So he'd slammed the car through the gate of the powerplant. And there they were, inside the powerplant, with four terrified engineers lying face down on the floor of the control room and forty thousand New York City cops gathering outside. The boy was scared shitless; the old man, his vision gear crushed, was lying hopeless and paralyzed beside the guards. "At least we've got hostages," said La Croy, fondling his gun, and Muzzi, staring around the control room of the nuclear plant, said:

"Asshole! We've got the whole fuckin *city* for a hostage!"

VI The job as companion and bedpan-changer to old Mrs. Feigerman paid well, worked easy and was generally too good to last. When it ended Nillie de Harcourt didn't complain. She turned to the next chapter in her life: bag lady. That meant eight hours a day sitting before a screening table in her pale green smock, chatting with the bag ladies on either side of her; while magnets pulled out the ferrous metals, glass went one way, to be separated by color, and organics went another. The biggest part of the job was to isolate organics so they would not poison the sludge-making garbage. The work was easy enough, and not particularly unpleasant once you got past the smell. But that was too good to last, too, because anything good was always going to be too good for Gwenna Anderson Vanilla Fudge de Harcourt. So when she saw The Man moving purposefully toward her through the clinking, clattering, smelly aisles she was not surprised. "Downstairs, Nillie," he said, flashing the potsie. "We need you." She didn't ask why. She just looked toward her supervisor, who shrugged and nodded; and took off the green smock regretfully, and folded it away, and did as she was told. He didn't tell her what it was about. He didn't have to. Trouble was what it was about, because that was always what it was about. She followed him into the waiting police car without comment. The driver in the front started away at once, siren screaming. In the back, the cop turned on a tape recorder, cleared his throat and said, "This interview is being conducted by Sergeant Marvin Wagman. Is your name Gwenna Anderson?"

"That was my name before I married de Harcourt."

"According to records, Mrs. de Harcourt, you have fourteen arrests and six convictions for prostitution, five arrests no convictions for shoplifting, two arrests one conviction for possession of a controlled substance and one arrest no conviction for open lewdness."

Nillie shrugged. "You're talking about fifteen years ago, man."

Wagman looked at her with annoyance, but also, Nillie noted, a lot more tension than anything he had said so far would justify. "Right," he said sarcastically, "so now you're a success story. You married the boss and went into business for yourself. Dope business, numbers business, bookmaking business."

"If I was all those things, would I have to get work as a bag lady?"

"I ask the questions," he reminded her, but it was a fair question and he knew it. He didn't know the answer, but then hardly anybody did but Nillie herself —and most people wouldn't have believed it if told. "You have a son named Marcus Garvey de Harcourt?" he went on.

Suddenly Nillie sat bolt upright. "Mister, did something happen to Marcus?"

The sergeant was human after all; he hesitated, and then said, "I'm not supposed to tell you anything, just make sure I've got the right person. But your son's in good health last I heard."

"Mister!"

"I have to ask you these questions! Now, did you ever work for Henry Gambiage?"

"Not exactly. Sort of; all the girls did, at least he was getting a cut on everything. But that was before his name was Gambiage. What about Marcus?"

"And do you and your husband work for him now?"

"Not me!"

"But your husband?" he insisted.

"Take the Fifth," she said shortly. "Anyway, you ain't read me my rights."

"You're not under arrest," he told her, and then clicked off the tape recorder. "That's all I can say, Miz de Harcourt," he finished, "so please don't ask me any more questions." And she didn't, but she was moving rapidly from worry to terror. Mentioning her son was bad enough; mentioning Gambiage a lot worse. But when a cop called her "Miz" and used the word "please"—then it was time to get scared.

It was all but physically impossible for Nillie to plead with a policeman, but she came as close to it in the rest of this ride as ever since the first afternoon she'd been picked up for soliciting a plainclothes on the corner of Eighth Avenue and 45th Street, fifteen years old, turned out on the turf just two days before and still thinking that some day, maybe, she'd get back to the Smokies of eastern Tennessee. She gazed out at the dirty, rainy streets as they whizzed by at fifty miles an hour through rapidly moving traffic, and wished she could be sick. Marcus! If anything happened to him—

Her view of the dingy streets was suddenly streaked with tears, and Nillie began to pray.

When Nillie prayed she did not address any god. What religion she had she had picked up in the Women's House of Detention, the last time she was there—the last time she ever would be there, she had vowed. It was just after the big riots in New York, and the first night in her cell she dropped off to sleep and found herself being touched by a big, strong woman with a hard, huge face. Nillie automatically assumed she was a bull-dyke. She was wrong. The woman was a missionary. She got herself arrested simply so she could preach to the inmates. Her religion was called "Temple I"—I am a temple, I myself, I am holy. It didn't matter in her church what god you worshipped. You could worship any, or none at all; but you had to worship in, for and to yourself. You should not drug, whore or steal; above all, no matter what wickedness went on around you, you should not let them make you an accomplice . . . and so when Nillie got out she went to seek her pimp to tell him that she was through. . . .

And found Dandy in far worse shape than she. No more girls to run. No money left. And both kneecaps shattered, because he had made the mistake of getting in the middle of a power struggle in the mob. So she nursed him; and when she found out she was pregnant by him she kept it to herself until he was able to hobble around, and by then it was too late to think about a quick and easy abortion. It was a surprise to her that he married her. Dandy wasn't really a bad man—for a pimp—though even for a pimp he damn sure wasn't a specially good one; but he wanted a son, and it was joy for both of them when it turned out she was giving him one. Uneasy joy, sometimes—the boy was born small, caught every bug that was going around, missed half of every school year until he was eight. But that wasn't a bad thing; in the hospitals were Gray Ladies and nurses to teach him to read and give him the habit; he was smarter than either of his parents right now, Nillie thought—

If he was alive.

She straightened up and rubbed the last dampness from the corners of her eyes. She recognized the streets fleeting by—they were in her own neighborhood now, only blocks from the candy store. But what had happened? The streets were littered with rain-smeared placards, and the smell of tear gas was strong. There was a distant bellow of bullhorns blaring something about evacuation and *warning* and nuclear accident—

The police car nosed across the LIRR tracks, with a commuter special flashing away along the maglev lines as though it were running from something. As Nillie saw that the car was approaching the power plant, she thought that it was probably time to run, all right, if there was anywhere to run to.

They parked at the end of the cul de sac, with barricades and police cars blocking off the road, and ran, dazzled by the spinning blue and white and red emergency lights, along one side of the street, across from the utility's chainlink fence, into a storefront. And there were cops by the dozen, and not just cops. There was supercop, the Commissioner Himself, giving orders to half a dozen gray-haired police with gold braid on their caps; and there was a hospital stretcher, and out of a turban of white bandages looked eyes that Nillie instinctively recognized as her husband's; and there was Mrs. Feigerman's sullen elderly son, David Tisdale, looking both frightened and furious—

And there, his scar pale and his lips compressed, staring at her with the cold consideration of a butcher about to put the mercy-killer to the skull of a steer, was Henry Gambiage.

The situation wasn't only bad, it was worse than Nillie had dreamed possible. If Marc was alive—and he had been, at least, a few minutes earlier on the telephone—he was also a hostage. Not just any hostage. Captive of one of the maddest, meanest murderers in the New York prison system, Angelo Muzzi. And not just at the mercy of the mad dog's weapons, but right at Ground Zero for what the convicts threatened would be the damnedest biggest explosion the much-bombed city had ever seen. The argument that was going on when Nillie came in had nothing to do with the hostages. It was among three people, two engineers from Con Ed and a professor from Brooklyn College's Physics Department, and what they were arguing was whether it lay within the capacities of the escaped convicts merely to poison all of Bedford-Stuyvesant, or if they could take out the whole city and most of Long Island and the North Jersey coast. The Commissioner was having none of that. "Clear them out," he ordered tersely. "The Mayor's going to be here in half an hour, and I want this settled before then." But Nillie wasn't listening. She was thinking of Marcus Garvey de Harcourt, age ten, in the middle of a nuclear explosion of any kind. Nothing else made much impression. She heard two of the police wrangling with each other over whether they had done the right thing by following Marcus with his bag of weapons to see where the escapees were, instead of simply preventing him from delivering them as soon as they realized the story of the candy-store holdup was a lie. She heard the Commissioner roaring at Gambiage, and Gambiage stolidly, repetitiously, demanding to see his lawyer. She heard her husband whisper—even harder to understand than usual, because his lips were swollen like a Ubangi maiden's—that Muzzi had made him get the boy to try to deliver weapons, had made him lie about the fake holdup and then had beaten him senseless to make the story more realistic. She gathered, vaguely, that the reason she and Dandy were there was to force Gambiage to get his criminals away from the powerplant by threatening to testify against him—David Tisdale the same—and none of it made any impression on her. She sat silent by the window, peering at the chainlink fence and the low, sullen building that lay behind it. "Listen, shithead," the Commissioner was roaring, "your lawyer wouldn't come if I let him, because if you don't get Muzzi out of that control room the whole city might go up!"

And Gambiage spread his hands. "You think I don't care about the city? Jesus. I *own* half of it. But there's nothing I can do with Muzzi." And then he went flying, looking more surprised than angry, as Nillie pushed past him. "There's something *I* can do," she cried. "I can talk to my little boy! Where's that phone?"

Marcus H. Garvey de Harcourt, king of the jungle, strong and fearless—Marcus who faced up every day to the threat of Dandy's cat-o'-nine-tails and the menace of bigger kids willing to beat him bloody for the dimes in his pocket and the peril of pederasts who carried switchblade knives to convince their victims, and stray dogs, and mean-hearted cops, and raunchy winos—that dauntless Marcus was scared out of his tree. Dead people, sure. You couldn't live a decade in Bed-Stuy without coming across an occasional stiff. Not often stiffs you had known. Not often seeing them die. Julius had not been any friend of his—at best, a piece of the furniture of Marcus's life—but seeing him sob and bubble his life away had been terrifying. It was all terrifying. There was old Mr. Feigerman, his seeing gear crushed and broken; the blind man was really blind, now, and it seemed to cost him his speech and hearing as well, for he just lay against a wall of the power-station control center, unmoving. There was his soi-disant father, Johnny Harvey, not jovial now, not even paying attention to him; he was standing by the window with a stitch-gun in his hand, and Marcus feared for the life of anyone who showed in Harvey's field of fire. There were the power-station engineers, bound and gagged, not to mention beaten up, lying in the doorway so if anyone started shooting from outside they would be the first to get it. There was that loopy little guy with the crazy eyes, La Croy, screaming rage and obscenities, shrieking as though he were being skinned alive, although he didn't have a mark on him. And there was—

There was Muzzi. Marcus swallowed and looked away, for Muzzi had looked at him a time or two in a fashion that scared him most of all. Marcus was profoundly grateful that Muzzi was more interested in the telephone to the outside world than in himself. There he was, looking like Pancho Villa with his holstered guns and the twin bandoliers crossed over his steel-ribbed flak jacket, yelling at the unseen, but not unheard, Mr. Gambiage. "Out!" he roared, "what we want ith fuckin out, and fuckin damn thoon!"

"Now, Moots," soothed the voice over the speaker-phone.

"Now *thit!* We had a fuckin deal! I keep my fuckin mouth thut about MacReady and you get me out of the fuckin joint!"

"I didn't kill MacReady—"

"You wath fuckin right there watchin when I gave him the fuckin ithe pick, tho get fuckin movin!"

Gambiage's self-control was considerable, but there was an edge to his voice as he said, placatingly, "I'm doing what I can, Moots. The Mayor's on his way, and he's agreed to be a hostage while you get on the plane—"

"Not jutht the Mayor, I want the fuckin Governor and the fuckin Governor'th fuckin kid! All three of them, and right away, or I blow up the whole fuckin thity!"

Just to hear the words made icy little mice run up and down Marcus's spine. Blow up the city! It was one thing to listen to Mrs. Spiegel tell about it in the third grade, and a whole other, far worse thing to imagine it really happening. Could it happen? Marcus shrank back into his corner, looking at the men around him. Muzzi certainly wouldn't have the brains to make it happen, neither would La Croy. The engineers and Mr. Feigerman might know how, but Marcus couldn't imagine anything the convicts could do that would make them do it.

That left Johnny Harvey.

Ah, shit, Marcus thought to himself, sure. Johnny Harvey could figure out how to do it if anybody could. *Would* he?

The more Marcus thought about it, the more he thought that Harvey just might. What little Marcus had seen of Nathanael Greene made him think that living there must be pretty lousy, lousy enough so that even dying in a mushroom cloud might be better than spending the rest of your life in a place like that. Or a worse one. . . . But it wouldn't be better for Marcus. Marcus didn't want to die. And the only thing he could think of that might keep him from it, if Muzzi blew his stack terminally and Harvey carried out the bluff, would be for him to kill Harvey first—"Hey, kid!"

Marcus stiffened and saw that Muzzi was glowering at him, holding the phone in his hand. "Wh-what?" he got out.

Muzzi studied him carefully, and the scowl became what Muzzi might have thought an ingratiating grin. "It'th your mom, thweetie. Wantth to talk to you."

The question of how it had all gone to hell no longer interested Johnny Harvey, the question of what, if anything, there was left to hope for was taking up all his attention. He sat before the winking signal lights and dials of the power controls, wolfing down his third hamburger and carton of cold coffee, wondering what Marcus had been wondering. Would he do it? Was there a point in blowing up a city out of rage and revenge? Or was there a point in not doing it, if that meant going back to Nathanael Greene?—or some worse place. He reached for another hamburger, and then pushed the cardboard tray away in disgust. Trust Muzzi to demand food that a decent palate couldn't stand! But those two words, "trust" and "Muzzi," didn't belong in the same sentence.

Trusting Muzzi had got him this far. It wasn't far enough. There was Muzzi, stroking the nigger kid's arm as the boy talked to his mother, on the ragged edge of hysteria; Muzzi with his jaw broken and one hand just about ruined, and still filled with enough rage and enough lust for a dozen ordinary human beings. You could forget about Feigerman and the engineers, they were just about out of it; there was Muzzi and that asshole La Croy, and the boy and himself, and how were they going to get out of here? Assume the Governor gave in. Assume there really was a jet waiting for them at Kennedy. The first thing they had to do was get out of this place and into a car—not here in this street, where there could be a thousand boobytraps that would wreck any plan, but out in the open, say on the other side of the railroad tracks, where there would be a clear shot down the avenue toward the airport. It was almost like one of those cannibals and missionaries puzzles of his boyhood. Johnny Harvey had been really good at those puzzles. Was there a way to solve this one? Let the first missionary take the first cannibal across the river in the boat—only this time it was across the railroad tracks—then come back by himself to where the other missionaries and cannibals were waiting—

Only this time he was one of the cannibals, and the game was for keeps.

The boy was still on the phone, weeping now, and Muzzi had evidently got some kind of crazed idea in his head, because he had moved over to the corner where Feigerman was lying. Callously he wrenched the remains of the harness off Feigerman's unprotesting body. The old man wasn't dead, but he made no sound as Muzzi began straightening out the bent metal and twisted crown. Then he got up and walked toward Johnny Harvey.

Who got up and moved cautiously away; you never knew what Muzzi was going to do.

And then he saw that Muzzi, glowering over the power-station controls, was reaching his hand out toward them; and then Johnny Harvey was really scared.

When Nillie got off the phone she just sat. She didn't weep. Nillie de Harcourt had had much practice restraining tears in her life. They were a luxury she couldn't afford, not now, not while Marcus was in that place with those men—with that one particular man, for she had known Muzzi by reputation and gossip and by personal pain, and she knew what particular perils her son was in. So she sat dry-eyed and alert, and watched and waited. When she heard Johnny Harvey on the phone, warning that Muzzi was getting ready to explode, demanding better food than the crap they'd been given, she looked thoughtful for a moment. But she didn't say anything, even when the Mayor and Mr.

Gambiage retreated to another room for a while. Whatever they were cooking up, it satisfied neither of them. When they came out the Mayor was scowling and Mr. Gambiage was shaking his head. "Do not underestimate Moots," he warned. "He's an animal, but he knows a trap when he sees one."

"Shut up," said the Mayor, for once careless of a major campaign contributor. The Mayor was looking truly scared. He listened irritably to some distant sound, then turned to Gambiage. "They're still shouting out there. I thought you said you'd call off the demonstration."

"It is called off," said Gambiage heavily. "It takes time. It is easier to start things than to stop them." And Nillie was listening alertly, one hand in the hand of her husband. Only when two policemen came in with a room-service rolling hotel tray of food did she let go and move forward.

"It's all ready," one of them said, and the Mayor nodded, and Nillie de Harcourt put her hand on the cart.

"I'm taking it over there," she said.

The Mayor looked actually startled—maybe even frightened, for reasons Nillie did not try to guess. "No chance, Mrs. de Harcourt. You don't know what kind of men they are."

"I do know," Nillie said steadily. "Who better? And I'm taking this food over so I can be with my son."

The Mayor opened his mouth angrily, but Mr. Gambiage put a hand on his shoulder. "Why not?" he said softly.

"Why not? Don't be an idiot, Gambiage—" And then the Mayor had second thoughts. He paused, irresolute, then shrugged. "If you insist in front of witnesses," he said, "I do not feel I have the right to stop you."

Nillie was moving toward the door with the cart before he could change his mind. A train flashed underneath the bridge, but she didn't even look at it.

She was absolutely certain that something was going on that she didn't understand, something very wrong—something that would make the Mayor of the city and the city's boss of all boss criminals whisper together in front of witnesses; but what it was she did not know, and did not consider that it mattered. She went steadily across the tracks and did not falter even when she saw crazy La Croy shouting out the window at her, with his gun pointed at her head. She didn't speak, and she didn't stop. She pushed right in through the door, kicking the powerplant engineers out of the way.

There they were, crazy Muzzi and crazy La Croy, both swearing at her, and sane but treacherous Johnny Harvey with his hand on a gun, moving uncertainly toward the food; and there was old Mr. Feigerman looking like death days past—

And there was Marcus, looking scared but almost unharmed. "Honey, honey!" she cried, and abandoned the food and ran to take him in her arms.

"Leave him alone, bitch!" shouted La Croy, and Muzzi thundered behind him:

"Fuckin handth up, you! Who knowth what you've got there—"

She turned to face them calmly. "I've got nothing but me," she said; and waited for them to do whatever they were going to do.

But what they did was nothing. Johnny Harvey, not very interested in her or his companions, was moving on the cart of food, the big dish with the silver dome; he lifted the dome—

Bright bursts of light flared from under it, thunder roared, and something picked Nillie de Harcourt up and threw her against the wall.

A shard of metal had caught La Croy in the back of the head; he probably had never felt it. What there was left of Johnny Harvey was almost nothing at all. Muzzi struggled to his feet, the terrible pain in his jaw worse than ever, and stared furiously around the battered room. He could hardly see. It had not just been a bomb—they wouldn't have risked a bomb big enough to do the job, in that place; there was something like tear gas in with it, and Muzzi was choking and gasping. But, blurrily, he could see young Marcus trying to help his half-conscious mother out the door, and he bawled, "Thtop or I blow your fuckin headth off!" And the kid turned at him, and his face was a hundred years older than his age, and for a moment even Muzzi felt an unaccustomed tingle of fright. If that kid had had a gun—

But he didn't. "Move your fuckin atheth back in here!" roared Muzzi and slowly, hopelessly, they came back into the choking air.

But not for long.

Two minutes later they were going out again, but there had been a change. Nillie de Harcourt stumbled ahead, barely conscious. Marcus Garvey de Harcourt pushed the wheelchair, and the occupant of the wheelchair, crown on his head, muffled in a turned-up jacket . . . was Muzzi.

And Marcus was the most frightened he had ever been in his life, because he could not see a way to live to the other side of the bridge. He could see the Governor coming toward them, with a flanking line of police, all their guns drawn; and he knew what was in Muzzi's mind. The man had gone ape. If he couldn't get away and couldn't blow up the city, the next best thing was to kill the Governor.

Halfway across the bridge he made his move; but Marcus also made his.

It wasn't that he cared about the Governor, but between the Governor and Muzzi's gun was someone he cared about a lot. He took a deep breath, aimed the wheelchair toward a place where the rail was down and only wooden sawhorses were between the sidewalk and the maglev strips below . . . and shoved.

Muzzi was quick, but not quick enough. He was not

quite out of the wheelchair when it passed the point of no return.

Marcus ran to the rail and stared down, and there was Muzzi in his bandoliers and steel-ribbed jacket, plummeting toward the maglev strips, beginning to move even before he hit, bouncing up, hitting again, and all the time moving with gathering speed until he flashed out of sight, no longer alive, no longer a threat to anyone.

I'VE BUILT UP A NICE LITTLE BUSINESS AS A sidewalk pitchman, sunglasses in the summer, earmuffs when it's cold, umbrellas when it rains. I've got an item to sell you for any season. The cops bust me now and then, sure, but that's just a normal cost of doing business. It's a pretty good life. I don't have a boss. If I want to take the day off, I take it. The work keeps me out in the open air, too, so I don't have to go to Coney Island to catch me some of that he-man tan. The only thing is, what's going to happen to me now? The way I see it, I'm heading right for Welfare as soon as they finish

The Blister

I The union guy's name was Ella Jennalec, and she wasn't a guy. Probably at least one of her grandparents had been black. She was short and she was hefty, but the weight was where it needed to be. She wasn't young. She had to be easing up on forty, which made her a good dozen years older than John Fitzgerald Kennedy Bratislaw the Third. So he thought, straightening up for a better view, although he could almost feel his wife's eyes boring into his back, because he was thinking that there was a lot of mileage left in some of those older models.

Roar from the foreman: "You, Bratislaw! Keep your fucking mind on the fucking job!" Bratislaw grunted and shifted position a little as the winch took a little more strain on the cable, and the rest of the crew leaned muscle against the cold, wet wind. All of them were sneaking looks at the same thing—not at the cable that curved up to the steelwork over Battery Park, but at the union guy, standing on top of the deadweight and hassling with an engineer from the contractors. She wasn't dressed for the weather, and the crew appreciated that; jeans hugged her hips lovingly, and so did their eyes.

The diesel blatted, the winch turned, the ratchet thudded, the foreman yelled: "God damn it, I said watch it! You, Carmen! Take the handlever in case it slips!" The old winchman looked up and nodded. He changed places with Bratislaw, the two of them sliding as they moved. The steel-toed shoes didn't grip the surface, and the wind was blowing—no, it was pouring —down the Hudson Valley. Almost all of it seemed to be funneled right to the little artificial island between Ellis and Governor's where the cable crew was putting stress on the line. You would expect that by nearly April things would be warming up a little. They weren't. The dirty gray waves broke into dirty gray foam that froze the crew as it splashed them. And the splashes stank.

"Watch it!"

The ratchet clicked over and hesitated before catching, and the whole crew yelled and scrambled for footing. But it was all right, and the crew boss, studying his strain gauges, ordered them to hold up for a minute. Ella Jennalec glanced down at the crew with a thumb and a grin, and went back to arguing bonus rates with the construction company's man.

The crew including Bratislaw—his friends called him Jeff, short for JFK—was reeving the cable-ends sunk into the deadfall to the spools of cable that, before long, would be pulled up the master line to the truncated top of the old World Trade Center, a kilometer and a half away and nearly half a kilometer straight up. It was hard work. Donkey work. Machines made it possible, but not easy. It took muscles. It took big men like Bratislaw and Carmen, and once in a great while a big woman like Merrimee, the old black grandmother. About a quarter of the crew wound up with a hernia after a year or two. For that kind of work Jeff

Bratislaw was well prepared. He had spent his child-hood on a dying Wisconsin dairy farm. It accustomed him to hard physical work in bad weather, because the cows had to be fed whether it was balmy June or blizzard time. When the warming winds had scoured the plains dry he came to New York, and found the hardest work in the city was child's play after the herds.

"Take another notch," the gang boss ordered, and the winchman started up the diesel.

The alloy-steel cable would have to stand a strain of more than two hundred kilograms to the square centi-meter and would have to stay exposed to the outside weather for fifty years. It was big and tough. Each strand of the cable had been frayed out, so that it looked like a steel fright wig. The individual strands were fed into a coupler, which consisted of a squat cylindrical steel barrel, with spikes projecting from a diaphragm inside. Once both cables had been matched in the coupler it was Jeff's job to hold the ends in contact while the linkup crew tightened down the cylinder. Then, as the coupler began to take the strain from the main length of the master line, to ease up on the clamps just enough to let the cable pull itself together. Hard work, yes, and dirty; but it was thirty-three-fifty an hour, and you didn't get that on a played-out dairy farm in Wisconsin.

But it wasn't enough for Heidi to quit working and have a baby on, and Jeff knew that very well because Heidi had pointed it out to him every day for the past two months.

So, as soon as the foreman nodded that all was secured for the moment, while the engineers argued over the strain-gauge readings, Jeff waved at his union rep. "Ella? I got to talk to you a minute."

She nodded and winked, and went right back to the hassle with the guys from the construction company. Whatever that was. Jeff leaned forward and spat into the cold Bay, and pulled his peajacket closer around him.

There was always a hassle. There always would be a hassle, for the next twenty years, he bet. When the Blister was built it would cover almost all of the island of Manhattan, and they said it would save sixty skin-tillion cubic feet of natural gas every year. Probably it would. But it was going to cost plenty of gas every day of every one of those years, because every union in the city was going to have to take some and give some, and most of all change some. Doming the city was going to change the way the city worked. Sanitation men wouldn't use trucks any more. Firemen were going to have a vertical city to deal with. Cops wouldn't have squad cars. Nobody else would have cars, either, because public transportation would be the only way to go, and a lot of the ways would be up and down; the transit workers and the elevator operators were squabbling that one out now, which was why Jeff had had to climb twenty-six flights to get to bed last night. But most of all and right now, it was a problem for the construction unions, because no job like this had ever been done anywhere before. Because what was it that they were doing? The skeleton of the dome was braced by cables—bridges had cables—so the old International Association of Bridge, Structural and Ornamental Iron Workers filed a claim. But it was also like putting up a big auditorium dome, so Building, Concrete, Excavating and Common Laborers took an interest; and the artificial islands had to be built on caissons, so here came the Compressed Air Workers, and the final product would be transparent, so there were the Glaziers; and the Blasters, Drillers and Miners; and the Stationary Engineers; and, because a few of the tallest skyscrapers at the fringes had to come down or be chopped shorter, the House Wreckers; and because of all the servomachinery, the Machinists and Aerospace

Workers—and about a hundred more—and then the Teamsters came in and offered to represent them all; and when you thought it out, Ella Jennalec's bunch had saved everybody a lot of headaches by putting together the One Big Union merger. The city liked it, because they only had one union to deal with. The builders liked it, because the city did most of the dealing. The workers liked it, because they didn't have to worry about which union to join; in fact everybody liked it, with the possible exceptions of the ABS and O.A.W., the C.A.W., the Glaziers, the Blasters and the Teamsters. They hadn't liked it at all, but they had been helped to get used to it through the hard work of some of the middle-management types like Ella Jennalec's associate, standing up there on the deadweight with her and the engineers. His name was Tiny, and he was taller than Jeff Bratislaw and heavier, and his scarred knuckles said he was probably better in other respects, too. In the table of organization of the new Elevated Structures, Tunnels & Approach Workers he was down as a clerk-typist. He probably might have been, once. But not any more, with those hands.

"Take five," growled the gang boss as the engineers finished their battle with Ella and beckoned to him. Ella herself hopped down beside Jeff, catching herself with his arm as she hit the slippery concrete.

"How they hanging, stud?" she grinned. "You want to see me?"

"Yeah. I'm Jeff Bratislaw—you know, we mambaed at the New Year's dance at the local—"

"I remember. You move good, Jeff Bratislaw."

"Well, I need a better job than this. Thirty-three-fifty won't make it any more, and I was thinking about deckhand on one of those tugs that keep people away."

"Come on, Jeff! Not our jurisdiction, a good union brother ought to know that." The EST&A Workers owned all the jobs that touched any part of the dome itself or its outliers, but the harbor tugs were outside their law.

"Then demolition, maybe." He jerked his head toward the diminishing southern shaft of the World Trade Center. "I hear those guys get forty-eight bucks an hour, portal to portal."

"And some of them don't make it through the first hour, asshole," she said cheerfully. "You ever try to take apart a prestressed concrete girder? You got a wife, don't you? Why do you want to make her a widow?"

"I want to make her a mother, Ella, but to do that I need more dough."

"To do that," she grinned, "all you need is what you already got, and when we was mambaing I noticed you got plenty."

"Yeah, but—"

"Yeah." She cut him off. "I ain't saying no, Jeff, but right now I got plenty of things to take care of. These jerks wanted to cut out hazard pay for your job, did you know that? And then there's that Grand Jury thing coming up. But listen, not demolition. Nobody knows where the tensioned cables are in those girders any more. You ever see a bomb go off? That's what it's like. I got twenty-two compensation cases right now from the top ten stories alone. And—"

She was stalling him, Jeff knew; but the stalling stopped.

Her hired muscle, Tiny, was edging her gradually toward the tied-up launch waiting to take them back to South Ferry; the engineers were listening frostily to explanations from the gang boss; no one was watching the winch. And the cable, stretching slowly, gave just enough of a fraction of a centimeter to make the ratchet slip one notch.

This time Carmen was watching the gang boss instead of his hand lever. The elasticity of the steel spun the geared-down hand drum a quarter turn for that one ratchet notch. The lever hurtled out of its socket.

Jeff Bratislaw heard the click and saw the drum begin to move. He dove for cover, sweeping Ella with him.

Tiny, a fraction of a second later, jumped too, but he was big and heavy for fast movement on the sleet-sprayed concrete. He fell sprawling, just as the hand lever flew a hundred meters through the stormy air before it splashed into the bay. Jeff was suddenly colder than the air around him. Two seconds earlier he was standing right in the path of that two-meter shaft of hard metal, and if that had struck his head what would have been left of it, hard hat or none?

"The hell," Ella said shakily, getting up. "Maybe demolition's not so bad after all. Thanks, Bratislaw."

You took your chances when they came. "So what about a transfer?" he demanded.

But she wasn't looking at him, she was staring at Tiny, sprawled on the slick concrete and sobbing, with one leg bent in a way that legs didn't bend.

Everybody was yelling at everybody else, but they got together enough to gentle Tiny into the launch, even though he screamed when they lifted him. Ella hopped in after him. Before it pulled away she lifted her face to call to Jeff Bratislaw: "Looks like there's a vacancy. Report to my apartment eight o'clock tomorrow morning. We'll try you out for a week, anyway."

II The elevators were running—the day was staying good. As soon as Jeff got back to his apartment he dropped his clothes in the bathroom and, stark naked, padded to the kitchen to make dinner. There was a note fastened to the refrigerator door with a magnetic clip: *Not fish again, please?* A little heart was drawn below it for a signature. Jeff considered his options, holding the freezer door open, and finally pulled out two large Salisbury steaks, part of the batch he had made the week before, each in its individual pouch. They were made out of one hundred per cent meat;

hell, it was a day worth celebrating! He pulled out three large carrots and a couple of potatoes, then took an empty pouch out of the hardware drawer and put it on the drainboard. A pot of hot water went on the stove, and while it was coming to a boil he put on the scraping gloves and rubbed the skins off the vegetables. They were nearly blemishless, city grown in the big sand-trays that used reject hot water from the 14th Street powerplant. He chopped them all into slices with the cleaver, and potatoes and carrots went together into the pouch, along with a chunk of butter and a sprinkling of salt, pepper and dried parsley. He zipped up the pouch and dropped it into the boiling water, set the timer and took his quick shower.

By the time he was out of the shower it was time to put the frozen meat in the same pot. He reset the timer, shaved, pulled on slacks and a tunic and had started mixing drinks when the bell rang.

Heidi didn't usually ring the bell; he peered through the peephole and saw a blurry female figure in a police uniform. "Hey there, Lucy," he said, opening the door; it was his wife's sister. "Didn't expect to see you tonight. You want to stay for dinner?" There was another steak in the freezer, and the vegetables, he calculated quickly, would stretch.

"I can't, Jeff. I won't even come in." But she did, just far enough to let him close the door. "I'm on duty, but I stopped off to see if you wanted to sign the petition now."

"What petition?" He knew, well enough; he just didn't want her to bring him down with talk about corruption in the city.

"For a Citizens' Grand Jury to investigate the Grand Jury—you know! We talked about it Saturday night."

He gazed down at the sheet of paper—two short paragraphs and then at least fifty lines for citizens' signatures. But there were only two signatures on the page, and one of those was Lucy's own. "Well, I don't know, Lucy," he said. "I could get in trouble with this—so could you, you know. Specially if you're canvassing when you're on duty."

"I'm not *canvassing*, Jeff, I'm just dropping this off, and I had to be in the building anyway—it's part of my beat. Look, I'll just leave it for you and Heidi, okay? And I'll come by for it when I go off duty."

"See you later," he said, which was not a commitment. He didn't see any way out of it, though. Lucy was the do-gooder in the family, an honest cop, never took a nickel or an apple; and Heidi was too proud of her to turn her down on a thing like that. And if Heidi signed, he might as well sign himself; the people that would get upset about signing the petition wouldn't stop to consider whether both members of a family had signed, they would just make a little mark against the lease form, and another against the park permit, and another against the names of the Bratislaws wherever they appeared. He dropped the petition on the windowsill, staring out at the city. There were red laser lights flashing at the tops of the unfinished dome skeleton, to warn off aircraft, and it was drizzling again. It was a pretty city to look at. Why didn't people just leave it alone?

When he heard Heidi's key in the lock he had dinner on the table. He greeted her with a kiss. "I got the job," he said.

"Aw, Jeff, that's great!" She was looking tired as she came in the door, but a smile broke through the fatigue. "Tell me about it." And then, when she took a better look at him, "Holy shit, what have you done to your face?"

He had not even known about the bruise until he was shaving. "Industrial accident," he said. "I fell. Now listen. I'm going to be assistant to the shop steward. White-collar work. I don't have to get into demolition, and I don't have to pull cable in the snow."

"And more money?"

Jeff hesitated. "Well, I don't exactly know what the money is yet."

She took a pull at the drink and then moved toward the dinner table. The fatigue was back on her face, along with a look of puzzlement. "Explain that to me, will you, Jeff?"

"The money's the least part of it," he said, dividing the pouches between their plates. "There's plenty of fringe benefits."

"Oh?"

"You know." He made up his mind to tell her; she would understand; she wasn't like her crazy sister. "When somebody wants to get a better job, you know? He comes to the union. And he pays a kind of, what would you call it, a finder's fee to the guy who gets it for him."

"A kickback," she said, nodding. "You're going to be taking kickbacks."

"Heidi, you aren't going to give me a hard time, are you? That's the way the system works. You take kickbacks or you pay them—I just happen to think it's better to take them."

"Um." It wasn't agreement, but it wasn't an argument, either.

"So are we going to do it?" he pressed.

She chewed, regarding him. Neither of them had to say what "it" was, because "it" had been a major topic of conversation for the past three months—ever since they got the genetics lab reports that showed them both fully fertile and without any seriously worrying defects. "Well, I'll tell you, old man," she said, "I would imagine we are. But let's finish dinner first."

Heidi was always three times as long in the shower as Jeff, which was fine with Jeff because the results were always worth it. While she was using up half their day's water allotment, he was putting the dishes in the washer, folding up the table, pulling out the bed. He stopped himself as he packed up the organic garbage for the chute: the strike. So it would have to go into the freezer until they settled that one. He smoothed the pillows, turned down the sheets, got out of his clothes and into the dressing gown that was his signal for sexual intercourse—Heidi's was pajama tops without the bottoms—and lit a joint, sitting on the windowsill. He could see the big Eiffel-tower sort of thing that had sprung up from Madison Square, first pylon for the dome; and he could even see, past the clutter of skyscrapers downtown, the twin lights of the Verrazano-Narrows Bridge, where Heidi spent her working days.

Heidi was a port dispatcher. She and the other twenty-five men and women in the control tower had charge of dispatching all of the tugs, barges, cargo vessels, workboats, dredges, pleasure boats, tour boats —everything that floated from the tip of Manhattan on the north to Sandy Hook and the Brooklyn shore on the south. Pleasure boats were the worst. Most of them did not carry radar targets, and so they could be controlled only visually. But if a pleasure boat got into trouble it was usually agile enough to get itself out of it again, and in any case the occupants were the only cargo that mattered, and they could almost always be saved in the worst case. The serious part of the work was the big bastards coming up from South America and the Gulf, and the few that came across the Atlantic, and the coasting traffic—and, above all, the barges that brought in fuel and industrial equipment. If you found two of them on a collision course you couldn't tell them to take evasive action. They couldn't do it. You had to think far ahead with them, point them in the right direction and sweep everything smaller and more mobile out of their way.

With the garbage strike her job was a little easier. The scows weren't being towed out, fourteen or fifteen long strings a day, to the dumping ground two hundred kilometers into the Baltimore Canyon offshore. Day shifts were better than night, too. It was easier to keep visual contact with the little vessels that didn't own transponders or didn't keep them maintained. But wet, windy weather canceled all the advantages out. It made some of the vessels harder to control; and above all it reinforced the known fact that the west tower of the Verrazano Bridge was the coldest place in the City of New York. The tower was heated, of course. But when freezing rain was sleeting in and visibility was patchy there was no substitute for taking the glasses out on the platform, into the wild, freezing winds; and it was in and out a hundred times a day. So Heidi always came home exhausted when the weather was bad. Jeff put out forty times as much physical energy as she did; but Jeff only needed a shower and a shave to be ready for anything, until any hour of the night. Heidi was a big woman, but she didn't have her husband's physical strength.

The shower sounds had stopped, and now there was a rattling of medicine chest doors and face-cream jars. Jeff stubbed out his joint, and reached to turn down the lights.

In the dimness he saw a pulsing green flicker by the door. Hell, he'd forgotten the mail! There wouldn't be anything worth getting except bills, anyway—

But Heidi would notice it, and she would want to see if there was anything from her mother. So Jeff walked over to the comm. desk and pressed the mail combination. The first three items on the screen were bills all right—and automatically paid by deductions from their bank account, so they didn't need any attention except to be sorted into the right stores for their tax returns. The fourth—

The fourth began with the heading:

FROM SELECTIVE SERVICE BOARD NO. 143

"Oh, shit," said Jeff.

When Heidi got out of the shower the lights were full up, Jeff was mixing himself another drink and the text of the letter was still on hold, displayed on the screen:

> From the President of the United States, Greetings.
> You have been selected for universal military service and are required to report for your final physical examination on Tuesday, the 3d of April, to the Armed Forces Induction Center at Number 1 Penn Plaza. . . .

"Oh, shit," Heidi said, taking the drink Jeff held out to her. She was wearing a robe, but Jeff could see that under it she had only a pajama top and a lot of warm, damp, pink skin.

"Of course we knew it was going to come someday," he said.

"But why now, damn it!"

Jeff put more ice in his drink and said, "I've been thinking. Of course, what I could do is sign up for the City Corps. So I'd be right here for three years, and after basic training I'd probably only be giving out parking tickets and like that for the first year or so—"

"At nine dollars an hour," Heidi said.

"Well, yeah. Maybe your sister could help me pass the sergeant's examination after the first year."

"Or you could take the eighteen-month field service hitch—"

"And maybe get my ass shot off in Puerto Rico or Miami Beach."

"But at least you'd have it over with. Oh, shit."

"Or I might fail the physical."

She looked at him, then pulled his robe open and punched him in his hard, flat stomach. "Fail for what? You should've got it over with in college, like me."

"I didn't go to college," he reminded her. "Oh, shit."

The evening that had looked so promising was suddenly down the chutes for good; and that was the moment when the doorbell announced Lucy's return for the petition. Realization smote Bratislaw; as he opened the door he said, under his breath, for about the twentieth time, "Oh, shit."

The sisters were kissing sisters, but while they kissed Lucy was peering past her sister's ear at Bratislaw. "What is it?" she demanded; then, guessing, "You forgot to tell Heidi about the petition."

Bratislaw was glad for the way out. "Yeah, that's right. I'm really sorry, Loose."

She shook her head. "But there's more to it than that," she went on, looking from him to her sister. "Come on. What?"

So Bratislaw told her about the draft notice, and told his wife about the petition, and by the time they had it all sorted out he was halfway through the second bottle of wine and it did not, after all, seem like a very good night to start a baby. But Lucy responded with righteousness. She was the do-gooder in the family, the one who had decided to become a police officer in the first place, against all wisdom, and to stay honest in the second—against all custom. "It's a good thing for you, Jeff," she said wisely, "and I'll help you get along, I promise. Now if you two will just sign—"

"Hold it," said her sister. "We can't do that, hon."

"Of course you—"

"No," said Heidi, "we can't, and if you stop and think about it you'll know it. You don't mind taking your chances; well, that's all right, you're past probation and your job's safe. Pretty safe. But what happens to Jeff if he signs that and then comes on the force? A draftee? With no rank? They'll have his ass, Lucy, and you know it."

Lucy looked at her sister, then at Bratislaw, anger growing in her eyes. "You two! Don't you *care?* Do you want the goddamn mob to *own* the city?"

"It already does, Lucy, and there's nothing we can do about it. And I'm sorry, but that's the way she goes. Good night, Lucy. Come and see us again real soon."

What was wrong was that she was right; Bratislaw

knew it, Heidi knew it, even Lucy knew it. Bratislaw wandered over to the window, gazing out at the city, then shrugged, reached for the light remotes and punched out a five-minute dim-down. The lights began to dwindle toward darkness and, yawning, he moved toward the bedroom, until his wife's voice stopped him. "Jeff, you forgot about the bills."

"What?" He turned, and the console was displaying the bills that had come in in that day's mail. "Oh, God," he groaned, "damn machine's on the blink again. They're all automatic pay, they should have just displayed and gone into memory. . . . Oh," he said then, staring at the CRT, "Oh, *shit.*"

That was time number twenty-one and the biggest of all, for under the lines of characters that represented the statements from the utilities, the installment purchases and the insurance company was a glowing red line that said:

BALANCE INADEQUATE

"Damn it! Heidi? Have you been drawing money out of the account without telling me?"

"Of course I haven't, Jeff." But even before the words were out of her mouth he knew that, for he was punching their banking codes for a statement, and the figures were already appearing for him.

17 MAY 1123 HRS ** WITHDRAWAL ** $1710.50 ***BALANCE $8.26

"We've been robbed," he cried. "Somebody broke into our code and cleaned us out! Jesus, this town is really going to the dogs!"

"I've been telling you," said his wife furiously, "we should've invested in a private cipher system."

There were not very many things that Bratislaw really wanted to hear from his wife at that moment. A reminder that she had told him so was about at the bottom of the list. Of course, all the other people they knew had double-locked their telebank systems with private ciphers, but they cost money, you had to remember code words—it was extra trouble. Everybody knew that computer crime was going skyhigh in the city—but some everybodies, or at least Jeff Bratislaw, went through life with the confident belief that it would be some other somebody who would be robbed. What an end to a promising day! The draft notice, the disagreement with Lucy, the robbery of the bank account; it was too much. And the dim-down had finished its cycle and he stumbled in darkness toward the bedroom where his wife lay staring at the ceiling.

Unaccountably, she was smiling.

"What's the matter with you?" he demanded, a long way from amiable.

She said to the ceiling, "I figured it out. Draft deferred. Essential industry."

He sat down beside her, puzzled. "What are you talking about, a draft deferment for me? Well, sure, but I'm not in essential industry—"

"You are," crooned his wife happily, "if that bitch you work for says you are. First thing tomorrow, Jeff, you put it to her—I mean," she corrected hastily, "you ask her to work that out for you. Now get in this bed, why don't you?" And actually, as it turned out, it wasn't such a bad night for starting a baby after all.

III   Ella Jennalec met him at the ground-floor level and a car was waiting. "You drive," she said, and climbed into the back seat after giving him instructions, and there wasn't much chance to talk the whole time until they arrived at the old penitentiary in Bed-Stuy. "You wait," she said, and disappeared up the walk to the entrance. A minute later she came back. "Fucker's in a police lineup," she said disgustedly. "I got to wait till they're through."

Obviously the "fucker" was a prisoner. "Friend of yours, Ella?" Bratislaw asked. She gave him a look.

"Anybody can do me some good is a friend of mine," she said obliquely, and then: "What about you? Can you do me some good?"

"I hope so, Ella." He explained about the draft notice and the fact that he and Heidi really wanted to have a baby. He didn't get a chance to go very far, because she understood what he was asking long before he got to that point.

"Hold it a second, ace," she said, and thought, gazing over at the Bed-Stuy City development with its black solar roof panels and its queer spiral windmills. She took her own sweet time, Bratislaw thought. It wasn't as if it was anything hard he was asking for! New York's police, like most city forces, had been federalized long since. When Selective Service got you, it was a choice between three years in the City and taking your eighteen-month draftee jolt with no guarantees about assignment, or rank—or even survival, if you got sent to one of the trouble spots. It was really no different from any other job. After basic you only worked forty hours a week. You started out with parking tickets, graduated to walking a beat with a regular cop—you could even live at home and maybe even moonlight. "Ace," she said seriously, "there's some good deals on the cops, you know. Smart fellow can make a bundle."

"I'd rather work with you, Ella," he said humbly. Not to mention that his wife's sister would crucify him if he turned out to be the kind of a cop that made a bundle. She smiled radiantly.

"No big deal, friend," she said cheerfully. "I'll put the word in today."

"What'll I do about the draft notice?"

"Tear it up. Now you just hang in here while I see my friend."

Bratislaw's job was not so much assistant as body-guard; if he had wondered why Ella Jennalec had picked him, he realized soon enough that his size was at least one of the reasons. Where she went he went, and she went everywhere. To Brooklyn, where Local 2432 of the Renewable Resource Energy Workers of America was threatening a strike because the dome was going to change the wind patterns in Bedford-Stuyvesant and endanger their jobs. To City Hall, where the Mayor's Commission on City Renewal was meeting. To 125th Street to inspect the northern hold-downs; to Jersey City to negotiate with the local across the river; to the top of the World Trade Center and to the great arch over Central Park, where the dome would reach its greatest height.

Sometimes Ella Jennalec's kid would tag along. It was a surprise to Bratislaw to find out that the union leader had a kid; he had not even known she had a husband, and indeed if there ever had been one he did not seem to be on the premises any more.

After the first day he formed the habit of picking her up at her apartment. It was a pretty nice apartment. Like every other apartment building in the city the sidewalk before it was piled shoulder high with ribbed-paper bags of garbage, waiting for the remote day when someone would come to remove it, and twice Bratislaw saw dirty brown rats scuttle slowly away as he approached. But there was a doorman, and closed-circuit television at every angle, and the first day Bratislaw had to stand around in the lobby for twenty minutes because Jennalec wasn't answering her phone just then.

When at last she was available she told the door-man to pass him right up. She met him at her door, hair wrapped in one turbaned towel and dripping, an-other towel wrapped around her damp body. "Wait in the living room, Jeff. There's coffee if you want it."

The living room was twice the size of Bratislaw's entire apartment. The carpet was wall-to-wall, thick, white. There was a video corner, and surround-sound acoustic cones in the molding overhead. He sat on a couch longer than he was tall—big enough to open into a king-sized bed but, he was willing to bet, not a convertible. Just a couch. He got up again restlessly, peering out the window—the Hudson River was gray between buildings—made himself a cup of coffee from the machine in the kitchen, sat down again. And waited. Bratislaw was not at all sure what he was waiting for, because that flash of golden thigh under the towel as Jennalec turned had started him thinking. But when she came out, fully dressed, jeans, boots, beret to keep her damp hair in place, she was all business. And he was not sure if he was disappointed or not.

When he got home that night and told Heidi about Jennalec's home, she said, "She came out *bare?*"

"Ah, no, Heidi. She had a towel around her."

"So did I," she said bitterly, "when you lived across the hall in Stuyvesant Town and I asked you to fix my window. But I knew what I was doing, and so does she."

So Jeff Bratislaw's work was to follow Ella Jennalec wherever her work took her, and where her work took her was everywhere the dome was going to go. That was all of New York—all of the *real* New York, that is to say, namely, Manhattan island. That was the city that had existed long before the Bridge let it swallow Brooklyn and momentum gave it the other boroughs; it was the New York that people from New Jersey and Texas and China meant when they said "New York." Once in a great while Jennalec went off the island, but there was plenty between the Battery and the Harlem River to keep her busy.

Exactly what she was busy at, though, was harder to

understand. Jennalec's position in the union was fogged. "Shop steward" was her title, but steward of which shop? She was as much at home at the Fordham pylon as at the World Trade Center truss. Sometimes she volunteered a reason for one of their errands—a hazard-pay argument near the old UN Building, a seniority dispute at the 59th Street Bridge site. When she didn't offer a reason Jeff sometimes asked. Not after the second day. "Jeffy doll," she said, squirming around in the seat of their car to stare into his eyes, "what you need to know I'll tell you, what I don't tell you is none of your business. Okay?" "Okay," said Bratislaw, and remembered it. It stood to reason. Everybody knew that there was a Grand Jury investigation about to pop, and if any of the mystery rides had anything to do with that, what would be the sense of talking about them? The TV reporters were already leaking stories from the Grand Jury every night. Let them have their fun, they'd never get anything on Ella Jennalec! Oh, sure, she'd do a favor for a union brother—maybe a favor for a boss now and then. One hand washed the other. How else were you going to get a big job done?

But to prove anything in a put-away-in-jail way—never. The more Bratislaw saw of Ella Jennalec, the more he admired her, and not just because of the way she filled out her jeans. She had guts. She had that kind of courage that obliged him to be brave, too, when she did things like climbing a hundred meters up the catwalk to talk to a rigger—Bratislaw gamely following, clutching the wire rail—or taking the bucket up to the top of the dome pylon itself. Bratislaw came along, but when she was chattering and gesticulating cheerfully with the gang boss Bratislaw's eyes were fixed firmly on the stately old condos across the river. He didn't look down until they were ten meters from the ground on the return trip. Jennalec nudged him. "I could probably get you on the high demolition now if you still want it," she said, and then grinned. "Just kidding. You're doing fine, sweetie. It's always tough the first time—oh, shit, now what's this?"

If Bratislaw had been a little less shaky he might have reacted faster, might have got between Jennalec and the little man with the blue legal paper. But he wasn't. The little man kept his eye nervously on Bratislaw as he tapped Ella Jennalec with the subpoena, and was watching over his shoulder as he turned and hurried away. Bratislaw opened his mouth to apologize, but Jennalec's grin had already come back. She blew a kiss after the departing process-server and handed the paper to Bratislaw. "Drop it off at the lawyer's on the way home," she said, "and don't look so shook up. What do you think we pay lawyers for?"

Of course, the TV had the news, and of course Lucy had it before them. She was waiting at the apartment when Bratislaw got home. It was Heidi's day off. The sisters had been baking something—good smells came from the stove—and more recently they'd been lounging around with a couple of drinks. Lucy was still in uniform, but her shoes were off, half the buttons of her blouse open and her pretty face flushed. "Jeff, dear," she said at once, "you really ought to get away from that witch."

"Ah, Loose, I've had a hard day. Don't make it worse." He gestured to the glasses and ice and watched while she made him a whiskey on the rocks.

"I know what's worrying you," she said, handing it over, "and it's the draft. Right? But honest, it's not that bad. You take city police service and I'll be your rabbi. True, the pay's lousy, but—"

"It's not the pay, Lucy."

"Well, it's sure not the pride in the job! Don't you know what's going to happen to Ella Jennalec? She's got a grand jury indictment for labor racketeering!"

"Frame-up!"

"Jeff, don't be a jerk. They've got the evidence. They've got witnesses and—" She hesitated, then

changed direction. "I know what they've got, and so
does she; she's looking at five to fifteen on a felony
charge."

He said, "What do you think we pay lawyers for?"
He got the words right, but the tone wasn't nearly as
smooth.

"Jeff. Listen," said Lucy, spacing her words as to a
child. "She's going to go before Justice Horatio Margov." Jeff almost choked on his drink. "That's right!
The Hanging Judge of Harlem. She's going to jail, Jeff,
and you'd better cut loose from her before you get
caught in her mess." Lucy wasn't gloating. She wasn't
the kind of person to do that, but Bratislaw's hackles
rose.

"Get off my case, Lucy. Ella's doing a great job for
the union."

"The hell she is! She's *scum*, Jeff. They've got—hell,
it's in the record anyway: they've got her on six counts
of extortion alone, not to mention two assaults with
deadly intent by her old goon, Tiny Martineau. You
want to get involved in that? Heidi! Make him listen!"

Heidi shrugged, but her gaze on her husband was
steady.

He protested, "She doesn't do anything everybody
else doesn't do!"

"And that's exactly what's wrong with the city! Too
many crooks in positions of trust, and nobody does
anything about it. Evil," she said sententiously, "re-
quires no more to triumph than that good men should
do nothing. That's a quotation."

"That's a crock! Ella's got friends with muscle. Do
you have any idea how many politicians owe her?"

"They're all going down the tube with her," Lucy
predicted. "Horatio Margov will take care of that.
Sure, there's plenty that owe her. She can get to the
Mayor, and the Commissioner and three-quarters of
the cops in my precinct. No problem! But it only takes
one honest judge and one prosecutor who really wants
to make a case, and she's blown away. Jeffy," she said

pleadingly, "use your head. The mob's in trouble. They've got nothing going for them in drugs since legalization, there's no prostitution worth bothering with, they can't even steal unless they can crack a computer code and they're mostly not smart enough for that. So what've the mob got left? Extortion and crooked unions! Once we get them cleaned up, they're out of business! So when we nail your girl friend that's the last step—I mean," she finished quickly, glancing at her sister, "I mean, I didn't mean anything when I called her your girl friend." But Heidi didn't respond. She just gazed at the wall, and her lips were tight.

It wasn't true, anyway. Ella wasn't his girl friend. True, Bratislaw couldn't help thinking that if a man wanted to make a move it could easily turn out that way, because Jennalec didn't ever seem to mind appearing before him in her underwear, or slacks without a top, or that towel; and didn't worry so you could notice it if the towel slipped a little. But he didn't make the move, and she didn't seem to give it a thought. She was probably getting plenty anyway, he thought, just her in that big apartment with her kid, and who knew who came in the door after he left her at night?

Which was, definitely, none of his business. His business was doing what she told him to do. When he tried to tell her what his sister-in-law had said, what she told him to do was forget it. "You like the job? Then just do it. Leave the law part to the lawyers." And he did like the job—not only was it interesting, but the draft deferment had whistled right through as promised, and the pay was a surprise. *Nice* surprise. Not only was it half again what he'd got on the winch gang, but half of it was in, of all things, cash. Cash! Off the books, and no tax to pay! "Just be careful how you spend it," she instructed. "Clothes, booze, parties, anything like that, fine. Or stick it in a safe-deposit box. But don't go paying off any bank loans, because once you get a transaction into the audit file they've got you. Now get the car, we're going up to a place in the South Bronx and you can come in with me. Maybe you'll learn something."

The name of the place was the Bellamy Wind Tunnel Test Facility, and the first and worst thing you noticed about it was the noise. What noise! Roaring like ten jets taking off at once, all of them in your bedroom. Bratislaw hesitated and Jennalec punched his shoulder. "Go," she yelled in his ear, pointing at a woman in a pale green smock, inside a glass cage. "Her. She'll explain it." And she disappeared into a door marked *Manager—No Admittance.*

Considering that Bratislaw had actually worked on the foundations of the dome, he knew astonishingly little about it. The wind tunnel itself was huge. It had to be, because the model dome inside it was nearly forty feet long. It was rotating slowly and irregularly on a turntable. The tunnel, Bratislaw realized, could not change wind direction, so the test table turned the model. The model didn't show Manhattan itself, only the dome that would cover it. It looked like two scoops of melting vanilla ice cream on an immense banana split—no—it looked like a wax model of a vanilla banana split that had been too long in a store window, with pockmarks and flyspecks all over its surface.

A voice over a PA system called, "Come on in here, why don't you?" and he looked to see the technician waving at him. Gratefully he joined her in the cage. The noise was still loud, but it no longer hurt his ears.

Before the technician was a smaller model of the dome, this one brightly lit in reds and blues that flickered and waxed and waned as he watched. "Hi," said the woman in the green smock. "I'm Marilyn Borg. How do you like it?"

Bratislaw admitted he didn't know enough to have an opinion. The woman smiled. "Ugly thing," she commented. "It would've been nicer to be doming Phoenix or even Los Angeles—so you could have a nice round dome, you know? New York's long and skinny, and it's got all those bridges, and it's got deep water all around it. Bad structurally."

"You mean it won't work?"

"Oh, hell, it'll *work*. But look at the pressure differentials!" The pits on the model outside, she explained, were pressure taps, with transducers that relayed their readings to the smaller model in front of her. Negative pressure showed red on the readout model, positive pressure, blue; the greater the pressure, the brighter the color. "See here, all this low pressure over the top of the dome? It's like an airplane wing. It wants to take off and fly. Then there's the high pressure where the wind impacts and again where the dome ends—wait a minute." She glanced at a digital clock, then punched in some commands. As the next sequence began white smoke appeared from each of the acne pits on the dome in the tunnel, streaming across the surface of the dome. She added another set of commands and the jets became a rainbow of different colors, showing how the smoke currents merged and flowed together. "Look at the old East River bridges! I wouldn't try going for a walk to Brooklyn on a windy day!" And indeed there was a great deal of turbulence at the base of the model, especially where the bridges came out. "They're going to have to beef up the skirts," Borg predicted gloomily. "'specially the Hudson. The Palisades funnel wind down the river when it's coming the right way, but we can allow for that. Hurricanes," she grinned, "are harder. And so's snow, and rain if it freezes there. You get a quarter of an inch of ice on the dome, that's maybe a hundred thousand tons over the whole surface." She leaned back and regarded Bratislaw. "You're a big one," she commented.

"And you," said Bratislaw gallantly, glancing at the way the smock draped over her breasts, "are a pretty good size yourself."

She tapped the model complacently. "My boy friend says he doesn't know whether I should study this or wear it."

Well, it never did any harm to jolly the girls along, thought Bratislaw, enjoying himself. Of course nothing would come of it. Well, nothing *had* to come of it, although the more he looked at Marilyn Borg the more he thought there would be a lot worth looking at under the green smock. It was a painless way to learn about the engineering and stress-resistance of the dome —the top, he discovered, would go right through the "boundary layer" of the atmosphere, where most of the turbulence was, but the dome shape would minimize the stresses. And about the wind tunnel, powered by three six-bladed propellers, temperature and humidity controlled, capable of modeling the stresses of a one-hundred-fifty-mile-an-hour hurricane or a two-foot snow load. And about Marilyn Borg herself, until a speaker over his head said, "Come on, stud, time to get out of here." And something about the tone suggested that Jennalec had been listening in.

In the car, Ella surprised Bratislaw by getting in beside him instead of entering the rear seat. "Where to, boss?" he asked, but she didn't answer at first. She was studying him, and for the life of him Bratislaw couldn't tell what she was looking for until she asked:

"How's your wife?"

"Oh, fine," he said, and she nodded as though it had been the final answer to a complex problem of diagnosis.

"I've got nothing going for the next couple of hours," she said, "and I think I owe you a home-cooked meal. You interested?"

He swallowed and grinned. "You bet," he said, and turned up the juice.

She didn't slip into anything more comfortable or play mood music for him; she slipped into the kitchen and left him to stare at the antique furnishings. "Five minutes," she called. "No more. I've got most of it made already." To Bratislaw's surprise the "home-cooked" meal was hardly cooked at all. It was salad and a tureen of soup, and the soup, he could tell by the smell, was fish broth. "It'll taste better than it smells," she promised. "I should've warned you, I don't eat meat."

He sampled it and it was true; it was a very thin soup, almost Japanese, but it made its appeal, and the salad was crisp and crunchy, with nuts and bits of what he guessed to be crisped potato-like nuggets. "How come?" he asked.

"You mean about the meat? Oh, I used to. Back in Bed-Stuy I ate it all the time, you know how kids are. But the first job I got was on the feedlots in Flushing Meadows. You know the place? Processing water hya-cinth. They mow it on the lakes, and dry it in the exhaust from the city heat pumps, and chop it up and give it to the cows. The cows love it. Makes great steaks, too."

"Well, then why?"

She looked disgusted. "I found out what else they gave them! Sterilized sewage sludge. SCP—that's single-cell protein; they grow it on the sludge from the sewers, and it's supposed to come out clean and pure. But I know where it comes from! And that's not all. Rock dust, would you believe it? Paper-mill trimmings! Their own shit! You eat a hamburger, and what you're really mostly eating is a cowflop brick mixed with confetti and weeds—no, thanks!"

"It was the same in Wisconsin," Bratislaw offered, "except they had all this whey left over from cheese-making. You don't know stink till you smell that stuff."

"And you still put it in your mouth?" She finished the last of her salad and sat back, lighting a joint and looking at him speculatively. "What all kind of stuff *do* you put in your mouth, Brat?" she inquired.

The best thing to do, Bratislaw thought, was to take it as a joke. So he laughed, around a forkful of carrot slices and raw cauliflower, and changed the subject. "Where's your boy?" he asked.

Ella nodded, as though it weren't a change of subject at all. "He's in school. Won't be home for three hours. Take a hit," she added, passing the joint over to Bratislaw and sitting up in her chair. "Help me put the dishes in the machine and then I've got something for you to do. See, Brat, Tiny had some special duties, besides driving me around. I haven't needed them much lately—but a couple of friends are out of town, and a couple of friends aren't friends any more. So, the thing is," she finished, getting up and taking his hand, "I think it's about time you found out what the special duties are."

If Heidi suspected that the nature of the relationship had changed she didn't show it. There was a tug captain's strike, and so her job was harder and longer than ever. When she got home at night she was tired. If Jeff Bratislaw wasn't home by the time she was ready to go to bed she went to bed anyway. It was just as well. Bratislaw was a reasonably horny man, but Ella Jenalec used him up pretty well—no long stretched-out orgies, but now it was first thing in the morning before they set out for the day, and usually again at night before he went home, and now and then an occasional joust somewhere during the day. Apart from that their relationship stayed about the same; she kept all the same engagements, did all the same work, spent all the same hours on the car phone between stops. But she talked to him more. About herself. About him. About the world. She even talked about her upcoming trial before Judge Margov, and the kind of courage she showed on the high steel was still there when she talked about the proceeding. "You're some woman," said Bratislaw, and the admiration in his voice wasn't feigned.

She was in the seat beside him, riding uptown. "Yeah," she said thoughtfully, looking at him. When she left him at the curb in front of a sleazy-looking loft building she was still thoughtful and when, half an hour later, she came back out she was grinning. He started to engage the electric motor but she stopped him. "Wait a second," she said, her hand on his; and he paused, perplexed. . . . And then he saw what she was waiting for. Out of the same doorway came a tall, white-haired figure, looking cautiously around before ducking into a subway station. It was Horatio Margov, the Hanging Judge of Harlem himself. He turned, startled, to Ella, whose grin was triumphant. "Just keep your mouth shut," she advised. "And next time listen to me when I tell you not to worry."

But he worried all the same, worried mostly about whether he would have the willpower not to tell his wife, and whether she would then be able to keep from telling her crusading sister . . . it was not a worry he needed to have. When he got home that night Heidi wasn't asleep. She wasn't even there. All the lights were on, and there was a flashing red message on the CRT: *Jeff, Lucy's been hurt. Meet me at Bellevue.*

It took him twenty minutes to get to the hospital and half an hour to find his wife, up in a sixth-floor waiting room that smelled of disinfectant and unwashed clothing. "Her head's crushed in," she sobbed. "Somebody mugged her. She's in intensive care, and they don't know if she's going to live."

"Oh, honey," he said, his arms around her.

"They let me see her," Heidi sobbed. "You couldn't even see her face, Jeff! What kind of animal would do something like that? The decentest, best human being I ever knew. . . ." She pushed herself a few inches away from him and looked up into his face. "And one other thing," she added. "I went to the doctor today myself, and I'm pregnant."

IV The police report was stark and skimpy. Police Officer Lucille R. Sempler had been on regular patrol duty on South Water Street, checked in by radio at seventeen hundred thirty hours, was overdue for her eighteen hundred hours report. In the interim she had made no calls nor were any transmitted to her. On failure to report a search was instituted and Police Officers William Gutmacher and Alicia Mack found her suffering blunt-instrument wounds to the head and several lacerations, apparently the result of a struggle, in an entryway. No witnesses. No known motive. Police lab was investigating physical evidence. The investigation would continue.

The police themselves were not much more informative, not out of policy but because they knew nothing. "Lucy was always looking for something wrong," said her precinct captain. "Probably it was somebody she busted. We're checking everything—and she was one hell of a fine lady," he added.

Bratislaw, too, thought Lucy was a fine lady. He knew that his wife felt more strongly than that; but he was not prepared for just how much Heidi cared.

Bratislaw knew about pregnant women; he had a sister sixteen years younger than himself, and he remembered the months before she had been born. Morning sickness he was ready for, and it came. A failing interest in making love he suspected, and that came, too. But his mother had not had a dear sister nearly murdered in her first month, and so there was nothing to prepare him for Heidi's unending, dry-eyed sorrow. She had given up gaiety. When he came home late at night she was almost always already in bed—and almost never asleep, though she pretended to be. He tested her to be sure. After a week of it, he rolled over in bed, changed position a time or two and then let his breathing become slow and nasal. Sure enough. A few minutes later Heidi slipped out of bed and retreated silently to the living room, where he found her sitting unmoving and unoccupied by the window. When he spoke she didn't answer.

Every day Heidi hurried from her work to the hospital to spend an hour at Lucy's bedside. She didn't ask Bratislaw to go with her, but worry made him volunteer. It was astonishing. In her sister's presence Heidi was Heidi again, sparkles and smiles and gossip and plans for what they would all do when Lucy "got better." And, of course, Lucy's mummy-wrapped head did not respond. Could not respond. Could only gurgle past the tubes in her mouth, or twitch the restless fingers on the sheet. When they were outside, Bratislaw said, "Honey? It's not much good making plans for when she gets better. She isn't going to get better. She doesn't even really hear you."

Heidi did not either flare up or cry. The mask was on her face again. "They're going to send her to a skinner," she observed detachedly.

"That's good," said Bratislaw, meaning, *That's the same as being dead, anyway, isn't it?* A lot could be done with the veggies by means of behavior modification, but what could not be done was to turn them into responsive, active, companionable human beings again.

Heidi understood his meaning. She said: "I'm tired, Jeff, and I don't want to talk. Let's go home."

The other thing Heidi did with her free time was nag the police. There were no arrests in the case and, Bratislaw believed, there was no real expectation that there ever would be. The average New Yorker's chance of suffering some sort of violent crime in any given year was one in sixty, and when it was a witnessless mugging, like Lucy's, the crime was rarely solved. Heidi didn't share his opinion, and so once a day she was on the phone with Lieutenant Finder at the precinct, demanding action. After three weeks of it Bratislaw tried firmness. "Heidi, honey," he began, "why don't you get off the lieutenant's back? He's doing the best he can."

She picked at the dinner before her and didn't answer. He tried a different tack. "They're going to send her to the skinner at Peekskill pretty soon, aren't they? I mean, there's no sense keeping her in the hospital any more."

"She said my name the other day," Heidi observed.

"Well, fine, but I talked to the doctors, too, and that's as far as she's likely to go. Honey? Shouldn't we be thinking about alternatives?"

She looked at him. "You mean cryonic suspension."

"Maybe. It's not such a bad idea. There's some hope that some day they could fix her up, you know, and then—"

"And then I'd be dead, Jeff, and so would you, and I'd never see my sister any more."

Bratislaw sighed and began to gather up the dishes, while Heidi retreated to the bathroom. An hour later, getting into bed next to the motionless form with the covers over its head, Bratislaw said, "I know you don't want to talk about it, but you're never going to be able to bring her back."

Heidi didn't move or respond. Then, as he sighed and rolled over, she said without moving, "You're right." As he fell asleep he wondered why her answer had not been satisfying.

Surprisingly, Ella Jennalec was a strong support to Bratislaw in his troubles, though not sexually. She never said their sexual relationship was over, or at least suspended pending the resolution of his family troubles, but it was. She simply did not invite him to her bedroom any more. There was intimacy, yes, but a different kind. When she invited him to stay for coffee her housekeeper was there, a waddling old woman from Kenya who admired Bratislaw's brawn and fed him up accordingly when she could. Or there was Jennalec's son, Michael, ten years old, bright-eyed and endlessly inventive. He had never seen a farm, and so plagued Bratislaw for stories about Wisconsin. They were more family for him than Heidi and (certainly) Lucy was. And there was that other intimacy, the political one, the one that was the core of Jennalec's existence and became pretty much Bratislaw's. As she let him closer and closer into the councils of power Bratislaw began to understand the significance of those strange errands to places outside her jurisdiction, involving trades and skills not under her reign. There was something brewing, and it was *big*. Intimacy did not extend to particulars, but there were a dozen unions involved, there was a timetable, there was going to be a decisive act—and the time was not far away.

For a solid week Jennalec's program took her to visit bridges—the George Washington, the Triborough, the East River spans first—and that was not surprising. All of them required special modification so that they could enter the vast dome when it was completed without destroying its geodesic integrity or producing the devastating turbulence he had seen in the wind-tunnel model. But what did the Verrazano-Narrows crossing have to do with it? Bratislaw didn't know. Jennalec didn't say. She left him at the base of one of the pylons while she went off on an errand to the working levels at the top. Heidi worked there—was there now, doing her job as a port controller; for a moment Bratislaw thought of dropping in on her unannounced. At one time it would have been a good idea. Now it didn't seem that way. So he stood in the lee of the pylon, shivering in the wet, hard wind in spite of the fact that it was full summer, and waited for Jennalec to come down.

She was scowling. "Your wife's a pain in the ass, do you know that?" she announced.

"Did you see her?"

"Didn't talk to her, if that's what you mean—but she's got the others scared. A regular whistle-blower, your wife! A big fan of UTMs."

Bratislaw was puzzled; Heidi was almost as much a do-gooder as her late sister—well, not *quite* late sister —but she had never mentioned any big feeling one way or another about the Universal Town Meetings. "I don't get you," he said.

"None of your business," said Jennalec sharply, pulling her sweater tighter around her. "Let's get the hell out of this wind—damn! Who needs it *now?*"

What she meant by that was none of his business, too, he found. But the things that she was willing to allow him in on were interesting enough, though scary. He had not realized how the kickbacks and payoffs mounted up, or what a network of union and public officials were involved in them, until he began adding up the lists of people Jennalec had surreptitiously visited. He was almost glad that Heidi wasn't much interested in talking to him these days. He would have found it hard to keep her from doing the same sort of calculation as himself, and who knew what conclusions she might have come to?

In other ways, the estrangement was nothing to be glad about at all. JFK Bratislaw was a healthy male in the prime of life who didn't like masturbating. When both his wife and his employer canceled sex he missed it badly—within a couple of weeks, desperately. He wondered what the technician at the wind tunnel was doing, thought of calling her up, wondered if Ella Jennalec would mind—did nothing.

The first upturn in his amative fortunes was when he came home almost on time one night and found the apartment full of cooking smells. Heidi was in good spirits. She made them both drinks while the microwave finished their baked bluefish and, responding to the look on his face, laughed. "You haven't noticed anything special about this week?" she asked.

He pursed his lips while he ran through his mental card file. Not Christmas and not Valentine's Day. Not their anniversary—

"Your birthday!" he exclaimed. "But that's not until Sunday."

She grinned and shook her head. "That's not what I mean, although there's something I'd like from you. You really haven't noticed?"

"Noticed what?"

"I haven't thrown up for a week!" And, indeed, she had never looked better. Or, it seemed, felt better. All through dinner she talked, just like old times, long, complicated stories about the string of LNG barges that had been misidentified at first as garbage scows, and what might have happened if they'd been allowed to try to make the passage under the bridge in the thirty-knot wind, about her co-workers, about how well Lucy was doing at the skinner, about when she could feel the baby kick. She not only talked. She listened. She let Bratislaw talk about the job, and the trouble with the hold-downs on Morningside Heights, and the twelve kilometers of cable that had failed the stress tests and been rejected, and Ella Jennalec's loathing for the Universal Town Meeting. . . . "Well, sure she hates it," Heidi commented. "It's what keeps her from running the whole city."

"Aw, hell, Heidi! She's got it made now, why would she want more?"

"Everybody *always* wants more, Jeff, that's what governments are all about. That's what the UTM's about, it's what keeps the power brokers and the bribers from taking over. Not just unions. Contractors. Builders. Everybody who can make an extra buck by breaking the law, or forcing the government to let them do something they're not supposed to. Lucy said—" She paused, then shook her head, smiling. "But let's not argue tonight, honey. Come on, help me get the dishes in the machine."

And as soon as they had the dishes in the washer and the garbage sorted and stowed they went to bed, without discussion or delay. Heidi's belly was beginning to plump out. At first Bratislaw found it disconcerting —but not incapacitating. Not even the first time. Much less the second and third. When at last they both had had enough they lay spoon-fashion, Bratislaw holding his wife in his arms, for a long time. Bratislaw was beginning to think Heidi had drifted off to sleep when she stirred and, without turning, said, "Honey? About Sunday . . ."

Half asleep, Bratislaw was not to be caught out. He remembered what Sunday was. "You mean on your birthday. What would you like?"

"Well—one thing, actually. Would you come up to see Lucy with me?"

"I would love it," said Bratislaw, and meant it at the time.

On Sunday, though, he wasn't so sure. The trip up the Hudson was fine enough because it was on an excursion boat all the way to Peekskill, up past the Palisades along the beautiful Hudson shore. The boat left from Battery Park, and for the first few miles Bratislaw was able to explain to his wife just where the dome was going, looking like two humps on a camel, the tall igloo one down around lower Manhattan, the lower connecting bridge from Canal Street to the twenties, the big elongated one covering midtown and Central Park. It was only the middle passage that had been mostly covered with its hexagons of plastic so far. North and south was still only steelwork, with some of the tensed cables strung so that it looked like lacy spiderwebbing as they sailed past. The boat was full of families on excursion, aiming for Bear Mountain or Indian Point. Cheerful, a lot of kids, and quite a few very small ones that Bratislaw noticed his wife observing with tenderness. It wasn't easy to fight their way into the boat's dining room for lunch, but the hostess noticed Heidi's thickening belly and eased them in early. The food wasn't all that bad, and Heidi even allowed herself a bottle of beer with the cheese omelette. When they were up to the coffee she said, "I've got a present for you."

After four years Bratislaw knew his wife's habits, but he protested, "It isn't *my* birthday."

"If I can't give you a present when I want to on my birthday, when can I? Hold still." And she pulled a tinsel-wrapped package out of her bag, opened it and displayed a carved wooden amulet on a golden chain. "It's the lover's knot," she said. "It keeps people who love each other together."

"I'll never take it off," said Bratislaw, touched. His wife nodded solemnly.

"Except maybe in the shower," she advised. "Jeff? It's mostly to thank you for coming here with me. I do appreciate it."

"I'm glad to do it," he said proudly. But half an hour later he wasn't so sure. He had never been at the New York Peekskill Facility before—what they called "the uptown skinner." As the taxi drove up the entrance road it was all green trees and flower beds, and if you noticed that the flowers were in ragged patterns and some of the borders were bare, well, that almost added to its rural charm. The buildings were pretty enough. Most of them were low-framed two-story garden apartments, with a pretty brick central building and people moving around the paths. It was only when you got close to the people that they became strange. On a wall by the entrance gate a skinny twenty-year-old man was snapping back and forth as though in an invisible rocking chair, thunk-thunk, like a metronome. A young man in a tank top and open fly approached them, smiling wordlessly to show no teeth at all. A terribly obese young girl, maybe fourteen years old, was lying on her belly in the middle of the path, unmoving; Bratislaw had to step over her to get by, and from her blubbery body in the warm sun, even in the open air of the Hudson River country, there arose a terribly unwashed stench. Heidi, who had been to the skinner before, watched her husband with concern. "Honey? There's a coffee shop over there. Why don't you go get a cup, and I'll find Lucy and bring her there."

"Sure," said Bratislaw gratefully, and accepted directions and an order to get for Lucy and Heidi. But the canteen was no better. He had had some sort of idea that it was off-limits to residents, except maybe Lucy, but the place was full of inmates. The boy with the open fly followed him in as he took his place in line, just behind a fifty-year-old woman with the unlined face of a teen-ager, who turned around to study him.

"What's your name?" she demanded; and when he told her, "What do you do? Who do you work for? What's she like?" It was not at all clear to Bratislaw that she listened to the answers. It was as though she were a parrot, socialized into the questions of social conversation but without any particular interest in the other person's part. He secured coffee for himself, iced tea and a Coke for Heidi and her sister and, as ordered, two large bags of corn chips. It was his fear that some of the inmates would sit down with him, and so he hurriedly propped the other chairs at the corner table he found. They didn't, but the boy with the open fly sat at the next table, licking up a sundae as though it were an ice-cream cone, still grinning toothlessly and without speaking at Bratislaw.

He wished desperately for his wife and sister-in-law to arrive, but when they did it was almost worse. He had not been prepared for seeing his sister-in-law in a football helmet with her name printed in large letters across the front, and painted again on the back of her police-academy tee-shirt. Pretty Lucy! Her face was as pretty as ever, and if anything her eyes were merrier and her expression more vivacious. The dedicated do-gooder look was gone from her face, and she didn't explain to Bratislaw the ways in which he should be working his ass off to improve society. She hardly spoke at all. She listened as Heidi chattered on about the clothes she was buying for the baby and how nice it was to have some breeze after all the terrible heat, and had the thunderstorms been as bad here as they had in the city? When Lucy answered it was almost always either "yes" or "no," like a binary bit in a solid-state computer. When she spoke it was only a word or two. "Friend," she said, reaching out to touch the arm of the huge black girl, six-foot-three at least, who came around to clear off their table. "Molly," Lucy announced, smiling prettily although the girl did not interrupt slamming cardboard plates into her trash bag to answer.

Heidi rescued her iced tea just in time. "Molly is going to graduate soon," she told Bratislaw. "Isn't that true, Molly?" But the girl didn't answer until she had finished mopping the table and was moving to the next, when she said over her shoulder, quite clearly and politely:

"That's true, Mrs. Bratislaw, and I'm really looking forward to it."

But Lucy was no longer listening. She had caught sight of the teen-ager with the open fly, now standing before them. He was exhibiting himself to the women, smiling proudly. Lucy jumped up. "Dan!" she cried furiously. "Teeth!" The boy's smile faded. He put his penis back inside his shorts, pulled a set of artificial dentures out of his pocket, stuffed them into his mouth and morosely walked away.

"Dan just hates to wear his teeth," Heidi told

Bratislaw conversationally, but he could hear the strain in her voice. The place was telling on her, too—and she had been coming up here three times a week for nearly two months!

There was a boat back every hour, and the return tickets in Bratislaw's pocket felt more and more precious; but he could not make himself take Heidi away. His mind was made up to pretend to be enjoying the visit—or at least to be generous and loving enough to want to prolong it. He was a victim of his own dissembling skill; twice Heidi asked him if he wanted to go and twice he lied. When Lucy suddenly stood up and said "Work time," he was all ready to smile and make his farewells, but Heidi said hesitantly: "Honey? If you really don't mind staying a while, I'd kind of like to see what Lucy's doing. You know, she's been promoted. She's really coming along very well."

And how could he say no to that? It did not relieve his depression that the job Lucy had been promoted to turned out to be feeding and caring for the bedridden inmates, but he was surprised to find that Lucy took the lead as they left the canteen. Out the door, down a golden walk, turned right at one whose concrete was striped black and white; it was only when she came to the next intersection that she had to stop and think. She shrugged almost as she always had, smiled at her brother-in-law and said clearly, "Where's the bedridden ward?" She had a sort of wrist-watch thing on, larger than looked sensible; from it a sweet, tiny voice whispered, "What color is the path, Lucy?"

"Came off black and white. Got red, got yellow with kind of wavy lines, got green with white dots."

"Take the green with white dots, Lucy. Turn left at the mess hall." And she was off again, her sister following, smiling gamely, her brother following and, last in line with no one to see his face, his expression sour. The bedridden wards! But there was a last-minute reprieve, because at the door of the low, cool building with its ominous smells coming from inside Lucy paused and shook her head.

Heidi translated. "This is kind of women's stuff, honey. Would you mind if you didn't come in?"

He was glad to accept the offer, and Lucy said happily, "Tour tape." That turned out to mean that if he chose to go to the administration building they would be glad to lend him a walking-tour tape machine for visitors, which would explain everything he wanted to know about the Peekskill Facility.

Actually, it explained far more. Bratislaw got the cassette, all right, but then he dared the canteen long enough to get a container of coffee—there wasn't anything stronger—and found a deserted section of the grounds to drink it in. It didn't stay deserted long. The youth with the open fly passed by several times, waving happily each time; his teeth were out again, Bratislaw noted. The woman with the white hair and smooth, untroubled face came to stare at him for twenty minutes straight, and she had brought a friend along, an ancient black man in a wheelchair, who muttered to the woman unceasingly in a thick, gravelly voice. But they didn't speak to Bratislaw, and he avoided eye contact, and eventually they went away.

To be replaced by other members of this parade of freaks, of course. He was glad at last to put the plug in his ear, close his eyes and listen to the cordial voice of the recorded tour guide, telling him in what ways the Peekskill Facility served its residents.

John Fitzgerald Kennedy Bratislaw the Third was a humane man almost always, and a generous one by instinct, and certainly he was thoughtful toward his family when he remembered to be. He had lovable traits. Heidi loved him enough to want to have his child, and Heidi was an intelligent and perceptive woman. When he listened to the ways in which the Peekskill Facility practiced behavior modification and social facilitation, and the enumeration of the skills taught and employed graduates, he found it profoundly satisfying. How wonderful that handicapped people could be so helped. That worrisome smell from the far edge of the grounds, he was pleased to discover, was nothing more sinister than a henhouse where batteries of poultry were raised for eggs and slaughter. The bright things that looked like cocktail toothpicks in the farm plots were markers for the people who weeded and picked: bright plastic cucumbers and tomatoes and avocados showed which plants to spare, and when they were ready to pick. There were off-reservation work parties that served the communities of Newburgh and Poughkeepsie, picking up and sorting trash and reclaiming the valuable glass and metals and organics. The skinner did not, of course, come anywhere near paying for itself, but it provided the inmates with one-quarter of their food, and twenty percent of their own supervision—with one person in each group of fifty detailed to such tasks as inspecting the others for haircuts, for bathroom habits, for birth control. There were special competitions—spelling bees for the under-ninety IQs, board games for the under-seventies. The residents with salvageable coordination were taught to crochet lace or string bead necklaces; the clumsier, but educable, ones worked on the farm plots or in the recycling rooms, and the money they earned helped keep the "tuition" down. Even the terminally senile and the dying were aided in large part by other residents, specially trained—and that was where Bratislaw's thoughts left the objective merits of the skinner and turned to what was left of his pretty, devoted, lively sister-in-law. Also his strong sister-in-law, strong in principle and, you had to say, physically strong, because not everybody would have survived so brutal and bone-crushing a beating, or should—

Or should?

Bratislaw clicked off the machine, now beginning its

third repetition, and started for the infirmary, because he hadn't liked the thoughts that had crossed his mind. He was early, and he didn't expect he would be let in, but evidently all the bedpan-cleaning and diaper-changing was over. Lucy was patiently feeding the last of her charges some gummy, gruelly porridge that looked like strained baby food. Probably was; and the old woman was dribbling and drooling it as thoroughly as any three-month-old. Heidi was sitting beside the bed, looking frayed, and Bratislaw thought indignantly that this couldn't be good for her, in her condition! "Good," said Lucy approvingly, and mopped off the old woman's bristly chin. "What dessert?" The old woman glared, so Lucy tried the menu: "Chocat puddin? Ban'a yogurt?" At the second suggestion the old lady glared, puffed, turned purple and managed an "Ess!" The banana yogurt seemed to take forever, but at last it was over, and Lucy was through with her chores for the day—and it was time, ah, blessed time!—for the walk to the taxi to the last boat of the day.

At the gate Lucy suddenly turned on the other residents who had been following at a distance, the black man in the wheelchair, his white-haired woman companion, Lucy's friend and roommate. She shooed them like poultry. "Go away, Molly, Dandy, Elise. Go away." It was the longest speech he had heard from her that day. Lucy's face was screwed up in concentration as she turned to her sister: "Baby all right?" she asked, as though Heidi hadn't been telling her all about the baby all day. Heidi nodded, "Oh, yes, honey, it's coming along fine." Lucy nodded. "Box?" she demanded, eyes squinting with the effort. "Yes," said Heidi, as though she understood, "it's all taken care of." "Come back?" And that was when Lucy seemed near to weeping. "You bet we'll be back," Heidi promised. "As soon as we can—but here's the taxi, and it's getting ready to rain!" A couple of farewell kisses— surprisingly warm and pleasant, if you didn't look at the football helmet or think about what Lucy had once been—

And at last they were free.

It did rain. It came down like the cloudbursts of the tropics, with thunder and lightning and gusty winds that made the old excursion steamer shudder. The decks were bare, all the holiday-makers crammed inside; there was no place to sit. The best Bratislaw could find was a corner by a window, where Heidi could at least perch on the sill and not much of the rain came through. He had things on his mind. "Honey," he began, "it must cost a bundle to keep somebody in that place."

The strain lines were deep on Heidi's face. "We don't pay it, Jeff. It all comes from the police disability fund."

"Well, sure, but there's a question of social responsibility here, isn't there? Especially since it's Lucy. Especially since she's so strong for good citizenship and all."

His wife said steadily, "Jeff, I know what you're getting at. You want me to take Loose out of the skinner. You want me to get her frozen like some boat person."

"For her own *good,* honey!"

"Oh, Jeff." She turned to gaze out the window. The rain began to beat in on her, but she paid it no attention. "Let me explain to you, will you? Freezing's not so bad for the boat people—they don't want to go back, they can't stay, anyway at least they freeze whole families together. And if you're in desperate pain, sure, get frozen. But there's a risk . . . and even if it works, even if a hundred years from now they figure out how to fix up her head, and bring her back, and she's as good as new—where will I be, Jeff? And she's my sister."

It was a rotten end to an already crummy day.

But there was still more to come. By the time they got to the Battery the storm was over. The streets were sloshy-clean, and there was a fresh, cool breeze. As they looked for a cab Bratislaw said, "I guess we'll do what you want about Lucy, honey."

She nodded, and then managed a smile. "We just won't talk about that any more," she agreed. "We've got plenty of better things to think about. Like us," she added, and put up her face to be kissed.

V The summer wore on, stagnant when it wasn't stormy. For Jeff Bratislaw, though, it wasn't bad at all. Heidi did not stop her pilgrimages to the Peekskill Facility, but she didn't stop the kisses, either. If Ella Jennalec was sometimes tense and abstracted, she was also convincingly annoyed when he asked questions. "You worry too much," she said. "I told you, we've got this indictment thing licked."

"Sure, Ella," he said obligingly. Since everyone was telling him not to worry, he didn't worry. Not even about the weather. The storminess kept coming. There were hurricanes boiling up out of the South Atlantic every four or five days. None of them hit the track that would take it up the Eastern Seaboard, but Bratislaw couldn't help wondering what would happen if one did. So he asked Ella.

"You mean after the dome's finished? Nothing. They claim it's safe for up to two hundred miles an hour. Right now, though—Jesus!" She was grinning with pleasure. "There'd be plastic falling in Portugal. That's why we're gonna win out, Jeff. I'm getting ready for a strike if they don't give us hazard pay any time the wind's over what they call Force Three, with escalations. Oh, and listen. Tomorrow I'm going to take my kid along with us, if you don't mind. He'll be home from camp tonight."

"Why should I mind?"

She nodded, acknowledging the justice of the question, then changed the subject. "I hear you were up to the skinner in Peekskill."

That was disconcerting. Bratislaw didn't want to ask her how she knew, but his expression asked it for him. She grinned. "I got a father up there," she said, "so I keep in touch. He's a mean old goat, but I kept him around as long as I could. Now, it's senile aphasia. He forgets things, like his name—he never did know mine real well," she finished bitterly. "Still, he's my dad, and I would've kept him longer if he hadn't started peeing the bed. They didn't skin him worth shit, though. I took him out for a weekend and he wet the bed worse than ever." She looked at her watch, then ordered, "So go on home to the pregnant wife, boy. I got company coming."

Company! Another lover? That would explain why she had cut him off—not that he minded, because the way things were with Heidi these days, who needed Ella Jennalec? But he was wrong about that, he realized as he finished parking her car. He saw a taxi coming in, and it contained Ella's kid, a mountain of luggage and an escort.

The escort was wearing a cast and carrying a cane, but Bratislaw had no trouble in recognizing him. It was Tiny Martineau.

Ella Jennalec didn't mention Tiny to Bratislaw, and Bratislaw said nothing to his boss. It wasn't a good idea to bother Ella these days, as the summer went through the hottest spells the city had seen for a decade or more. She was edgy, irritable—just plain mean sometimes. Bratislaw began to wonder if being drafted into the City Patrol Corps would, after all, be so much worse. There were more and more meetings to go to, and neither Bratislaw nor any of the other bodyguards/thugs/administrative assistants were allowed inside. Even the union officials had to pass through metal detectors. They were searched and their briefcases were fluoroscoped, while the muscle men lounged around in hallways and anterooms, sizing each other up speculatively.

There was a new organization being born, a Metropolitan Trades Action Council, and its birth pangs were private. That all sounded reasonable enough. Doming the city made big problems for the unions, because it involved great physical changes in the way the city worked. Once the dome was up sanitation men wouldn't use trucks any more: there went one job classification. They would get more deeply involved in recycling on-site, maybe—unless that was turned over to private-sector operations—unless the unions were able to forestall that before it got off the ground, or anyway get a piece of the action if it went private. Organic waste would now go into sewage, and there were big possibilities in the sludge-handling trades, but what about the men who had run the barges? Industrial wastes would be stockpiled and maybe mined, perhaps with bioconcentration via algae, etc.—the technology was complicated and Bratislaw wasn't sure he understood it. But neither did the union leaders, and they needed to know about it so they could mark off their spheres of influence.

All that made sense, but in the chatter with the other muscles Bratislaw confirmed his opinion that the primary topic in the secret meetings had little to do with any of the above. The big concern was the Grand Jury. Ella wasn't the only one who had been subpoenaed. Their lawyers were manufacturing delays and postponements with great skill. But that couldn't last forever. The news broadcasts said so. The trouble with that was that the newscasters gloated over the Hanging Judge of Harlem's white-hot crusading determination to wipe out organized crime in the unions of the city, and Bratislaw had not forgotten whom he had seen coming out of the secret meeting.

More than anything else he wished he still had Lucy to serve as his social databank, and maybe a little bit even his conscience. Lucy was the one who had explained to him that with most of the drug laws repealed and all the prostitution statutes, so that cocaine was sniffed even at the Mayor's fund-raisers and the Yellow Pages had a fifteen-page listing under "Sexual Services," more than half the revenues of organized crime had gone down the toilet. The unions were about all they had left. There were still a couple of unions in the city that had not become gangster-run but, offhand, Bratislaw couldn't think of which they were.

Ella's kid came back from his camp in the Rockaways tanned and heavier than when he left, and Bratislaw found baby-sitting added to his duties. Not often. Just when Ella Jennalec was going to be tied up all day in one place, whereupon the union car and the union driver, namely Bratislaw, might as well be doing something more useful than just sitting around outside the hall. So Bratislaw got to climb the Statue of Liberty, and point out to Marvin the bridge where his wife worked, and the hold-downs in the harbor where he himself had once toiled. He went to the Bronx Zoo and the American Museum of Natural History and the Planetarium. They even went to prison together, or at least to visit the great Nathanael Greene Institute for Men; and the days wore on toward the end of summer. The boy was a bright spot in Bratislaw's life. His wife Heidi was another. "I think I'm going to take early maternity leave," she told him one night as she was just out of the shower and he just about to go in.

He patted her belly, rounding up nicely now and still dewy from the bath. "Aren't you kind of rushing the gun?"

"There's so much to do," she apologized; and, indeed, she was looking gaunt in the face, though nowhere else. She was worrying too much about her sister, Bratislaw reflected as he sudsed and rinsed, and he got out of the shower to tell her so, still toweling and dripping water on the rug.

Heidi was in the bedroom but not in bed. She was bent over something, and when he came in she jumped up, startled. She had his amulet in her hands. "You *scared* me," she cried. And when his look told her he had a question, she added, "I was just polishing it up. You sweat so, Jeff."

He was touched: she was keeping their love bright. And so, he vowed, would he; and for some time after that he worked at it, and she fully cooperated.

The hurricanes had started in June. Alfred pooped out on the way to Bermuda, Betsy wandered into the Gulf of Mexico, Curtis creamed Cuba and threatened all of Florida, then madly backtracked and lost itself in the mid-Atlantic. By Labor Day they were up to Michael, tracking stolidly up the coast but more than two hundred miles offshore, and Ella decided it was time to give her son the promised treat. Not the big dome. Not even the little tube-shaped dome that connected the two big ones. But there was Aqueduct racetrack with a dome of its own, and Ella claimed herself entitled to a day off. The boy Marvin wasn't interested in betting, but he was thrilled by the horses themselves, and by the power of his mighty mother, demonstrated in her obtaining for him a pass and a guide which let them go into the stables and the owners' enclosure at the paddock. Ella Jennalec stayed with them for a while, but her love of the breed stopped at picking winners. Long before the first race she was up in her box, studying the forms and placing her bets on the daily double.

Bratislaw and the boy watched the grooms bringing back the horses from the first race. The winner was a roan gelding, three years old. While all the other horses padded quietly enough to their stalls, the gelding was conducted to a shed where a man in a white coat pulled back its lip and dabbed at its teeth with a white pad. "What's that all about?" the boy asked, and their guide, a twenty-year-old groom whose horse had been scratched, explained:

"That's the spitbox, where they take the winners to get a saliva test."

"You mean they might be doped?" the boy demanded, thrilled.

"Who knows? Anyway, it's the law. That's a pretty horse," she added enviously; and, as the boy moved closer, warned, "Don't touch him now, though."

"Why not?"

"Because he's not through with his tests, that's why." And as the boy followed the handsome, sweat-darkened horse she lagged behind and whispered to Bratislaw: "You sure you want the kid to see this?"

"See what?" But she didn't have to answer, because the horse was in its stall, and a man with a shiny metal can on the end of a long pole was chirruping and shuffling his feet through the straw. The boy stared in delight as the horse's immense sexual organ extended itself. The man quickly slipped the can under the horse's penis and caught some of the splash of urine.

"Jesus," said the boy. "Wonder what ma would say to *that?*"

"I think we ought to get back to the clubhouse," said Bratislaw.

The boy grinned. "Can't stand the competition?"

But he followed obediently enough, and for the next hour or two was content to pick horses for his mother and make trips to the refreshment stands to score sodas, hot dogs, fish and chips. But he wasn't good at picking winners. Ella, who was having a bad day, was getting more and more irritable. "What do you say, sport?" she asked her son. "Time to go home?"

"Ma! You promised! You said I could go up on top of the dome—"

"It's too windy," said his mother, "and I've got a bad feeling. We're going."

"Too windy" the boy might have argued with; his

mother's bad feeling he did not. He simply sulked. On the drive back to the city Bratislaw tried cheering him up with promises—"Another time, maybe? Maybe tomorrow?"

But that tomorrow never came.

By the time Bratislaw finished parking the car the storm had broken. He heard Ella yelling before he got inside the door of the apartment, and when he looked a question at the housekeeper she only shook her head. The boy was in his room, hiding. Ella was screaming and throwing things in the living room. She paused only to scream at Bratislaw: "That son of a bitch! That Jew bastard crook!"

Her eyes were enormous and the look she gave him was pure hatred. Bratislaw couldn't help flinching. "Is something wrong?" he managed.

"Wrong!" she shouted, and the next thing she threw was at him. He dodged a 1939 World's Fair souvenir ashtray and heard it splinter the mirror on the back of the door. "The son of a bitch froze himself, that's what's wrong! Look what I find waiting for me!" She jerked her thumb at the TV console, beeping softly and flashing its red urgent-message light. "Read it for yourself! And stay here until I come back."

She disappeared into her office and slammed the door behind her; the faint murmur told Bratislaw that she was on the phone, and no doubt shouting, for the sound to come through those solid doors. He turned to the TV, which was set on one of the datafax channels, and read the news item:

FEDERAL JUDGE UNDERGOES
CRYONIC SUSPENSION
Justice Horatio Margov was admitted to the Bronx General Suspension Facility at five P.M. this evening. A spokesman for the family issued a statement saying that the justice, who is sixty-one years old,

had received a diagnosis of inoperable pancreatic cancer, and had elected to place himself in cryonic suspension until such time as surgical procedures for his condition, which at present are believed to carry a hazard of more than eighty per cent mortality rate, can be sufficiently improved to permit a cure. Justice Margov, sometimes called "Harlem's Hanging Judge," achieved a reputation as a crusading fighter against political corruption.

However, a source in the District Attorney's office states that questions have been asked concerning Judge Margov's role in the current investigation of labor racketeering. "If he had not been frozen he would have been asked some questions," said the source, adding that the District Attorney's office has moved to sequester all of the judge's estate, including all documents. A full investigation is promised. Another spokesman for the District Attorney's office, however, stated that the legally ambiguous position of a person in cryonic suspension will handicap further investigations.

When Ella came out of her office she was no longer raging, but there was a frozen anger, and when Bratislaw tried to question her she simply said, "Wait a while." She sat him down next to the ruin of the mirror, and herself sat across the room, smoking and refusing to answer questions. When the doorbell at last rang she motioned to him to get it.

It was two goons from the hiring hall.

It was obvious that Ella had been expecting them. She didn't get up, or slow down the pace of her smoking, or even look surprised. She just said, "Go along with them, Bratislaw. You've got no choice." And then, just as the door was closing behind them, he heard, or thought he heard, one thing more:

"Good luck."

Good luck was what he needed. Once they got him down to the basement garage they paused to work him over—not viciously, not with intent to maim; one held him while the other punched him half a dozen times in the belly and chest and kidneys, they reversed roles and the other took his shots. It was bad, all right; it was as much pain as Bratislaw had ever felt, and when he was through vomiting and gasping they pushed him into their car with the world swimming around him.

But they hadn't broken any bones.

It was because of that that, when the car pulled up next to the union headquarters and his captors led him to the private entrance in back Bratislaw did not resist. There was also the question of whether he would be able to, because their scientific punchup had left his entire torso radiant with pain. As the guard at the private entrance slammed the door behind them. Bratislaw wondered if he would ever see the other side of it again; but that was only fear, not reason. Reason told him that if they wanted him dead they would have found some better place to do it in.

They didn't, evidently, want him dead—at least not yet. They didn't even beat him any more. They took him to a room in the subbasement, and for a weird moment Bratislaw thought perhaps it was a clinic. Perhaps they were going to bandage him and poultice him and maybe even apologize to him for the misunderstanding. That was wrong, too. The clinic had other purposes. The two muscles sat down in one corner of the room and said nothing and did nothing further; the action was in the hands of three competent-looking people in white coats. They slipped a needle into Bratislaw's rump and wrapped him with tubing and strapped him with damp pads on arms and neck; and for three hours one of them asked him questions, from a written sheet, while the other two studied the traces of instrument pens on rolling paper.

They did not *tell* him anything at all. Not then, and not even when it was all over and they were whispering among themselves, while he was at last unstrapped and permitted to smoke a cigarette and the hazy, giddy numbness that had struck him as soon as the needle went into his skin began to go away. Some things they didn't have to tell him, because the questions were themselves an answer. There had been a leak. Someone had evidence, somewhere, about the connection between Judge Margov and Ella Jennalec. The connection had something to do with an act of homosexual rape the judge had committed twenty-five years before; Ella was blackmailing him, and that was all new to Bratislaw. Perhaps the startlement when he was asked about that was the biggest factor in Bratislaw's favor. At last one of them disappeared to another room to make a telephone call. While they waited for him to return Bratislaw had plenty of time to think; the clouds were lifting from his brain, the pain in his belly and ribs had not become less but had at least become familiar. He was in trouble. Ella was in trouble; she was suspended from all union offices, and therefore her personal attendant was down the tube no matter what else happened—no more job, no more draft exemption; the best he could hope for was that he would be allowed to live. . . .

And he was. Without explanation; without apology. He was taken to the same rear door and pushed out onto the sidewalk, and the door closed behind him.

There was something he had to do. Whether doing it was smart was a whole other question. The answer would depend on how far and fast the word had spread. He pulled himself together, studied his face in a store window, brushed some dried flecks of something or other off his jacket, took his amulet off, wadded it with its chain in a pocket and walked around to the front entrance.

The guard at the metal-detector nodded and waved him in through the private entrance. Vastly relieved, Bratislaw shook his head. "I just want to borrow your fluoroscope. We took this off a wise guy, and I want a look inside."

"Sure, Bratislaw." The guard took the amulet and

put it on the rolling belt; Bratislaw crowded up beside him and looked at the CRT.

The image slid into view, the hard, dark picture of the gold chain, and the ghost of the amulet.

But the ghost had a skeleton. Two tiny reels, some wiring, a solid blot that was probably the recording head, the filmy outline of magnetic tape.

"Looks like you caught yourself a bugger," said the guard, smiling enviously.

"I guess so," said Bratislaw, trying to look triumphant when what he wanted to do was scream, or run, or hit something. Failing any of those, what he wanted most of all was a confrontation with the person who had got him into this mess. He wanted it badly, and right away.

VI

It was Heidi's good luck that she wasn't at home. All he found was a note on the CRT:

NIGHT SHIFT< I 'LL BE BACK
AROUND FIVE A.M.

But Bratislaw couldn't wait until five A.M. He couldn't go out again the way he was, either, so he stripped the clothes off his aching body, stood under the healing hot shower as long as the timer would allow and dressed clean. Halfway through he poured himself five ounces of Scotch and sipped at it. It made him realize he hadn't eaten for nearly ten hours, so he broke two eggs into a pan; but before they had begun to cook he had changed his mind. He dumped the mess into the organic disposer, swallowed the rest of the Scotch and went downstairs to hail a cab.

The driver grumbled all the way out through Brooklyn about having to leave a fare in the middle of the

Verrazano-Narrows Bridge. Bratislaw didn't even listen. He was icy calm and walled inside his own thoughts, which were unpleasant. When they arrived at the pylon he thrust the money at the woman there, didn't wait for change and headed for the pier elevator. "You got a pass, Mac?" the guard asked, but Bratislaw had his story all prepared. He shook his head.

"No pass, friend, but it's kind of emergency. See, my wife's a controller topside. She's pregnant and she left her medicine at home. I sure don't want anything to go wrong. It's our first—"

Whether the guard was convinced or not Bratislaw could not tell, but at least that got him into the elevator and up to the working levels. He had not expected to be let into the control tower itself, and wasn't. But he was put in a visitors' room with thick bulletproof glass between him and the controllers' room. He could see Heidi before a multicolored console, fingers dancing over a keyboard, speaking into the microphone pinned to her blouse. When the guard spoke to her she glanced up at Bratislaw and nodded.

A few minutes later her relief took over and she joined him in the room. "Hi, honey, what's up? I've only got ten minutes—this'll be my pee break."

"What's up," he said, "is you bugged me. I've been carrying a taper around in that amulet you gave me. You pretty nearly got me killed, and it could happen yet."

She nodded. It wasn't a frightened nod, or an apologetic one—not even a startled one; it was as though he had told her that the co-op had been out of swordfish and so he'd got salmon steaks for their dinner that night. Information received, reaction none. She sat down on a bench facing him and folded her hands in her lap. "I was afraid they'd suspect you sooner or later," she said.

"Suspect me! They fucking *pulverized* me! They even scopped me."

She was nodding again in that same absent way.

213

"Yes, I thought that might happen too. So it was better if you didn't know about the bug. That way you wouldn't have to try to lie."

"Heidi!"

Her expression still did not change, but two tears were gathering on her eyelids. She took a deep breath and said, "I've thought about what would happen when you found out—when they caught you, or whatever. You're entitled to know what it's all about." He laughed, sharp and bitter, but she did not respond, simply kept on with her prepared address. "Your boss is going to hold a pistol to the city's head. She wants to abolish the Universal Town Meeting, and she's going to do something violent."

"Come on, Heidi! Of course she's against it, but that doesn't prove she's going to do anything illegal."

"Proof was the trouble. My sister didn't have any," said Heidi, and the tears that slipped down her cheeks were replaced by two new ones. "She got that amulet made and she wanted me to get you to wear it. I refused. Then when Ella Jennalec had her beaten up—"

"She didn't!"

"She did, and if you think about it you'll know she did. Anyway, Lucy can't do it any more. I have to do it for her. I've given every one of your tapes to the D.A."

Bratislaw gasped, appalled, "They'll kill me!"

"They'll give you protection if you agree to be a friendly witness."

"I'll be a friendly corpse!"

Steadfastly Heidi said, "You have to take that chance, Jeff." She glanced at her watch. "I'm sorry, Jeff, but if I had to do it over again, I'd do it. Now we pregnant women have our problems, so I'd better use the rest of my break the way it was meant."

Bratislaw slept little that night. Before daylight he was up and dressed and out of the apartment, because he did not want to see his wife again. It wasn't that there were not things he wanted to say to her. What he feared was the things he might do to her.

That was not all he feared, for the day that was just dawning, in rain and wind, was full of things to be feared. The chances were excellent that he was now unemployed; what would that do to his draft status? Surely Heidi would now tell the D.A. that he knew about the tapes; subpoenas would be flying, and what would he do about the one with his name on it? He nursed a cup of coffee in a diner on the far West Side, gazing out at the skeletal dome building over the river and the rain lashing at it, and thought bleakly that none of those things were the worst. The worst was that when Jennalec found out what had actually happened the thugs would no longer want information from him. They would want his life. And this day just beginning might quite possibly be the last he would ever see.

It took all the courage Bratislaw had to show up at Ella Jennalec's apartment at seven-thirty that morning.

But the funny thing was that the day that had begun so badly brightened fast. Jennalec wasn't apologetic. The most you could say was that she was just, or trying to be, but it was more than Bratislaw had expected. "Mistakes happen, Jeff," she said, standing by the table, a slice of toast in one hand, hot coffee in the other. "Hazards of the trade. They thought it might be you that was talking."

Bratislaw opened his mouth, but she kept on talking. "You better not work for me any more though, Jeff. Pity. I'll miss you. But you wanted high steel work anyway, didn't you? And they're putting on extra shifts. The man you want to see is Woody Vult up at Governor's Island; he's expecting you, better get up there right away."

And ninety minutes later Jeff Bratislaw was working on the dome itself.

The rain was only an occasional sprinkle now, blown one way or another with the veering wind. Not a good day to go up on the bulging whaleback of steel framing that lay before Bratislaw, but the other men didn't seem worried about it and the foremen shooed them all into the lift cage together. Bratislaw felt his chest try to settle into his gut as the acceleration hit. The lift wasn't straight up. It was up and over the great ground bulge of the skeletal dome, changing thrust as they climbed. The cage was gimbaled inside its split-cylinder shell, so the floor remained down. But the shell rocked like a carnival ride.

They stopped less than a third of the way up and the men spilled out onto a stage. Bratislaw felt a hand on his shoulder. "You, too," said the foreman. "Shoe up!" And then, watching Bratislaw turn the dish-shaped plastic over in his hands in puzzlement, "Oh, shit. Come over here, you!" Out of earshot of the others, negligently touching with one hand a cable that Bratislaw was clinging to for dear life: "You ever been on the high steel before? No, I thought not. Damn that Ella!" He glared furiously at the other men, chattering among themselves, his face scowling while he thought. It was a dark face but not Negroid, and his accent was more New England than black. "I've got two choices. I can kick your ass off here. That's what I ought to do. Or I can take a chance that you'll kill yourself. Which do you want?"

What Bratislaw wanted he didn't want to say, since it was to be off that place where the wind thrust raggedly in all directions and the vents moaned and whistled and screamed. Woody Vult gave him what he said was the easiest job on the shell. It was to attach bundles of optical fibers to the structural members of the dome. When stressed, the transmission of laser-light through them varied and the strain registered on monitors below; when they broke, it called for a repair crew. So Bratislaw went out with his bowl-shaped shoes laced to his boots and a reel of colored sticky tape over one shoulder, dragging the fibers behind him as he pulled and rappelled himself across the dome with the hand-lines. It was a job for a man with at least three hands, preferably a man, like Vult, with Mohawk ancestry. Bratislaw had none of those. What he had was a determination to stick with it, and for the first hour, as he clung desperately and sweated fiercely and shook with fright, it didn't seem enough.

But as the day warmed and the sun came out, it began to seem not so bad. Bratislaw had never been so high in the open. Five hundred feet below the bridge and the river were toys; out across Brooklyn and Queens he could see planes taking off and landing and a thin knife-edge of blue that might be the Atlantic Ocean. All around him, on the swell of the dome, he could see other crews at work, sliding in the transparent panels and tacking them down, rappelling themselves with a grace and ease he so desperately envied. He couldn't do that. His grip on the lifelines was still tetanic. The others didn't fail to notice it, and when he returned for more cables every half hour or so he was the butt of jokes. Sometimes advice, too, or even information: "One hand for you, one hand for the job—never forget it!" "Every hundred feet up means one extra mile per hour wind." "Push is cube of wind speed—twice as much wind, eight times as much push —you wait till it gets *strong*, boy!" And always, from the foreman, "You guys get your ass moving! We got a schedule to meet!"

The schedule wasn't important, really—construction jobs are *never* on schedule. What was important was the weather. If the dome had been covered in on time there would have been no problem, for once it had its integrity it was aerodynamically proof against winds of a hundred and fifty miles an hour—more than had ever been recorded anywhere near New York by far. But with half the hexagonal panels in place and half missing, a really big wind would get right under and scoop it up. It would become an airfoil on its way to Oz—with, to be sure, hell's own mess of catastrophes left behind as pylons fell and cables snapped and great acre-sized sails tumbled and scraped across the city. So far the weather had spared them. But it was storm time.

"You! Bratislaw! What the hell do you think you're doing?" It was the foreman, Vult, scuttling up behind him. "Jesus, look at the way you've put them in, so loose the whole damn dome'll come down before they register!"

For nearly half an hour Bratislaw had been concentrating on the work and the odd sense of satisfaction it gave him to be up so high and fear it so little, but all of a sudden he realized he was fifty stories high in a growing wind. "I'll do it over," he gasped.

"You'll do shit! I'll get somebody who knows what he's doing! Anyway, you're transferred up."

"Transferred up?"

"What I said! Jennalec wants you on top, and she sent somebody to get you." And Bratislaw turned and looked past the foreman, and there coming toward them along the lifelines was Tiny Martineau.

If Bratislaw had thought fast he could have told the foreman to stick his job up his nose and made a safe, if unheroic, retreat. He didn't think fast. By the time he decided that was what he wanted to do the foreman was well out of earshot and Martineau was grinning. "Up you go," he said comfortably, interposing his body between Bratislaw and the way down. Although the cast was off, he still favored that leg.

"Look, Tiny," Bratislaw began, measuring him for size. He wasn't as big as Martineau but the difference wasn't much. In a fair fight they'd come out even enough—

"Up," grinned Martineau, and showed the blade in his hand. It was a sleeve knife, razor sharp. The fight would not be fair. Bratislaw edged back and up, his eyes fixed on the steel.

"Tiny," he said, "you and Ella've got this all wrong. I don't know what you think, but I'll never testify!"

"Right," said Tiny cheerfully. "Just keep going up and we won't have any trouble."

That did not seem likely to Bratislaw, especially as there wasn't anything he could see up higher along the dome that was worth going to. They were getting out of the area where the plastic had been put in place, and his snowshoes had become useless. "I can't go any farther than this, Tiny," he said.

"Sure you can. Take off the shoes. We don't have much further to go."

Bratislaw, one hand on the cable, bent down to release the lashings with the other. He kept his eyes on Martineau. It wasn't hard to do; there wasn't anybody else around to look at, and Martineau obligingly kept his distance.

As Bratislaw slipped out of the shoe he missed his grip and the wind caught it. It sailed away, down through the open metalwork where the plastic had yet to go. Some citizen far below was likely to have a nasty surprise. "Tiny?" he offered. "I think we better talk to Ella."

Tiny shook his head regretfully. "She don't want to talk to you any more, Jeffer," he said, uncoiling a cable from his waist. Bratislaw was surprised; it was a safety line, and for a minute he thought Martineau was about to offer it to him. Wrong guess. The big man clipped one end to the lifeline and the other to his belt.

"You can't do this!" Bratislaw yelled, retreating a step along the catwalk.

"Sure I can," grinned Tiny. "I got my orders from Ella, that's how I know it's okay. Now, you just hold still a minute—"

And Bratislaw might have done it, monkey caught in the python's glare, but the wind was whistling around him and the chill steel was slippery; he moved away and stumbled. He fell flat on the catwalk, hugging it as he'd never hugged a woman, scared as he had never been in his life.

And there was Tiny Martineau galloping toward him. The knife was back in his sleeve, no longer needed to do the job he had come to do. The expression on his face was serious and thoughtful as he drew back a foot to kick Bratislaw loose from the catwalk.

It wasn't skill. It was terrified reflex. Bratislaw kicked first. He caught Martineau on the ankle that had been in a cast; the slippery steel slipped; the giant yelled in sudden rage and fright; he fell across Bratislaw, missed a grab for the steel. And was gone.

When Bratislaw looked over the edge of the catwalk he could see Martineau dangling helplessly from his lifeline, fifty feet below, bobbing up and down and yelling, and wholly, completely unable to do anything to prevent it as Bratislaw, gasping, got to his feet, retrieved the one remaining snowshoe and slowly, carefully, slipped and clung his way back down the dome.

VII When the baby was two weeks old Heidi declared herself ready to travel and the child to be shown off to his aunt. They took the train to Peekskill and a taxi to the B-mod farm, and Lucy was waiting for them at the gate. She wasn't alone. She was pushing a wheelchair that contained a middle-aged woman who lacked arms and legs. "I'm Dorothy," said the woman, "and I'm a kind of counselor here." The halt leading the dumb? thought Bratislaw, but said not a word. He didn't have to. Lucy's scrambled brains had not forgotten how to greet a new child, and she was stroking the sweet, soft cheek and burbling over the little snorts and sighs that were all John Fitzgerald Kennedy Bratislaw the Fourth's vocabulary so far. "Nice kid," commented the woman in the wheelchair. She looked Bratislaw over carefully. She wasn't really without arms or legs, he saw, but they were no more than flippers at the shoulder, and what they were at the hips he could not see for the lap robe that covered her.

But they surely were not full-scale legs. "Congratulations," she added.

"It was my wife's doing," he grinned.

"I don't mean the baby. I mean the trial."

"Oh. Yeah," said Bratislaw, but the time had passed when he preened himself at that kind of remark. Ella Jennalec's lawyer had been the old-fashioned kind. He didn't cross-examine. He pulverized. He tried every tactic a fertile imagination and a lenient court allowed him to demolish Bratislaw's credibility as a witness, and not the least of his weapons was the testimony, irrefutable, because it was true, that Bratislaw had spent a lot of time in Jennalec's bed while his poor, pregnant wife worked overtime to pay their debts and save money for the child. Of course, it didn't change the outcome of the case. The amulet in Bratislaw's pocket had still been running, and Tiny Martineau's admission on tape that Jennalec had ordered the killing pushed the last reasonable doubt out of every juror's mind—not to mention all the other tapes, and all the other evidence from a dozen sources that had been building up the pattern of extortion and conspiracy and crime, which had made the verdict easy.

Heidi Bratislaw was not an unusually jealous woman, but it had taken a lot of the easy trust out of the marriage. Not to mention what it had done to Lucy. "Yeah," said Bratislaw again, looking down at the sisters bent over his new son, "but to tell you the truth, I kind of wish none of it had happened, for all the trouble it caused." And Lucy looked up at him. The pleasure went out of her pretty, empty face. She bit her lip and contorted her cheeks. Her eyes squinted with the effort and her jaw trembled, but at last she got it out:

"Was worth it," she said.

I WAS A DEPRESSION KID. I WAS BORN DURING the War to End Wars—the 1914 one. I started prep school the autumn of the 1929 stock-market crash, and transferred to the public high school in 1930 because Dad didn't have tuition money any more. By 1933 I was out of school entirely. I had to work for a living, when I could find it. Bad times! There were the breadlines, Okies fleeing the Dust Bowl, veterans on the Bonus March, poverty, fear—I hated the gritty, grimy world I lived in. You know what kept me going? Movies. Especially movies about the future. When I was in the theater sitting through two or three showings of Just Imagine or Things to Come I could shut the real world right out. I could imagine I was actually living in one of those great sparkly cities of the future where everybody was happy and healthy and rich and you lived like a king under a

second-hand sky

I And when the dome was complete it made a new world. A magnificent one, with magnificent new temptations. It was a magnet, and Jamespercy Nutlark one of the filings it drew. "Stay in Atlanta, Jimper," his friends in the club begged him. "You don't want to go to New York! They catch you hanging in New York, they *hang* you!"

But he emigrated anyway. You had to go where the work was, and anyway New York was the Big Blister and what hanger didn't want to try his wings on *that*? So he brought the old works with him when he moved and, as soon as he had a locker and a bed and a job, in that order, he was off to try the air. So he found the right high-rise and took the express to 75, with his Macy's shopping bag casually in his hand and his heart pounding. There was a wait for the local, and he walked over to the skywindow.

It was the right place, all right. There was Central Park spread out below them, with the construction crews busy getting ready for the Fair and, Jesus!, easily two hundred meters and better of clear open air! He couldn't wait. So he made himself wait—stretched and yawned, and glanced irritably at his watch and scowled and generally made himself look like a hard-working citizen with too much on his mind to be thinking of breaking the law. The policeman in 75's transfer lounge was a draftee, no real threat, a lot more interested in trying to chew the wad of tet gum in his mouth without moving his jaws than in anything Jimper might do, but all the same the cop was gazing at him. Jimper decided not to linger. He moved to the back of the local as soon as the doors were open. The cop lost interest. The car filled quickly, the doors closed and Jimper was the only one to leave the car at the 79th floor.

"Suite 7900," the fellow in the bar had told him. "It'll cost you twenty dollars and he's a real prick. But he's got the right window."

Suite 7900 was a solid metal door that said *T. J. Hallen and Co.—Imports,* and it was locked. Jimper shifted the Macy's bag to his left hand and knocked hard. When he heard the spyhole click he smiled at the invisible person behind the little glass eye and said, "The Baron sent me."

Silence. Then, hard to hear, a man's voice through the door: "Baron who?"

Jimper scowled. "How would I know Baron who? I was just told to say the Baron sent me. And twenty bucks."

More silence. Then the successive snicks of three locks being turned—did this choot think he was living in the Dark Ages?—and the door opened about twenty per cent of the way and Jimper squeezed through. The man inside took his arm, pulled him out of the way of the door, peered outside and then closed it. This time he didn't lock it. He looked at Jimper consideringly for a moment, as though he certainly knew a wolf from a bedridden grandmother and was just deciding how to expose his masquerade, then snatched the Macy's bag. He rummaged under the empty cigarette cartons on top. When he saw Jimper's works he relaxed enough to say, "Fifty dollars."

Jimper, who had already been reaching for his change purse, arrested his hand. "What do you mean, fifty? I was told the price was twenty."

"Good-by, friend," the man said softly, his hand on the doorknob again. But when Jimper didn't move he didn't open it. He said, almost apologetically, "I don't know you, do I? And, listen, you don't know the steam I've been taking. Twenty bucks don't cook it. Fifty don't cook it, either, but I got to live. So hand over the fifty and suit up, and the minute you go out the window I go out the door, and if there's any questions I never saw you before."

He counted the coins Jimper handed him quickly, and nodded. "All right, now make it rapid. And jump straight out when you go."

What did it matter, after all? Jimper left the man standing and made for the window, or anyway the place where the window had to be behind thick drapes. Jesus! You take an office on the 79th floor and you cover it up with drapes! And ratty old polyester-velvet at that, stuff you'd never use for clothing. Maybe for trim, a collar, bands around the wrist—

He realized he was stalling, and pulled the drapes aside. The window was a delight, three meters across at least, plenty of room for the works. It didn't look as though it would open, but it did. Jimper eased himself through, twisting to get the works out a corner at a time without bumping them against anything, and knelt on the edge of the void, breathing hard with pure delight

224

and that lovely little scatter of goosebumpy fear that always got you just before you went. Shoulder straps tight, belt cinched. He adjusted the tarbush around his face so that he could see but, with luck, not be seen by the police spotters, or at least not well enough for a conviction. And he was ready.

He heard the door thud closed at the other end of the room even before he brought his feet up, released his grip on the upper window and launched himself out into a quarter of a kilometer of beautiful, heart-stopping, empty air.

Now, this was the part that made it all worthwhile! A quarter of a kilometer of clear air above him, to where he could see the maintenance crews working on the panels of the dome, a quarter of a kilometer below, with the bikes and vodkars creeping around the construction sites in the park, and the wind whistling in your ears and the wings snapping out and locking just right! He fell fluttering for half a dozen stories. The step-back on the sixtieth floor was beginning to look worrying—then the wings began to feel the air. He had an updraft.

He soared out over the cool greens and blues of Central Park and its lakes. He was absolutely alone in the sky! It was true that out of the corner of his eye he could see two or three other illegal hang-gliders, off toward the west side of the Park or up north; but they were alone too! That was why you did it, that sting of solitary adventuring, just you and your gear and the dome far above and the ground far below.

There was a startling, ear-slitting whistle from the Fair grounds site. Jimper tumbled for a moment, coordination gone; but then he straightened. It was just a noise-polluter invading the Fair's sound system, not some supercop. But he had dropped nearly a hundred meters. He turned back toward 59th Street to catch an updraft from the tall old hotels. The draft was there to be found, although there was also a flash of strobe light from the roof of the Plaza—some cop with a long-range camera. No matter. The tarbush hid all of his face but his eyes, and he had long since removed the numbers from his wings. They'd never ID him that way. The only real danger would be when he landed, and for that he had plans. First-flight dummies might aim for the middle of the park, where the park cops could see you from a kilometer away and get to you before you could stow your wings. You could lose your works that way, even if you didn't get tagged yourself. Jimper Nutlark was smarter than that. He'd cased the whole midtown area for the perfect landing place on his first day in New York. Any choot could hang—it was the wise ones that kept their wings to fly another day! And he spiraled slowly up toward the dome roof in the vertical, and looked down on the city below, and peace entered his soul. Coming out of the top of the updraft at three hundred and eighty meters by the altimeter on his wrist, he gazed longingly south over Times Square and the midtown high-rises. You could see where the uptown dome curved down to meet the lower connecting bubble that joined it to the other big one south of Houston Street; one day, he vowed, he would take off from somewhere around here, glide through the connection and not land till he was at Bowling Green! But not this day. He didn't know his air yet. So he turned north and west, with the pretty colors of the park beneath. Some part of Jimper's mind was noting the colors and automatically translating them into fabrics that would become blouses and slit-slacks and belly-bands. But most of his mind was simply empty, accepting the tranquil delights of the sky. Atlanta dome had never been like this!

The temperature under the Big Blister averaged twenty-five degrees Celsius, a balmy May afternoon. (The fact that it was a balmy May afternoon outside the dome just then was, of course, irrelevant.) There were heat waves when it got to twenty-seven degrees or twenty-eight degrees, and in the depths of winter it sometimes plummeted as low as fifteen degrees. Then the New Yorkers put on their long-sleeved shirts or even light jackets, and chattered excitedly to each other about the chill. At sundown, sometimes the moisture in the air condensed at the plastic undersurface of the dome, and what didn't trickle away into the conduits as it was supposed to occasionally fell as fat, gentle raindrops. Snow fell never. Not inside, at least, although anyone with field glasses could see all he liked, any winter, scudding fiercely over the transparent sections of the dome.

Across the park—picking up an updraft from the big apartments along Central Park West—a quick turn over toward the dome edge itself, disappearing into the river past Riverside Drive. So many marvels to explore! And so pretty! Many of the newest buildings were very tall, right up to the curving dome itself, helping to keep it rigid against wind-stress. Because they were so tall fewer of them were needed, and so open spaces grew. From above, more than half the area of New York's West Side was in parklets—though some of them, of a dozen acres apiece and more, were thirty stories above the ground. Jimper marked out blocks and neighborhoods to explore on foot. Maybe on Joan-Mary's next day off—

But he had forgotten that Joan-Mary had decided to stay in Atlanta; such tricks the mind plays on the unaware. And it dampened Jimper's mood.

In any case, there was no sense pushing your luck the first day up in a new dome. The longest Jimper had ever stayed in flight was three hours and fifty minutes in Atlanta—all the way up to almost touching distance of the Atlanta dome itself. But that was a baking August day with a radon flush going on, the upper vents pouring out the old air while new came in around the skirts, and the updrafts so strong that he had almost feared being sucked into the vents themselves. This day was glorious, but not up to that standard. So Jimper picked up enough altitude over West End Avenue to soar back across the park, circling the huge pylon going up to support the Rainbow Bridge (what a place to launch from!—but the police would never let you get away with it). He reached Grand Army Plaza down to a hundred meters, and just barely in range of the place where he had planned to land.

Jimper made a quick turn over the fountain, between tall buildings, and there was the roofed tenth-floor pedestrian bridge over Fifth Avenue. The rest was tricky: glide close to the buildings on the West Side, a steep left bank, and he would be down on the roof of the bridge, running to lose momentum. . . . But the turn was steeper than he had expected. Twisting and straining, the folded tarbush came out of his collar and whipped across his face. He lost grace. He flung himself to the right to correct, bumped his head against the wing strut and knew he was in trouble. The tarbush nearly blinded him for a critical moment. He misjudged his height, and the bridge was there before he was ready for it.

It was not a serious accident. He tripped, fell and slid, but did not go over the edge. But his right wing was crumpled and the frame bent, and blood ran down his leg where he had scraped the knee raw.

Jimper shucked the quick-release harness and gazed at the wreckage of nine hundred dollars' worth of rig. He caught a glimpse of someone watching disapprovingly out of one of the wide windows on the east side of the avenue. The window opened; the person leaned out toward him. He glared at her, half stunned. "Leave the rig," she ordered. "Come on into my office. I'm a doctor."

So she was. She was a hundred and sixty centimeters of a doctor at the most, so that even as he was sitting on her examining table she had to look up at him to bawl him out. Dark mousy hair, brown gentle eyes—but angry ones. Her touch was not angry, though. She carefully cleaned away the ragged scrape, sprayed it with something that stung, touched it with two seconds of ultraviolet, then, immediately, sprayed it again but this time with something else that took the sting away. And all the time she was telling him what a choot he was. "All you did this time was skin your knee. The luck of drunks and fools, I guess."

"You think losing your gear's lucky?" They were almost brand-new, nine hundred dollars and twenty hours of his own modifications.

"You lost your gear before you touched down, dummy. There was a cop team on the thirtieth-floor deck watching you. If you had stayed there one more minute you'd be telling it to the desk sergeant right now." She was wrapping neat spirals of bandage around his knee as she talked. "Do you know that's a confinement offense? Plus confiscation of your works. Plus license revocation if the judge is in a bad mood, so you can't glide even outside the dome—where was it worth it?"

Jimper's leg was beginning to throb now, and the fuse on his temper was getting short. "I guess I owe you a favor," he said, "but I don't have to take all this steam. You don't know what it's like up there or you wouldn't tell me it wasn't worth it."

She slapped the bandage to show she was finished— the slap hurt!—and stepped back. "If you had kids playing in the park and never knew when some choot was going to drop a shoe on their heads, you'd know why it was against the law."

Jimper shrugged and slid his legs over the side of the examining table. He stood up experimental- ly. It didn't make his leg hurt any worse. "Well, thanks," he said grudgingly. "You want my Medcard number?"

"In my office," she said, pointing. On the way he

sneaked a look out the window, and his wings were gone, all right. Now he really needed to get to work—it would take him weeks, anyway, to save up for a new pair.

When they were both standing Jimper was a good quarter-meter taller than she. Although he was lean, she was tiny. While she was processing his card through the terminal he looked at the framed objects hanging on the wall. A picture of herself with a small, not very pretty, kid next to her—the picture was queerly off center, as though there had once been a third person she had decided to remove. A diploma from New York University School of Medicine that told him she was a fully accredited internist and manual surgeon, and that her name was Jo-Ellen Redfan. A photograph next to it told him more than that. "Oh, hell," he said, looking at a shot of Dr. Jo-Ellen Redfan hanging from a General Dynamics Thirty-Oh-Three, "why didn't you tell me you were into hang-gliding too?"

She handed him the light-pen for signing his bill. "Not under the dome, I'm not. Off the Palisades, sure. You can stay up longer, you don't get steamed for it, and if you boob the only one you kill is yourself." She stopped him as he turned to leave. "You ought to stay off that leg for the next hour, and besides if you go out now with your shorts all bloody the cops are going to notice you. Go back in the examining room and stretch out for a while."

"Why, thanks," Jimper said, startled. He looked at her in a new way, readjusting his image to allow for the fact that she was human, after all. She flushed under his gaze.

"I've got patients outside," she said, turning to open the door—

And just on the other side of it, poised to knock, were two cops, a skinny young woman in regular force blues and a brown-suited auxiliary, and they looked right at Jimper Nutlark. Jimper sighed. "Well, thanks for trying," he said to the doctor, and sadly went out to meet his fate.

In the elevator on the way to the station house on the top floor, the cop key in the controls to make it run express, the regular cop shook her head, studying Jimper's ID. "Just up from the boonies," she mused. "You farmers give me a pain. Well, you'll find out how we do things in New York City, and I will be a very surprised person if you like it a bit."

II "Thirty days," said the judge at the hearing, "or five thousand dollars. You farmers give me a pain. Next case."

Jimper hadn't expected an acquittal, but he hadn't expected that, either. Five thousand dollars! Thirty days would be even worse, when he needed to make a living. He backed away from the dock, lifted his wrist to his lips and talked to his lawyer. "That's preposterous!" he hissed. "I haven't got five thousand dollars!"

"It's a disjunctive, Nutlark," his lawyer said wearily. "Thirty days *or* five thou. Did you bargain yet?"

"Bargain?"

"Oh, for God's sake," said his lawyer crossly, "don't you ever listen when I talk to you? I told you you had to make your deal after the sentence. Look for the window marked 'Contract Negotiations,' all right?"

Jimper lifted his head to search the room, then crossed to the door to peer into the hall. It was right there. Three or four other defendants, now sentenced, were standing in a line before it. The first in line was immersed in a hand-waving, head-shaking argument with the person beyond the window. "I see it. What do I do now?"

"Make your damn deal!" the attorney said. "Now,

231

remember, the best way to figure it is, say, your time's worth twenty dollars an hour, so don't let them give you more than, let's see, twenty into five thousand—"

"Two hundred and fifty hours?"

"That right? If you say so. If I could've handled math I'd be an engineer or something instead of a goddamn lawyer."

"I wish you'd do the talking for me," Jimper said.

The attorney sighed. "You pay for personal appearance in court, you get it. You don't pay, you settle for phone consultation like this. Tell you what. If your adjuster tries to hand you anything over two-fifty hours call me back. Now I've got a client in the office." And he cut the connection.

By the time Jimper got to the head of the line he had time to study the liquid-crystal sign over the window. The numbers changed slightly from minute to minute, but not enough to signify, Jimper thought. It said:

Current Exchange Rates

CLASSIFICATION	$100 EQUIVALENT
General clerical	13.4 hours
Sanitation	7.1 hours
Emergency auxiliary	5.3 hours
Teaching*	8.5 hours
Transit, operating*	8.0 hours
Park/farm	10.5 hours
Ombud	16.2 hours

*Available only to convicts with appropriate qualifications.

By the time Jimper stopped quaking over that unpleasant word "convicts" he was at the head of the line, and the man behind the window was reaching for his ID. The clerk punched up the identification number and gazed at the screen. "Oh, hell," he muttered, "what are you, cherry? You mean I got to explain the system to you?"

"We don't do things this way in Atlanta," Jimper apologized.

"That I believe. Well, so listen. You make a choice. The first choice you got to make is decide if you want to serve your time in the slammer. Allowing for good time that might get you out in eighteen days, give or take. Or you can pay the five thousand. Or if you don't want to do one of those, the other thing you can do is work off your debt to society, and that's what I'm here for. Work-offs," he droned on, leaning back in his chair as though he no longer needed to listen to what he was saying, "work-offs are on call, day and night, every day until they're paid up, and you got to work the full time—whatever the exchange rate is, as posted, times the number of one-hundred-dollar units in your fine. You got that so far? Okay, now let's talk about what kind of job you can handle, not that I expect much. You farmers give me a pain."

The haggling took quite a while, especially since Jimper insisted on having every job explained to him, and then tried to get a break on the exchange rates. By the time he left the window the line was fifteen "convicts" long behind him, and the comments they were making were no longer restrained. But he was grinning. He paused at the end of the corridor to dial his lawyer one more time to gloat. "Hey, Mr. Seymour, this is Jimper Nutlark, and I think I made a good deal. Of course, now I've got to wear this transponder thing all the time so they can know where I am and reach me when they want me—"

"Nutlark, I know how the system works. So what did you get?"

"Not bad at all, Mr. Seymour. I beat them down to a hundred and thirty hours, what do you think of that? Not bad for somebody right up from crackerland!"

Pause. Then, cautiously, the lawyer asked, "Mind telling me what kind of duty you signed up for?"

"They call it 'emergency auxiliary,'" Jimper said proudly.

"Oh, my God," moaned the lawyer. "If you'd only— Well, it's too late now, and maybe you'll learn something out of this. But listen, Nutlark—if you ever do this again, next time pay the difference so I can be there!"

For three days the transponder was silent, and Jimper almost forgot he was sentenced. Not that they didn't remind him. By the time he got back to his windowless, airless little room that night there was an official message on the console to confirm that he had accepted one hundred thirty hours commandable, which meant that he could be called at any time as an auxiliary cop, as a sweat laborer if they wanted him, and the long paragraphs of what would happen if he failed to respond, or failed to wear his transponder at all times or in any other way offended the majesty of the City of New York went on for three frames. But he was too busy to worry. He had come up from Atlanta because of the Fair, and he spent half his time walking around the growing exhibits, talking to supervisors and liaison persons, offering his services for design of any kind. Most didn't want to hear, but there were so many of them that he began to be hopeful. He would peer into the ditches they were digging for the Russian pavilion— it was going to be a reproduction of part of Leningrad, canals and bridges for the Venice of the North—or study the animal cages that would be Australia's koala and wallaby habitats. Then he would go back to the corner of an office he had rented as a studio and whip up drape and costume sketches, pull hard copies and run back to the Fair to thrust them under the noses of anyone who would look. Even when they turned him down, he was having a ball. The city was a ball. He liked the leg-powered bikes and trikes, and the vodkars with the exhaust of the alcohol-burning Stirling engines smelling like Sunday morning in a saloon; he liked the open, flat-bottomed trams, flywheel powered, that you leaped onto when you wanted a ride and leaped off again when you were there—no fares, no seats, no frills, just a chance to rest your legs when you were tired of walking. He liked poking into the queer neighborhoods of the city, ethnic or churchly or culty, though some of them scared him. What he would have liked even better was someone to share all this with, or even someone who wasn't interested in sharing anything but a bed, but Joan-Mary was still in Atlanta. Although he had struck up a few conversations with New York women in bars, most weren't really attractive to him; and farmers, it appeared, gave most of the others a pain. Not that Jimper Nutlark was a farmer, or anything like it. But New Yorkers seemed to think that everything that was not under the Big Blister was covered with meter-deep cow-flop.

It was not so much that New Yorkers disliked other people, he discovered. They didn't like each other much, either, or so it appeared from the orffiti on the public-speaker systems, maniacal screechings and bird-calls interspersed with yells of "Brooklyn sucks!" and "Death to Stuyvesant Town!" . . . and the spray-painting on every flat surface which, if you collected a representative anthology, would denounce Jews, blacks, Irish, southerners, New Englanders, Arabs, Chinese, English, Brooklynites, midwesterners, Swedes, Californians, Italians, women, men, gays of both varieties and members of every religious denomination in the Yellow Pages. Why they were so mean to each other Jimper could not say. They certainly had a nice place here, at least to visit. The Big Blister was far better climate-controlled than Atlanta. New York had achieved optimal conditions, defined as humidity always comfortably between mildew and skin-itch, temperature at which you could sit around in your underwear and make love without getting under a blanket. . . .

If you had anybody to make love with, that was.

That was denied to Jimper, but he had other solaces, and among them, yes, a real live job prospect! The name of the company was Mawzi Frères. They had the contract for the British Pavilion at the Fair, and they needed clothes for the staff. Lots of them. There would be ushers and demonstrators and lecturers; there would be waiters at the New Simpson's and barmaids at Ye Olde Englysshe Pub; and it was important that every garment be *British*. Not British made, necessarily, and under no circumstances British designed. But they had to convey that unique quaint and trendy British air, somewhere between Carnaby Street and the Tower of London. So decreed fat old Rasfah Mawzi, waving his hands to explain what words could not, and so Jimper spent a whole day begging swatches of British (or British-like) fabric from every dealer he could find. He fed the specs on each into his datastore, and then sat crumpling the swatches, one by one, in his hand, visualizing the Shetland wool and the Scottish cashmere and the Midlands cottons, dyed and patterned and cut and pleated and gathered in a hundred ways. It was important to design the garment to the cloth. Each fabric had its own weight and "hand" and resistance to crease or wrinkle. You couldn't design, say, a Household Guards uniform without knowing how supplely it would drape, or how hot it would be to wear in the steady May warmth under the dome. The fabrics were all so *heavy*. Jimper, frowning, drew in a couple of practice kilts with his light-pen, keyed in the specifications for the most lightweight weaves he could find, then draped them on one of his stock model programs and caused the little figure on the screen to walk and turn. The kilt moved nicely, he acknowledged. But what about the poor son of a gun who had to wear it?

Was it true that you weren't supposed to wear anything under the kilt, and wouldn't it itch terribly?

He looked up irritably. There was an unpleasant smell in the room. He checked his wastebaskets, and looked around at the desks of the other free-lancers. Nothing appeared to be burning, but the smell was there—a little like scorched wood, a little like asphalt, a little as though someone had set fire to a heap of automobile tires and old used condoms. He turned up the air circulator by his desk, frowning, and went back to his drawing screen. A pair of military shorts, now. Something in bright colors, but with dignity—

"James Percy Nutlark, attention."

He almost dropped the light pencil as the commanding voice sounded in his ear. He had not heard it before, but at once he knew what it was. "You are activated!" it snapped. "Report at once, Water Street station, where you will receive equipment and orders. Prepare for a prolonged tour of duty."

III The tip of Manhattan Island had been growing like a tumor for more than four centuries. What had once been an island became Battery Park. What had once been deep, sweet river water, with sturgeon the size of sharks, became landfill . . . and the fill was whatever happened to fall into the river. There were bricks and rock. There was dumping from excavations and dumping (illicit) of trash. There were old piers and scuttled ships. There was every sort of trash one could imagine. It was the old piers that were the worst. They had been creosoted against marine worms and driven deep down to hard surfaces to support weight, and then they had been buried just as they stood to get them out of sight. When they had started to burn it was like a Pennsylvania coalmine fire. They burned, and they kept on burning. Some of those old underground fires had probably been smoldering away for a hundred years, damped now and then by the seepage of river water, until they boiled the last of the water away and grew white-hot again. They did no great harm . . . until they reached open air.

And open air was what the City of New York had provided them. For the thousands of expected visitors to the coming Fair the city was building new hotels. Luxury ones in Central Park West. Medium-cost ones in the East Village. And down here, a long subway ride from the Fair itself, the cheapies. The cheapest of the accommodations amounted to nothing more than a three-meter-long file drawer that a man could climb into and close off, each with its own air vent and light and luggage rack and pillow and abiotic mattress. Since there was no money in their budget for such frills as windows, there was no reason to poke these constructions up into expensive domed airspace. So they went down.

Unfortunately, they went down into made land, where the old pier fire was still smoldering. Great gray stinking clouds of smoke began to pour into the sealed inner space of the dome.

The Water Street station was crowded when Jimper got there, more than a hundred work-off convicts like himself. Not all very like. There were blacks and whites and Hispanics and orientals, two high-iron Mohawks from Red Hook, a pair of grave, bearded gays from Yorkville holding hands and blushing as they averted their eyes from the nakedness of other men, plump and puffing Japanese businessmen rousted out of their Wall Street offices, hassidim kissing their phylacteries as they took them of and indignantly refusing to remove their skullcaps, women in purdah robes and women in minikinis, young ones, old ones—it was a cross-section of the city, or anyway the mildly criminal element in it, working off their various offenses and bitching most loudly. The regular force cops paid no attention. "Shuck your duds and hit the suds," they droned, and, "Move your asses!" When the convicts had stowed their possessions in the assigned lockers and run quickly through the showers, they filed to a supply bay.

Jimper was not surprised to be issued fire-fighting gear, but not particularly pleased, either. "I don't know anything about being a fireman," he commented to the convict next to him.

She looked at him with scorn and disgust—fifty years old if she was a day, with a sagging, pear-shaped body. "Do I look like *I* do?" she demanded. "My God, what will they think of next? Yesterday a rat hunt and now this—and, listen, it was a bum rap, too. The thermometer was out of order, how was I supposed to know I was violating thermal guidelines?" But Jimper wasn't listening. His attention was taken up with the garments he was supposed to be putting on. Long cotton underwear, like thick pantyhose. Stiff, scratchy work pants that fastened around the ankle. Steel-tipped boots, and by no means new—they were scarred and seared, and the zip-it fastenings were clogged with the congealed souvenirs of some previous draftee's miserable ordeal by mud. A face mask and an air pack—"Hey," Jimper squawked to the professional firefighter who was urging them on, "this looks dangerous!"

"Shut your face and move your ass," the man droned. Twenty at a time he moved them out and onto wide-bodied vans, standing room only; and the driver engaged the flywheels and they rolled down the avenues to the fire.

They were very near to the base of the dome, and stinking black smoke was pouring out of an excavation. Jimper wondered if the heat from the fire could damage the plastic of the dome and, looking up, was surprised to feel warm spray in his face and see that the emergency flaps in the vents were open. Rainy spring air was coming in. But everyone knew you only opened the vents a few times a year, to flush out the accumulations of radon gas, when the weather conditions were just right. If the hope was that the smoke would pour out through the vents, the hope was misplaced; it flowed at ground level, oily and choking, and when the fireman in charge of their contingent bawled "Masks on! Move your asses!" Jimper was glad enough to comply. Slipping and swearing, they descended a muddy earthen ramp toward the fire.

They were not, of course, allowed to do any real firefighting. There were professionals for that, manning the stiff, writhing hoses, pouring dense CO_2 blankets on the rubble nearest the face of the fire, spraying quick-dry thermosetting concrete across the glowing face itself. What the convicts had to do was stoop labor, and of the meanest kind. The first regular crews had been in there with their water hoses and inert gases, and most of the visible fire was long subdued. But not out. Even this side of the face, almost concealed now in its smoky, hot wall of cement, there were pockets where the coals were still live, bits of smoldering rubble concealed by the extinguished rubble. It would wait patiently until it dried out the wet and let the anoxic vapors blow away, and then, if allowed, it would start up again. What the convicts had to do was keep it from starting up again.

So they had to remove all the stuff it fed on. Bulldozers could have cleaned out the cut in minutes. But bulldozers could not recognize the difference between ashes and coals, and it would have meant only removing the fire to another place—not to mention the fact that they were so near the dome's edge that Jimper could see the shoulders of the vast supporting concrete structures, and no one wanted to run heavy bulldozers where they might bring a whole edge of the dome down! So they had shovels. A few of the more proficient had air-hammers to loosen the rock-hard dried mud and stone and trash. Most of all they had their hands, stiff in the heavy gloves. The firefighters from the regular force kept shouting their orders: "Pick up everything that's loose! Break off anything that's hanging! Tote it out of here—and if you hit a hot spot don't fool with it, yell for a pro!"

The problem, or one of the problems, was that Jimper couldn't really see very well in the face mask. The other problems were fatigue, and unaccustomed muscles, and clumsiness, and most of all the smoggy, smelly, sauna heat, with the air about them clouded with smoke and steam and stink. The air packs gave them oxygen, but they couldn't give them coolth. Even the air was only enough for half an hour at a time, but that wasn't so bad, because a half an hour at a time was about all that Jimper could stand. He measured his life by the breaks to recharge the pack, and stalled around adjusting the face mask and the valves as long as he possibly could before the fire-pusher's yells began to get really nasty. At that, he was better off than most of the convicts. After the first hour the contingents in the air packs began to dwindle, as more and more of the older and weaker were put to running the dumpsters that lifted the excavated trash into portable bins for disposal. After his third or fourth change of air packs Jimper glanced up and saw that the dome vents were closed again: some kind of progress, anyway! After the sixth, or it could have been the tenth, he noticed that the outside of the dome was getting dark, and tardily remembered that the man from Mawzi Frères had been expecting to see his sketches before the close of business that day.

If he had been less bone-deep exhausted he would have been terribly upset . . . as it was, he sighed and snapped the mask and went back to scavenge some more of the rubble.

When the fireman slapped his shoulder and pointed to the waiting inertial-drive van, Jimper did not at first understand that the ordeal was over. When at last that penetrated, he was too weary for exultation.

Back in the station house, with the other auxiliaries,

Jimper stripped off the firefighting gear, got a receipt for every piece and took his turn in the showers. He was a mass of muscle aches, and the water stung as it hit parts of his back and rump—he dimly remembered taking a fall. Or had it been two different falls? But his mind was on other things.

Specifically, the firefighting gear. Did it have to be so extremely uncomfortable? Not to mention ugly? Couldn't there be something lighter, less abrasive, maybe, my God, even with some attempt at *design,* that would work just as well? Something with one of the newer semi-syn fabrics from the sea plants, maybe, more flexible so the sizes wouldn't be so critical?

Of course, he thought, gingerly touching his right buttock where it smarted worst, the most important quality for these garments was toughness. So there couldn't be too much give, or at least not in all directions—but a polymerizing fabric that would stretch as much as you liked in one dimension, but maintain its dimensions in the other, might work just fine. . . .

He looked at his fingers and discovered them smeared with watery blood, rinsing away under the spray from the shower.

"Oh, hell," he groaned, peering under his lifted arm and twisting his torso to see that he was abraded and bleeding from rib cage down across the buttock out of sight. He had hardly felt it, but as he did not want to bleed all over his own clothes he wrapped a towel around himself, took his place in the first-aid station and flopped on the first free cot.

Lying on his belly, he felt someone dab at his wound, spray it and then gently tap his shoulder. "This is getting to be a habit," the voice said.

He squirmed around. Dr. Jo-Ellen Redfan, the woman who had taped him up after the hang-glider fall. And she was wearing the brassard of an auxiliary—another felon working off a sentence, just like himself! "What did they get you for?" he asked.

"None of your business." But her tone was pleasant enough. She bandaged him and slapped his rump to tell him he was all through—but as he was leaving the first-aid room she winked good-by.

He took his time dressing, and as he was leaving he was handed a printout by the duty officer. It had his name, his ID number and a notation of credit: "5 hrs. 41 mins. served. 124 hrs. 19 mins. still due."

He was far too tired to walk. He jumped on a flat-bottom bus and leaned against the rail, staring sightless at Tribeca, Soho and Chelsea as the inertial-drive vehicle moved placidly up Hudson toward the 23d Street transfer. 124 hrs. 19 mins. Maybe it would have been better to serve his time. Still, it was the law in New York City that employers had to give work-off convicts time to do what they were commanded to do, although whether or not Mawzi Frères would be willing to consider themselves "employers" in that sense was a whole other question. At 21st Street the vehicle slowed to let someone jump off, and Jimper's eyes focused for the first time.

It was the woman doctor. He didn't stop to think, he swung over the rail after her. "Jo-Ellen!" he called, and, as she turned, amended it to, "Hello, Dr. Redfan. Do you live around here?"

The expression on her face did not match the friendly good-by wink she had offered. It wasn't hostile. It wasn't interested, either. She nodded absently—remotely, a nod wholly detached from any recognition of his presence as a living human being. It was a little chilling, but Jimper pressed on. "Tough day today," he said, shaking his head. "I think I'm about due for a nice cold beer—how about you?"

Jimpercy Nutlark was of at least normally good looks and personality, and knew it well enough to possess some self-confidence in dealing with young women. They might not respond, but they were almost never repelled. So he smiled and waited while Jo-Ellen

Redfan frowned and glanced at her watch, and was not really surprised when, after that, she shrugged. "A beer is all it's going to be, champ," she said, but amiably enough, "but you're right, it has been one hell of a day."

It was her own neighborhood, and Jimper was content to let her lead the way. This far over to the Hudson side of the island, the dome was not very high, therefore neither were the buildings. Chelsea still had many of its ancient row houses, with little gardeny parks in the middle of some blocks, and along Eighth Avenue the buildings were low and the storefronts ethnic. All kinds of ethnic; between a Lebanese grocery store and a Moslem religious-objects outlet was what was called the Bank of Ireland Bar, and there was real sawdust on the floor and a real old jukebox against the wall. "So what were you in for?" asked Jimper, grinning.

She shrugged. "No reason not to tell you. It was creating a disturbance."

"Ah." He nodded as he took a sip of the beer, letting her infer the question.

She grinned. "I wasn't drunk and disorderly. Actually, there were two men fighting over me, if you want to know."

"I can understand that," he said gallantly.

"Sure you can, champ." But she didn't expand on the remark, only listened, politely and interestedly enough, while he told her the traditional singles-bar story, namely his autobiography. She was attentive enough to ask the right questions: "Well, what made you go into clothes designing?" "Were you serious about this girl in Atlanta?" "Do you think there'll be a lot of tourists for the Fair?" But she was working her way down to the bottom of the beer, and when she reached it she looked at her watch again. "Jimper," she said, "I'm sorry, but one beer's all the time I've got. There's somebody going to be getting home about now and I need to be there."

"Ah," said Jimper philosophically, accepting destiny when it forced itself on him, but she shook her head.

"It's not my husband," she said. "I'm not married or attached, but I don't date, either."

"Ah," he repeated, and she shook her head again.

"I'm not gay or frigid, either." She grinned. "You can't win 'em all, champ. No, don't get up—I live just around the corner, and I can make it by myself really well."

He watched her go out of the door, admiring the way her body moved under the scarlet, translucent sundress, and thought that it was a terrible pity that she was whatever she was that had men fighting over her but didn't want to see more of one of them.

Or at least of himself; but Jimper was philosophical about that, too. He was cheerful enough as he left the bar and collided with a huge, smiling man who seemed to have been standing right there. "Oh, sorry, sir!" cried the man, beaming down on Jimper. "It's all my fault. I apologize."

Jimper was quite pleased to find this immense person so genteel. "No harm done," he said, moving to get out of the way, but the man put a bearpaw hand on his shoulder.

"I think I ought to buy you a drink," he said. "Just to show I'm sorry."

Jimper was surprised and a little touched. But then he remembered the aches in his bones and the stiffness in his butt. "I'd just as soon take a raincheck," he said politely. "I was on duty putting out that fire downtown all day, and I'm pretty beat—I just stopped off to have a drink with somebody from the first-aid station there. I don't think I could handle another one."

"I see," said the man jovially, and stood aside to let Jimper pass on the way to his bus. Jimper turned and saw the man still standing outside the bar, beaming at him. Now, thought Jimper in pleasure, that's a nice man. Who says New Yorkers are standoffish? He probably was going to like this town, he decided. At least it began pretty well.

IV And, as a matter of fact, as the days passed he began to feel more and more at home. Twice he was called up for auxiliary duty, but both times it was easily done—an hour of helping to hand out parking tickets way up in East Harlem, four hours of standing around to direct fans in and out of Shea Stadium for a double-header. And Mawzi Frères were quite decent about his failure to show up on time with the designs. Better than that. They liked the designs. Better still, they recommended him to a couple of other contractors; best of all, old Rasfah Mawzi turned out to have a daughter. Her name, according to her father, was Fatima, but she said, "Please, call me Doll," and though she neither leered nor winked she gave off the impression that the doll liked to be played with. Unfortunately she gave her father the same impression, and whenever Jimper managed to get within a meter of Doll the old man's eyes made exactly the same sensation as an ice cube applied to the back of his neck. Doll was tall for an Egyptian, or Iraqi, or whatever she was—Jimper couldn't quite figure out which was which—but still tiny enough to have to look up at him. She was not in veils and robes, but she wasn't wearing hip-huggers, either: a well-behaved skirt almost to the knee, a buttoned blouse of material far heavier than anyone needed under the dome. "Daddy dresses me for home," she explained, leaning over him to watch his light-pen sketch out lingerie. "Home's Edinburgh."

"You don't sound Scottish." Or Arab either, Jimper thought.

"Daddy wanted me to get my degree at Columbia, so how should I sound but American? Speaking of

246

Daddy," she added, "he's coming over here, so you'd better make some fast adjustments in that lady."

It had come to look a lot like Fatima; Jimper lengthened it and fattened it and changed the hair color to blonde just in time. It had stopped looking like Fatima only to begin looking like Jo-Ellen what-was-her-name, the doctor with the hangups. Jimper sighed. Life had been a lot easier in Atlanta. What was wrong with all these New York women, anyway?

The best thing that happened to him was that the classifications clerk at the parole board had come to recognize him as a regular. "Volunteer, choot," he advised Jimper. "Volunteer for everything easy, don't wait to be called up."

"I don't even know which jobs are easy," Jimper admitted humbly. The clerk sighed and told him that farmers gave him a pain, but then relented enough to tick off the best bets available. Rat patrol was bad, but laying out the pipes before the drives was good. Patrolling in the entertainment areas around Times Square and 14th Street was bad. Patrolling around the docks was good. The best thing available, as long as he could get days off, was lifeguarding; and so Jimper found himself sitting on a tall chair at the Municipal Baths on Asser Levy Place for eight hours at a stretch. The only thing he had to bother about was calling a cop if someone made a disturbance, and as it was under the dome he didn't even have to worry about getting a sunburn. He could even catch up on his sleep, twenty minutes at a time or so now and then; which meant that he could also volunteer for night duty patrolling the docks at the toe of the island.

Atlanta wasn't a seaport. The volume of traffic that went through the bays and rivers of this city amazed him. From the inner catwalks of the dome he could look down and see squat, square submarines slipping under the surface, traveling the calm sandwich layer to resupply oil rigs in the Baltimore Canyon. Outside the dome were the barges up from the Delaware Bay and the Jersey Shore, freezers of meat and produce for the ship's bellies, and the fuel, and the raw materials the city's industries fed on, and the videospecs and the music plugs and the game disks and the typewriters and the washing machines and the shoes and shorts and sealing wax that went into the city's stores. Upstream, under the chopped-off skeleton of the World Trade Center, the huge submersible garbage scows came in at night. They pumped their holds dry of ballast, surfacing like great bloated dead whales until the coupling crews pumped another twenty-five hundred metric tons of foul-smelling tarry waste into each of them, and submerged them; then they too slipped away, silent as sharks, bound out for the dumping grounds at the edge of the continental shelf. When seeing the sights got boring, there was always a chance to find a comfortable doorway and take a little nap, until the noise of the crabbers woke him up as the tide went out and the crabs came in.

They were the big business there, first thing in the morning. They swarmed along the river's edge, inside the dome or out, wherever the water was shallow enough to drop their traps. There seemed no limit to the crabs they could haul in, great eighteen-centimeter brutes that moved like whippets and pinched like a vise if they got the chance. When Jimper saw one of the crabbers dumping a bucket on the sidewalk to sort out his catch, he learned not to volunteer to help.

The only time his official presence was needed was when two of the crabbers dumped their loads together, and the crustaceans scattered in all directions. It took Jimper half an hour to settle the arguments about which was which. Then the old men turned friendly and invited him into the shadow of the dome pylon to share a joint. When Jimper praised the size of the crabs, one of the old men exhaled deeply, coughed and said, "They like the sewage."

"Sludge," said the other, holding his hand out for the roach.

"Starts out as sewage. Piss and shit and God knows what. The sludge barges dump here."

Jimper took his turn, and puffed out a thin blue curl of smoke. "I thought they were supposed to clean the holds out at sea."

"Sure they are. Supposed to open the hatches fore and aft and steam for twenty minutes in a straight line. All they are inside is like a great big sewer pipe, you know. The sea'll come right in and scour them clean. But they don't do it. If they go five minutes it's a lot, because they get paid by the load, and naturally they don't get all the way clean. But that's all right. The little bit of sewage they dump here you'd never notice, unless you were some little sea creature that's glad to have it. Then along comes the crab, and he's glad to have *him,* and Marty and me're glad to have the crab." He peered into the bucket, watched his chance, then dived in with both hands and pulled out a pair of claw-waving monsters. "Here. Take 'em along. Your lady'll know how to cook them."

The trouble was, Jimper didn't have a lady. The girl from Atlanta didn't answer his letters. The doctor woman was not in her office when he called her, and didn't call back. And Fatima-Doll was busy at graduate school. The crabs were definitely losing vigor by the time Jimper made up his mind to offer them to her father, who was grateful enough, the next day, to offer Jimper a package. "Sandwich," he said. "Crabmeat salad. Your crabs, made by Fatima. Very good."

"Thank you," said Jimper, drugged by lack of sleep, and sat over the light-board for another half hour, altering sketches without much improving them, until it occurred to him that crabmeat salad should not be left indefinitely without refrigeration. He began to eat, too fatigued to notice whether or not it was good. Almost too fatigued to notice that there was something in the crabmeat salad too tough to be meat and too flexible to be shell, and when he took it out it was a sort of

Band-Aid, and when he pulled it open there was a folded slip of paper inside:

> Tonight, 1730 hours, New Gotham Tower East, 83d floor, DOOR.

New Gotham Tower was one of the ethnic neighborhoods, in the ethnic's usual battle with the freethinkers, counterculturists, arts-hopefuls and soi-disant Bohemians who liked cheap rents and enough grime to prove superiority to material values. The 83d floor was an express stop, with the usual sprinkling of shops, fast-food stores and sidewalk vendors. It took Jimper only a moment to find the place he was looking for. The sign on the door said

DOOR

all right, but it wasn't really a door, it was a cloud-curtain. That is to say, it was a flow of air containing large, light organic molecules, pumped out of slots at the top of the frame and sucked into slots in the floor. Some projector somewhere laid the cloud over with a curious dark-hued scene, a bare turf with a standing figure whose shadowy back was to Jimper as he approached. It was vague. But it looked real. Jimper almost braced himself for contact as he entered, but all he felt was a warm draft raising the hair at the nape of his neck.

When he glanced back it was the face of the shadowy figure he saw, female, with tufted hair that looked almost like horns, wearing a tee-shirt that said:

> We Sell Magic
> Not Tricks
> Magic

What a strange place, Jimper mused. The lighting was dim, but all his other senses were being assailed

Musk and pine, garlic and stranger, more easterly scents; sitar music in the background; and, suddenly, a flare of angry red flame as a clerk at the back of the store demonstrated a pinch of something tossed into a brazier. There was only one other salesperson, talking to a customer. Jimper approached her.

"Excuse me."

She glanced irritably at him and went on talking. "I'm so glad you came in tonight! We just got some graveyard dirt."

The customer was a teen-aged boy with acne. "How much for a quarter kilo?"

"Twelve-fifty," she said apologetically.

"My God!"

"But it's the real thing," she cajoled. "From—" she lowered her voice "—you know the old Portuguese cemetery on Eleventh, street level? From there. And legal. And certificated."

The boy pursed his lips and tapped them gently with two fingers. "I'll have to think about it," he said, and drifted away. The clerk sighed and turned toward Jimper, her eyebrows raised.

"I'm looking for Doll," he said.

"Oh, sure. Wax? Male or female? Or, if you have something of the affected, hair clippings, whatever, we do a custom for forty dollars up—"

"Not *a* doll. Doll. Fatima Mawzi," he said.

The salesperson lost interest. "In the back room," she said, with so little concern that Jimper wondered just how many times that particular transaction had taken place. And then he was at the end of the long, narrow store, and in the back room—with a real door this time, with a real lock—and there was Doll, inhaling deeply on a water pipe, and looking up at him through the hashish fumes, and wearing no clothes at all.

The business of magic, real magic, no tricks, must not have been all that profitable; the back room was set up for exactly what Doll had chosen it for, and how she

251

had come to know about it Jimper never asked. The technology of the room fascinated him. Handheld TV cameras that let you watch on a large screen what was going on in parts of your bodies inaccessible to the eyes. Gadgets that shuddered and gadgets that pulsed. Electronic gadgets that overrode the flagging hormones when the body was ready to quit but the brain wanted more. Beds that moved, and harnesses that made a bed unnecessary. Liqueurs. Scents. Tapes of herculean performances, even of your own if you chose to save them. The first four times Jimper and Doll visited the room he was kept so occupied they never had a chance to talk at all; and even afterward Doll was not conversational. Her stolen moments for Jimper were scant and scarce, and she did not want to waste them on blab. Her time in New York was limited, she told him. Quite soon she would be sent back to Edinburgh to marry the boy next door. "What kind of a man is he?" Jimper asked, lying on the bed that still quivered from their exercises. Doll pulled the robes over her head and looked at him.

"A man. Very strict. Very religious. Very likely to refuse to marry me if he finds out what I do in New York. And also very, very rich."

The veil was the hardest to put on, but it completed the ensemble and made Doll just one more strictly religious Moslem woman in a Moslem neighborhood. "Doll?" he asked. "Won't he expect you to be a virgin, like?"

"Not in front," she said, studying herself in the mirror, and moving toward the door. "And the room rent runs out in ten minutes, Jimper, so get your ass in gear, will you? I'm off to the Fair."

Doll was never in the drafting offices any more, so Jimper went against the good advice of the parole clerk and volunteered for guarding the Fair site. It was nearing the time to open. The great Rainbow Bridge stretched clear across the park now and teams of engineers making stress tests were crawling along it every day. The main pavilions were completed now, Iceland with its foamed lava structures and artificial geysers, the Saudis with their fake Red Sea beach in miniature, and tiny icebergs being towed to it across the Fair's central lake. The fast-food stands and novelty booths were hauled in and set up, and the concession-aires squabbled about their locations and complained about the weather. The dome took most of the risk out of rain, shine or gloom, but it was not any help at all when dust clouds filled the skies and at noon the sky was dark. "Dark day, no pay," a taco seller informed Jimper despairingly, as he hesitated over how much corn flour to order. "If it doan get bright, we doan get no sales."

"It's bound to get better," Jimper reassured him, out of no knowledge at all, because Atlanta was not usually in the dust storm track. He smiled benignly, adjusted the angle of his red beret and moved on to admire his costumes at the British pavilion.

As the staff began to practice their tasks in dress rehearsals, Jimper watched when he could be there, and smugly acknowledged that the designs were good. The kilts hung smartly and moved well with the wearer; the Union Jack blouses made the most of whatever the women inside them had. He had picked up what might almost be called a clientele. When his sentence was served, when the Fair was over, when these temporary interruptions in his career had run their course, then, he was quite sure, he would become one of the reliable, successful designers of the city, and he was already shopping around for a good location for his boutique. Things were going well enough, he realized compla-cently.

With one exception.

As he caught sight of Doll's back and moved toward her he discovered she was staring up at the sky, and observed the exception. High over the park a dragonfly skimmed and soared. A hanger. Hard to make out in the dusky afternoon, but clearly an expert who was taking advantage of every thermal and every breeze. "Go it, old soul," Jimper muttered, yearning toward the glider above, and Doll gave him a quick glance.

"I wish I were there," she announced.

He took his eyes off the glider for a moment, caught by surprise. "I didn't know you were a jumper."

She shrugged, and didn't answer. From behind Jimper her father answered for her. "Fatima has done such things, yes," he rumbled heavily. "But now that she is of age to marry it is no longer suitable." Jimper smiled, excused himself and drifted away, watching the hang-glider as long as he could and praying for the safety of his landing when the figure was out of sight.

He had an idea.

There was very little that could be done between two consenting persons that he and Doll had not already done, in that little room behind DOOR; but there was one experience they had never shared. It was silly. It was dangerous.

It was wholly and completely desired.

From his tiny apartment in the East Village to the New Gotham Tower East was only a short ride on a hydrovan, and all the way Jimper was staring at the dome. It was dark, though the time was high noon. When he got to the little room behind DOOR Doll was there before him, already undressed, the hookah going and the smell of hash powerful in the tiny room. "What's the matter with you, Jimper?" she asked, passing him the mouthpiece. He took a deep drag before replying.

"The Mid-Day Dark," he said.

"Brings you down, does it? Take another hit," she commanded, "and we'll see if we can bring you up again."

And of course they could, at least physically they could. But while Jimper's body was active in one area, his head was turning over the Mid-Day Dark. If the Earth was warming up, as they said it was, why were the farmers constantly nagging with their petty complaints of cold? Look at the lousy stuff in the super-suq. Lettuce brown around the edges, potatoes that you damn well knew were going to be all black or holey inside, limp carrots. And if you complained to the checkout clerk all she said was it's the weather.

And the weather was supposed to be getting warmer!

Jimper had followed the documentaries about it well enough. The atmosphere was a heat engine. The more heat you poured into it, the more violence it produced. Heat engines do not work on temperature but on *differences* between temperatures; that was what they called "Carnot's laws." If you piled seventy-five multi-megawatt powerplants and fifteen million gas-burning vehicles into one slice of a state in the west, such as California, and left two or three states a few hundred miles away pretty much alone, such as Nevada and Utah, a temperature differential was built up. Air would not accept that. Air wanted to be the perfect democracy, every molecule bounding around at the same velocity as every other. That was entropy. Air scooped up heat from Malibu and transported it to Salt Lake, and on the way it blew the roof off your house, if you happened to live in the way. Then it roared across the plains, and lifted the topsoil into the sky to float over Kansas and Connecticut. Or New York. Or else it muscled its way through Canada, where it dropped its water and dried out as cold as a Platonic hell, and slid down into Arkansas and Mississippi and froze the revelers at the Mardi Gras. Meanwhile Fairbanks thawed and Honolulu sweat, but that didn't help the farmers in the Midwest. The food-growing states were chilled and windy. The growing season was short. And tens of millions of tons of their topsoil came east to visit, and made the Mid-Day Dark. It floated over their heads, borne on the breezes, rising with the thermals.

"We can do it if you want to," said Doll.

Jimper came back to the room with a start. He gazed up at her. "What?" he managed to say.

She was standing, rubbing her spine and looking at him. "You were talking about flying," she said.

Jimper nodded, trying to fasten himself to the moments that were fleeting past. It was not easy. He had had quite a lot to smoke, he realized.

"I think my back will take it," she said.

He nodded agreeably, although he did not have the faintest idea what she was talking about. Or what he had been talking about, either. Something about her back? Doll was short, vivacious, tiny, but her breast development was impressive and she was already complaining about back aches. Had they been trying something particularly hard on her back? He couldn't remember.

"Anyway," she said, "I've got wings stashed away, and my friend told me where there's a good window. Only thing wrong, you've got to jump out blind. But it's a sheer fall, and good winds."

"Oh, yeah," he said, nodding as though he understood.

"So get dressed," said Doll, "because the old man's away all afternoon, and we'll never get another chance like this."

It occurred to Jimper that he was doing a lot of nodding but, as he could think of no more cogent contribution to make to the dialogue, he continued to do so, all the while Doll was getting into her own clothes and driving him into his.

It had been a lot of hash. Jimper was in that biddable state where everything looked like a good idea, especially if all he had to do was say yes to it. Unfortunately Doll wanted more than a yes. She wanted him to move. She was in that other stage where everything that looked like a good idea had to be done right away, and right away was when they did it all: clothes on, out of the room, down an elevator, across a flying bridge, up another elevator—Jimper might have stayed in that second elevator forever, gazing at the pretty patterns the floor buttons made, if Doll had not dashed back in to collect him just as the doors were about to close. It wasn't until he was actually belting into the rented hang-glider that he began to break through the hashish fog. "I don't know if this is a good idea, Doll," he said; but his fingers were checking the buckles, touching the wings, looking for frays and loose fittings—old wings but well kept; there were none.

"Come on," she said, tugging him toward a great wide window. Strange that so obvious a jumpoff had not been spiked long since, he reflected, and said, "It seems kind of dangerous to me—"

About that he was right. He knew it at once, as soon as hand in hand they leaped, and he heard the funny slithering rattle and saw something spring up before them, and felt the buffered jar, and realized they were in a net. They hung there for ten minutes, bagged like bunnies in a trap, before three grinning regular-force policemen hauled them in.

"You, young lady," said the judge, "are paroled in custody of your father, and if I see you here again it will go hard with you. And as to you—"

He looked down over the bench at Jimper, and you could almost hear the workings of the judicial brain as it clanked toward a sentence. "Recidivist," he said. "Second offense. No extenuation. Ninety days or fifteen thousand dollars, next case."

V

Recidivists didn't have it as easy as first offenders. Their opportunities to volunteer for easy jobs were limited; they went where they were sent, and they had other penalties first offenders were spared. One of them was in the building marked *Municipal Hospital— Emergency Clinic & Rehabilitation*. And there Jimper waited more than two hours for his turn.

It was the man ahead of him who took up most of the time, because he wanted to talk, and, Jimper thought, appalled, had certainly a lot to talk about. "After I put my, you know, my hand on her," the man was saying, "she told me, she like told me she was scared."

"Scared of you?" the counselor asked, looking down to make notes to show that he was following the story.

"She was scared her mother would find out. But I didn't stop." But he did stop there, for a moment; he stopped and wet his lips and looked out toward Jimper, on the far side of the file cabinets that were all the counselor's office had for a wall. Jimper tried to look as though he hadn't been listening, though every convict in the waiting room was obviously intent.

The little man made eye contact with every one of them before turning back to the counselor. "I didn't stop," he repeated, wiping his lips against the back of his wrist. "Then, when I had her panties off, I—Like, I—Like I took the, uh, the thing—"

"The butcher knife, yes," the counselor prompted.

"Yes, I took the butcher knife, and I stuck it in—I like, stuck it into her—"

"You penetrated her sexual area with it," the counselor finished for him. "I see, but there's one thing that puzzles me, Willy."

"What's that?" the little man asked eagerly.

"Weren't you aware that that would hurt her? Maybe even kill her?"

"Oh, sure," the little man agreed.

"But you said you loved her, this five-year-old girl."

"Well, I couldn't do the other thing. She was only five," Willy explained virtuously.

"I see." The counselor made a note on his memo plate. He thought for a moment, then leaned forward benignly. "You do know this is all a fantasy, don't you, Willy?" he asked.

Willy's expression clouded. "Oh, hell, sure I know that," he mumbled.

"Because before your interview I called her mother to make sure. Sally is quite all right."

"I know that! It's just that the judge told me I had to come and talk to you when I—When I get these kind of ideas—"

"Of course," the counselor beamed. "You've been very good about that, Willy, and I appreciate it. Is there anything else on your mind?"

The little man hitched around in the chair for a moment as though he were about to get up, but didn't.

"Yes, Willy?" the counselor encouraged.

"Well—Don't I have to get punished?" Willy pleaded.

"Ah!" The counselor shook his head in self-reproof. "I almost forgot! Thank you for reminding me, Willy. Let's see, I would say that calls for a fine—say, twenty-five cents. Now, you'd better pay that up right away!"

The man reached gratefully into his pocket, and on his way out he beamed at Jimper, the next in line. "That's one great doctor," he confided.

The one great doctor was mournfully dropping the quarter into a large jar. By the sound of the falling coin, it had a good deal of company inside. "Name?" he said without looking up, and when Jimper responded he sighed and tapped out the name on his memo plate. "What's your problem?" he asked, waiting for the data file to come up.

"I don't have a problem. All I have is two convictions for hang-gliding inside the dome."

For the first time the doctor showed interest. "No murder fantasies? No acting out antisocial impulses?"

"No nothing, including a decent lawyer," Jimper groused.

The doctor studied his face more carefully. "You think you got an unfair trial? You want to take it to the Supreme Court, maybe?"

"Doctor," said Jimper, "I don't even have *that* fantasy."

The doctor shrugged. "Heaven knows where the Supreme Court is, anyway—Houston, last I heard." He scowled at his memo plate. "What's the matter with this thing? Did I spell your name wrong?" Scowling, he reached to key the name in again, and then drew his hands back, his expression scandalized. "Oh, *God,*" he moaned, "that's the last straw. First case I get all day that isn't some kind of wacko, and somebody else steals him away."

"Steals me?" Jimper asked.

"Volunteered to take you off my list," the counselor said bitterly. "I should have known! Always look a gift horse in the mouth, right? And she's such a sweet little thing—"

Jimper said, "Look, friend. I was told to report here for counseling, because that's the way the law is for second offenders. Outside of that I'm not interested in your problems. Counsel me and get it over with, will you?"

"If only it were that easy!" The counselor shook his head mournfully. "Your new doctor, in the next office. Name's on the door, Dr. J. Redfan. Move along, please. Next!"

J. Redfan. The name was familiar, in a sort of way, but it wasn't until he had worked his way up the second line—mercifully shorter—and was allowed into the office that he attached the name to the face. "Hello, Jimper," said Jo-Ellen Redfan. "I was wondering when you'd show up."

He sat down, feeling suddenly relaxed. "This I didn't expect," he admitted. "I thought you were in private practice."

"When you're working off a conviction," she said, "you do whatever you have to do. Listen. The reason I took your case on, I understand you're a painter, right?"

"Well—I wish I were, anyway. Actually I'm a fabric designer mostly. Not enough talent to get into the Met, I'm afraid."

"But you do know how to paint?"

"Well, sure—" But she wasn't listening. She was dialing the phone, and spoke into it as soon as it answered.

"Hello, Willy? I'm bringing company home for dinner, so go out on the balcony and catch us about a dozen big ones and I'll make chirpy chili. See you in about half an hour."

"Chirpy chili?" Jimper asked, baffled.

"I'm taking you home for dinner," she explained. "There's no problem. You're a recidivist so you need some therapy, right? The best therapy is work therapy —and, Jimper, have I got a painting job for you!"

Home for Jo-Ellen Redfan was a really nice apartment, high up in the twenties, three big rooms and a wide balcony. It was what they called a Canadian co-op, meaning that she paid a quarter of her income for the apartment and it was hers forever. Or until she stopped paying, or decided to move away. "But I won't do that," she explained, putting water on the stove to simmer, "because they gave us the apartment in the first place when there were two earners in the family, and now with just me it's a real bargain. Will! I'm ready to blanch!"

The bedroom door opened and Will peered out. He was holding a keyboard in his hand and had all the look of a young man doing his homework. "They're on the balcony, Jo."

"So bring them in from the balcony!"

The boy sighed, set down the keyboard and marched through the living room, past the kitchen and out on the balcony. Jimper wandered after him, admiring the view and listening to the cricket song that came from the cage at one end of the terrace. A smaller cage was near it; the boy picked it up, delivered it to his mother with an aggrieved air and said, "Now can I finish my algebra?"

"Go," said Jo-Ellen, cautiously opening the top of

the little cage. One by one she fished the lively crickets out and dropped them into the boiling water for a moment, then took the pot off the stove, drained the contents and began to shell their dinner. "So you got caught by the old net trick," she said over her shoulder. "Don't feel too bad. Every farmer gets caught once. When you open the window it cocks the net and rings an alarm."

"I didn't pick the place," Jimper said defensively, looking for something he could do to help. But Jo-Ellen seemed to have dinner under control; there was a pot of onions, beans and tomatoes already beginning to heat up, and as she shelled and diced the cricket meat she dropped it in.

"What happened to your little friend?"

"Her father sent her home," said Jimper. "I think she's getting married over there." He had lost something, but he didn't feel particularly bad about it; he seemed to be gaining something else, if the indications were trustworthy, and this something had her own apartment. Well, almost her own. But the kid probably went to sleep early?

"Pity," said Jo-Ellen. "Listen, do you know how to pick palm hearts?"

"I'm afraid not, Jo-Ellen."

"You farmers! Well, come along and I'll show you."

Jo-Ellen Redfan was quite a farmer herself, Jimper decided, and enviously studied her home. The balcony turned out to be a cornucopia of food far better than anything you could buy in the supersuqs. Coppiced palms yielded their tender hearts, along with tender young lettuce to make a salad to go with the chili. For dessert there were papayas, picked ripe and put in the freezer for a moment to chill them; for the table, there were flowers from the borders around the balcony. The important thing, she told him, was to get a balcony with southern exposure and a low railing, so that the sun could get at the crops even in winter—and, of course, to plant the varieties that would thrive under the diffuse glow that came through the dome. There was wine with the meal and thick, sweet coffee out of a copper pot after it; but then the time for relaxation was over. The time for the painting job had begun.

The painting job was the kitchen. "See, Jimper," said Jo-Ellen, putting away dishes and swabbing the wall where the water vapor from the hydrogen stove had dampened it, "we're not quite tall enough. You're *nice* and tall. Will? Where's the drop cloth? Jimper, go give him a hand, will you?"

Jimper went willingly enough. An hour or so of painting a kitchen was not a bad tradeoff for a good meal, not to mention the prospective fringe benefits. His calculating eye could not, however, figure out just where the fringe benefits were likely to be found. There was only one bedroom with two beds in it—one obviously apiece for the two occupants of the apartment. There was no other bed in the place. Not even a couch; the living room had only chairs, and most of them simple uprights. The third room was fitted up as a sort of a doctor's office—evidently Jo-Ellen practiced at home sometimes—and it did have a sort of examination pallet, yes. But nothing that one could very well share. The balcony? But surely you would crush the plants. It was a puzzle—but, Jimper was confident, Jo-Ellen would have solved that puzzle before, in spite of all the things she had said. It would be interesting to see how she worked it, but that it would work some way or another Jimper had very little doubt. No woman invites a man to paint her kitchen without further plans for the evening.

With the three of them at work the job went fast, Jo-Ellen moving the drop cloths around as Jimper moved with the spray cans, Will shaking them to have them ready as the old ones wore out and catching little misaimed spatters where they didn't belong. With the skies still shaded from the remnants of the dust storm Jimper lost time, and was surprised when, as soon as the last cloth was picked up and the painting equipment stowed away, Jo-Ellen said, "Good lord, Will, it's past your bedtime. I hope you finished your homework."

"I'll finish in the morning," the boy promised, yawning. "Good night, Jo. Good night, Jimper." And Jo-Ellen brought out the last of the wine and a couple of joints, and when the boy had finished in the bathroom and closed the bedroom door behind him, she leaned back as far as she could in the straight-backed chair, lit up, passed the cigarette to Jimper and said:

"Listen. This is a little embarrassing."

"What is, honey?" he asked.

"Well, calling me honey is, for one thing. Remember, I told you I don't date."

It was the very worst of bad manners to scowl and sulk when a woman let you know she wasn't interested, and Jimper had always tried to be polite. So he maintained the smile as he inhaled the joint, but when he spoke his voice was less friendly than he had planned. "It's your decision, Jo-Ellen," he said.

She sighed in exasperation. "Look, it's not you. You're not a bad guy. You might even be a really nice one. And it isn't a moral question, and I'm not in love with anybody else, and I don't have a communicable disease."

"Then—"

"What I do have," she said bitterly, "is an ex-husband."

It was also bad manners to look as though the person you were talking to had just said something incredibly stupid, but Jimper couldn't help himself. Half the people he knew had ex-husbands, or ex-wives, if not indeed current ones who were not working at it. He said something of the sort, and Jo-Ellen shook her head.

"Not like Dinny. He didn't want the divorce, Jimper, and he's never accepted it. He follows me around. Half the time when I go out I see him hanging around the elevators. He's got field glasses, and he found some landings in the buildings across the square where he can see right into this apartment; and if I pull the drapes I start getting phone calls where there's nobody on the other end when I pick up. And—" she frowned in embarrassment—"the bad part, Jimper, is that if I actually get, uh, involved with somebody else, he beats them up."

It was not the best news Jimper had ever heard, not to mention that it was hard to believe. He could not help darting a quick look at the open drapes and the lighted windows beyond them.

"But tonight he's in Chicago," Jo-Ellen observed.

Jimper reached for the joint and started to relax.

"But I never know whether or not he's got somebody else watching when he isn't around," she finished, and then laughed. "Look at you! You're all relaxed and ready, then you tighten up, arms across your chest and knees together, then you close up, then you open again—"

"Jo-Ellen," said Jimper, beginning to feel the effects of the joint, "what do you want from me? Is this how you get your kicks, some kind of game?"

"No! I'm just telling you what the score is."

"Like a tennis match, right? First the ball's in this court and then in that and I'm running back and forth to try to stay in the game?"

"I didn't mean it that way, exactly. I guess all those psych courses show up—I get interested in watching how people react to stimuli—"

"Speaking of psych," he went on savagely, "how would you diagnose a grown woman who shares a bedroom with a ten-year-old son? Do you have any idea what you're doing to his chances of maturation?"

She laughed. "Funny," she declared. "Every man who comes up here tells me I'm screwing up Will's sexuality, when actually it's their own they're worried about."

"And what are you worried about, Jo-Ellen?"

She stubbed out the half-smoked joint and confronted him. "I'm worried about my ex-husband! I'm worried that he's going to beat somebody else up, and I'll be in the middle of it again, and I'll get another conviction for public disorder. I'm worried that Will's going to grow up terribly bent, not because his mother sleeps in the same room with him but because his father makes him a spy! Look at this place! I've taken out everything that might encourage a man to start fooling around—and even so, Dinny says there are all those pillows and how does he know what I do with them on the floor? And— And— Oh, *shit*," she said, and began to cry.

Jimper stood up, hazy from the dope, keyed up from the talk, his reflexes confused. What he wanted to do was either to take her in his arms and comfort her or walk out and never see her again.

It wasn't until he found himself actually drawing those heavy drapes that he realized he had opted for course number one, and then things went along without further planning. The examination table wasn't necessary. The pillows were just fine. It was all just fine, as a matter of fact, with just the one little nagging worry, and so it was not until, hours later, he was leaving the building and glancing around for lurking figures, and finding none, that he was convinced that Dinny the Ex-Husband had indeed been in Chicago that night.

Ninety days' work equivalent wasn't all the punishment Jimper suffered. There was a penalty beyond the legal one, and that was the terrible wrath of old Mr. Mawzi. Mawzi Frères was no longer interested in employing the despoiler of Mawzi's daughter, and the bills he presented for work already done got somehow stuck in the accounting department. Worse. The other prospective customers Mawzi had turned him onto had got the word. He wasn't received with cordiality any more. Usually he wasn't received at all.

So the ninety days' sentence was a boon, for he got paid for the work he did. Minimum wage, to be sure.

But minimum wage was a lot more than zero, which is what he was getting from all other sources. The way he had to earn that minimum wage, though, was something else again. They put him where they needed him each day, and they needed him in places where he did not much want to go. Graffiti cleaning, which meant climbing the balconies and trellises of high-rise buildings to scrub off someone's spray-painting. (The longest and hardest was fifty stories up under the lower dome, where someone had managed to decorate what was left of the World Trade Center with the three-meter-high legend *Don't Deface Our City!*) Compliance inspection—touring a hundred businesses and residences a day in a particular volume of the city to check on whether they were observing safety regulations, sanitation, maintenance of public services and all the other things they were required to do. "Pied pipering," which turned out to be distributing high-frequency sound generators in rat-infested sections. Well, all the sections were rat-infested, more or less—every city always was—but although the Pied Pipers couldn't win the war against rats they could cause them to blunder around, disoriented, so that they could be trapped, poisoned or clubbed fairly successfully. Jimper didn't mind laying out the sound generators, or helping evacuate invalids, pets and children from the areas about to be pipered; clubbing the clumsy, ugly creatures when the generators had destroyed their normal caution, however, was the worst job the authorities gave him. Almost the worst. "Lift maintenance" was at least as bad. That didn't mean anything to do with the machinery of the elevators itself—only specialists did that. It meant getting down into the pits to clean out the refuse that collected there, while the huge cages swooped down at the work crews, popping their ears with pressure and scaring them half to death—they always *had* stopped in time, but would they always continue to?

On the other hand, he had Jo-Ellen. Sort of had

Jo-Ellen, or at least almost had Jo-Ellen—would have had her if it hadn't been for the Jealous Ex-Husband. Dinny did not make any further trips to Chicago, and Jo-Ellen flatly refused Jimper entry to her apartment while Dinny was in town.

It took Jimper a week to figure out what to do about all that, and so he counted up his money, decided he had enough and made a trip to the 83d level of the New Gotham Tower. It cost more than he expected to reserve the little room for two hours.

But it was worth it. It was well worth it, he decided, drowsily relighting the hookah when Jo-Ellen and he had worked off the most urgent of their pent-up needs. He smiled fondly at her as he passed the mouthpiece over.

But she refused it. "Jimper," she said, "this is all pretty nice, even if a little weird—"

"Did they try to sell you graveyard dust?" he chuckled.

"—but do you understand that what I told you is *real?*"

"What's real, doe-deer?" he asked comfortably.

"Dinny's real, Jimper. It's all right this time—I *think* it's all right—anyway, I was careful about coming here, and I'm pretty sure I wasn't followed. But if we keep coming here, sooner or later he'll catch us."

"So we'll go somewhere else. It's a big city."

Jo-Ellen sighed and nuzzled closer to him for a moment. They were lying flesh to flesh, both of them with skins still damp and sticky, and Jimper felt no urgencies or apprehensions at all. But then Jo-Ellen stirred and got to her feet. "I have to show you a poem," she said, rummaging in her shoulder bag.

"A poem?"

"A poem that Dinny wrote," she said firmly, and handed him a bound sheaf of creamy white paper, each page with two neatly calligraphed lines on it. Aw, hell, thought Jimper, what does she want to show me somebody else's love poetry for?

But it wasn't exactly love poetry. The first page read in its entirety:

A's for an Axiom that's easy to see:
If you put out for him, you put out for me.

"What the hell is this?" he demanded.
"Read on," she ordered.

B's for the Bargain that follows on A.
If you don't keep it, sweetie, I blow him away.

C's for that Cute little rascal of ten.
Call for a cop and you won't see him again.

"My God," Jimper breathed, "the man's a psychopath!" He riffled through the rest of the alphabet. All the pages were the same—no, not true; some were worse than others! "What's this about forcing you to realize there's no such thing as divorce?"

"He says he didn't agree to it, so it's not binding on him. I mean," she clarified, "as far as Dinny is concerned, we're still conjugal. You know? He says he won't stop me from making love. Only every time I do it with someone else I have to do it with him, too, he says."

"You— Uh, you—"

"But I don't want to do that, Jimper! So— Well," she said, looking away, "I had this idea that maybe I could do it with somebody I didn't like very much. You know? So I wouldn't mind if Dinny creamed him."

Jimper swallowed. Then he swallowed again, words this time, because all the things that occurred to him to say were things he didn't want to say.

"I know," said Jo-Ellen grimly. "That's why I tried to warn you. He's put two men in the hospital already."

Two men! So (Jimper calculated swiftly) those were two he *caught;* and tried to estimate (a) Jo-Ellen's total score and (b) his own prospects of getting put away. "The best part of our relationship," said Jo-Ellen—"I mean, the *safest* part, is I don't think he's ever seen you with me. So if I'm really careful—and you're, anyway, a little bit careful—"

"Yeah," said Jimper. He remembered to drag on the hookah, but the hash had burned itself out and all he got was a stale, sour taste—no staler or more sour than his mouth had registered already. Two men in the hospital. A wacko ex-husband. He riffled through the bound couplets. "It's lousy poetry, too," he complained grimly, and only then realized that next to him on the waterbed Jo-Ellen was crying.

Well, that put a whole different face on the matter. Jimper was of that class of males who melt. There were surely wrongs that could not be forgiven for tears, and impediments that tears would not wash away—but not many of either. The only thing he could possibly do at that moment was comfort her; and then, of course, one thing led to another. When they were at rest again he said earnestly—having thought the matter out with one part of his mind, while the rest of him was fully engaged elsewhere—"You ought to go to the police, love-love."

"You saw what he said! Anyway," she said, "I already talked it over with a lawyer. I can't prove he wrote this—it isn't his handwriting, he had somebody else letter it for him, *he* didn't give it to me. I just found it on my desk one day."

"But still—"

"But still, he's Will's father. Oh, I'm stuck, Jimper. I wouldn't blame you if you cut out right now and never saw me again!"

And of course, when she said that it made what had until then seemed a reasonable option quite impossible. "Not a chance!" he said staunchly. "But I just can't imagine what sort of man would do this."

She hesitated, then sprang from the bed, slim bare back a pretty arm's-length away while she rummaged again in her bag. When she turned around it was to hand him a framed picture. "I borrowed this from Will's room," she said, "because I thought you might want to see what he looked like. But he's bigger than he looks in the picture."

"I know," groaned Jimper, looking at the face of the man who had bought him a beer around the corner from Jo-Ellen's home.

That night, as Jimper crossed a street open to the dome on his way to bed, a startling flicker of ruddy light made him look up. The great overhead dome was flashing dull red. It was a warning. The next day there would be a radon flush. So when he reported in the morning for his work assignment, he was not surprised to be sent to the Fair grounds to batten down all that was loose in the construction sites.

There was plenty to do, and hard work doing it. Jimper was glad enough to do it—roping down unsecured roofs, chasing flyaway bits of lightweight plastic, shoring up temporary walls. With no hang-gliding allowed he wasn't getting enough physical exercise, and he welcomed the sweat. There was plenty of it, for the dome controllers picked warm, still days to open the vents and replace all the air inside the structure, so that the slow accumulation of radon gas could be vented. In half an hour he was drenched, and so was the rest of the work crew. They took a break and lay back, muscles sore, between his two favorite exhibits. The lavish affair of cement troughs on one side was for Saudi Arabia; when it was done the troughs would be filled with water, and one-tenth-size icebergs would glide along them, towed by toy tugs, to supply cooling water for air-conditioning and drinking and irrigation water for everyone. The Iceland pavilion, on the other side, was foamed lava structures, showing how they built windbreakers to create microclimates, warmed by hot springs, and so Reykjavik now called itself "the Waikiki of the Atlantic."

Overhead the cables of the new Rainbow Bridge

271

were singing slowly in the gentle updraft toward the vents. When it was done the cables would be invisible within the balloon-like fabric that people could walk on—that great floats would roll along, and vehicles would use for a hundred years after the Fair was over. The key to the bridge's stability was dynamic strengtheners—"turgidifiers," the individual cells were called; when the sensors detected too much sway or an off-balance load, fluid under pressure would stiffen the cells where they were needed. Around the cables three ultra-light flyers were buzzing, stopping their motors to glide when they could, starting them again when they needed to change direction or gain altitude. Jimper gazed at them with what he intended to be humorous disdain but that turned into, he realized, longing. Stinkpots of the air, sure—but they were *in* the air! If only he could get a job doing what they were doing—

The construction foreman was a huge man, middle-aged, who looked at Jimper as though he were out of his mind. "What do you want to fly around in one of those things for?" he demanded; and then, discovering that Jimper's sentence was for hang-gliding, merely shook his head in incomprehension. "It's not my department anyway. I stick close to the ground."

"Well, Mr. Bratislaw, is there any chance of another job around the Fair? I'm a good designer—"

"Not while you're a work-off," Bratislaw said, kindly enough. "Why should we put you on the payroll when we can get you for minimum wage?"

But he promised to keep Jimper in mind if anything turned up, and that was the closest Jimper had come to a friendly reception since getting in the bad graces of the influential Mr. Mawzi.

So when, over the next weeks, he could get himself assigned to the rapidly completing Fair, Jimper seized the chance. Twice he was set to pied-pipering, since the Fair administration was determined to keep the grounds a rat-free zone. Once he managed to get himself put to work in the motor pool. He knew too little to work on the engines of the smaller cars—electric for the buggies, low-temperature Stirling engines, burning only alcohol, for the small trucks. But the big tour buses were momentum propelled, with wide, dense flywheels, and needed little work except to be washed and swamped out after every trip.

And, of course, there was Jo-Ellen. She agreed, reluctantly, to one more visit to DOOR—after that she positively refused. It was too risky—especially now that Jimper had admitted the Jealous Ex-Husband did in fact know who he was. That removed one impediment, anyway. There was no longer any reason why they could not be seen together in public—in the most aseptic and generally temptation-free public places there were. So sometimes they rode together on the vans, or lunched in a busy terrace restaurant, or walked, in broad daylight, down by the waterside or along one of the open skywalks. But they always, and conspicuously, departed in quite different directions after these meetings. More intimate dates required great care and forethought. Now and then there was a lucky break, as when Jo-Ellen was sent to check out radiation levels in the Nathanael Greene Mushroom Farms across the river, and they had more than an hour to themselves, alone and in the dark, in the soft ammoniac air of the caverns.

And then there was a whisper of a possible job in a fabric plant in New Jersey, and at that same time Dinny elected to take the boy overnight. A whole night together! So Jo-Ellen made an excuse to take the bullet-train to Philadelphia, to come back less openly by way of Atlantic City and the coastal hydrofoils; and Jimper took the more conventional hovercraft to Sandy Hook.

As the nineteenth century Germans learned to make the most colorful dyes out of stinking coal tar, so some of New York's most beautiful fabrics came out of the city's sewage. So did some of their food.

All that was used was the liquid effluent, and the problem was halved at the outset by keeping industrial pollutants out. No crank-case oil poured into a gas-station sump. No PCBs or acid wastes; no heavy metals, no dyes, no pesticides. The liquids that came out of New York's sewers were ninety-nine point nine per cent pure shit, piss and corruption. In the recycling tanks it bubbled and stank, and the algae loved it. It made them fat. Each citizen's bowels reliably manufactured several hundred grams of fecal solid each day, which equaled almost as much algal protein in the settling tanks, which equaled the daily ration of *Spirulina* algae for a chicken, a small rabbit or about one-twentieth of a hog. It wasn't the lack of fecal solids that kept the Sandy Hook plant from producing more food. It was the lack of space to keep its flocks.

So not all the effluent went to food; and that was why Jimper was there. "They're just starting to make fabrics," he explained to Jo-Ellen when he met her at the hydrofoil dock. "It's a brand-new field, and I can get in at the bottom of it." He noticed that she was turning her head from side to side, and made a guess at what was the matter. "There's no chance Dinny could have followed us here," he reassured her.

"Oh, never say that, Jimper," she protested. "But that's not it. I was wondering why I don't smell anything."

"Because it's a nice clean plant," he said with pride. "Here, up this road they've got some tourist cabins. I've already checked us in. My appointment's in half an hour so there's no time for, uh—"

She didn't respond, only looked around the cabin curiously, excused herself to use the bathroom for a moment and came out looking rather glum. Well, they weren't the grandest accommodations in the world—but a lot better than, say, the aisles in the mushroom farm! "Come with me," he suggested, to cheer her up. "It's interesting."

"I don't want to mess up your interview—"

"It'll be all right. Mr. Bermutter seemed like a nice guy over the phone—here, you take the scanner while I sort out my samples—"

Bermutter was a nice guy—young, fair-haired, full of confidence about the future of sewage fabrics, enthusiastic about the quality of Jimper's designs. "Nice colors," he said, switching from one shot to another quickly enough to keep it from being tedious, slowly enough to convince the creator of the designs that he was really looking at them. "What do you think of my shirt?"

He extended one arm so they could feel the sleeve. "It looks like what I wear in the operating room," said Jo-Ellen.

"Very acute! This is one of the first batch we were able to sell—nurses' uniforms. Are you a nurse?"

"A doctor, actually," smiled Jo-Ellen. "Can you make the fabric in different colors?"

"Well, that's what we've got you here for," he said, nodding affably to Jimper. "The only thing is, it's a little early for us to be designing actual garments; we were thinking more of meter goods. Still— Let me show you how we do it!"

And he led the way out of the office section into a long, low shed. There was a sound of moving liquids, but all concealed inside pipes, most of them opaque. The smell was not bad, only surprising, rather like a hotel room you've stayed in too long. Bermutter lifted a hatch and plunged his arm into the pipe, pulling out what looked like a string of gelatinous seaweed. "This is the stuff. We dry it and spin it, and it comes out like my shirt. It'll wear forever. Very light. Very strong. The weave we're using is a little too fine, I think, so you can't sweat through it and it feels a little clammy in hot weather."

"We never have hot weather under the dome," Jo-Ellen pointed out. He grinned a little apologetically.

"Even in fairly warm weather, I'm afraid. Still—that's something we can fix." They let him explain the process. Bacteria, he said, wore sort of little suits of armor to protect them against phage viruses. The "armor" substances were called polysaccharides; they appeared in envelopes of what he called hydrated gel. You could get the bacteria to grow any sort of polysaccharides you wanted—insect-shell chitin, collagen, whatever. Some bacteria were better at doing the trick than others. They had started with what he called klebsiella, switched to something called Acetobacter mylinum—they still used some of those, which were what made the rotten-fruit smell Jimper had noticed. "Here," he said, pulling the shirt over his head. "Feel it."

Nice texture, nice drape, nice "hand"—"I'd love to work with this stuff," said Jimper enthusiastically.

"Well," said Bermutter, leading the way back to his office, "I hope you'll get the chance. Not right away, I'm afraid. We've got to straighten out the weave and a few other things—"

"When do you think there might be an opening, then?" asked Jimper.

"It's hard to say. I do like your work, though—on the other hand, Dr. Redfan, we're going to need a house medic when we get into full production, and probably we should hire the medic soon to help with planning. So if you're interested—"

So all in all it was not the best tryst Jimper had ever heard of. He didn't get the job, though Jo-Ellen got a firm offer. When they got back to the cabin she explained to him that, unfortunately, she seemed to have started her period that morning. And as they checked out the next morning, Jimper's card in the machine produced not only the printout of a bill but a message on the screen. "Funny," said the clerk, reading it. "Looks like you got a call from somebody named

Dennis Redfan, but he didn't want to be put through to your cabin, just to leave a message."

"Oh, my God," said Jo-Ellen; and Jimper said: "What was the message?"

"Well, that's funny, too. All he said was, 'Hi.'"

For the next couple of days Jimper worried uninterruptedly because Dinny might at any minute show up and bash his brains out.

Dinny did not appear; so for the next few days Jimper worried even more, in a quite different way, because Dinny did not. Now that All appeared to be Known, there was no particular reason why they should not be seen together even quite often—in public places. In Jimper's opinion, there wasn't much reason to avoid being seen quite privately, for that matter, but he was unable to convince Jo-Ellen of that. "It just isn't worth it," she said, stabbing Jimper to the heart, "and I don't want to take the consequences"—stabbing him again, in a different place.

"If he wants to take it out on me, let him try," he growled. Jo-Ellen shrugged. "As to the other thing, I certainly don't want you to be—"

"Now, hold it right there," she commanded. She was wet and irritable, having been drafted to give emergency medical services in a 55th-floor apartment fire. The fire had been put out easily enough—every structure had its built-in sprinkler systems, with plenty of water in the rooftop swimming pools—but she had had to give resuscitation to three smoke victims, sloshing around a swampy apartment. "You don't have any rights in me, Jimper!"

"Of course I don't," he acknowledged sulkily. "But I would think that as a matter of keeping your self-respect—"

"*Jimper.*"

"I was only trying to say—"

"Soak it, Jimper!" She waved the fork one more time

at the almost untouched salad, then put it down. "This was a mistake. I'm tired, I'm dirty, I don't want to argue—I'm going home," she finished. Stood up. Came around the table. Hesitated, then brushed her cheek against the prickly top of his head before striding off through the restaurant.

Fiercely Jimper returned the stare of other diners, who averted their eyes. He looked glumly at his plate, but the water-chestnut quiche was no longer attractive. It was an unfair day. Jo-Ellen wouldn't listen to reason about their relationship. She had told him in detail about the penny-ante fire and he had listened tolerantly. But when he tried to tell her about the funny thing that had happened to him on his job the day before—and it was funny; he'd been on compliance inspection, smelled what he thought was a health violation and called the cops and it turned out only to be some kind of Vietnamese fish sauce—she wasn't listening. And she had forgotten to pay her check.

Jimper was far downtown, and perilously close to overstaying his lunch hour. Glumly he settled the bill, descended two floors to catch the uptown express tram and stared wistfully at the buildings he passed. There were no tall ones to speak of between the lower-city bubble and the rise of the big one at midtown, but once he was past Madison Square they began to get impressive again. Just right for launching. . . .

But that was out of reach, too. He dropped to ground level at Grand Army Plaza and hurried out into the park. Under the distant second-hand sky of the dome the Fair was beginning to take shape. Opening day was near, the tempo had picked up, the pavilions and stands were almost ready . . . his punishment job, in fact, was about the brightest spot in his life. Which said unkind things about his life, but that was hardly necessary. Jimper himself was saying unkind things about his life.

And yet—

To Jimper's surprise, his spirits were beginning to lift. A Fair was, after all, a Fair—by definition, a place to have fun. And people were having fun, as some of the attractions gave previews to specially fortunate people, or even specially unfortunate ones—a whole caravan of handicapped adults, each in his own little electric go-cart was rolling through the plastic pyramids of the Mexican pavilion, oohing and ahing as the elephants were brought in to their private island, ready for the opening-day parade, and gorging themselves on gaucho pies, soft ice cream, funnel cakes, steaming corn on the cob, baklava, appleade, stuffed potatoes— or at least on such of the available feasts as their diets or prostheses allowed them to handle. Jimper was drafted to help the dollies in and out of the Native American pavilion, where a young man, wearing a loosely tied scarlet sash, a scarf and long, black hair, said over and over, "I am your guide for today. I am a member of the Lenni-Lenape nation, and my name is Alexander." Between times, Jimper gazed enviously at the fluttering flyers still hovering around the Rainbow Bridge, while Alexander repeated his spiel—

"—when my people lived here, before the Dutch and the English came—"

—and reassured himself that, badly off as he was, he had nothing to complain about, in comparison to these unfortunates. Some were limbless. Some were tied to artificial hearts or lungs or kidneys. Some were blind, with sonar dishes on their heads.

"—these huge canoes were hollowed out by fire—"

He became aware that, outside the Native American pavilion, Jeff Bratislaw was standing and watching him. Now, what was that all about? Jimper searched his memory to see if he had been doing anything wrong, without success.

"—spread wet clay all around the top of the log to keep the fire contained, then place burning coals all down the trunk—"

Bratislaw was coming over to him. "You through here?" he asked. Actually, Jimper realized, he was; the last of the preview crowd had already gone through the pavilion. "Good, then we'll get you a shovel. I've got another job for you. Aren't you the one that wanted to fly?"

Jimper's heart leaped as he followed the supervisor. "Yes! You mean you're going to let me—"

"Not right now," said Bratislaw over his shoulder, "but maybe there's going to be something for you. See, on opening day they're going to release a thousand balloons. The dome people have complained about that—say they'll clog the vents, interfere with circulation. Do you think if we got you your wings and something like a light spear—oh, hell!" he interrupted himself. "Somebody's tapped in the P.A. system again!" He pulled his phone out of his pocket and began barking orders—over the noise of the squeaks and squawks and outlaw tape snatches of music that were coming over the speakers. "Hate those bastards," he growled, putting away the phone. "Well? What about it?"

"Oh, sure!" said Jimper, happier than he'd been in weeks. "You want me to pop the balloons that cause trouble, right? No problem! Glad to do it!"

"I thought you would be," smiled Bratislaw. "You'll get double time for flying, too—and maybe I can get you some overtime if you want to clear up your work-off fast."

"That'd be fine," said Jimper enthusiastically— better and better. "Only—you said a spear, didn't you? You don't want me to pop the balloons with this shovel?"

Bratislaw looked perplexed, then grinned. "Oh, I see what you're thinking. No, those are two different things. You don't have to worry about the balloons till opening day. What you need the shovel for," he said, opening the gate to the elephant pen, "is here."

VI Opening day! The Fair was coming alive! Overhead the hatches in the dome released a glittering snowfall of dry ice, and laser beams struck brilliant patterns of color through the haze. Under the old fountain at the corner of the park the New York Philharmonic was doing the *1812,* a polka band rocked its floating platform in the lake, marching groups blatted Sousa and Dixieland as they circled the exposition area. A million and a half New Yorkers and tourists surged outside the admission booths, waiting for the signal to open. The air was thick with smells—funnel cakes frying and barbecue sauce boiling, caramel and curry; animal whiff from where the parade was lining up, old city underground smells from where the refuse pits were being dug. Noise and sights, smells and the good-humored tension of the waiting crowd—if there was a graph of excitement in the city it was rising to a peak. Jimper collected his superlight wings from the enclosure where the pent-up balloons were waiting under their nets for release and found himself caught up in the excitement. It was going to be a great day! Way up on the Rainbow Bridge where he would launch he could see Jo-Ellen and her son waiting for him. Tiny dolls, they were waving in his general direction. He waved back, picking up his gear—

"Hello there, James Percy," said a smiling voice from behind him.

"Oh, my God," said Jimper. Even before he turned he knew who he would see. "Now, look, Dennis!" he began. "I don't want any trouble, and what you're doing is a criminal offense—"

"What am I doing, then?" Dennis Redfan said reasonably. He gestured with the gas-hose he was holding. "We're all work-offs together, right? I fill the balloons, you pop them, if we've got any personal business we take care of it some other time. Right?"

Jimper retreated a step, holding the flimsy powdered

wing right in front of him like a shield. A fight he could have handled—one way or another; this sudden reason-ableness from his dating friend's ex-husband was hard-er to deal with. "Right," he said at last. "I didn't know you were working here."

"I knew you were," Dinny observed pleasantly. "You know these balloons go up in, let's see, twenty minutes? So you better get on up to launch, right?"

Jimper tarried. He wasn't sure why. Considering how little he had wanted to see Dinny Redfan, he surprised himself by not vanishing as swiftly as he could. But Redfan was already turning away, spreading another balloon over the hose and knotting it full with a shriek of compressed gas. He didn't look at Jimper again, but over his shoulder he said, "Nutlark? Why are you pushing your luck?"

"Right," said Jimper, backing away. He didn't turn until he was at a five-meter distance, and even then his shoulderblades twitched nervously until he was in the lift to the Rainbow Bridge. All the way up to the 50th-floor level he was debating with himself whether he should say anything to Jo-Ellen in front of the boy.

It was an unnecessary worry. "*Damn*, Jimper," young Will cried breathlessly, "I thought *sure* Dinny was going to cream you down there!" He looked more pleased and excited than dismayed, Jimper thought, but Jo-Ellen supplied enough dismay for both.

"What did he say to you?" she demanded, and listened worriedly while Jimper relayed the highlights of the conversation. She shook her head and took the monocular away from her son, pointing it down into the park where Dinny Redfan was cheerfully popping one filled balloon after another into the net. "He doesn't look mad," she reported. "But then he never does. He just starts punching with a smile on his face."

"That's nice," said Jimper dismally, shrugging his arms into the harness.

"I don't think he'll do anything to you, Jimper," the boy advised sagaciously. "He's already got about a million hours to work off. Last time it was aggravated assault, they said, because the guy could have died."

"Just get that buckle for me, will you?" Jimper begged.

"Yes, but the thing you have to remember is he just can't afford another conviction. He wouldn't just get a work-off, they'd transport him."

Jimper backed away, as Jo-Ellen and the boy locked his extended wings in place and tested them. "You think so?" he asked hopefully.

"No doubt in the world!" Will assured him. "He won't touch you here, and that's for sure!" And then, as Jimper touched his starter button and the hydrogen turbine began to shrill and he leaned forward to his take-off jump, the boy added: "Of course, if he catches you alone when nobody's looking, that's something else."

He had taken too much time getting in position; the balloons were already drifting up out of the nets before he was airborne. They didn't rise very fast. They weren't meant to. Some inert gas had been mixed with the helium so that they were only marginally lighter than the air they floated in. All the same, they were a good distance away from the end of the bridge. So Jimper twisted his body to incline the wings, and soared clumsily toward the tall buildings he had just left. What he needed was an updraft. The ultra-lights could climb, but not very rapidly; a good thermal would get him out over the flock of balloons, where he could pick them off at his leisure. . . .

No. There would be nothing leisurely about it, he realized. There were hundreds of them, and they were not staying in a neat cluster. They were less than a hundred meters up when he turned back to meet them, but they were already all over the sky. They simply didn't rise fast enough to remain a unit. Each vagrant puff of air, each rising bubble from a taco stand or a tempura kettle fluttered them this way and that.

The one common motion for all of them, though, was up. There was no point in trying to attack them at the hundred-meter level. They did no harm there. It was only up at the vents on the dome itself, half a kilometer overhead, that they were an annoyance; the thing to do was go up there and wait for them to arrive. Some of them would pop by themselves from the altitude. Many would have lost themselves in trees, buildings, bridges, walkways—on the stony chins of old carved gargoyles, on the stubs of outworn TV antennae, on the metal fittings of the dome panels themselves. He only had to worry about the survivors, and of those only the ones who arrived near a vent in great enough numbers to be a problem. The thing to do was to go up there and wait for them.

It was also, of course, a thing that Jimper Nutlark was happy to do. He figure-eighted over the Fair grounds, seeking thermals, exulting in the freedom of the air, rising faster than the untidy sprawl of balloons, as happy as he had ever remembered to be. The whole midtown city was beneath him now. There was the old dome of the Planetarium, and across the greenery the chunky shape of the Metropolitan Museum of Art, with Cleopatra's Needle unrecognizably foreshortened beside it. There was the parade already halfway across the Rainbow Bridge, with elephants plodding behind horses prancing and bands playing—already the sound thinned and blurred by the distance. He was above the wall of old hotels at the edges of the Park, almost above the newer openwork skyscrapers built after the dome was finished. There was the old Waldorf Tower, with its twelve-room suites where ancient presidents and generals had waited to die; there the face of the Citicorp's solar panels, turned away from him and now forever blind; there the needle of Chrysler and the bland oval of Pan Am. The crowds surging into the Fair had blended into a slow trickle of polka-dot color, creeping between the rides and the pavilions. Farther up the Park were the flowering ginger and banana trees of the botanic garden, beyond them the wilderness created by Olmsted long before. Take it all in all, Jimper was having the best ride of his life—and it was *legal.*

A quick flash of green and blue nearby reminded him that it was also just a little bit dangerous. He was up in the haze area now, where the condensation from the CO_2 crystals still left a smudge of mist, and the laser show was playing through it. It would be no fun at all to catch one of those beams in his eye. He slipped the quick-dark glasses into place, and checked the cable that lashed his spear to his belt—what a missile it would have made if dropped into the crowd!

The first couple of surviving balloons were soaring toward him, not more than a hundred meters below. Jimper grinned up at the TV cameras on the dome, two or three of them turning to keep an eye on him, and yelled: "Tally-ho!" He leaned forward, extended the spear and dove into the cluster, pop-pop-pop, three in a row.

If there was a better way of working off punishment time, he had never heard of it. It wasn't punishment. It wasn't even work. It was the thing he liked best to do, with trappings of the medieval tourney. He imagined he could hear faint cheering from the crowds far below as he turned and climbed slowly again to catch the balloons he had missed.

A couple of dozen balloons later it no longer seemed quite as much fun. They were coming fast now, faster than he could easily handle; the expectation that most of them would pop with altitude hadn't worked out. He was coming closer to the vents than was prudent; the drafts there were a lot more violent than his flimsy ultralight was built to stand, a lot stronger than the tiny hydrogen turbine could fight. And there was a queer smell that he couldn't identify—maybe the smell of the fabric of the dome itself, maybe something from the turbine exhaust at his back; it made him dizzy.

At that point the lasers started again.

From the ground it must have been beautiful—red

and green and violet shafts of light, cutting through the faint remaining CO_2 haze, bouncing off the balloons as they bobbed upward. At close range it was scary. Each time a beam came near him, each time even one struck a balloon and the reflections came back, his glasses went black for a moment. It saved his eyes, true. But it wrecked his reflexes at the same time. He blanked out at just the wrong moment and missed a cluster of three; turned, took aim again and pierced two of them.

He found himself spinning, caught himself, swung violently around the harness of the ultralight and straightened out.

What was the matter with him? It couldn't be the altitude—there wasn't enough of it inside the dome to bother even a first-flyer. Not the exertion . . . not anything he had eaten, surely . . . not anything he could think of; but the balloons blurred in front of him, and his reflexes were definitely slowed. *Flash,* and the goggles blacked out; *pop-pop,* and two more balloons burst at the point of his lance—and somebody was calling his name. *Jimper! Jimper dear—*

Now, who could be speaking to him up here? It was impossible. There was no one near, no single human being visible at all. It hardly sounded like a human voice: too loud, too distant, too blurred, as though it were coming from several places at once.

It was. It was coming from the intercom speakers at the remote TV pickups, and it was the voice he knew. It sobbed, *Oh, Jimper, come down—please! Dinny's put stuff in the balloons—*

Why, thought Jimper with pleasure, that would explain the funny smell, wouldn't it? But it was a silly idea, he considered. What could anyone put in the balloons that would do him any harm? It was ridiculous. It could not possibly account, for instance, for the fact that he was fluttering back down to the ground, wholly out of control, the Fair spinning before him and the tall buildings whirling around, impact only a couple of hundred meters below—

By the time he realized it was more important to do something about the problem than to try to understand its cause, he had barely flying room enough left to straighten the frail, whipping wings, slow down the plunge, try to miss the huge trees that caught at him. His brain was still fuzzed. He didn't know whether he had saved himself or not until he discovered that he was floating in a lake, his arms tangled in the harness, the stilled hydrojet trying to sink him. It might have done it, too, if the lake had been more than a meter deep.

And when he had waded halfway to the shore there was Jo-Ellen splashing muddily toward him, with the boy sloshing enthusiastically after; "You were some great horror show coming down like that!" cried Will; and, reaching to pull the harness away from where he had gouged and pitted himself, "This is getting to be a habit," said Jo-Ellen. And when he was (almost) clean and (thoroughly) bandaged and back at the Fair, there were the tanks of nitrous oxide that should have been plain nitrogen, and the Fair guard, a work-off like himself, proudly explaining: "So when the doc phoned down to say what she'd seen from the bridge I nabbed him right away; that's about his fifth offense, and he'll be working it off in Idaho. Maybe the Aleutians! Maybe ten years!" And when they had turned their backs on the Fair and were back in Jo-Ellen's apartment, the boy said importantly, "I know what you're going to want to eat, so I'll go out and catch a bunch of big ones!" And when he returned with a colander of chirping, leaping big ones he gazed at Jimper on the couch, head in his mother's lap, and said, "I've been thinking, choot. A boy needs a father, true? And it looks like I won't have my regular one for a while. Think you might know where I can find one to fill in?" And Jimper Nutlark (farewell, Atlanta lady; good-by, daughter of Mawzi Frères) relaxed and smiled up at the woman who owned the lap and said, "Matter of fact, choot, I think I do."

I'M EIGHTY-FOUR YEARS OLD, THOUGH YOU wouldn't think it to look at me. Over the years they've repaired my pipes and restored most of my senses and taken the Struldbrug look off my face. Although it's fifty-seven years since I graduated from Columbia Law I still practice when I have to—or, to tell it more truthfully, on those very few occasions when someone who happens to need a lawyer happens to get referred to me. I've seen a lot of changes. I've seen eighty per cent of the felonies on the statute books abolished, and most of the causes for civil actions ameliorated away. I've seen computers replace law clerks—even replace a judge or two, now and then—and I've even seen contracts and wills written in language you don't need a lawyer to understand. But I'll tell you the truth. I never expected to see anything quite like

gwenanda
and
the
supremes

I The prosecuting attorney was a mouse, the defendant was a born brute and the whole day was turning into a cow. For one thing, the Supreme Court chamber was grossly packed. It was a day when the candidates for the next term were herded into the auditorium to see how a day's judging went, so there were forty of them there. Plus, the usual drift-ins. Sometimes Gwenanda liked it when the house was SRO. If you got a lively bunch and a lot of cross-chatter you could really have some fun with a case. Today they were all bored petrified. Half of them weren't looking at the witness at all. They were reading, or drowsing, or even staring at the continuous strip of glow-light mottos that circled the dome of the courtroom. Now it was spelling out:

"Covenants without the sword are but words and of no strength to secure a man at all."—Thomas Hobbes.

Gwenanda sighed and ducked behind her bench for a quick hit to anesthetize some of the tedium, just as Chief Justice Samelweiss passed her on the way to the toilet. She knew it was Samelweiss. None of the other justices would pinch her butt when she wasn't looking. "The twitch is guilty as hell," he muttered in passing, "and isn't this day *ever* gonna end?"

"Turn on your set, old an," said Gwenanda as she straightened up. You never knew when some legal-eagle defendant was going to holler mistrial, just because a judge forgot to turn on his walk-around headphones when he went to take a leak. This particular defendant was just the type to do it.

In fairness to Samelweiss, it was true that nothing was being said that any sensible person would want to hear. The brute of a defendant had begged for twenty minutes to make a statement, and Samelweiss, the old fool, had let her have it. Probably just wanted time to go to the can. So the statement had gone on for six or seven minutes already. Bor-*ing*. All she did was complain about the myriad ways in which society had so warped and brutalized her that whatever she did wasn't really her *fault*. Now she was only up to the tyrannical first-grade teacher who had hung the label of thief on her—

A loud beep interrupted her—one of the Tin Twins. "Hold on there a minute, sweet-meats. You did swipe the teacher's wallet, didn't you?"

The defendant paused, annoyed at the interruption. "What? Well, sure. But I was only a child, Your Honor."

"And then you did, the way it says here in the charge, you did stab your marry to death, right?"

"Only because society made me an outlaw, Your Honor."

"Right," said the Twin, losing interest. It was

Ai-Max, Gwenanda saw, peering down the curve of the justices' benches. She envied him. When one of the human judges fell asleep you could usually tell because you heard him snore. The Tin Twins could power down without external sign, so they got away with murder.

Murder. Oh, yeah. The case. "Move it, chotz," Gwenanda snapped at the defendant, and glanced down to get her name, Donna Maris Delius. "You, Delius. Get along with it."

The defendant gave her a look of resentment, blinked, studied her notes for a moment and proceeded: "At the age of eight all the other kids had video playmates, but my family was too cheap—" Gwenanda sighed, wishing Samelweiss would come back and give her a fast count. Under the rounded dome of the courtroom the glow-light was displaying a new motto:

"We are under a Constitution, but the Constitution is what the judges say it is."—Charles Evans Hughes.

Gwenanda sat back, looked around and furtively punched out a new code for her memo plate. Obediently it displayed a map of North America. Tracings in bright red extended from the Yukon down through half of Mexico, over the legend:

NARRO

THE NORTH AMERICAN RIVER REDIRECTION OPTION

She studied it glumly. Why weren't there any decent rivers in the eastern half of the continent? Why did Kriss have to be a riverine hydraulics engineer, anyway? And if there were good reasons why those two problems couldn't be changed, why couldn't she go with him when he moved on to follow the work? It wasn't just the beast of a defendant that was ruining her day, it was her personal life, too. It hadn't been all that great in Tucson, maybe, but from the day she got her draft notice and reported to the Supreme Court Candidates Corps—it was in Atlanta then—things had been messed up. Supreme Court Justice sounded pretty good, when you considered the alternatives, but when you were just considering the alternatives you didn't know about Chief Justices that pinched your behind and days when you pulled two murders, a record-juggling and a two billion dollar lawsuit all on the same calendar. What was that thing they'd flashed about the sword enforcing covenants? Right on, said Gwenanda to herself, bring on the sword!

And just then the sword fell. The twenty minutes were up. The speaker system beeped a time-up reminder, and the defendant's microphone went dead in mid-syllable.

Samelweiss, scuttling back to his high bench in the middle of the row, got there just in time to hit his override button. His amplified voice filled the hemispherical hall: "Right," he said. "I'd call this a case for summary judgment if we ever saw one, and I'll start the ball rolling. Guilty. How say you, gang?"

The defendant nudged her lawyer furiously. He looked alarmed. "Uh, Mr. Chief Justice," he began, "there's lots more evidence—" But he was drowned out by the chorus of "Guilty"s from the court.

"That's what I like to see," approved Samelweiss, gazing affectionately around at the other justices. "Now we get to the sentence. I'd say freezing, myself. Anybody have any other— Wait a minute. What's on your mind, counselor?" he added, scowling, because the attorney for the defense was waving frantically. Worse than that. His client had her mouth to his ear, and she was scratching her fingernails against his lavallière mike. The courtroom filled with squeaky-chalk static. Samelweiss's finger hovered dangerously over the cutoff switch.

The lawyer nodded and cried: "E wants to know what you're going to do with the kid."

Gwenanda was leaning forward, with her mouth all ready to concur in the verdict of freezing. She changed plans in mid-vocalization. "What kid?" she demanded.

"Uz kid. Uz and uz marry's—uh, the deceased's, I mean. E's three years old, the kid. Female. Do you want to make um an orphan?"

Faint, considering beep from one of the Tin Twins. Thoughtful cough from Justice Myra Haik at the end of the row. Reflective silence from all the rest of the court, until Gwenanda broke it. "Obviously," she said, "we got to think this over a little more, you guys. I say we reserve judgment for a while."

There was an approving murmur from the entire bench. Samelweiss confirmed it. "So ordered," he said. "Let's see, what's the next case, the nut that wants to sue us for two billion dollars? Right. Tell um to get uz ass in here on the double." And gazed with satisfaction at the current legend making its way around the domed ceiling, which said:

"Why should there not be a patient confidence in the ultimate justice of the people? Is there any better or equal hope in the world?"—Abraham Lincoln.

Very little ever got decided in the Supreme Court of the United States of America without a squabble. That was held to be one of its great present virtues: that every point of view was reflected in the variety of justices, and so no argument went without an advocate. What they were squabbling about just now was whether to proceed with the loony who wanted to sue the United States for two billion dollars or break for lunch. Gwenanda stayed out of the battle, because all of a sudden she had something more important on her mind. With her eyes she watched Donna Maris Delius hysterically pursuing her lawyer with reproaches as he fled through the door; with her fingers she was tapping out instructions to her benchtop data plate. The defendant's name and vital statistics sprang into glowing color: Donna Maris Delius, 28 years old, *m.* Dale Lemper (*d.*), 1 child *f.* Gwenanda hit the reject key and got the next item in the dossier, coroner's report: fourteen major blows with a blunt instrument and eight penetration wounds. The woman had not only beaten her husband to death with a brandy decanter, she had broken it on his head and stabbed him with the jagged remnants. Gwenanda tapped again—flick, flick—more reports—flick—a wedding picture of the brute and her victim, five years earlier—flick—

There it was. A picture of a three-year-old girl, one finger in her nose and a beat-up toy rabbit in her hand, staring at the recorder. A nice-looking little kid. Or was then, anyway; Gwenanda punched another key for dates and discovered the picture was a little more than a year old. The child's name was Maris Delius Lemper and, at four, Gwenanda thought swiftly, she would be well toilet trained, should be talking up a streak, probably ready to start pre-school classes if she hadn't done so already—

"What?" said Gwenanda, looking up as somebody called her name.

Chief Justice Samelweiss said sternly, "You have to pay more attention, Gwenanda, because we're taking a vote. We've got this two-billion-dollar loony coming up and I for one want to see what this joker looks like, but Mary Joan—"

"Mary Joan didn't get any breakfast today," Mary Joan Whittier snapped from the other side of the row, "so e wants to take an hour for lunch. How say you, pups?"

"Oh, lunch recess for sure," said Gwenanda. "I got to get to a telephone."

Gwenanda was the last of the justices to get back to the bench, and Chief Justice Samelweiss gave her a mean-hearted look. He didn't say anything, though, because he was too busy looking forward to what was coming next. "Bailiff," he called, "bring in the loony."

All the justices were acting a little more expectant and almost party-cheerful—not counting the Tin Twins, of course. Even Gwenanda sat up straighter and fussed with her huge fluff of hair, in spite of the fact that half her phone calls hadn't got her the person she wanted to talk to, and the other half left her feeling half mind-made-up and half Jeez-do-I-dare? The courtroom was packed again, and everybody was giggling and rubbernecking and whispering as the loony came in. The loony was a man in his late fifties, conservatively dressed in long pants and shoes and a dark-colored blouse, and he beamed affably around the room before raising his eyes to the glow-writing on the dome.

It was, "There is hardly a political question which does not sooner or later turn into a judicial one."— Alexis de Tocqueville.

The loony studied it thoughtfully, shrugged and then turned to the justices.

The expression on his face chilled. He swallowed, stumbled over his lawyer's foot and took his seat, still staring. "All right, now," Samelweiss said impatiently. "Are you the, what do you call it, the plaintiff?"

The loony whispered worriedly to his lawyer, who said out loud, "Just get up and tell them what you want, okay?"

"Well," said the loony, rising, "all right." He bowed to the bench. "Ladies and gentlemen," he said— whispers from the justices, a couple of actual giggles from the spectators—"honorable judges, I mean, my name is Horatio Margov. *Justice* Horatio Margov, that is, since I had the honor to serve the bench myself in my previous life. I ask your permission for my attorney to approach the bench."

The bench giggled in surprise, all nine of it, and Gwenanda craned her neck for a better look. This sort of thing had not been covered in basic training, or even in the hard six months of cadet school. She turned to see how Samelweiss would handle it. The way he was handling it was whispering to the Digital Colleague next to him. "Oh, sure," he said, nodding. "I get it. E wants Wally Amaretto to come up here and talk to us. Come on, Wally, what's this all about?"

Amaretto was big, black and easy-going, and the nearest thing to a staff lawyer the Supreme Court had. He sighed and came forward, nodding to the justices. "Hi, Sam, Gwenanda, D.C., how's the chess game going? Listen, any chance you can fire me and get another lawyer for this chotz?"

"No way," twinkled Samelweiss. "What's uz problem?"

"Which one? Like, the first one is, e didn't really expect to see you all looking like this."

Samelweiss was honestly perplexed. "Like what?" he asked, glancing around at his colleagues. "We've all got our robes on."

"I think it's the Tin Twins mostly. E says e's used to human beings for judges, not a garbage can and a vacuum cleaner. And e says in uz day courts were right up in God's good sunlight, that's what e said, not a thousand feet down like a bunch of goddamn moles."

"What are 'feet'?" Gwenanda asked.

"It's what they used to measure with," Amaretto explained. "But that's only the start. E says e wants a thirty-day postponement so e can get uz witnesses ready to testify."

All the justices were shocked now. "E can't *testify*, Wally! We've got no time to hear a bunch of chotzes *testify*—no offense," Gwenanda called to the loony, who was listening to the exchange with an expression of rage and disbelief.

"That's what e says. Says a proper trial has to be conducted according to case law and the rules of evidence, that's all there is to it."

"You sticking up for that prunt?" Mary Joan called.

Amaretto turned to her, his expression rebellious. "That's another damn thing e expects. E says under the adversary system I'm supposed to take uz side no matter what. And then some other lawyer takes the other side and we both lie and fink any way we can to get the verdict we want. I mean, e wants."

Gasp from the spectators. "Ah, no," cried Gwenanda in disbelief, and Samelweiss echoed her:

"You must've got that wrong, Wally. What if your side doesn't have a case, like?"

"Even then," the lawyer insisted.

There was a silence while the justices digested this, broken by a beep from the far end. "What do you want?" Samelweiss asked, and then, grinning, added, "garbage can?"

"I think it was D.C. that was the garbage can," Wally put in helpfully. "Angel was the vacuum cleaner."

"Whatever," nodded the Chief Justice, and Angel's voice said suspiciously:

"What's e hanging around down there for? Why doesn't e come up and talk to us like Wally?"

"No way," declared Samelweiss. "Wally, you go back where you belong and we'll start this trial. Margov! What are you suing for?"

The plaintiff stood up, breathing deeply. He was obviously trying to control himself. Obviously he had had a lot of practice, because he succeeded tolerably well. When he spoke his voice was easy and self-assured, like a professional actor's: "Honorable justices," he said, "I understand that there have been many changes in the juridical procedure since I was frozen, and so I ask your pardon for any errors I may commit. As I understand it, you justices have been chosen through a form of selective service rather than the conventional process of—"

"Margov," Samelweiss interrupted, hand on his Chief Justice's volume control so that his voice drowned out everything else, "just tell us what you want, okay? We've been here half an hour already with this bullshit."

Deep breath. Then, "Yes, Your Honor. The facts are simple. I will present witnesses to prove—"

"The hell if you will," snapped Gwenanda. "We want to know anything, we'll go ask them."

"As you wish, ma'am," Margov said gamely. "Anyway, these are the facts. I was frozen fifty-eight years ago due to serious medical problems not curable at that time. Two weeks ago I was revived, treated and discharged. I have since learned that, through an error in record-keeping, I received not only the treatments proper to my case but also an entire series that had been intended for another occupant of the freezer, also revived at that time. As this is a clear example of medical malpractice, resulting in grave physical and mental harm—"

"Hold it a minute, chotz," said Angel, his voice thin and reedy because he was doing several things at once and could manage only a narrow-band communication. "Where's this other person?"

Margov said gravely, "He has disappeared."

"Ah, come on. Nobody disappears." Margov shrugged. "I think we ought to talk to um," Angel said.

"Not here you don't," said Samelweiss, looking at the clock on his data plate. "Say e really has disappeared. Say they really mixed you up. What about it?"

"This other person," Margov said indignantly, "was a boat person from Baja. Heaven knows what diseases he may have carried! So they gave me a complete series of antibiotics and vaccines and heaven knows what all. My arm was sore for days! Not to mention—"

"Whatever it is, don't mention it," ordered Samelweiss. "So what's worth two billion dollars?"

"The diseases, your honor! He evidently was suspected of having herpes, syphilis, yaws, tuberculosis—"

"I told you not to mention all that stuff!" yelled Samelweiss. "Listen, that's all crap. You got a sore arm and you got your feelings hurt. I'd say you've got a claim, all right, maybe fifty dollars. Maybe a little more."

"Your honor! But I can prove—"

"You can't prove anything in this court," Samelweiss said reasonably, "unless we let you. I'm not about to do that."

"I want to talk to the other guy," Angel put in obstinately. He was taking it seriously, too; he had turned up the bass on his voice filters so it came out all grave and majestic.

"Oh, dog," sighed the Chief Justice, looking around the rest of the court. "Any of the rest of you got anything to say?"

Gwenanda raised her hand, and thought for a minute while the rest of the court looked at her. She decided to take the plunge. "Two things," she said. "First, I vote we put off the loony's case until Angel does what e wants to do. Second, I figured out how to handle that Delius an, so let's get um back in here for sentencing."

Samelweiss stared at her. "Are you loony, too? E's long gone."

"E's not," said Gwenanda, "because I told the bailiff to keep um here during the break. Bring um in, Sam." And when the woman was back in the dock, glaring sullenly at her persecutors, Gwenanda said, "Delius, what you did is too bad to sweep under the rug, I guess you know that."

"But society—"

"Society," said Gwenanda, "my ass. So we're going to freeze you. You get automatic review every eighteen months, and sooner or later the Parole Board or the Prisoners' Redemption League or somebody will get you defrosted and then you'll get another chance. But this chance, pups, you've all used up."

The woman's lip quivered nervously. "I have a very low tolerance for pain," she said tremulously.

"Oh, hell, it doesn't hurt. I *think* it doesn't," Gwenanda amended. "You can ask that old judge if you want to, but I think they just like knock you out and that's all you know until thawing-out time."

"Yes, but my baby—"

And Gwenanda grinned. "That's the best part. I'll take um to raise myself."

"You can't do that!" cried the woman, looking to her lawyer for reassurance. He smiled regretfully to say that sure they could, and she repaid the smile with an expression probably much like the one she wore when she picked up the brandy decanter. "Well, I'll have to think that part over," she said firmly.

"Actually," Gwenanda said, "you don't, because it's all settled. It is the unanimous verdict of this Court, delivered by me—unless some of you jokers don't agree?—that you freeze, and your kid is adopted by me as soon as you're iced, which will be any time tomorrow. You can take um away, Sam. And get um a nice dinner," she added kindly, "because it'll have to last um a long time."

II The place where Gwenanda lived, or at least the place where she slept most nights, was a condo-commune about thirty stories up over what had once been called the Five Points. The reason it wasn't exactly where she lived was that, officially, she lived in the residences provided all justices of the United States Supreme Court, two hundred stories straight up from the underground Court itself. The reason it was where she usually slept was that Kriss lived there.

Good smells came from the common rooms as Gwenanda let herself in. The video monitors were carrying the current UTM discussion—dome repairs, for or against luminescent panels to make the night bright—and the cooks of the day were half watching while they got the food ready. She collared one of them and asked, "Seen Kriss?"

"Swimming," he said over his shoulder, concentrating on mincing cucumbers, parsley, garlic and shallots together for the *gazpacho*. It looked so good that Gwenanda decided to stay for dinner, no matter what. So she punched in on the work roster—dishes, cleanup, food storage—for that night before she shucked her clothes in Kriss's room. She glanced at the mirror for reassurance, and was reassured: foxy female from the bicentennial past, her hair feathered out two feet wide, each nail on her ten fingers and thumbs a different iridescent shrieking color, her eyebrows narrow enough to inflict a wound. Gwenanda liked to dress to be seen. And succeeded; but she didn't need clothes to look good. Confident of her appearance at least—a lot less than confident about the success of her plan—she let herself out on the pool balcony.

The architect who designed the condo-commune had not intended it for people to live in. Offices, it was supposed to be, for doctors, dentists, lawyers and psychiatrists. The enclosed square of garden and pool was planned as a touch of charm to remind the afflicted patients that better times would come again. Since there weren't enough practitioners of the sad professions left to need all the space that had been built for them, most such suites had been converted to suit other needs. Like living. Like living well, as Kriss was obviously doing, playing water volleyball with a dozen others, mostly kids. She stood and admired him for a minute. Pencil-slim figure, brown down on his chest, and those darling, round, firm chubs that you wanted to pat and squeeze and hang onto. "Hey, Kriss!" she yelled. "Here I come!"

She launched herself off the balcony into the deep end, a little extra optimism lacing her mood as she saw how much fun Kriss was having with the kids. A good sign! She parted the water neatly, swam under the surface to where Kriss's long, lean legs were thrashing, tweaked him a friendly hello and rose to take a breath.

He gave her a wet kiss while the ball was in the other court. "They voting yet?" he asked.

"Uh-uh. Hey, Kriss? I want to ask you a favor. Big favor. I want it very much." He only had time for a quick questioning look at her before batting the ball back across the pool. The return from the other side went far and wide. While one of the children was clambering out of the pool to retrieve the ball, his expression was running the spectrum from surprise through uncertainty to affection. He promised, "I'll be through in five minutes. Go get us some drinks."

Gwenanda climbed out, shook herself semi-dry and settled down at a poolside table with the bottle of wine and two glasses. She watched the game for a bit. One of the players was a stranger—female, youngish, very pale and, apparently, not very well. She missed easy shots and coughed from exertion, and the most interesting thing about her was that Kriss was helping her out. Cheerful, encouraging, *kind* Kriss, thought Gwenanda, and derived optimism from the thought. She switched on the poolside monitor and watched the dome debate on the UTM until Kriss came out of the pool. What a beautiful man! Sideburns straight down to the jawline, then flaring out in a waxed curl, with crystal drops from the pool flying off them as his head shook from laughter.

To Gwenanda's surprise, he brought the stranger with him.

"Hello," she said, discouragingly.

Kriss was oblivious. "This is Dorothy," he said. "E just got here. E's eighty-seven years old."

Well, she obviously wasn't eighty-seven, or half that, but she wasn't as young as she looked at a distance, either. She was stumbly, fumbly young, like a newborn calf trying to figure out what its legs are for, but she was not young in the face. "What I wanted to talk to you about," said Gwenanda, cat's-eye look of *keep off!* to Dorothy, "was private. Important. Personal."

"I'll go away," the woman said at once, but Kriss stayed her.

"Pay no attention to um," he advised. "E's just out

of the freezer, doesn't know a thing. You can talk in front of um."

Well, Gwenanda didn't *want* to talk in front of her, but she realized that under normal circumstances she wouldn't have minded. That was one of the reasons she and Kriss got along so well together. Kriss was a gentle, kindly, outgoing person, and so was she, by dog! "I'll get another glass," she sighed, rising, and detoured by way of the toilet. Yes, the test-tab said she was coming up on time for a flush, which accounted for the little irritability. Although Gwenanda disliked taking pills she swallowed a trank, as well as the regular pre-flush capsule, washed her hands, found a third glass and went back to the pool. "Pups," she said sunnily, "what I want is for us to shack." Kriss shrugged amiably and started to speak, but she forestalled him. "I've got a kid coming," she said.

He gave her his full attention then—surprised but not, Gwenanda was pleased to see, hostile. "What did you do that for?" he asked, eyebrows high in astonishment.

"I don't mean pregnant," she explained. "Adoption. There was this beast in the court today, killed uz marry, has a little kid. Well, we have to freeze um, but then there's the kid to think about. I want to adopt um."

"Why not do it, then?"

"No. No, you don't follow. I want *us* to adopt um."

"Ah," said Kriss, nodding. "Oh, I see what you mean." He pursed his lips, then remembered to fill Gwenanda's wine glass. "Here's to the kid," he said, "but look, honey, what happens when I go to the West Coast?"

"That might not happen," she pointed out. The river redirection program had been on the back burner for decades already, she knew; it might easily stay there for the rest of their lives.

"I think it will happen," he said, chewing the idea over thoughtfully. "The Ob–Yenisei project is working

302

out just fine, isn't it? So why shouldn't America do the same thing?" He took a sip of his wine before asking, "Nice kid?"

"I haven't met um yet," Gwenanda admitted, "but e looks pretty nice in the picture. E's a shemale. Four years old."

He looked at her with amusement and doubt. "Well, hell," he said, "just bring the kid here."

"I thought of that," she said, "but that's a bummer for um if we don't do it then, don't you see? I mean, e's just lost one parent, I don't want um to think e's got a new one and then lose that one too."

"I promise," Kriss said solemnly, "that I won't act like a parent, at least until we figure out how to handle this."

"But—" began Gwenanda, and didn't finish because the other woman's glass slipped out of her hand and crunched on the floor. Claret splashed all up along Gwenanda's bare calf.

"Oh, hell," Dorothy said dismally. "Look, I'm really sorry about that."

"Not to worry," Kriss said comfortingly, patting her shoulder. "I'll clean it up and, listen, anyway, they're getting ready to vote on the dome. So we'll talk about this later, all right, honey?" And whether it was all right with Gwenanda or not, it was the way it was, because Kriss was already gone to fetch something to clean the mess up with.

The voting took half an hour, because there was a lot of emotion on both sides of the question, especially on Kriss's part—large-scale engineering projects were what he loved best, and he was downcast because the random selection hadn't given him a chance to be heard in the debate. And then there was dinner, and then it was Kriss's job to vacuum the pool while Gwenanda took her turn at cleanup as promised. The woman out of the freezer was on the same job, and it was continu-

ally surprising to Gwenanda, although she tried not to
stare, to see how clumsy Dorothy was. "Watch it!"
Gwenanda cried, as a stack of dessert plates began to
teeter on its way to the washer. The woman grabbed
just in time.

"My fault," she apologized. "See, they unfroze me
eight months ago, and I'm not quite used—I mean, I
don't know how—The thing is," she said, "I was
phocomelic."

"Say what?" asked Gwenanda, astonished.

"Phocomelic is the word. I was born that way, you
know. No arms or legs, just little flippers? So when they
unfroze me there was a lot of work to do, opened up my
bones, stuck me full of hormones—here I am. But I
need practice with these things." She levered her arms
out in front of her like canes to look at them.

"Wow," said Gwenanda, suddenly all sympathy.
"Did it hurt?"

"Hurt?" Dorothy demanded. "Who cares if it hurt?"
She grinned at Kriss, just coming in the door. "Com-
pared to what I used to be, listen, this is *paradise*. . . .
Although I surely do wish that old woman would leave
me alone."

"A real prunt, that one," Kriss nodded, leaning
against the sterile food cabinet and licking a juice
banana. "You ought to see um, Gwennie."

"Oh?" said Gwenanda, suddenly less sympathy
again. "You know this old an?"

"Well, sure. E waits table where I eat sometimes,"
he said, nodding toward Dorothy, "and e had to go for
a flush and didn't know exactly where to go. So I
walked um over to the clinic."

"Uh-huh," said Gwenanda, aware the washer was
signaling the dishes were clean, aware also that it was
Dorothy's job to empty it, not at all inclined to help her
out.

Dorothy was paying more attention to Gwenanda
than to the washer. "We met because I live here now,"

she explained. Gwenanda nodded judiciously. "Well, I went to where you have the—flush?"

"Pucky-flush, yes," Gwenanda supplied.

"And she was there. Outside the place. Yelling and screaming. Her name is Jocelyn Feigerman. I knew who she was, right away, and I figured she was up to her old tricks, so I tried to stay out of her sight. She was trying to persuade some of the women not to have a flush."

Gwenanda was getting interested in the subject more than in the relationship now, hovering between astonishment and annoyance. "That's dumb," she said. "If a female an doesn't have that each month, it is very messy, and also I think there is a lot of discomfort."

"God, don't I know that! But it wasn't the discomfort. Jocelyn said they would abort any pregnancies they might have."

"Well, of course they would."

"And she thinks that's immoral. You see, that's how I knew her, in the old days. She used to be on television a lot when I was a child, campaigning for a constitutional amendment to make abortion illegal—"

"Illegal!" Gwenanda cried, now slipping over into full shock and outrage, and Kriss grinned as a person does who is seeing the reaction he expected.

"—illegal, and I was kind of her example to point to. I was born deformed, but I had a pretty face. So Jocelyn took pictures of me, and she would get me on the network news and say, 'Aren't you glad you're alive, honey?' Well, what did I know? I'd say, 'Oh, yes, Mrs. Feigerman, I surely am,' and then she'd pat my cheek and turn me over to the woman who took care of me. Her group paid the woman's salary, so I got something out of it, anyway. But I wish she'd leave me alone now."

Gwenanda said indignantly, "You can *make* um leave you alone. That's the Thirty-first Amendment!"

Dorothy sighed. "I don't want trouble," she complained, "so the best thing is for me just to stay out of her way." And that reminded her of nearer concerns, so she added, "Are we finished cleaning up? I think I'll go to my room and lie down."

"Tactful, anyway," Gwenanda commented, looking after her. "Well, pups? Have you thought about it?"

"About the kid, you mean. Sure I have, Gwennie. But I really would like to see um . . . and even then . . ."

Gwenanda nodded. The kid would be the best card she could play. "We could go see um tonight if you wanted," she said, "but it's uz last night with uz muddy. How about tomorrow?"

"Absolutely! But there's NARRO to think about, don't forget—and honestly, Gwen, I care about you a whole hell of a lot, but that's where my work is."

"If it happens," said Gwenanda, clutching at straws.

"If it happens," he agreed, and grinned, and said, "How about us going to our room to lie down, too?"

Since Gwenanda had lived most of her life under the thermal dome of Tucson, Arizona, she was not against the Yukon project at all. In fact, it was one of the things that had made her and Kriss take an interest in each other in the beginning. He was full of stories about the work he'd done in Siberia, finishing the diversion of the Ob and Yenisei rivers so that they flowed south to the arid tundra instead of north to waste themselves in the Arctic Ocean. Gwenanda had heard of the North American River Redirection Option, of course, for a full-scale continent-wide Universal Town Meeting on the subject had been announced for the future. But it had not been one of her major concerns, until she met this man with his satchel of plans for diverting far-north water all the way from the Mackenzie and Yukon rivers all the way south to the salty fields of Mexico. She was thrilled with the idea of actual rivers flowing past Tucson and Phoenix.

The more she thought about the project, the better

she liked it—except for one aspect. Physically it was great. The Ob–Yenisei work had removed fears about damage to the Arctic environment, because there hadn't been any. The water in the far northern wastes of North America did no human beings any particular good. Large parts of the Midwest were too dry to farm without irrigation; irrigation water was scarce; the salting of the land from irrigation water used too often had poisoned much of California's rich valleys. Clean, copious flows south would mean more food, more wealth, more of everything for everybody—especially including the Canadians, who were driving sharp bargains for their rivers.

The only reason Kriss was in New York was that he was working on that small job, no more than a handyman's afternoon chore to a big-scale engineer like Kriss, of damming the ends of Long Island Sound so that it would fill with water from its rivers, clear itself of brine and begin to be the fresh-water lake, a hundred miles long, that it had been in the geological past. Restored, it would take care of the region's drinking-water supply for the next century. But that was nearly done. The bad part of NARRO was that if it went through Kriss would move on. While Gwenanda, as long as the Supreme Court was sitting in New York and her six-year stint had not run out, had no choice but to stay. You could always resign, of course. But then you had to take some other selective service job, probably a lot less interesting and important, and who was to say that a Supreme Court justice's work was not as important as any engineer's? "So look, honey-he," she said, as they were sharing a relaxing joint before getting ready to go to sleep, "what about damming the Hudson or something instead of going out to Seattle? I mean if it happens."

"Because they won't let me just do it," he said, grinning. "They have to vote, and you know as well as I do that the continent's not going to want to give this area another big project when we just finished Long Island Sound."

"E's a real sweet kid," she said wistfully, and then sat up. "Hang on," she said, dialing her special code that was one of the fringe benefits of her job; and in a moment the monitor displayed the solemn little face of Maris D. Lemper.

"You do keep coming back to the same subject," sighed Kriss comfortably. "What do you want from me, love? What's this sudden parenting urge?"

"It's an urge normal people get," she flared. "I—hold on, what's the matter?"

There was a hesitant, persistent rapping on the door. "Come on in," Kriss called, and the door opened. Framed in it was a short, sallow man in a fluffy bathrobe, unshaven, coughing. He said peevishly:

"Could you see what all the noise is about, Kriss? I can't sleep, and I really don't feel good."

"You look lousy, Harl," Kriss corroborated.

"I *feel* lousy. Make them stop the racket, will you?"

Gwenanda reached for her dashiki as Kriss was wrapping a kilt around his waist. "Wait for me," she called. Now that the door was open, the noise was very apparent; it was people shouting, and one of the voices was Dorothy's. "It's the prunt," Kriss growled indignantly. "Why doesn't e leave um alone?" And Dorothy's voice repeated the same message, loud along the corridor:

"Won't you please leave me alone, Mrs. Feigerman? I don't like what you're doing and I don't want any part of it."

"But you're my proof," said another voice, a controlled, elderly, woman's-club-speaker voice. The woman glanced at Kriss and Gwenanda as they came into the room but returned immediately to Dorothy. "You prove just by your existence that abortion is wrong, don't you see that? My dear, your case was as tragic as any in history—not counting stillbirths—and look at you now!"

"'E wants you to get out of here," said Kriss sternly. "Will you go, please?"

"Young man," said the woman clearly, "I don't like the way you are dressed and I am having a private conversation. You are being rude." Gwenanda, a step behind, saw Kriss's shoulders hunch and settle and was amused; the prunt didn't know what she was getting into! Seemed like a nice, quiet-looking old lady, too. Frosty-faced, used to getting what she was after, you wouldn't pick her to split a joint or hear your troubles, but still it seemed out of character for her to be making scenes in public. Gwenanda reached out and touched Kriss to slow him down.

"Feigerman," said Gwenanda, "get out of here or I make nice scar-lines all down your face." She held up her ten brightly colored nails. "We live here, you don't, we don't want you, we have the right to eject you, People versus Gargiano, 562 Fed. Stat. Rev. 1993. So go!"

The woman looked shocked, then indignant, then cautious. "I'll go," she said, "but Dorothy, I'll be seeing you again—"

"Not here," Gwenanda said firmly.

The woman stood her ground long enough to say, "I will see you again too, young lady, and if you don't mend your manners it may well be in court!"

"That is a lot more likely than you think, chotz," grinned Gwenanda. She closed the door behind the woman and beamed at the others. "You can go to bed now, Dorothy. It's all over."

Kriss chuckled. "Honey, you were great. What's that People versus Gargiano stuff you were saying?"

"No idea," said Gwenanda, taking his arm. "That kind of stuff, I just make it up as I go along."

III By the special mercy of Providence the next day's calendar was a sweet pup. There were only seven cases scheduled, none of them serious, and for a wonder all eight of the other justices were willing to spend the day in court. "So can I have the day off for personal business, C.J.?" Gwenanda wheedled over the phone, and the Chief Justice shrugged.

"As far as I'm concerned. If it looks like we're going to deadlock on anything I'm going to call you back, though."

"So don't deadlock," she said, switching him off with pleasure; by phone was the best way to talk to Samelweiss, since if he did you a favor on the phone he couldn't pinch you for payment.

She took the uptown tube to Fordham Road and was astonished, coming out of the station in the undomed far north of the city, to find snow drifting across the road. "Wow," she said, pleased, and then less pleased as the cold reached her. Coming from Tucson, Arizona, Gwenanda was not used to an outside-the-dome climate like this. Domes were meant to keep out heat. Outside temperatures never got cold enough to freeze rain into snow—even assuming there was such a thing as rain—and of course she wasn't dressed for it. Fortunately, there was a van loitering at the tube station, and in two minutes she was at the freezatorium.

She nerved herself up to go in, prepared for a bad scene. She was spared. The first thing she learned was that Donna Maris Delius was already at fifty degrees below zero Celsius, all functions stopped, her internal body temperature dropping steadily toward the liquid-hydrogen levels where she would remain until some optimist decided to give her another chance. "The kid?" Gwenanda asked, and the reception clerk pointed to a little waiting room.

The little girl was contentedly reading a book. Gwenanda peered in without speaking, then pulled herself together. "Maris, honey? I'm Gwenanda. Your new muddy."

The little girl looked up politely. In person she was, if anything, cuter and prettier than in the picture; she was a year older, and a year more civilized. "Hello," she said. Too late, Gwenanda wished she had slicked down her hair, taken off some rings, tried to find a simple slack suit or maybe even a dress in her wardrobe. The contrast between the mousy murderess and the trendy Supreme Court justice was bound to give the child culture shock—to add to all the other shocks she had experienced! But the child showed no sign of shock. She read one more page to finish the story she was looking at, and then closed the book. "Kay," she said, getting up and taking Gwenanda's hand. "That's my suitcase."

The apartment, which was Gwenanda's until her hitch on the Supreme Court ran out or the Court moved elsewhere, was certainly large enough to house a child. It was large enough for six of them and maybe a husband or two as well, for there were eight rooms and three baths. "Guest room," said Gwenanda, checking them off as she led Maris through the tour, "my study, junk room, kitchen, that's my room, that's my bath, this is your bath, sun porch—and here," she said, bringing the child to a halt, "I thought this one could be yours, loves. We'll fix it up for you real pretty. I've got a friend who's an artist, and e'll make you bunnies or clowns, or anything you like on the walls."

"It's very big," said Maris politely. She looked up at Gwenanda for permission, then carefully pulled open one of the six big drawers in the smallest of the chests in the room. It was empty. The reason it was empty was that Gwenanda had been up at six to move all the dashikis and ski clothes and no-longer-worn blouses into closets and boxes. "Can this drawer be mine?" Maris asked.

"Honey, they're all yours!"

Maris looked at the drawers, then at her suitcase, but did not comment on the overkill. "It's time for my lunch now, I think," she said politely.

Lunch! Lunch was fine. Lunch was not a department that Gwenanda was worried about. Maybe it was the *only* department she wasn't worried about. She had set out biscuits from the freezer and picked papayas from the porch and put them in to chill, and it was as pretty and tasty and nutritious a lunch as any kid ever got, Gwenanda was certain. The little girl ate politely, solemn-eyed, not inquisitive, not volunteering for anything, though when Gwenanda gave her a cut papaya and a big spoon Maris was diligent about getting the seeds out. "E had a temperature," she announced as they were putting the dishes in the cleaner.

"What say, puppy?"

"My muddy had a temperature. They almost didn't ice um, because e was sick."

"When they take um out again," Gwenanda promised, "that's the first thing they'll do, fix up anything that was wrong with um." And what better way to bring a temperature down than the liquid-nitrogen coolers? But change the subject! Sure the kid had to talk about it, how else would she get it out? But not now! "What we're going to do this afternoon," she said quickly, "is get you some stuff, and then I want you to meet a friend of mine. E's an engineer, loves. You know what Long Island Sound is? It's all like part of the ocean, and what e's doing is closing it up so it will fill up with fresh water and then it will be a pretty lake for us to drink out of."

"What stuff?" Maris asked.

"To get you? Well—clothes, you know?" There had not been much in the suitcase. "We'll buy you whatever you need."

"I've got clothes. They're where I live— Knickerbocker Hostel eighteen, apartment forty-eight, only now they're in the storerooms in a big trunk."

"You live here now, pups," Gwenanda sighed, and then corrected herself. "Anyway, you will if you want to. Give me a chance, will you?"

"Sure," said Maris D. Lemper. "I think it's time for my nap now."

What Gwenanda should have been doing while the little girl was sleeping was preparing progress tests for the next batch of Supreme Court candidates. That was one of the assigned duties for second-term justices, but she couldn't keep her mind on it. She kept listening for sounds from Maris's room. When she wasn't doing that she was feverishly making lists of things she needed to get and do, coffeemaker on one side of her desk, ash tray on the other, three joints in a row burned up to calm her nerves. A nursery school. An afternoon play group for the days when Gwenanda couldn't get out of court. A playground ID—for Gwenanda to get in and out, not for the little girl. A quick trip to the stores for extra underwear and pajamas and socks—dog, what else did a child need? A child needed everything! A pediatrician. A children's dentist. A dancing class? Piano lessons? Some friends—Gwenanda sat back, dismayed. You could order up almost anything, but how did you go about ordering up friends?

Of course! She punched out commands on her memo plate, and in a moment it displayed every household within six floors up or down in the building which had young children. She found six such families and only stopped herself in time from dialing the first on the list to audition the child. Maybe three joints had been too many?

But there was still so much to do. Maris would need trips to the zoo, new shoes, swimming lessons (or could she swim already?), probably more books, probably more dolls, probably ribbons for her hair . . . and, oh, yes, a father.

So when Maris woke up from her nap and was

toileted and fed, Gwenanda dressed her bait in the best she had bought for her that morning, brushed her hair, wiped the crumbs of toast off her face and took her downtown to dangle her before Kriss.

The only thing wrong with the plan was that they couldn't find Kriss. Gwenanda left Maris in one of the common rooms, where some tenant's infant slept in a crib before the big Christmas tree, and went hunting for him. At the pool she found Dorothy, not swimming, diligently studying something on the data screen. "Oh, Kriss?" she said, looking up. "He took that other fellow to the hospital. I guess he'll be back pretty soon; he didn't say."

"Uh," said Gwenanda. "Ah. I wanted um to meet somebody."

Dorothy sighed and stretched and clicked off the screen. "It's all so complicated," she complained. "I'm trying to get caught up on what a person is supposed to do, you know, like the Universal Town Meeting and the Cafeteria Income Tax."

"Don't let me keep you, Dorothy."

"No—No, actually, is it the little girl you're talking about? The one whose mother killed her father?" She saw Gwenanda's look and said quickly, "Kriss said something about her this morning before he took off for the hospital. She sounds really nice."

Gwenanda, mollified, flashed thirty-two proud teeth. "Come and see for yourself," she said, and led the way.

Maris was polite to the new grown-up, but it was clear that she was getting along just fine by herself. She had appointed herself guardian to baby Don, who had waked up and was watching her cheerfully as she shook his word-rattle. *"Hel-*lo," it said. *"Good* kid. *Mud-*dy."

"She's very sweet," said Dorothy wistfully, pouring coffee for Gwenanda and herself.

"Sure e is," said Gwenanda, recognizing Dorothy's good critical judgment. "Aren't you working now?"

"Only for lunch today," said Dorothy, watching the children. "I guess I lost count. Is it really Christmas?"

"You mean because of the tree? No. It's February. They just decided to leave it up for pretty." And it was pretty. The tree had been coaxed to grow in seven lush green tiers, with a spike of pure white needles at the top. Gwenanda waved the room lights down, and as they dimmed cold gold and silver flames licked at the branches. "Pups?" she called. "You like the tree?"

"It's very pretty, Gwenanda," said Maris, stroking a cat behind the ears. It began to purr, its yellow eyes looking at her with appetite. Baby Don hung on the bars of his crib to watch. Gwenanda studied the scene thoughtfully.

"I wonder," she said out loud, "if I'm going about this thing the wrong way? What have they got here now, three kids?"

"I think it's three. There's a five-year-old boy, I know, and I think another one—although," Dorothy added, "it's not always easy to tell who lives here and who's just visiting. Where do you live, Gwenanda?"

"Government housing, uptown. It's what they give you when you're a Supreme Court justice, but I could move if I wanted to . . . what's the matter?"

Dorothy was staring at her. "Did you say Supreme Court? You mean of the whole United States?"

"Sure, Dorothy," she said suspiciously, returning the uncertainty on Dorothy's face with a scowl from her own. "Anything wrong with that?"

"Good heavens! Nothing wrong. It's just that I'm— well, impressed. Where I come from—*when* I come from, that's so important it's scary. I mean, you have to watch yourself with big shots."

"Nobody said you don't have to watch yourself with me," said Gwenanda darkly, and then, reaching out for her, "Aw. I keep forgetting you're just new here." She hugged the other woman before sitting back on the couch. "Listen," she said, "until a couple years ago

315

what I was was a securities analyst in Tucson, Arizona, about to get fired because I thought the dumb job was stupid. Then my number came up, you know?"

"But I don't know," said Dorothy. "Is that what they call the selective service?"

"Exactly it is. 'Greetings. You have been selected for a term of national service as—' Fill in blank—'report for orientation so and so, your salary will be so and so, good luck, don't try to get out of it, get your ass over there.' It could have been worse. I got on the judicial panel, see, and I qualified for major judiciary, and so here I am. The pay's good and the work's easy."

"Really?" Dorothy hunted for the inoffensive way to say what she wanted to say. "I thought that to be on the Supreme Court you had to have, I don't know, anyway a law degree."

"Hell, pup, we get basic training!" Gwenanda was uncomprehending. "That's mostly to teach us how to get the law out of the datastores when we're not sure. We don't even need that, much, because we get clerks to help us with the hard stuff. Samelweiss, e's the C.J., has six of them, and e's trying to get two more so e can have uz own baseball team. When you come right down to it, it's mostly common sense. That's what the Second American Revolution was all about, right?"

But Dorothy was still impressed, tickling Gwenanda very much. "Do you see the other VIPs? Like the President?"

"Sally Kamperstein? No. I mean, I've met um, but e's in Washington right now."

"Is there still government in Washington?" asked Dorothy, surprised. "I thought it decentralized all over."

"Sure it did. Still does—we won't stay here forever. Sally, e just took uz family there to see the sights. It's all fixed up like an amusement park now." She leaned over and patted Maris, who had adjusted herself at Gwenanda's feet to play with the cat. She dangled a tangle of silver-silk from the tree before the cat, which batted at it, making Maris giggle with pleasure. Then, as the cat's long claws raked across her arm, giggled again. That was pleasure, too, but a different and pleasingly scary kind. Those soft and blunt claws could never scratch flesh, but they looked as though they could. "We could buy you one, pups," said Gwenanda, and the little girl's look changed and deadened as she looked up.

"No, thank you," she said.

"Why not, lovie? They don't make any mess or anything."

"Because I had a cat once and my muddy broke it. Excuse me," she said politely, and got up again to watch baby Don being changed and fed by his father on the far side of the room.

Gwenanda sighed. "Keep an eye on um for a minute," she asked, and headed for the toilet. There was no use rushing things, she told herself, because when the kid was ready to show affection she would. And maybe not that far from now because, look, hadn't she just curled right up at her feet a minute ago? She was a nice kid, and like any kid she would come to love the person who took care of her, only— Only why didn't it happen right away? And then she checked her tab, and came back scowling at the results. "Dorothy," she said, "I have to get my pucky-flush today or tomorrow, but I took all day today off so I'd better be in court tomorrow."

"Yes?" Dorothy asked politely.

"So I think I'll go down there now. What I was wondering was whether you wanted to come with me."

The woman looked embarrassed. "What for?"

"Well, in case your corpsicle's still there."

"I don't want to see the woman!"

"E might want to see you," Gwenanda pointed out, "and maybe it's better if I'm with you."

Dorothy looked rebellious. She was quiet for a

minute, then she stood up. "Oh, *hell,*" she said, and Gwenanda understood it as intended to mean agreement.

Don's father had agreed to keep an eye on Maris, and Maris was more than willing to stay in the condo-commune for an hour or two; they took the elevator up and a cross-bridge van to the clinic. Dorothy wasn't a bad person, Gwenanda thought, at least not when you got to know her. It was even sort of fun showing her around and explaining things.

The city had changed immensely while Dorothy lay frozen. It was easy for her to recognize the new buildings—not because she remembered the old, for she had seen little enough of the city from her wheelchair, but because the new buildings were different in kind. They were thin-walled and sometimes almost wall-less; they had less glass and more thin-strip screening, with terraces inset for planting. "So much to get used to," Dorothy sighed, looking around.

"It's not so bad, is it?" Gwenanda probed, not because she was in any doubt—dog, when had the world ever been better?—but because she wanted Dorothy to understand how lucky she was.

"It scares me, though. I mean, suppose they draw the numbers again and I get drafted for something?"

"Why not? We've got Angel on the Court, e's been around as long as you have."

"The one that's half machine? Oh, sure, but he's been *living* the whole time. So he's had a chance to get used to all this, but I don't know what I'd do if I got drafted to Congress or something."

"Congress isn't bad," Gwenanda said reflectively, lighting a joint and passing it to Dorothy, who shook her head. "No? Anyway, that's okay. You really feel like you're doing incrementals there, unpassing laws all the time."

"Unpassing laws?"

"Sure. There's too many, you know, so the big job is getting rid of them."

"I wouldn't know how to do it," Dorothy said decisively.

"Nothing to it! You can only do so much at a time or it's all boxed—haste makes waste, right? So each year your congressun gets a piss-off list—" Dorothy's eyebrows went up—"a list," Gwenanda explained, "of the laws that people think dump on them. And the staff people compute how much trouble it would cause to change each one. They figure it a dozen different ways. So then the congressuns get together in committee, maybe six or eight at a time, and they talk it over. And each one gets a hit list—"

"A hit list?"

"A list, see, of the people who sent in a quantum about that particular thing—a quantum's a short statement, like no more than twenty-five words, see?—and then e calls up the ones that sound like they have something to say. Then they meet again. Then the whole Congress chews it over for a while. Then they vote."

"And that's all they do, and then the law's unpassed?"

"Dog, no! Who'd let them do that all by themselves? No, then it goes to Universal Town Meeting, see. If there's a good consensus they pass it. If there isn't, well, then it's back to the drawing board and you can't win them all. But mostly by the time it gets to Meeting it's all pretty clear."

She looked up, then ground out her roach and stood up. "This is the place you saw here before, right? So let's get out."

And sure enough, there the fool person was, marching back and forth on the promenade in front of the clinic, wearing a sandwich board—a sandwich board!— for dog's sake!—that said, *I Beg for the Life of Your*

Baby. An E.S. was watching her numbly, only remonstrating with her when she darted across the walk lanes to catch an entering clinic customer by the elbow. Jocelyn Feigerman had learned something about how things operated, it was clear. The big-character wall behind her glittered with another of her messages:

MURDER
is a sin
ABORTION
is murder

Dorothy stopped short. "I can't handle this," she said.

"Come on, pup! I'm with you. E won't do anything."

"No, Gwenanda, please. I just can't. I—I'll see you later."

Shaking her head, Gwenanda walked slowly past the woman with the sandwich board, half hoping she would try one of her arm-clutches. But she was busy complaining about something to the E.S. Catch her later, maybe, thought Gwenanda; entered the clinic, slipped her O-G card into a reader, was assigned a cubicle, took off as much of her clothing as necessary and settled in.

Actually, Gwenanda rather enjoyed her monthly pucky-flush. It didn't take long—twenty minutes or less, unless you had conceived. Then it might go twenty-five. The temperature of the liquids was warm, the force gentle, and besides there was a mild analgesic and a pepper-upper in with the hormone solutions and the refreshers. Most women spent the time reading or making talk-only phone calls—that was the only kind of phones the cubicles had, due to some prudishness in the management. Gwenanda simply let herself feel good. She lay back and allowed the shed cells to wash themselves away, already loosened by the pre-flush pills. Didn't worry about Maris. Didn't worry about

Kriss. Didn't worry, least of all worried, about the Court's upcoming cases, or even about what she wanted to eat for dinner that night. She finished with a shower and clean biks out of her shoulder bag and, very cheerful, signed out . . . and there was Dorothy sitting in the waiting room.

"Thought you went home?"

"I decided to keep an eye on Jocelyn," with a little toss of the head. "There's no reason for me to run away from her. I have as much right as she does."

"More maybe," Gwenanda encouraged. "That fool person still here?"

"Go look."

Oh, yes, the fool person was still there, and foolisher and nastier than ever. She was shrieking at a young bearded man, who was yelling back. "I've got a right!" he cried, waving at the big character board, which now said:

> Geoffrey,
> I Love You!

"I demand," Jocelyn screamed, while the Emergency Services person whispered into her radio for instructions, "that you remove that obscene, perverted message!"

"Obscene!" shouted the youth. "Perverted! It's uz *birthday,* for dog's sake! What's perverted when you love somebody to wish um a happy birthday?"

"What a barf case," sighed Gwenanda, and introduced herself to the E.S. "You want me to take care of this?" she asked. The E.S. was delighted at the prospect. "Kay," she said, turning to Jocelyn. "Now look, you. You're new here so you can be excused, a little bit. But e's right, it's uz turn and if you want to put something on the board again you just have to wait."

"Never! Not for such indecency! And that's not the point anyway," said Jocelyn, shifting position so that

321

the half-dozen passersby could hear her better. "The point is that helpless innocent unborn children are being *murdered* in this place."

"Well," said Gwenanda reasonably, "not usually. Anyway, this is the way we do it."

"A sinful, vile way!"

"Aw, dog," sighed Gwenanda. "Look. One, it saves us female ans a hell of a lot of mess and trouble, you know, and, two, it means if you want to have a baby you have to decide to. What's wrong with that?"

"If God wanted women to decide to have babies He would have made us different!"

Gwenanda was getting irritated in spite of herself and the recent relaxing flush. "See, you even called God a hemale! What's hemale got to do with female business?"

Jocelyn pursed her lips into a thin line. "I could ask you the same question. What have you got to do with my business?"

"I'm a justice of the United States Supreme Court, is what, pups."

"And I'm doing nothing wrong! Never mind. I see it does no good talking to you," she announced, gauging the crowd with her eye, and took a deep breath.

She swung her handbag at the glass louvers of the front of the clinic. The glass didn't break. Jocelyn grunted angrily and kicked at them with her foot, several times. That was more satisfactory; she broke one loose from its hinges.

"Aw, dog, what did you do that for?" Gwenanda said in annoyance as the E.S. squeaked. "Now I got to arrest you. Day after tomorrow, Supreme Court, ten A.M.—ask anybody how to get there. You want the E.S. to write it out for you?"

"No!" cried Jocelyn in ringing tones. "In fact, I welcome it! I want to make my case public!"

"That's fine," said Gwenanda, "if you do it there.

But if you keep on doing it here the E.S. will probably have to take you into the hostel for the night, because that's, uh, that's probably contempt of court, I think. Come on, pups," she added over her shoulder to Dorothy.

"You dealt with her pretty well," said Dorothy in the van.

"Hope so," muttered Gwenanda.

"What will you do to her?" asked Dorothy, studying Gwenanda curiously. She was not used to such sudden changes of mood, could not reconcile them with her image of what a justice of the Supreme Court should be.

"Do to um? Dog, pups," cried Gwenanda, "I've just put another case onto the calendar, when old Sammy's been complaining about overload already. Question is, what will Sammy do to *me?*"

IV   By the time they reached the condo-commune Gwenanda had other worries, for there was an Emergency Services van at the elevator and half a dozen medic bicycles scattered before the entryway. "Oh, jeezie! Where's Maris!" Gwenanda cried, and ran into the common rooms.

It wasn't Maris, though, or not particularly. It was everybody. Five E.S. people with red-cross armbands were shepherding the two dozen inmates of the condo into some sort of order so that they could give them spray-shots in the wrist and take germ-samples from their mouths. "Maris!" Gwenanda shouted, and then saw that Maris was sitting quietly enough, and on Kriss's lap, at that. "E's all right," grinned Kriss, half embarrassed and half proud of himself. "We just have to get splashed a little, that's all."

"Splashed for what?" demanded Gwenanda, trying

to decide whether to yield to her newfound maternal urge to grab Maris up out of Kriss's arms or allow body-chemistry to do its work on him. Consequently she only heard part of what he was answering. When he took Harl to the hospital the place had been a madhouse; they couldn't say exactly what it was that Harl had, but whatever it was a lot of people had it. They kept Harl. They sent Kriss home, and sent along with him a medic E.S. van, calling in some roving E.S. personnel to help out. Everybody who had been near Harl in the previous twenty-four hours had to get a broad-spectrum anti-bug splash from the sprayers.

"It won't hurt, pups," murmured Gwenanda, making up her mind to leave Maris where she was on Kriss's lap, but leaning over to pat her. "Won't even tickle, hardly. Then you take a sip out of that little bottle, it's just distilled water, won't even taste like anything, and you don't swallow it. You just—"

"Goodness, Gwenanda," said Maris, "*I* know how to give a mouth sample. We do it all the time in school."

"But I don't," said Dorothy humbly from beside her. "So would you please finish explaining?" It was Gwenanda's first impulse to say no, because all her attention was on Maris, but that looked like something that might get Kriss busy explaining to Dorothy instead of paying attention to the little girl. So Gwenanda gave her the pitch. The little yellow bottles held sterile water; you swished it around your mouth and spat it back, and then they analyzed it in the clinic to see if you were sick. About to be sick. Exposed to someone who was real sick. And, although Gwenanda could see nothing in Maris's looks or behavior that suggested she might have been infected, she was cursing herself out for having brought the child to this sinkhole of pestilence without making everybody take a physical first.

Kriss was holding the child out to her, explaining that he had to cook. "No, no," said Gwenanda hastily, realizing that everybody had now spat and been sprayed, "I'll take your turn, pups, because you two look *so* comfortable just the way you are. Dorothy, you come help."

Wingbean pâté with prawns, a krill stew thick with cream and butter, bacon bread with a puree of vegetables—Gwenanda cooked up a storm when she felt like it. All the condo people complimented her, but Maris sighed at each course, a chore to be got through. "You don't have to eat anything you don't like—" faint smile of unconvinced thanks—"no, truly, piglet dear. Tell you what? Is there something special you'd like? For dessert, maybe?"

"I'll think about it," said Maris judiciously, dipping bacon bread into her stew, and Kriss said,

"Aw, leave the kid alone, sweets." And patted Maris soothingly on the head.

"Of course," beamed Gwenanda, delighted at the way things were going. Well, the way *some* things were going. She still had not got over being revolted at the itch's behavior in front of the flush palace, and there was a creepy sort of false jocularity in the room. Nobody mentioned Harl. Everybody thought about him. Sickness! Godlies, thought Gwenanda, when was the last time they had an outbreak of *sickness?* It was like the Dark Ages!

As chief cook of the day Gwenanda had decreed a buffet-style dinner, to make sure that she and Maris and Kriss had a cozy little spot of their own. They had pillows to sit on, strewn around a coffee table for the food; and when you looked at them from across the room, as Gwenanda was in her imagination delighted to do, they looked exactly like a *family*. How strange it was, she thought, that she had not realized years earlier that that was what she wanted! "Would you like more stew, Kriss? Maris? Some salad?" The little girl sighed and put her spoon down.

"I think you're pushing too hard," Kriss observed.

"E's got to eat, doesn't e? Look, pups, you just tell me what you like and I'll get it. What did your muddies feed you, then?"

There was a moment's dogged chewing and swallowing of what was left in Maris's mouth before she answered. "Different things."

"Meat? I could've given you meat. Hate the stuff myself, but," Gwenanda said charitably, "lots of good people like it, so at home I keep it in the free—" Oh, *wait* a minute!—"I keep it around."

"You can say the word," the girl remarked. "I know my muddy's in the freezer."

"Ahhh—" Gwenanda kept up the spacing-out noise for a moment, looking at Kriss for help, trying to decide if this was heart-to-heart time. It was. "I'm sorry about um, pups," she said tenderly.

"For what?" The little girl shrugged. "E certainly asked for it, didn't e?"

Kriss finished his stew and smiled at the girl. "Do you want to tell us about it?" he asked, and Gwenanda flared:

"Course e doesn't. Leave um alone!"

She got a perplexed look from Kriss, and from Maris a forgiving one. "Mits Gwenanda," she said, "I don't mind talking about it, or um, or em, but, honest, it's *boring*. The shrinkers and the kid-keepers have been talking to me about it now for *weeks*, ever since it happened." She paused, thinking hard, and Gwenanda got ready for the dramatic breakthrough. Then, "I decided," she announced. "What I want for dessert is ice cream!"

The leftovers away, the waste separated, the table tidied, the two of them were on their way. Just the two of them. Kriss had work to do. Gwenanda had work to do, too, but when she proposed they do it together at her place he shook his head. Gwenanda gritted her teeth. Damn that damn Kriss, he was just digging his feet in! So it was only Maris and Gwenanda who went down the el, out across the Rainbow Bridge in a slung-under car, up again to the high-rent, high-rise that was Gwenanda's courtesy home. "To bed, pups," she caroled gaily, "or, no, wait a minute. Toothbrushing first! Bath before toothbrushing! Make the bed before the bath!" What a lot of work it was to get a little girl into bed at night! But it was all done at last, and Gwenanda looked sentimentally in at the warm, quiet little lump in the middle of the big white jellybed, her heart filled with love.

Then the tests for the cadet justices were still to be written and Gwenanda conscientiously bent over them.

Kriss . . . Maris . . . quizzes . . . that itch Jocelyn— there was too much on Gwenanda's mind, and right in front of her were the incomplete lists she had begun that afternoon. She swore softly to herself. Too much! She switched on the newschannel, heading for music, but stopped when she caught the word *emergency*. "—emergency," the newscaster was saying, "was declared at twenty-two hundred hours tonight by the Mayor and Council. Full immunization. So what you have to do, folks, is get your asses over to a clinic if you haven't been sprayed already. This means you, no shit! Do it, you hear?"

Wow, thought Gwenanda. The real stuff! She touched buttons until she found the detailed takeout she wanted. They had found the body of what they called the "primary vector" hours earlier. It wasn't hard to find it. The body called attention to itself by falling twenty-four stories out of a garden terrace onto a cross-building skyway. Because the immediate cause of death was pretty obvious, the examination of the remains waited until a biotech felt able to take time off from administering spray-shots to look it over. Then, since he didn't believe the results of his first cultures, it took nearly half a day more.

Virus flu.

Virus flu was a killer.

The great plagues of the past swept through whole cities—through whole countries, even continents—and the dead fell like reaped grain. Of course, this time there was no chance of that. Gwenanda was almost positive there was no chance. The city had not had a real pestilence for nearly two centuries, and it was not about to have one now if it could help it.

Still, the odds looked worrying. This "primary vector"—they didn't seem to know who he was, which was just plain unbelievable—appeared to have got sick nearly a week ago. Say six days. Say ten million people in the city and one center of infection. Gwenanda thoughtfully punched out the arithmetic. One center of infection walking around could brush up, close enough to maybe infect them, to probably fifty people an hour. Each of those people would move on. Subtract the eight hours a day each of them presumably spent sleeping—optimistically, alone—and in those six days there was time for $6 \times 16 = 96$, let's see, 50^{96} contacts. Well over enough chances to infect the whole city. Or the world. Or the galaxy.

Of course, medicine was quite capable of dealing with any infection, even an obsolete one—in small numbers. Large numbers became a problem, because the specific antibiotics did not exist in large numbers. The broad-spectrum sprays were less effective; the specifics had to be found in other cities and hurried in. Or they had to be made. Meanwhile there were life-support systems that would keep almost any flicker alight almost indefinitely (but how many of them? not ten million!) and as a last resort there were the freezers (but nobody had ever tried icing a million people in a week!).

Wow.

Gwenanda sighed, dumped all her memos into storage, threw off her clothes and jumped into the shower. What a mess. It would probably screw up a lot of things tomorrow—like nursery school? Certainly like nursery school! She certainly was not going to send Maris off to a nursery school, where half the kids might be carriers already, never mind how many broad-spectrum shots she'd had! She determined to keep Maris with her that day, and fell asleep grateful that this particular problem wasn't hers.

Staying alive, though. That was her problem, all right, and now it was a double problem because she had to provide for the protection and survival of two people, not one. Being a muddy wasn't all fun, was it?

V "This," Gwenanda told the child, "is where muddy works. How do you like it?"

"It's nice," said Maris politely, looking around the great hemispherical chamber. The circled spectator seats, laid out like a planetarium, were almost empty, because this was an arguments day, not a public hearing day. The nine curved desks were waiting for the other justices to arrive. "Gwenanda? When we took that elevator here, didn't we go way down in the dirt?"

"Way down, pups, uh-huh. Two hundred meters. Whatever city we're in, they dig out an underground chamber for the Court—it's kind of a tradition, if you know what that means."

"No," said Maris, with a different question on her mind. "Gwenanda? Is this a real good job you've got?"

"You bet, honey-buns."

"Can I be one when I grow up?"

"Well, no, it doesn't exactly work like you pick the job. It's more the job picks you. See, first you have to get drafted for government service, right?"

"What's 'drafted'?" The little girl was listening intently, but her eyes were on the justices' door, where

Mary Joan Whittier had just appeared. No judicial robes today; she was wearing a sort of muumuu and her hair was in curlers, and she was looking wistfully at the child. She waved. Maris blew her a kiss in return, and Gwenanda told herself sternly that she couldn't go on being jealous of a child's affectionate gestures just because they were going to someone else. She said:

"That means they pick out a bunch of people at random. I mean, like they pick the names out of a hat, only actually it's a computer. Then they assign you to different things, depending on how you do on your tests in basic training. They made me a cadet for the Supreme Court here, and then the computer sorts things out so all kinds of people get represented—and I was one of them picked. So I've got six years on the job. I'm just finishing my fourth. Pretty soon the senior class, that's the C.J. and Myra Haik and Angel—e's one of the Tin Twins, you'll see them in a minute—anyway, they'll retire, and we get three new ones, and then I'll be one of the three senior members for my last two years. Then I'm through."

Maris nodded, her eyes now on the endless circle of mottos and adages that illuminated the court's deliberations. This one said:

"The skill of making, and maintaining commonwealths, consisteth in certain rules, as doth arithmetic and geometry, not as tennis-play, on practice only."—Thomas Hobbes.

"I don't know if I agree with that one," said Gwenanda doubtfully, following the child's eyes, but Maris had already given up on the hard words.

"Is it a lot of work, what you do?" she asked.

"Aw, naw. There's two kinds of things we do. One is when people come up to the Court because they can't agree on something. That's kind of dim, because they only get here when they won't take on-the-spot arbitration or something, so they're usually stubborn people and, personally, I'd just as soon they fit it out with bicycle chains instead of bothering us. But the criminal stuff, that's good. I feel good when there's some really wicked an that we can stick in the freezer or—aw, *damn.*" She stopped, conscience-stricken.

"It's all right, Gwenanda," said the little girl. "I know you had to ice muddy."

"I didn't mean to say that. It just slipped out."

"I know." The courtroom was filling now, not with audience but with lawyers and litigants, and Maris was busy looking at everything that could be looked at. Even the latest circling maxim. "Oh, I can read that one!" she cried, gazing up at the glow-letters:

"If it is not right, do not do it. If it is not true, do not say it."—Marcus Aurelius.

While Gwenanda led her pridefully up to greet the other justices, Maris was spelling out the words. She was still rehearsing them to herself when summoned to meet the Tin Twins. Gwenanda's introduction was nervous—damn, what if the kid *said* something? Those two weren't what you met every day. What if she tried, like, to shake hands? When neither one of them had any?

But Maris was too polite to do anything like that. She gave each of the mechanicals a polite smile, and she said, making polite conversation, "I liked that, what e said, that Mark-us Orrel-us."

Of course neither of the Tin Twins could smile back. You could tell when Ai-Max was feeling genial, though, or at least when he was approving. When he was bored and paying only fractional attention his voice was flat and thin. When all his circuits were engaged it was majestic. "Marcus Aurelius," he corrected, voice rich and filled with harmonics. "A great human philosopher, 121–180 A.D. E was adopted by the Roman emperor Antoninus Pius and so e became emperor too, but is best known for uz Stoic philosophy. This was moral and often admirable, as you can tell by the quotation just given."

331

"Was Catholic, too," cried Angel, his lights flashing, "like my momma. E said the same thing always, 'Don't do bad, don't tell lies—' Oh, I should have listened."

Gwenanda beamed, hoping Maris had noted that adopted kids really could do well in the world, and hardly noticed the quick argument between the Tin Twins that broke out when Ai-Max tried to tell Angel he was probably confusing Marcus Aurelius with Constantine. What she noticed was Mary Joan Whittier calling her name fretfully: "Now, honestly, Gwenanda! We're all waiting for you!"

Gwenanda gave Mary Joan a poisonous look tinged with concern—dog, what had she been doing to herself? looked like *shit!*—and to Maris an anxious one. "Will you be all right sitting here by yourself, pups?" she demanded.

"I'll be fine, muddy," the child replied. "You go ahead and do your work."

Muddy. Gwenanda made her way to her bench in a haze of joy.

This day the Court had set aside to hear arguments, which, in the case of this particular Court, meant *arguments*. The dozen lawyers were trying to get some justice to listen to them, Samelweiss was doing his best to get a bet down on the two o'clock race with anybody in the room, Mary Joan was stammering with anger as she quarreled with Pak Il Myun over whether a bank embezzler should get frozen or just lose his credit identity for a few years, the Tin Twins, having given up on Marcus Aurelius, were now squabbling about some crossover interference in their circuits. The cheerfulest one in the room was Gwenanda. The other justices looked at her uneasily, but she beamed on because her heart was singing. *Muddy.* "Are you tranked out?" Myra Haik demanded. "I've been asking you the same question ten times!"

"What question is that, love?" Gwenanda inquired

gently. Forgivingly. Myra couldn't help being a prunt, because everybody knew she was having trouble in the love department. Not with her husband, the textile chemist, not even with her lover, who was one of the pages, big, coffee-cream fellow who almost made it in pro football, but with her girl friend. But even the Digital Colleague didn't know who the girl friend was, except that it might be one of the groupies who followed the Court around from city to city, and if the Digital Colleague didn't know, considering what he could do with other people's telephone calls when he wanted to, then nobody would know—"What?"

"I said what's this *damn* case you stuck on the docket?" Myra screamed.

Gwenanda gazed at her sweetly while she got her head back to present time. Then she remembered. "Oh, yeah," she said. "That Jocelyn an. Hey, C.J.," she called across the Court to Samelweiss. "I forgot to talk to you about that one. Uz name's Jocelyn Feigerman. E thinks every time a female an conceives e should go ahead and have the kid."

Her voice cut through the babble, because she had put her microphone on override, and produced incredulous snickers from all over the courtroom. But the Chief Justice was shaking his head. "E's a prunt, all right," he agreed, "but e has a right to think whatever e wants. Thinking isn't against the law."

"Breaking windows is, though. Also e's bugging a friend of mine really bad—keeps following um around and yelling at um." And Gwenanda, conscious of Maris's grave eyes observing her, punched out commands for the glow-screen, so that the next words to circle the dome were:

"Nobody has any right to dump on anybody else."— The 30th Amendment to the Constitution of the United States.

"Dog, Gwenanda! I know what the Constitution says," the C.J. complained. "You know what else I know? I know we've got a full calendar for the next two weeks, and Mary Joan here walking around like she's stoned—" Mary Joan, chin on her hands, quivered but didn't look up—"and some of the other justices busy with their private fights—" faint protesting beeps from the Tin Twins—"and taking days off whenever they feel like it—"

Gwenanda refused to come down from her high. "Sweety-bumps," she said sunnily, "e's already summonsed."

"Damn!"

"Anyway, e'll be kind of fun, I think, like that chotz that wanted to sue us. Besides, I won't take any more days off," she promised. "Now, come on, pups! All of you. Let's hit the docket so I can get out of here and buy my kid some ice cream!"

For a wonder, they all did—even half-asleep Mary Joan, even Angel, whose voice was flat when he voted because he was using big chunks of his circuits to display pictures of his great-great-great grandchildren to Maris, in the front row. They cleaned up a couple of dozen motions in half an hour. For the cases they couldn't resolve on the spot, they split up research and investigation chores fairly—more or less fairly—Mary Joan was hardly answering to her name when the C.J. tried to give her the job of checking out the facts on Justice Horatio Margov, the loony with the billion-dollar suit, so Samelweiss gave up and turned it over to Ai-Max. Samelweiss himself seemed to be spending as much of his time watching Gwenanda as he did on ramrodding the other seven and the score of attending lawyers and litigants. When at last he slapped the tape systems off and crowed, "Court's adjourned," he crooked a finger at Gwenanda. She was halfway down the dais to where Maris was sitting already, but she gave the child a wink and sidled over to the C.J.'s bench.

For a wonder, he didn't complain about anything. He

didn't even pinch her bottom, just said, "You're getting to be a real take-charge judge, Gwennie. Have you ever thought about being C.J.?"

Gwenanda gave him an open-mouth stare. "Me? You mean *me*? Dog, Manny, I can make enemies easier ways than that!"

"Somebody has to do it," he persisted. "Figure it out for yourself. My hitch runs out in a couple of months, Angel and Myra too, so your class comes up. C.J. doesn't *have* to be one of the three senior judges, but e always is, so who've you got?" He counted off. "There's Pak. Not bad, but e doesn't get along with people. There's Mary Joan. A real dummy, not counting being spaced out like e is. And there's you. Which one would you say, sweet-lump?"

"Pak," she said firmly, and then reversed herself. "Or Mary Joan. Why not? E just doesn't feel good today."

"E sure doesn't," agreed the C.J., watching Mary Joan stumble toward the robing room. "Hope e doesn't have that damn flu—did you know they found the chotz that started it?"

"No! Are they going to summons um for it?"

"Can't," chuckled the C.J. "Found um dead. *Real* dead, you know, like three or four days, and just lousy with diseases, all kinds. One of the lawyers was telling me—anyway, what about it? C.J. for you?"

"Absolutely no way," Gwenanda declared. "Positively. I mean it. Anyway, that's not your worry, you know."

"No, you're wrong about that. Sure, the next Court elects its own Chief Justice, but I want to make sure it's done right. You've got the votes if you want them. I already talked to Pak and the juniors—"

"Now, *damn*," cried Gwenanda, "you had no right to do that!" She was getting really upset, the good mood from the kid calling her "muddy" blown away, ready to rip right into him. The only thing that stopped her was the child's voice, along with a beep from the Tin Twins.

"Gwenanda," Maris called urgently. "Angel says there's something wrong with that judge—" And Angel's booming voice, full attention register sounding, confirmed:

"It's Mary Joan. E's in the hall, passed out cold! I'm getting a remote that says e's really sick!"

Naturally the C.J. put in a priority call for help. Naturally the Emergency Services van was there in ten minutes, to take away the patient and to splash all the contacts with anti-virals and immunizations. Naturally Gwenanda didn't wait for any of that, because both she and Maris had already had their splashes and her most urgent thought was to get Maris out of there.

What she wanted was to take her home, and "home" at that moment sounded like Kriss's condo-commune. They didn't take a van or a shuttle. They took a three-wheeled minicab, driver over the electric motor in front, Gwenanda and Maris sharing the passenger seat behind. All the way up from the Court to ground level Gwenanda held the child away from the other passengers crowding the elevator, and when they were in the cab she worried about whether there was any infection still at the commune. Shots were supposed to keep you from getting sick, sure. But who knew if the shots always worked? To conceal her own nervousness she tried to point out interesting sights to the child, but Maris had been seeing them all her little life and anyway what was interesting wasn't the city, it was what was happening to it now. Gwenanda swore to herself and gave up, flicking on the news plate on the back of the driver's seat.

Bad. More than eighty thousand flu cases reported in the city, it said. Hospices overflowing. Clinics swamped. Vaccines running out. All Emergency Services people on twenty-four-hour call, and the next year's class of in-lieu-of-taxes E.S. workers being summoned up early. Gwenanda spun through the news stories, looking for reassurance and not finding much. The most perplexing thing was that the dead vector had been found, all right, but was officially unidentified. "Now, that's *dumb*," Gwenanda complained out loud. "How can they have the stiff and not know who e is?"

"Everybody's somebody," agreed Maris.

"Damn true e is. You can tell in two minutes who. All you have to do is get uz fingers or eyeprint or DNA spectrum—what do they mean 'unidentified'?" she demanded fretfully. "What a chotzy *mess*."

The mess Gwenanda meant was the simple mess of not being able to make an ID on a routine stiff, but what inflamed her irritation was the far bigger mess the city was in. There had not been an epidemic, or even a threat of one, in so long that the city didn't know how to take it. Laugh it off? Flee the plague spot? But there were too many wretched victims to laugh, and there was an instant quarantine of the whole city that wouldn't let you run. So, since the city didn't know how to take it, it took it all wrong. Took it by panicking (a few), or by making sick jokes that no one found funny (more), or by trying to pretend that it didn't exist (almost everybody—until somebody sneezed nearby, or even looked unwell, at which point the citizens of the third kind immediately switched over to being citizens of the first; no leper was ever shunned with more vigor than any New Yorker who, that day, happened to clear his throat out loud).

Two hundred meters up from the Court, halfway across the city, pay off the cab, another hundred meters to the commune—and Kriss wasn't there. He wasn't at work, either, because when Gwenanda called the municipal Water and Sewage Authority the message machine informed her that the office had been closed for the day. That left a possibility Gwenanda didn't much like. "Come on, pups," she said darkly. "I'll get you the ice cream now." And all the way to the terraced restaurant where Dorothy worked her jaw was set grimly.

When she saw that Kriss wasn't there her suspicions shamed her. The restaurant was a nearly empty, cheery place high over the park and the Rainbow Bridge, and Dorothy saw them at once and came over in that Tin Woodman walk of hers. Gwenanda summoned up a friendly smile for her, but it hardened when Maris ran to Dorothy to be kissed and vanished entirely when Dorothy said, "You just missed Kriss, but he said he'd be back in an hour or so." The suspicions came back full force. Scowl time. Tooth-grinding time. Was the damn an trying to take both Kriss and the kid away from her? It was not Gwenanda's best hour, and what was coming over the restaurant's sound system was beginning to get on her nerves. When it wasn't high-tech music, it was what sounded like adjurations to the employees: "Now, breakfast is the most important meal of the day, so what do we do about it? We try to make it a *pleasant* one for our guests."

"Hello," said Gwenanda ungraciously. "What's that damn noise?"

Dorothy's sober, unlined face clouded over, but she responded civilly, to the words instead of the tone. "It's something they do to help train us. We're mostly just out of the freezer here—though the others," she said wistfully, "seem to catch on faster than I do."

Maris was watching Gwenanda's face with an expression of—dog, could it be *fear?* well, sure it could be fear—what else would you expect from a kid whose muddy not only beat the child up but Xed her marry when she got sore? "Aw," said Gwenanda, realizing she was being unfair, remorsefully trying to put everybody at ease, "I bet you do just fine, pups."

Dorothy, absently stroking Maris's hair, considered the point. "Well, I can do waitressing and I can even do short-order. I don't panic when a crowd comes in and I don't mix up the orders. But I do break a lot of dishes."

"You'll do better," Gwenanda promised.

"I hope so. Well, what'll it be—I mean, what may I bring you?" she corrected herself, glancing up at the loud-speakers. And when she had the orders—a mango split for Maris, a bottle of beer for Gwenanda—she was off, stiff-legged, arms swinging awkwardly at her side, but smiling.

Gwenanda sat back and compelled herself to relax, ignoring the speakers—

"—as soon as the diner reaches uz table, don't wait, come right up to um and say, 'Would you care for some coffee?' And have the pot in your hand, ready to—"

"This is a nice place," she commented brightly as Maris looked around. "Can you see over the park there? That's our building, see it? The greeny-glass one? Well, we're about twenty stories higher than this, right above that setback with the palms?"

"I see it," said Maris politely, and excused herself to go to the bathroom.

She took a while to come back, and worked on the mango split only slowly. By the time Kriss showed up she was still finishing it. "I came back early," he said genially, "because I thought you pups might be here." He kissed Gwenanda and moved along to nuzzle his nose in Maris's hair. He sat down, beckoning to Dorothy to take his order, and said, "It's getting gritty out there. I was a little worried about you two."

"Not half as worried as I was," Gwenanda snapped, noticing how Kriss winked at Dorothy as he asked for a glass of wine. But she had decided against jealousy, she reminded herself; it wasn't worthy of her, and besides

Kriss wouldn't put up with it forever. But today he wasn't taking offense. Probably he understood she was a little on edge because of the sickness in the city, not counting trying to learn a muddy's role in a hurry, and not doing too well at it.

"I thought we might all go to the track this afternoon," he said, one arm on the back of Maris's neck as the child worked slowly at her ice cream. "Can't, though. It's closed down because too many jockeys are sick."

"That's bad news for the C.J.," said Gwenanda. She waved for another beer, beginning to feel relaxed again. She leaned closer to Kriss, fondly rubbing her ear against the curl of his sideburns; damn, how good just his being around made her feel. "I wish you weren't going to Seattle," she said wistfully, while over the sound system:

"—in the event the wine steward is busy, you may display the list, but during dinner do not take orders—"

He grinned at her. "Who knows? It may not get past the UTM. Speaking of which, have you been practicing your quantum, just in case?"

"Sure I have." And she had, Gwenanda reassured herself, though not much since she took over care of Maris. Her heart wasn't really in it, of course. Why should she make arguments in favor of the thing that was going to take Kriss away from her? Of course, it might not pass no matter what she did.

But it also might. No matter what she did. She watched wistfully while Kriss leaned over to the little girl. "Kittens," he said, "you're not doing much with that sundae. Would you rather have something solid?" He turned on the table-top telly and caused it to display the roasts and stews and salads that made up the specials of the day. Maris gave it a horrified glance.

"Oh, no," she said faintly. Kriss, looking concerned, switched the telly over to news, and the paella on the screen was replaced by an index sheet.

"Wow," he said. "A hundred and twenty thousand sick!"

That was a shocker—why, not even an hour ago it was only about eighty thousand. The city was plunging into the deep shit, all right, thought Gwenanda—

"—knife to the left, sporks to the right, chopsticks across the top of the plate—"

—and tardily she saw that Maris, looking distressed, had stopped eating entirely. Gwenanda licked her lips. "I'm sure glad you got Maris her shots," she said; and Kriss, startled, stammered:

"But I thought it was you—"

That was how the nightmare began.

For a long time afterward, whenever Gwenanda set a table she felt a cold wind strike at her heart; whenever she held the child on her knee, she remembered how shifting Maris from lap to lap had cost her her shots; every time she saw a mango split her stomach twitched as it had when Maris, without warning, threw up all over the table. When Gwenanda clutched her, the little girl's forehead was burning.

What was absent in Gwenanda's later recollections was the memory of herself doing anything. As far as she could recall, she was a spectator, paralyzed. That couldn't have been true, but it was Kriss who snatched up the child and hurried toward the door; it was Dorothy who stripped the next table—crash of crockery, rattle of silverware to the floor—for a cloth to wrap around Maris and napkins to clean her off as she followed. When they called Emergency Services (was it Gwenanda who had done that?), there was a two-hour wait for a van; "Downstairs!" yelled Kriss, heading for the elevator. When they got down to ground zero and Kriss, scouring the throughways, at last found a vacant three-wheeled cab, all four of them crowded into the two-person seat. When at last they approached the nearest E.S. clinic, it seemed that every vehicle in New York was there before them. For the last quarter-kilometer Kriss trotted with Maris in his arms—hours later, Gwenanda remembered to wonder if they had paid the driver.

The waiting room was jammed. Never mind the emergency room itself; they couldn't get through the wheezing, sneezing, groaning and sweating mob that overflowed to the van rank outside. "Stay here!" cried Kriss. "I'll get somebody!"

"I'll help!" echoed Dorothy, and Gwenanda was left with the hot lump of sick child in her lap as they pushed and trotted away.

The news reports had not kept pace with reality. Exponential growth was sweeping through a population that had never needed resistance to the virus. The reported sick were not a hundred and twenty thousand any more, they were a quarter of a million—and growing every minute—tens of thousands of new cases limping or being carried to report themselves sick as fast as they could get to a place to do so. A handful of E.S. medics were crawling through the crowd, spray-guns in each hand; they gave a shot, felt a forehead, once in a while took a temperature, felt a throat for lumps or peered into a mouth. But—beds? "Dog, chotz," gasped the E.S. Kriss finally managed to drag over, "we haven't had a *bed* all day!" She pressed the spray against Maris's arm, pulled down an eyelid, held a hand against a cheek. "Needs bed care now," she said. "Take um home! Check the telly for instructions, keep um warm, keep um quiet, keep um full of fluids." And, as she was turning to the next case, "Oh, and check your loo numbers, because if you're draftable you're drafted!"

One more damn thing! And, yes, when Kriss shouldered his way over to look at the big-character screen it was displaying emergency orders:

"If you have an in-lieu-of-taxes obligation and your class number appears below, report at once for Emergency Services duty."

Kriss's number was there. "Ah, shit," he groaned, and disappeared in search of a supervisor. Gwenanda sat on the edge of a stack of emergency folded cots—a teen-aged boy, breathing with horrible rasping gasps, was stretched out on top of it—and rocked Maris, the child's head burning her breast through the thin dashiki. "Aw, baby, sleep," she crooned, scared as she had never been in her life before. What did you do with a sick child? Get help, right? But there were fifty people just within sneezing distance that needed help as much as Maris, and help had run out. "Muddy's here," she whispered. "Sleep, sweet-cheeks, sleep. . . ."

Dorothy was the first one back. She didn't bring a medic but something far more valuable, a paper cup of watered down juice, held high with one unpracticed hand, somehow saved from spilling as she edged through the crowd. "Prop her head up," she ordered. "I'll see if I can get her to swallow some." And while they were coaxing the last drops into the unresisting child Kriss appeared. He was towing a frazzled-looking woman, the two of them arguing all the way.

"Gwenanda!" he cried. "E says I have to report to take care of sick. I said we've got a sick of our own and I want to take um home and take care of um. E said that's not good enough, they can't spare an able-bodied an for just one patient, and anyway what they need is beds. They're requisitioning some underoccupied homes, and—"

"My place!" cried Gwenanda. "Sure, pups! We'll take um there and you can send up others! It's a big apartment, there's easily room for twenty or thir—— for at least a dozen," she corrected herself, dazzled with the first good news in what seemed like years. Sharing Maris's care with Kriss! Who cared if there were a few others? And even while the supervisor was checking her facilities and making the arrangements for Kriss to transport beds and blankets and medications and bedpans, Gwenanda was selecting her guests.

"That one," she said, pointing to a young boy, "and that one, and—no, not that one, but the one next to um—" And led the way to the van, still scared, but more and more hopeful, even, almost, happy.

The City of New York, in its half a millennium since the Dutch, had lived through pestilences. Not all of its citizens did. Yellow fever sometimes took one in ten, typhus one in five; in the last great influenza epidemic, right after the first of the World Wars, many thousands died and many more, decades later, suffered the twitches and speech problems of Parkinson's syndrome as a consequence. But that was long ago. Medicine had honed its skills and multiplied its resources for more than a century since the last bad one. The therapies and remedies for almost every communicable disease were known, and they were effective. What they were not was readily available. Who could have guessed that they would be urgently needed?—when nearly every such disease organism was as extinct as the great blue whale? The resources were scattered all over the continent, in a hundred disease-research centers—really, they might almost better be called museums of antique ailments. The medicines could be brought to bear on the city's sickness, but not in an instant.

Meanwhile half a million New Yorkers were sweating and sneezing and tossing and turning in achey efforts to sleep. Gwenanda didn't wind up with a dozen of them in her care, or even with twenty or thirty. At maximum there were fifty-one patients in her apartment. It wasn't Kriss who shared their tending, either, because Kriss was kept busy all that day and most of the long night in staggering in with loads of cots and supplies, and patients to fill them. Dorothy was Gwenanda's only helper for most of that time. She was clumsy, all right—spilled one whole six-liter kettle of simmering chicken broth and had to spend an hour mopping it up, dropped things, fumbled things. But she was strong, stronger than Gwenanda when it came to lifting a fat old man off a stretcher. And as devoted to Maris's care as Gwenanda herself. Between coaxing a child to swallow juice or spooning broth into a semiconscious face or wiping sweat from a fevered brow, they took turns to look in on that tiny but most important patient of all, asleep in Gwenanda's own huge bed. They refused to let her share it, though every flat surface in the big apartment had a patient or two on it now—the beds, the couches, the chairs big enough to be pushed together; Kriss brought in camp cots for another twenty, and mattresses to spread on the floor for the rest.

For the first hours, both Dorothy and Gwenanda were running to the telly every few minutes to check nursing instructions on the emergency band. But the job was not that complicated. Every patient had already had a broad-spectrum shot of antibiotics and antivirals. It was just a matter of letting the medicine work, and meanwhile keep them warm, keep fluids in them, take temperatures, listen for choking, watch for convulsions, sponge them cool if the temperature got dangerous . . . it was Gwenanda and Dorothy all that day and all that night, doing it all. What neither of them did was sleep. A catnap now and then, sitting beside the bed jealously reserved for Maris—that was as much rest as any of them got, never more than a minute or two, and then up and at it again. It seemed to have no end.

But at dawn a hastily drafted E.S. temporary appeared to share the labor, and a real, genuine nurse!! The work didn't actually get easier then, though, because by that time the bedpan problem and the changing sweated sheets problem and the general cleaning up spills and stains problems were all beginning to get acute. It was the hardest work Gwenanda had ever done, and the dirtiest, and it seemed to go on the longest. It took her some time to realize that, if not ending, at least it had stopped getting worse. A trickle of new patients were still coming in, but some of the earliest and least sick were beginning to sit up, and sometimes fend for themselves, and even, a few of them, declare that they were able to be up and about and so weakly totter off home.

At eleven that morning the nurse chased both Dorothy and Gwenanda, one after another, into the shower—not yet to sleep, but at least to do the next best thing. Slightly refreshed, Gwenanda sat for a minute, chewing cold, dry toast—made an hour before, but then the woman with the hacking cough had begun to strangle on her own mucus—and remembered her real job. Dog! Call the Court right away! When she did she found the Court was closed for the emergency. Two justices were out sick, plus any number of pages, clerks, lawyers, complainants, defendants—all cases were rescheduled for Monday morning.

Gwenanda put the phone down. She wandered away from the forgotten toast, automatically heading for Maris's bed. The child was sleeping easier now, but her temperature was still high. Sponging her down, Gwenanda wondered fretfully which of the justices had got it besides Mary Joan. Not one of the Tin Twins, of course. Pak? Myra? She reached with the damp cloth toward Maris's brow—

"Oh, please don't!" sobbed the child, flinging herself away in terror from Gwenanda's hand. "Please muddy, don't hit me again!"

At the door, Dorothy almost dropped the bedpan she was carrying past. "Oh, what's wrong?" she cried, hurrying in.

"Don't *know*," Gwenanda moaned. She wanted desperately to touch the child. She didn't dare, for Maris was straining away from her, searching her face with frightened, imploring eyes. "No more, please!" she begged; and then, the tension ebbing from her crouched limbs, in a different voice: "Oh, it's you, Gwenanda."

And lifted her face to be kissed; and went peacefully

back to sleep; and an hour later her temperature was down to normal.

More tired than she had ever been, Gwenanda allowed herself at last to stretch out on the bed beside the child. Her sleep was snore-deep, but her face was smiling and her dreams were good.

All the same, Gwenanda did not allow herself to sleep very long. When she woke, the temperature of the whole city was down. Doctors and medical supplies had poured in from Philadelphia and Boston and Baltimore. There was a hundred per cent prophylaxis by now—with specific vaccines, located freeze-dried as soon as the specific virus had been identified, flown in, reconstituted, administered. It had taken an immense effort, but now the people who had not already come down with the flu never would, and the influx of new cases had ceased. The nurse—short, dark Palestinian from Omaha—had the situation under control and reported that he didn't need sleep for an hour or so yet, so Gwenanda, after checking on Maris, allowed herself to remember she was starving.

Dorothy was in the kitchen ahead of her, making heavy work out of trying to scramble eggs. But she refused Gwenanda's help. "I have to learn to use the damn things," she said, glaring at the pieces of shell her clumsy hands had allowed to fall in the bowl. "Might as well be now. I'll put in a couple more for you, honey."

"Dog, yes! Please," Gwenanda added, and sat down to allow herself the pleasure of watching somebody else work. "It's been a tough night," she sighed.

Dorothy grinned. "It's been two of them," she said, "and two days, too. I guess we just weren't watching the time."

"Aw, really? Then this is Saturday?" Gwenanda tried to remember why Saturday was important, but it wouldn't come to her. She dismissed the thought completely when Dorothy said:

"Maris was up for almost an hour while you were

sleeping. Seemed pretty nearly fine, but I told her to try to get to sleep again. And she did, soon as she hit the pillow."

"Aw," said Gwenanda, delighted at the report, disappointed that she had slept through the event—but a lot more delighted than disappointed, she decided. "I guess maybe the worst is over," she offered.

"It looks that way," said Dorothy, carefully pouring the beaten eggs into a pan. "And, oh, wow, Gwenanda, it's been kind of wonderful. Would you believe that?"

"Believe what?" Gwenanda asked suspiciously.

"I mean, everybody getting together like this—the whole city pitching in—even the whole country!"

"Dog, Dorothy! Why wouldn't they? We're *civilized* people, you know, not like the damn *animals* where you came from!" And then, penitently, "Aw, my mouth's too big. I didn't mean anything, pups—"

"Of course you didn't," Dorothy said comfortably, tipping the eggs into two plates and carrying them carefully over. "I know you pretty well by now, Gwenanda. You yell when you're mad, and you hug when you're feeling affectionate—you don't have to apologize for that. Gwenanda? I *like* you, just the way you are. Now eat your eggs."

"Aw," said Gwenanda, embarrassed, mouth full of eggs—delicious, too, and who cared if you bit into a tiny piece of shell now and then? "They're fine, Dorothy."

"And another thing," Dorothy said suddenly, "I like Kriss, too, but not the way you do. I mean, he's a lot too young for me, wouldn't you say? Even if he took an interest of that kind, which he doesn't."

"Aw," said Gwenanda again, again embarrassed at being so transparent, searching for the right way to repay sweetness with sweetness, finding only: "You've been a real big help this time, pups, do you know that?"

"Uh-huh," said Dorothy complacently. "And I be

you don't know how good that feels to me. You know what my life was like? I had to be fed, I had to be dressed, I had to have somebody sit me on the damn *toilet*—every day—for forty-six years! You just can't know how nice it is for me to be taking care of somebody else for a change!" And she grinned, and dove into her cooling eggs, and didn't mind at all that now and then some of them spilled back onto the plate from her shaky fork.

"I'll do the cleanup," said Gwenanda tenderly, "because now it's your turn to get some sleep."

By that Saturday evening half of Gwenanda's tenants had taken themselves home, and all of the rest were mending fast. They had not been the sickest, of course. The really hard-hit victims were still in intensive care and more than two thousand persons had actually died—irreversibly dead, some of them, though most had been quick-frozen for a better day, when the doctors decided that a spark remained but the immediate prognosis was bad. The crisis was over. The called-up E.S. people were beginning to get their releases. Kriss celebrated by tumbling into the bed in Maris's room, just vacated by a recovering tourist couple from the island of Maui. Gwenanda, with the nurse from Omaha, labored to get the cots and mattresses stacked for pickup and the apartment somewhat tidied up, then stretched out beside Maris again and allowed herself once more to drift off into a nap.

When she woke, Maris was standing beside the bed. She had bathed herself and changed her clothes and brushed her hair, and she held out a glass of juice to Gwenanda. "Drink it, muddy," she commanded, "because you have to keep taking fooids."

"Aw, thanks, sweet-cheeks," Gwenanda cooed, struggling to sit up on the edge of the bed. With one hand she reached for the glass, with the other pushed hair. "Pups! What are you doing out of bed? Are you feeling all right?"

Maris supervised the swallowing of the juice before she answered. "The nurse said it was all right to get up, 'cause I feel fine. E said don't eat too much, don't get too tired, go back to bed early, drink a lot of fooids," she recited, and then, "Gwenanda? Can I tell you something?"

"Sure you can!" Gwenanda caught sight of herself in the mirror behind the little girl and shuddered.

"I'm sorry I yelled at you."

"Aw, you didn't really *yell.*" Gwenanda pushed hopelessly at the disintegrated dreadlocks; dog, she looked like somebody had sat on her head!

"If I did yell," Maris said determinedly, "it was only because I was dreaming and I thought you were um. My other muddy, I mean. I thought e was going to hit me again."

"Aw, pups!"

"E didn't *mean* to be hitting me all the time, you know. Daddy said it was just because e was sick. E said until e got better we mustn't tell anybody about it, because they'd take um away from us—"

"*Aw.*"

"But then e—Then e took the bottle and—" Maris swallowed. "Anyway, e died, so it wasn't a secret any more, but I never told anybody, Gwenanda, honest." She paused, while Gwenanda strained the child wordlessly to her chest, and then added, "If—if you got sick sometime, Gwenanda, and had to do something like that—I wouldn't tell on you, either."

Gwenanda found herself muttering something hoarsely. It wasn't in words. It wasn't even an "aw!" It seemed to satisfy Maris, though. The child allowed herself to be held tightly for a moment, then gently tugged herself free. "You prob'ly want to get cleaned up, muddy," she said practically, "and I promised to help the nurse." She kissed Gwenanda gravely on the cheek, and then left to do her duty.

Gwenanda, rubbing her eyes, sat for a moment, then sighed and got up to start the repairs on herself. It was a sad, wistful little sigh, but when she had breathed it out of her she had breathed out all the sadness she felt, and what was left was feeling good. She had had a scary and exhausting two days, with no more than a handful of hours of interrupted sleep; but in the shower she was singing and lathering up a storm, letting the hot water pour down on her healthy, fine body, when the curtain was snatched aside and Kriss leaned in, bleary-eyed and excited. He yelled, "It's the UTM, Gwennie! It's on!"

"Oh, *dog*," Gwenanda cried, conscience-stricken—how could they have forgotten that?

"So get out of the damn shower! They've started random selection for quanta—you have to be ready if they call you!"

VI They should have postponed the UTM! New York City wasn't ready! Those ten million people under the dome and in the underground warrens across the river and out in the suburbs—they had had other things on their minds these past few days than what to do about some damn rivers in Alaska! Gwenanda was tsking with vexation as she tried to dry herself, against Kriss's urgent hurry-up noises.

But, of course, this wasn't one of your little local meetings about some damn dome or transportation scheme or zoning change. This was the Big Time, continent-wide, tropics-to-Pole high! All of the United States, all of Canada, a big wedge of northwestern Mexico were all affected, one way or another, and all the quarter-billion people who lived there had an equal right to be heard.

The fact that you had a right as good as anybody else's didn't mean you had a very good *chance*. Not when the universe of this particular Universal Town

Meeting added up to the population of a whole continent. The odds were terrible. The permissible Quantum of Debate for each person selected by the random-access computers was thirty seconds. The time allotted for all the vox-populi quanta put together was only six hours—twelve segments of half an hour each, spaced over the twenty-four-hour span given to deciding the fate of NARRO. That meant that precisely seven hundred and twenty persons could be heard. Subtract from the total population the twenty per cent or so who were too young to participate. Subtract again the sixty per cent, more or less, who had nothing to say on the matter, or at least had failed to put their names in for the draw.

What was left was some fifty million people, all of whom wanted to be heard. $\frac{50,000,000}{720}$ = barely one chance in seventy thousand that any one name would come up in the draw, so that its owner's cogent or significant or rambling or even demented quanta could be heard.

And, actually, the odds were far worse now, because they had slept through most of the UTM. It was prime time now—eighteen hundred hours in New York, fifteen in California—they were coming up on the last half-hour segment for vox-populi soundings, and the last rounds of voting would take place within the next two hours. Most of the continent had been following the debate for hours. So Kriss rushed Gwenanda out of the shower and into a robe. No time to do her hair properly. Hardly time to turban a towel around it. There were still drops of moisture running trickling down her forehead and over her nose as she sat herself down beside Dorothy and Maris, already glued to the screen in fascination. "This one's from Miami Beach," Dorothy announced, "and I don't think he's for it."

"That's two in a row," Kriss groaned. The man from Miami was a construction worker who wore a hard-hat tipped forward over a scowl. His jaw was aggressive, his voice hoarse with resentment as he said,

"—somebody else's turn at the trough! The Gulf Stream Power Takeoff is proved technology. Dollar for dollar, it would be a better investment than NARRO, and I say California is—"

But his thirty seconds were up. He disappeared from the screen, and whatever he was going to tell the continent that California was went unheard beyond the room he was in.

"Bunch of bullshit," Kriss said, diagnostically unkind. "Are you ready in case they call?"

"Dog," groaned Gwenanda, "how can I be ready, haven't even had any coffee, didn't brush my hair—"

"I'll get you some coffee," Dorothy said, and Maris snuggled up against Gwenanda.

"You look fine in the hat," she announced, and gratefully Gwenanda hugged the child to her. Kriss was leaning forward, dividing his time between the small screen next to the telly, where he had displayed the text of his quantum, just in case, and the main screen, where a schoolteacher from Pennsylvania was exercising his rights.

"Oh, wow," Kriss grumbled in dismay. "Listen to this prunt!" The schoolteacher was telling the continent that Pennsylvania didn't always get enough rainfall, either, but the good people of Allentown weren't going around trying to steal other people's rivers. "Dog!" snarled Kriss, "that's the *third* in a row against the whole project! You think the computer's screwing up?"

Swift chance of *that!* Gwenanda eagerly accepted her coffee from Dorothy, and made reassuring noises for Kriss's sake. The computers for the UTM used algorithms almost identical with the ones for Selective Service. Every applicant was tagged as to age, gender, occupation, sexual preferences, education, IQ and AQ—all the qualities that distinguished one segment of the population from another. If eleven per cent of the population were left-handed, then of the 720 selectees some eighty, more or less, would also be southpaws; if three per cent had doctoral degrees, then so would twenty or twenty-one of the faces on the screen. The computer took no note of preferences on the issue. It was meant to randomize opinions, and it did. Always. Even if, as now, three people in a row turned up dead set against NARRO.

For the first time Gwenanda felt a thrill of wicked hope. Dog, what if it got *beaten?* What if there wasn't any NARRO, so Kriss had no reason to skylark off to Seattle for the next dozen years, so that he might stay right here where they could all be so happy? What if the sampling had been right on, and the good people of the continent in their wisdom were going to reject this harebrained scheme?

Of course, the good Gwenanda whispered in the real Gwenanda's ear, drowning out the voice of the temptress Gwenanda, NARRO really was a good thing. You get a big job like that done, and in the long run it's good for everybody. . . . "What's going on?" she demanded.

"They've recessed for a vote," Kriss snapped. "That prunt from Miami Beach did it!"

He had. The town-meeting computers had taken note of his remarks about the Gulf Stream project—great slow turbines sucking energy out of the flow of the world's hugest river to make electricity for the land—and had tallied the volunteer call-ins in favor of it, weighting them for where they came from and what kind of people made them, and decided that there was enough sentiment for the Gulf Stream to warrant calling a question. So there was a vote. The acting chair of the congressional supervisory commission, looking chipper if sleepy, announced the question: "Yes or no, folks. The idea is, if NARRO passes, we start engineering studies for the Gulf jobber and follow it up if they look good. Say whether you think that's a good idea," and she gave instructions on how to dial to cast a vote either way.

Sounded like a good idea to Gwenanda—as good a

anything that would take Kriss away, anyway. She punched in her vote for the rider; so did Kriss; then the two of them headed for the kitchen to replenish their coffee cups, leaving Dorothy, delighted to be taking part for the first time in so huge a decision, carefully keying her ID number and aye vote.

The count was fast, but there were still a couple of minutes to wait for the result. "E didn't sound in favor of it," fretted Kriss, "I wonder how many of them feel the same way? Even if they vote for the rider?"

"It'll be all right," Gwenanda soothed, and wondered if it would. Wondered what "all right" meant. Wondered if there was some smart way to get the best of both worlds, have Kriss happy, have herself happy, have a home for Maris.

"Sure it will," said Maris from behind her, startling her. "Can I have a glass of milk?"

"Oh sure," said Gwenanda, but Kriss was already getting it out for the child. *Aw,* thought Gwenanda to herself, building fairy castles in her mind of the two of them parenting Maris together, just this way, forever. . . well, until the kid got big, anyway. . . .

"Gwenanda?" called Dorothy from the other room. "What does it mean when your name comes on at the bottom of the screen, like red letters crossing along—"

Gwenanda's jaw dropped. *"Dog!"* yelled Kriss, slamming the milk down in front of Maris, jumping for the door. In a moment he shouted back:

"It's you, Gwennie! They've called you! You're on in two minutes!"

Called! Two minutes! "Dog *shit,*" Gwenanda moaned, and shook her head. And felt the turbaned towel loosen at the back of her head. She clutched at it. "It isn't *fair!*" she bawled, meaning having to go on the telly looking the way she did, meaning having to do anything when she was prunty *exhausted,* meaning the world.

"What's the matter, Gwennie?" asked Maris.

"Aw, pups, what am I going to do? Kriss wants this so much—but he'll have to go off to damn *Seattle*—but —Aw, *damn.*"

"It's just what e says," said Maris, putting down her milk to take Gwenanda's hand. "That Mark-us Orrel-us."

"The which?"

"What e said where your job is. If it's true say it, if it's not don't. That's right, isn't it?"

"Aw," said Gwenanda, nuzzling the child's hair, her heartbeat fluttering with love. "*Aw.*"

She held Maris's hand as the two of them went back into the big room looking out over the park, with the opal curtain of the dome far away. Kriss was all nerves. "Careful you don't run over your time," he fidgeted, and, "You can use my quantum if you don't know what to say," and, "Dog, Gwennie, are you *ready?*"

"I'm ready," she said, as the red light pulsed off the seconds till her turn. At the last moment she pulled Maris onto her lap, and the two of them faced the telly as the ready light told her she was on.

"I think," she said steadily, "that we should say yes to NARRO. The water doesn't do anybody any good going north, and it will do a lot of people a lot of good going south. It's a big, expensive job, but we can afford it, and then it's good for a couple hundred years. The other thing I think is we shouldn't load it down with a lot of promises for other projects in other places, otherwise we'll tie ourselves up in knots we maybe will want to get out of. And the last thing I think—" watching the timer with one eye—"is we should be glad to have a chance to do so much good so easily." And she closed her lips into a faint smile just as the ready light winked off—seconds before she turned her head and flopped the soggy towel down over her eyes.

"You were *great!*" Kriss cried adoringly.

"Sure I was," said Gwenanda through the toweling

but not altogether happily, because she was wondering just what she had done.

What she had done, probably, was not all that much. Gwenanda's quantum of debate was only one out of seven hundred and twenty—thirty seconds total out of all the long hours of argument and polling and mediation. Certainly the handsome dark Supreme Court justice with the fair, pretty child in her lap made an appealing picture. Certainly what she had said made sense. But could one person, really, influence the decision of a quarter billion?

Maybe not. But one person could surely be *part* of it.

There were six more phone-in votes on changes in the closing hours of the Meeting. Every time the question was phrased a little differently, and after each vote the mediators gamed variations through their computers to find a better formula.

But after the second phone-in, the issue was no longer in doubt. If the Canadians could be satisfied on the payments for their rivers—If the people of Alaska and the Northwest Territory and the Yukon were assured of an adequate minimum retention of flow—If the Mexicans were promised a low enough salinity in the residual waters for their crops—If the Midwest got a share of the hydropower, and the East a priority on the Gulf Stream project—if all those interests could be reconciled, then the necessary sixty per cent aye vote would come. . . .

And it did.

By the time the UTM got to its final vote Gwenanda and Kriss were sitting side by side in front of the telly, Maris half asleep between them, Dorothy with her clumsy legs in the lotus position on the floor by their side. The apartment was quiet. All the flu victims were long gone. In breaks of the debate all four of them had stacked folding beds, dumped linen into a pickup basket, moved furniture back to where it belonged. By the time the continent had expressed its will and the final tallies were coming in the apartment looked once more as it always had. It was stately, it was elegant, and it was much, much too vast to be a home for a Supreme Court justice whose lover was far away.

NARRO won with more than fifteen million votes to spare. Maris flung her arms around Kriss. "Hooray for you!" she cried, and allowed herself to be swung exuberantly nearly to the high ceiling. And in her good-night glass of milk she took a drop of the wine Kriss opened to celebrate.

When Maris and Dorothy had gone off to sleep, and both Kriss and Gwenanda were beginning to feel the need of the same for themselves, they finished the last of the wine. They were shoulder to shoulder on the lanai that looked out over the Rainbow Bridge, both very silent until Kriss said abruptly, "How much longer have you got to be on the Court?"

"Four months to the end of this term," said Gwenanda gloomily, "and then two more years on my hitch."

Kriss digested that thoughtfully. "It'll probably be three or four months before they're ready for me in Seattle," he said.

"Uh-huh."

"But then there's the other two years."

"Uh-huh," said Gwenanda, who had long since performed the same calculations. They sat silently for a moment, gazing out at the convalescing city.

"Aw, dog," said Kriss at last. "Let's go to bed."

"Uh-huh," said Gwenanda hopelessly.

Accumulated exhaustion put them dreamlessly out. At daybreak Gwenanda woke, wholly and quickly. Kriss's heavy arm was across her rib cage and Kriss's downy beard against her shoulder. She extricated herself gently, pulled on a robe and found Maris already in the kitchen. The child had picked a couple of ripe papayas, and split them and chilled them in the freezer

One empty skin was on the plate in front of her, and swiftly she got up and brought out another half for Gwenanda.

"Dog," said Gwenanda, gazing at the melon.

Maris was concerned. "Didn't I get all the seeds out?"

"Aw, sure, it's just—" It was just that for a moment the damn thing had looked so much like a damn *mango*. But she couldn't refuse what her kid had made for her, after all. . . .

She had squeezed the fresh lime over the fruit and scooped out the first juicy spoonful when she paused, the spoon halfway to her mouth.

She stared unseeingly before her, her eyes widening. All of a sudden the sun outside had become brighter, the tropical aroma of the fruit sweeter, the entire world more kindly.

"If it isn't the seeds, then what is wrong?" Maris worried.

Gwenanda flashed thirty-two strong white teeth at her, enchanted with the wondrous idea that had just come to her. "Aw, pups! Nothing's wrong," she cried. "It's just that everything's so damn *right!*"

VII Two hundred meters down in the silvery Manhattan schist, the great hemispherical chamber was cool and quiet, but the people in it were ebulliently warm. Gwenanda paused on the way to her robing room to open the justices' door a crack. Like any actor, she cased the house. Looked like a good audience. Not cadets this time, but litigants, lawyers and a good number of ordinary citizens come to see justice done—and all of them with that special *well-we-beat-the-devil-this-time* jolliness that was the aftermath of the epidemic.

She sang to herself as she dressed, and then admired herself in the mirror. Too bad the robe covered up the spectacular black-and-red dashiki, *damn!*, but the flower lei around her neck, the forty neatly bobbing dreadlocks—they were *fine!* Gwenanda stared at the handsome, haughty female in the glass. Then she softened, grinned, blew herself a kiss and whirled out to take her place with the other justices.

It was Samelweiss's conceit that when the Supreme Court of the United States entered its hall of justice it should do so with ceremony. Fully robed. In single file. Majestically, and, of course, with the Chief Justice himself coming first. Samelweiss was followed by his two senior colleagues, then Gwenanda and her cohort, last of all the freshmen. As usual, the Tin Twins were grumbling to each other in high-pitched, high-speed beeps, since they were a lot less mobile than the organic colleagues; but they did what was expected of them. Even wore robes—or as close to robes as they could manage, which was to say some sort of doilies of black attached to their upper surfaces. That was Samelweiss's whim, too.

Like the gathering audience, the justices were all in a survivors' mood, laughing and nudging each other into place. When Gwenanda sashayed up, Samelweiss made a swift, jolly grab at her bottom—missed, because she was quicker than he—and said jovially, "Pups, you were *grand* on the UTM last night!"

"Oh, did you see me?" asked Gwenanda, gratified by her brush with fame. She preened herself as the other justices congratulated her, then got serious. "I have to talk to you about something, C.J."

"That's what I'm here for," he beamed.

"I'm thinking about a deal. Suppose I take the C.J. job next year. Does that mean I can pick the place where the court sits?"

"Getting too hot for you in New York, sweets?" he twinkled, and then saw she was in earnest. "Well, it's not up to me, of course, but that's usually the C.J.'s privilege. Assuming you get elected C.J., that is."

"You've got my vote," said Pak behind her, "although I do hope you don't want to move to Houston—I spent thirty-one years there already, and that's enough."

And the Digital Colleague chimed in: "I will gladly vote for you, Gwenanda. I don't think the junior members would object . . . only, will I have to wear this damn throw-rug when you're C.J.?"

Caught between the D.C. and Samelweiss, Gwenanda said only, "We'll have to see about that later." But with the eye away from Samelweiss she tipped the Digital Colleague a broad wink.

"So there's no problem," said Samelweiss, his tone a little dejected as he contemplated a future in which someone other than himself would inherit the mantle of John Marshall and Charles Evans Hughes. "Where do you want to move to?"

"Why," said Gwenanda, "Seattle, of course! Where else?"

Half a million people in the city had felt the chilly breath of death on their necks, but the morning's chief defendants had not been touched. Of course not, thought Gwenanda as she glowered down at the two of them, sober and hostile in the midst of the celebrating mob in the spectator seats. Those two were probably so full of old germs they were like city rats, too scummy mean to be damaged by trap, bug or poison! They had chosen to sit together, an oasis of ice in the warm courtroom. Even their lawyers, flanking them on either side, were leaning away from them as they chattered with their neighbors, or called greetings to the justices. "How's it going, D.C.?" cried Wally Amaretto, lawyer for the two-billion-dollar loony, Horatio Margov. "Say, did you know Tim Kapetzki here is this other prunt's lawyer?"

"Yes," said the Digital Colleague. "It's in the record. How are you, Tim?" Since the Digital Colleague was playing remote chess with one of the pages, out in the robing room, and at the same time calculating race-horse form on the afternoon's card for the Chief Justice, his circuits were taxed. His voice had only a narrow band of frequencies, and so it sounded as though he were talking through a tin cup and string.

"Fine, thank you," said Kapetzki, ignoring the gasps and glares from the two clients. "How's the game going, D.C.?"

"Mate in twenty-two," piped the Digital Colleague.

"Damn good, D.C. Listen, can we get these cases heard so we can get out of here?"

"Now, now," said the Chief Justice benevolently, "you have to wait your turn, because we have a really full calendar today what with the UTM and all. Let's get on with it, all right?" he said, sweeping his eyes over the ranks of his colleagues. "Court's in session!"

Wait their turn they did, though not with good grace. As the cases raced through the Court machine Margov and Jocelyn Feigerman watched with hostility, and contempt, and finally pure shock. There were plenty of cases. There was a reckless hang-gliding, and an ingenious credit-embezzling, and three or four other minor misdemeanants who hadn't been willing to accept the rough justice of the nearest E.S. patroller. There were no fewer than twenty-eight separate challenges already filed against various parts of the weekend's UTM decision on the NARRO project. There was a murder, and a child-molester, and a particularly nasty case of a loo-job assignments clerk who had been caught taking bribes to credit people with work they hadn't done. Gwenanda reluctantly disqualified herself in the case of the child-molester, for she could not help seeing Maris scared, hurting and uncomprehending, as one of his victims. (But she was delighted when the other eight justices were unanimous to freeze the prunt, and used the free time to look up apartment listings in Seattle.

The clerks and pages had already run all the NARRO challenges through the computer, and the Tin Twins reported there was no merit in any of them, just last-gasp attempts by die-hards of one kind or another. Five minutes was plenty for the C.J. to gavel them all out of existence. Even so, the Court was more than two hours getting through the minor attractions of the day and Gwenanda, gazing absent-mindedly at the moving adages—

"All that is needed to remedy the evils of our time is to do justice and give freedom."—Henry George.

—was beginning to find hunger distracting her from her lovely, leisurely musings about the future in Seattle. Then she became aware that the loony with the two-billion-dollar suit was making a wasp of himself again: "Mr. Chief Justice! Sir! I do believe we were here long before many of these other good folks!"

"Why, sure you were," said Samelweiss amiably. "I'm glad to tell you that the two of you are next—as soon as we come back from lunch."

"Lunch!" rumbled the ex-corpsicle, as though the word referred to some depraved lunacy these future weirdos had invented.

"Lunch," ruled Samelweiss, and grinned. "And I've saved you two for dessert."

Samelweiss, Gwenanda decided, had something up his sleeve. He was really polite to Horatio Margov, smiled at him, urged him to take his time making his speech—"I mean, delivering your what's it, *statement,*" he corrected himself—and all the while was smiling the secret smiles of a cat that's been lapping up cream. Gwenanda, who had actually been lapping up cream, the heavenliest kiwi-fruit pie ever, with at least three centimeters of whipped cream on top of it to end one of the nicest lunches she'd ever had, was sated enough to be tolerant. Even amused, as all of the Court was obviously amused, though some of them tried to hide it. "I am, honorable justices," the loony was declaiming, "formerly of your estate myself, as you know—" And went on like that, and Samelweiss never told him to get the hell on to the point.

What a *damn* great lunch it had been! They'd gone to where Dorothy worked, bustling and partyish now, as the whole city was; the same people as before, Kriss and Maris with her, Dorothy waiting on them and sitting down for a minute now and then when she got a chance. But what a different feeling! Gwenanda wondered if she'd made a mistake inviting Dorothy to come to Seattle with them, maybe live with them and help take care of Maris until she got herself settled—dog, what if Kriss didn't think she was too old for him? But that wouldn't happen. She lifted her head and smiled at the two important people in her life, sitting way at the back of the auditorium under the bright red letters that were spelling out:

"Justice is truth in action."—Benjamin Disraeli. They smiled back, and it was all Gwenanda could do to keep from jumping down from the bench to hug them.

Instead, she made herself pay attention to the loony. What the loony was doing was reciting great slabs of autobiography. Now, that was *pe*-culiar. Old C.J. didn't let people do that on his time—if he did, he was off to the lavatories until it was over, but this time he was smiling and nodding through all the stuff. "—a person of some stature. I was a State Senator for eight years, then a member of the Governor's cabinet. My name was mentioned as a candidate for Governor myself, as a matter of fact, but I chose what I believed, and still believe, the more honorable profession of judge. As a jurist, I had a certain reputation for being severe on serious and recidivist offenders—in fact, the press labeled me with the sobriquet 'The Hanging Judge of Harlem.'" He twinkled at the nine justices. "After what was generally considered a distinguished career, I discovered that I was seriously ill and elected to have myself placed in cryonic suspension, since my

364

doctor could not undertake to be responsible for treatment at that time."

"You came out pretty healthy," commented the C.J.

"Only after much therapy," said the Hanging Judge quickly. "And that is the essence of my case, Your Honor. Too much therapy! Serious and even life-threatening repetitious doses of vaccines and immunizing agents of all kinds, causing me great pain and loss of function. I am prepared," he said, "to place in evidence certain records to establish—"

"Oh," said the C.J., interrupting, "we've already got them."

"I beg your pardon?" said Margov, rattled.

"We've got the records," the C.J. explained. "Not 'certain' ones. All of them. You can shut up a while, because there's some other stuff. Wally? Would you come up here and say out loud what you told me in the bar, while we were waiting for our lunch table?"

Wally Amaretto stood up and approached the bench, licking his lips as he looked at his client. "E's going to be pissed, C.J.," he said gloomily.

"Tell the truth and shame the devil, Wally," said the C.J. sunnily. "Or, in this case, shame your client."

"Well. . . . Well, what e said, when we were talking about uz case, was e said it cost um plenty to fugger up the records at the freezatorium."

Gasps and babble from the courtroom, while the Hanging Judge stuttered in rage. The C.J. looked pleased. "Now, you just keep shut up, Margov, while we straighten this out. Did e say why e'd do a thing like that?"

"E said it was so they couldn't find um in a hurry. I think e was in law trouble, then."

"Uh-huh. And tell me, Wally. Did you report this to anybody?"

"Oh, sure. I told um." He pointed to the Digital Colleague. "All the rest of you ran off to lunch, but e doesn't eat, you know. So e was just sitting there playing thirty-board simultaneous chess the way e does. I told um, then I went out to catch a drink and I saw you there."

"I protest!" Margov yelled.

"You shush. D.C., what about it?"

"That's right," the Digital Colleague boomed. He was playing no chess now. "So I called the freezatorium and got them to search their records. It took a while—they've been busy the last couple of days!—but they found out Wally was right. This defendant fuggered the records."

"Now, that's enough!" bellowed Margov, and needed no microphone to be heard. "I protest the unethical behavior of this attorney! I want him disbarred. And I object to the prejudicial statements of this justice, for I am not a defendant. I'm a plaintiff!"

"No," boomed the rich, full-attention tones of the Digital Colleague, "you used to be a plaintiff, but that suit's going to be dismissed. The freezatorium records show that you caused your ID file to be concealed under the case history of one Chrétien Entier, and when they thawed you the records were still bollixed so you got all uz shots and e got none."

"Right," said Samelweiss in happy indignation. "It was your own fault, Margov, case dismissed. Now we have to figure out what to do to you for this record-fuggering business."

"Objection!" cried Margov. "Exception! I intend to appeal this ruling!"

Samelweiss stared at him in honest puzzlement. "Appeal to who? This is the *Supreme* Court, chotz."

"This rinky-dink crowd? Supreme?" sneered Margov.

"We're the supremest you've got, chotz," the C.J pointed out. "And you're beginning to give me a pain Some of you criminals are as bad as the lawyers, the way you act!"

"I am simply insisting on my right to be heard by competent authority!"

"You already were! Look, we don't have all the time in the world, you know, we've got—what is it now, D.C.?"

The Digital Colleague was flashing for attention. "I only wanted to suggest that we hear um out, C.J. This is a rather important case, after all."

Samelweiss shrugged, and the Hanging Judge looked both pleased and faintly worried, at the same time. "I appreciate the courtesy, Your Honor," he said, addressing the Digital Colleague, "although if you are referring to this matter of the error in the records, I must say I am astonished to hear it called an 'important case.' Surely a fifty-dollar fine, or perhaps only a reprimand—At any rate," he said, responding to Samelweiss's glare, "I will take very little of the Court's time. All I wish to say is that I am a stranger here. I am not familiar with your customs. In my day a court was headed by a *judge*. A judge who had legal training, who usually had many years of experience as a trial lawyer or a corporate attorney—some sort of practice that he was actually working at. Then I come up against you people! None of you are lawyers, really. You're certainly not judges. You're just average citizens—well, to be frank, some of you are not anywhere near what I would call 'average.' No offense to any of you. You've been picked for this job like, my God, I don't know what, like being drafted or something. As I understand it, some for God's sake *computer*—no offense, you two gentlemen—just picks your names out of the hat, and you're the Supreme Court! My God! How can you be expected to know anything about the law?" He stood silent for a moment, scanning the nine justices. His strong, photogenic, politician's face had softened into a less distinguished, but much more human, expression of worry. Gwenanda found herself almost feeling sorry for the chotz, until he spoke again. "I guess that's all," he said humbly. "I withdraw my suit. As to the other matter, I suppose I did wrong and I'm willing to pay my fine or whatever—although considering my record I should think a suspended sentence would be the maximum you would consider imposing."

"About time," Samelweiss grumbled—"Oh, what is it this time, D.C.?"

"I'd like to respond to uz remarks, please," said Ai-Max.

"For what?"

"As a courtesy!" boomed the Digital Colleague. "Also there are other matters. First, we *are* the Supreme Court, because we're about the only court there is. The only one that's needed, because there aren't all that many laws any more, and most things get settled on the spot. Second, we do know the law, real well, or anyway the Court computers do, and the clerks are really good at letting us know whatever we need. Third, the reason we hear rinky-dink cases like yours is we don't have much else to do—because of the fact that there aren't that many laws now, and people usually try to get along by themselves. And fourth—" The D.C. paused, before going on: "Fourth, there's some stuff we haven't talked about yet. This Chrétien an, who didn't get any shots at all, e was unfroze and released to population with all those dirty old organic bugs still in um. E was the stiff they found. The flu vector, C.J. E was the reason the whole city got sick, pretty nearly, with all that trouble and worry and cost, and considering all the other diseases e was carrying we were damn lucky it was just flu. So there's more for Margov to worry about than the old records business, because e's the one that put us through it all."

The whole courtroom was thunderstruck. There weren't any gasps. There certainly weren't any snickers. This was a whole new aspect to what had been a light farce. Around the room a new adage was circling—

"The people made the Constitution, and the people can unmake it."—John Marshall.

—and Gwenanda wondered absently if the D.C. had

ordered that one up for Margov's benefit, but mostly, like everyone else in the room, she was almost in shock.

The Chief Justice was the first one to act. His eyes were narrowed. His brows pulled themselves down toward the bridge of his nose. His lips pressed each other into thin lines. He slapped the cutoff for all lawyer and litigant circuits. For the justices' ears only he snarled, "Now it's not funny any more. Freezing's too good for that prunt. What'll we give um?"

"Forfeiture of all uz property," offered Ai-Max. "E's from a property time, you know, so that's what will mean the most to um."

"Twenty years' draft service, with no lieu-of-taxes credits," snapped Pak.

"Exile um to Los Angeles," Myra Haik proposed, and Angel hissed:

"It's not enough! Let's stick um the whole shaft—give um all of them, and then when they're all served we pop um back in the freezer!"

Now, *damn,* thought Gwenanda, staring at the Tin Twin, that was kind of perplexing. Why would Angel get so upset? She ignored the buzzing of the justices, trying to figure it out—of course! Angel was the other one who'd been taken sick! Somehow or another, there was enough of the meat human being inside that tin can of prostheses and life-support systems to catch a disease, and so Angel had a very personal reason for wanting a way-up-high shaft job on the Hanging Judge.

And yet, she thought disconsolately, it really wasn't right to crucify the prunt. In spite of the fact that, personally speaking, remembering the terror of clutching her sick child, she really felt that they didn't have a punishment bad enough for him. She stared loathingly at Margov who, far from repentant, was furiously berating his lawyer, pausing only to accept sympathy and share resentments with the other prunt, Jocelyn Feigerman. The whole courtroom was buzzing now. The word had got out, and the telly crews were there with their news cameras, and the print media, and the foreign correspondents, and the citizens' interest observers. They were all going to be on the screens that night, thought Gwenanda, pausing to sneak a look at herself in the monitor and poke the dreadlocks into place . . . but it was still wrong. Wasn't it? "Hey, C.J.," she called, overriding the other justices. "How about if we cool off a little bit?"

"Now, Gwenanda," said Samelweiss, turning his good profile to the cameras, "why don't we just finish this up and get um put away good?"

But the Digital Colleague chimed in, "I urgently support Gwenanda on this, C.J. True, e's a prunt. But we're talking lynch mob now, not U.S. Supreme Court."

"So what we can do," said Gwenanda quickly, "is hear my chotz's case. It won't take long, I think, 'cause e's guilty as hell."

"Well. . . ." The Chief Justice looked around, then shrugged. "So ordered," he said, opening the mikes. "Get on with the other prunt then, gang. Tim? You want to say anything for your criminal?"

Tim Kapetzki stood up slowly. He glanced at his client, sighed and, as he approached the bench, took out a joint and lighted it. "Let's all mellow out a little," he proposed, passing it around. And for a wonder, the C.J., who always disliked smoking in his court because it made him sneeze, only smiled, directly into the camera. "Okay," said the defense lawyer, "let's get to it. E did what you said e did, sure."

"You mean e wants to plead guilty? So we can get right to the sentencing?"

"Well, now, C.J.," Kapetzki sighed, "that word 'guilty' covers a whole lot of shit. There's 'guilty' like somebody takes a gun and kills somebody, and there's 'guilty' like e got a little mixed up and did something, like, almost by accident. I admit e clings to what you'd call an outmoded life style, and of course that messes things up for other people—"

"That's the Thirty-first Amendment, right?" said the

Chief Justice. He fiddled with his controls, and in a moment the circling letters spelled out:

"Nobody has any right to dump on anybody else. This takes precedence over everything else."—The Thirty-first Amendment to the Constitution of the United States.

Kapetzki didn't even look at it. "But e didn't *realize* e was dumping," he said, without very much conviction. "Tell you what. How about if you let the old girl talk for umself?"

"Well, sure," said the C.J. hospitably, grinning into the cameras again; but Gwenanda flared:

"Girl? What's this *girl* shit?"

"Excuse me, Gwenanda, you're right, but e calls umself a 'girl.' Like, 'we girls used to do this' and 'when we girls get together' and so on. You ought to talk to um sometime, Gwennie. E's really interesting—only I don't see why I always get all the yoyos."

"Now, now," said the Chief Justice indulgently. "We said we'd let the, uh, *girl* talk for umself, so let's do it. Come on, Feigerman. This is your chance, so don't blow it."

So Jocelyn Balmer Tisdale Feigerman composedly stood up and identified herself. She did not show her wickedness to Gwenanda's eyes—damn, would the rest of the Court see what a prunt she really was? She was no taller than a twelve-year-old and plump as a baby, and her eyes were a sad, pale brown. "I do not know," she said, "why I am here, for I certainly committed no crime. What I did may have been against some minor ordinance, but it was done only to uphold God's law."

"Old Thirty-one's no damn minor ordinance," snapped Gwenanda, but subsided when she felt the C.J.'s eyes on her.

"It is possible," said Jocelyn bravely, "that unfamiliarity with your present customs may have caused me to offend in some worse way than I realized. I can only apologize, like Judge Margov, and ask that you give me, as you did him, the opportunity to tell you about myself, so you will understand my motives and take into consideration my past record.

"I was brought up as a God-fearing Presbyterian," she went on, settling into an oration. "I married young, to a man who died in the service of his country. Some years later I married again, to a distinguished engineer and philanthropist, and remained his wife for nearly thirty-five years. I was his wife at the time I was admitted to cryonic suspension. In all that time I was active in community affairs, and particularly in attempting to prevent the sin of murder of unborn children. Although I was only able to have one child myself, I raised him with a mother's full devotion and—"

"Hold on a damn minute," Gwenanda cut in. "Let me get this straight. You were shacked with two different marries, altogether maybe thirty, forty years, and you didn't flush or anything and still only had one kid?"

The C.J. turned up the amplification on his mike. "Now, stop it right there, Gwenanda," he said sternly. "It's the, uh, girl's turn now, you can kick the shit out of her later." And over the private line came the whispering voice of one of the Tin Twins in Gwenanda's ear—she could not tell which:

"Gwenanda? I wonder if you want to disqualify yourself—after all, you were the arresting officer."

"Aw, damn," said Gwenanda, and was moodily silent while Jocelyn Feigerman went on.

"I was a good wife," she said strongly, "but I was also mindful of God's law. Reverend Arbneth used to say that the best birth-control device was a silver dollar. Hold it between your knees and never drop it, and you'll never have a problem. He was right. Girls today—I mean, girls then, before I was suspended, they should have taken that advice, and then there wouldn't be any need for legalized murder, and I'm sure that's still true now, whatever else has changed. Murder is a sin, and it's also a crime. You should prevent it! Put them in jail if they can't live decently! What kind of a world would it be if you let people do whatever they wanted?"

And she stood silent, with her eyes downcast.

When the Chief Justice realized she was through, he cleared his throat and looked around the Court. "Any questions, gang?" he asked. There were no questions. Samelweiss began to smile. "Well, I'll tell you what we're going to do. We're going to retire to our chambers for a while, and maybe pass around a joint and mellow out while we figure out what to do with these two, uh, *unusual* cases." And led the way out, smiling, because if there was one thing Samelweiss knew, especially when the media people were right there watching, it was how to build a dramatic climax to an interesting case. And, no doubt at Samelweiss's contrivance, as the robed justices marched or lumbered out, over their heads the circling glow-lights spelled out:

"Nobody can rule guiltlessly."—Louis de Saint-Just.

So there was time, there was plenty of time, for furious whispering between the defendants and their attorneys in the front bench, so that Jocelyn and the Hanging Judge began to appreciate what deep shit they were in, and for Kriss and Maris, hugging each other in the back, to let each other know how proud they were of Gwenanda, and for the media people to get all the reaction shots from the audience they needed; and then the justices filed back in.

They were grinning.

When he was quite sure the cameras were on him, Samelweiss said, "Myra, the Court is ready."

Myra Haik put her two forefingers to her lips in thought for a moment. If you looked quick at Myra Haik she seemed like everybody's mother, but inside that motherly forty-six-year-old head was a dangerous lady. Both defendants discovered that as they met her gaze, and then she said: "Jocelyn, we do you first. By rights it ought to be Gwennie doing this sentence, but e

373

took umself out because e tagged you in the first place, so I asked to do it. Tell you why. I got to thinking that if I'd been born a little earlier my life might've been quite a lot like yours, and I sure thank God every morning of my life that it isn't. Well. Anyway. Here's what we have for you. We're going to give you a marry. And you're going to be uz, what you call, uz 'wife.' If e's in a bad mood, you're going to live through it. If e snores, you'll go short on sleep. If e drinks too much at a party, you'll stay sober enough to get um home, and if e wants to make love then and can't because e's too blind smashed to make it, you'll hang in there. You probably won't have to worry about your damn silver dollar," she said charitably, "because while they fixed you up so most of you functions fine at the freezatorium, they probably didn't think you needed to ovulate any more. Of course, you can go back and get that done if you want it. Anyway. E won't be handsome. E won't be smart. E won't be any kid, either, and as e's going to be getting along in years you're going to hear a lot about uz prostate and uz hemorrhoids and a lot of other stuff that's really kind of tacky. Well, shit, Jocelyn, you get the idea. And that's the easy part.

"The hard part is this: You'll keep um in line. You'll give um sex when you think e deserves it. You'll clam up and keep um guessing what you're mad about when e does something to make you mad, like not picking up uz clothes or talking too much to some other shemale an at a party. You'll tell um how all the other marries in the world take better care of their bodies and get farther in their business, and if e ever thinks e's done anything special you'll be sure to explain to um why it isn't, after all, much. And you'll do that every day you live and e lives and we won't give you any divorce, and that is the order of this Court."

Bang of the gavel. "So ordered," cried the C.J. happily. "Now you do the other one, Gwenanda."

Gwenanda winked proudly at Kriss and Maris before returning her gaze to the defendants. They were a lot less cocky now. Jocelyn looked both smiley and faint, as though she thought she was getting off easy and, at the same time, didn't know if she could live through it; the Hanging Judge looked merely scared. "Horatio," said Gwenanda, "the easy thing to do with you, with both of you, would be just to pop you back in the freezer and let tomorrow worry about straightening you out. But, shit, you'd probably be just as bad when they thawed you again. So we've got something special for you.

"You're going to be the hemale marry e's married to."

And she grinned meltingly into the cameras; and, with a twitch of the dreadlocks, tore the robe off and marched down through the crowded courtroom, the red and black dashiki glowing and smoldering, to where Maris and Kriss were waiting. They kissed. They led the way to the public elevators, arm in arm. And they kept their arms around each other all the way up the long ride, up out of the layers of abiotic rock, past the first prokaryotes and eukaryotes, past the crawling things that lived only to eat each other and spawn and die, past the rocks where the bellowing reptiles were entombed, past the beginning of mammals, past savagery, past history, all the way up, and out, into the clean, kind, civilized air.

About the Author

FREDERIK POHL, one of science fiction's greatest authors, has several times won the Hugo and Nebula awards, the field's highest honors, for his novels, which include *Gateway, Beyond the Blue Event Horizon, Man Plus,* and *Jem.* In addition, he has been honored for the genre classic, *The Space Merchants,* written in collaboration with C. M. Kornbluth, has won the Hugo for Best Editor three times, is an American Book Award winner, and has been awarded the Prix Apollo in France. In 1982, he was elected a fellow of the American Association for the Advancement of Science.